CARRIE HUMPHREY

Fanged and Confused

~Christina~
Welcome to Briarberry!
[signature]

Interior design by Cover Me Darling
Formatting by Athena Interior Book Design

To my Husband: Not once did you ever question the characters that played in my imagination. You only encouraged them. Watched them grow and applauded when they made their grand appearance on paper. Thank you for that.

To my children: I may be a highly unusual mother, but you seem to not notice. I hope each of you shoot for the stars and end up within galaxies of endless possibilities. My love is never ending for each and every one of you!

To my family and friends: Thanks for not locking me up when the voices got too loud. You guys rock.

To the moose to my squirrel: You know what you did so thank you for all of it.

Your soulmate is not someone who comes into your life peacefully. It is who comes to make you question things, who changes your reality, somebody who marks a before and after in your life. It is not the human being that everyone idealized, but an ordinary person, who manages to revolutionize your world in a second.

~Anonymous

CHAPTER
one

Okay, you can totally do this, Kedah thought as she shifted her backpack to the front of her body. No one was guarding the room. It was as simple as sneaking in, grabbing what she needed, and getting out. Easy.

Taking a huge gulp of air, she tried to rid herself of the nervous hiccups that appeared and ran for the door. It was unlocked, as it had been in the past, so she slipped into the cool dark room with ease.

Going over to the standup cooler, she grabbed what she needed, filling her pack so much she almost couldn't zip it shut. She quietly rearranged things inside the fridge to make it look like nothing was missing, hopefully. As with the previous times she had been here, things seemed to be going without a hitch.

"Stop." A voice demanded from somewhere in the dark shadows of the cold room. She hadn't noticed anyone in here, but then, she thought it was safe to think no one would be lurking, aside from her.

Holding her backpack just a little closer, she began to frantically look around for the body that belonged to the voice. She would have thought with her heightened senses that she'd have no issues identifying a body in the room. She thought wrong.

"Are you stealing blood?" The male voice asked. He didn't sound angry, just slightly amused, which was odd. Confusion clouded her thoughts as she tried to think of something clever to say, because 'yes, I'm stealing blood' just sounded pathetic. If only her current health condition came with the superpowers she expected, she'd have been good as gold to just leave without anyone catching her.

Well, she thought, when all else fails, lie.

"Yes, but because my mother needs a transfusion and insurance isn't covering it." As lies go, it was the best she could come up with. Even though it was pretty lame.

"Right," the man laughed as he stepped into her view. He was tall, had wide brimmed black glasses, ruffled dirty blonde hair, was strikingly handsome, and he glowed. Not like glowed, glowed, but had an aura about him that she'd only seen one other time. "Even a human would find it hard to choke down that lie. Because darling, you are a terrible liar."

She sighed and realized that some things just never change. Bad liar as a human and even worse now. "Are you going to call the cops? Cause I'll just run and I'm pretty sure they won't catch me."

"I bet I'll catch you before you can finish your next thought." He smirked. "The cops on the other hand won't stand a chance, of that I am sure." Cocky SOB, she thought. Then he disappeared before she could continue her mental rant and reappeared behind her, wrapping his arms around hers and her pack, his lips beside her ear. "Now, why are you really stealing blood? And for the record, I have fangs as well so lie again and I won't hesitate to use them."

She paled and froze. He had fangs and moved faster than she did. He was just like her. "I'm hungry." She muttered, no longer attempting anything but the truth. She was hungry, after all. This was her only source of food. Humans were a no-fly zone for her. She tried the animal thing but that tasted like rotting cattle, and left her with the urge to vomit for days.

"Hungry?" He asked, startled. "What do you mean you're hungry?"

8

Kedah sighed and closed her eyes. She was, in fact, starving. "I've not had, er, liquid, in days and I'm hungry. This is my only way to get what I need. Please," she pleaded. "If you are what you say you are, let me just go on my way and take what I need."

The man holding her let go, spun her around, and looked deep into her eyes, which had now snapped back open. "Excuses me if this sounds harsh, but why are you starving and reduced to stealing? Surely your Sire is providing for you?"

She growled at the mention of the person who had turned her. He drained her, turned her and left her. "Well, he isn't and no, I don't want to talk about it."

"Unfortunately, I can't just let you go. Most of us live by a code of ethics and I'd like to know why your Sire feels the need to be excluded from that." The man stated. He was becoming increasingly persistent and she was becoming increasingly irritated. She just wanted to leave and be on her way, alone.

Though it would be nice to know a fellow vampire, she was not about to lose what little control of her life she still had. Ever since the accident, she spiraled out like a tornado on a path of destruction and only now, four months later, was she gaining a foothold. She'd gotten a night job, moved to her basement, found a local blood bank to "borrow" from and had one friend in the world who knew what was going on and still loved her.

So who exactly was this guy, anyways? Where was he when she was turned? Those nights of hell when all she wanted was to be burned or staked to get her out of the pain she'd felt. That was beyond the worst torture she could have ever imagined and she still wasn't sure how she survived. Shuddering, she took a step back. "I'm fine. Can I go, or are you going to call the cops?"

"The cops? Really? What do you think I should say? Hey, there is a woman here stealing blood because she's hungry. We'd both be arrested, or at least they'd try. I wouldn't be caught, but you're young, you may. And what would you do in prison? Ask nicely for bags of blood?" He laughed bitterly. "Seriously, though, I really need to know who you are and why you're stealing blood." She watched as he pushed his glasses up onto his nose and crossed his arms over his chest.

Glancing to the door that was lit with a dim exit sign, she took a deep breath, trying to, yet again, calm her nerves. Whoever this was, it was obvious he was not about to let her go. But, to be fair, he wasn't attacking her either. She hugged the bag tighter to her chest and closed her eyes. However this would go down, she needed to not lose the bag, or she risked the life of her best friend back at the home.

"Let me at least introduce myself, okay? I'm Jensen, local vampire. And you are?" There was nothing threating about his voice, nothing that suggested to her that she was in trouble, and yet worry clouded her thoughts. The only other vampire she had met had turned her and left. Her view on the species as a whole, wasn't great.

She had been fine alone, or at least okay, but a deep need to belong was beginning to push forward in her subconscious and it was getting hard to ignore. Maybe, just maybe, Jensen wouldn't disappoint.

Maybe he could help.

"Kedah." She made no move to shake hands, but neither did he.

"Alright Kedah, I'm going to go out on a limb here and say that you maybe didn't have a good experience turning." He took a step back and held her gaze. "It seems you have little to no reason to trust me, which I understand. I can offer you help, if you're interested."

Before her brain could tell her no, her mouth opened and spoke words she didn't stop to think about. "A good experience? Are you kidding? It was the worst thing I have ever felt and I wished and prayed for death. Where in the hell were you to answer that prayer? I should have died, I wanted too. Even now, I don't feel like I should be here, yet here I am, stealing blood because I don't even know how to bite someone. So trust you, no. I don't even come close to trusting anyone because I have had to do this alone while no one cared. Where was your help then? You're a little late." She snapped her mouth shut to stop talking but her eyes were wide and her emotions all over the place.

To his credit, Jensen remained calm through her rant and continued to hold her gaze. "Kedah, I am sorry that happened to you. I am. But you made it, you did it alone. That's impressive as hell. Trust me on that. Though I couldn't help you then, and I intend to find out why you were left alone, I can help you now. Here."

If her heart still beat, it would have started to race when he began to reach for something. She choked back a hysterical laugh at the sight of a business card that he pulled from his pocket. A vampire that carried business cards. Cute.

Her hand shaking slightly, she reached out and grabbed the card and briefly gazed down at it. The Den was written in solid black print and in tiny lettering underneath it said The Briarberry Estate. She paused, confused. "Wait. The Briarberry Estate? Like the one that doesn't exist?"

Jensen laughed and shook his head. "Oh it's very much still there. Trust me."

"No offense, but I've been going to the briar patch where the estate used to be since I was a kid. It's not there." She said stubbornly.

"It's there and it's someplace that will help. I work there. Come by and check it out." Jensen smiled as he grabbed his phone from his pocket, gazing at it quickly. "I have to take this call. Help yourself to whatever you need here. Next time just go through the front door and tell them Jensen said you can have what you need. After all, I do own the company." Answering the call, he turned and left without another word.

She stood still, clutching her backpack, staring after the vampire that just walked out the door like nothing was out of the ordinary. He casually strolled out like she wasn't in the process of stealing from his company. His company, which of course he owned.

So, what exactly was the place on the business card he handed her? She's been to that location a dozen times and nothing was there. Was this just a huge joke, she wondered. But, before her thoughts could gather any more information of what had happened, the lights in the room flared to life, causing her to jump in surprise.

"Oh, I'm sorry. Jensen said that you may need a cooler and that he wanted an Uber to take you home." A lady in a white lab coat handed her a discrete looking fabric cooler and smiled. "Keep the cooler and the ride has been paid for. Have a wonderful evening." The woman smiled again and turned, walking out.

Several seconds passed, maybe minutes, with Kedah just standing there, holding her backpack and the cooler, doing nothing more than staring. Her mind whirled with thoughts on the turn of events this evening. The lab coat lady popped her head back through the door and spoke softly. "Your rides here."

Kedah stumbled to the door, still in a daze from the last few minutes, backpack and cooler in hand. They gave her the cooler, free blood, and a ride home. It was too good to be true, and with her luck, something was going to bite her in the ass, it always did. For now, she was just going to ride this out.

As she was reaching for the door, a cool hand touched her shoulder. She turned her head to see the women in the lab coat smiling at her.

"I just wanted to say I've known Jensen for almost 300 years, sweetie. He doesn't give things away lightly, and only does it when he sees someone with promise. He must see something in you. Take that for whatever its worth." She nodded happily and left Kedah alone with her thoughts, which were jumbled and non-coherent.

A horn blared in the distance, reminding her that her ride was here. Scrambling to the car, she muttered her address to the driver, and tried to relax in an unfamiliar car that held the stench of too many travelers and regrets of decisions they all made. At least it wasn't a taxi.

Pulling out her phone, she noticed three missed calls and ten texts from her roommate. All of which was her freaking out that something bad had happened. Her personal favorite text to date was something along the lines of, you're not dead, again, are you?

Typing a quick message back explaining that it was a weird night and she was on her way back, she leaned her head back and closed her eyes. Even though she shouldn't be tired, it was, after all, the middle of her day, at midnight, she still felt drained. Lack of blood and the weirdness of the night wasn't looking to be a good combination and she couldn't wait to get home to fix at least one of the several issues bouncing around her head.

Jensen walked into his office followed closely by the manager in charge when he wasn't around. "Well, that solved that issue as to where the blood was going." He muttered as he sat heavily behind his desk. The night was long and strange and hadn't even really begun yet.

"I'm glad. I was really beginning to wonder what in the world was going on. It was the damnedest thing." The manager said as she stood at the edge of the door.

"I'm just confused as to how there are vampires within my region that I don't know about and have no one aiding them. I really couldn't care that she was stealing, better that than murdering people, but I do care that she seems to be alone and absolutely clueless about her very nature." He pushed a piece of paper around on his desk and sighed loudly. Really the last thing he needed right now was a bunch of baby vampires running around untrained and unaccounted for. Where there was one there was always more to follow.

"I'll let everyone know to keep an extra eye out in case we see anyone else coming in for a snack. You're right though, better to be taking what they need than causing issues within the human world." She agreed. He looked up at Natalie and smiled. It really was a good decision to put her in charge, she was level headed and calm under pressure and kept everything running smoothly since his duties took him to the Den more than they allowed him to stay with this business.

"Thank you, Natalie. You have been a wondrous help." He said in appreciation.

"You're welcome, sir. Anything else I can do for you tonight?" She asked.

"No. I'll just take care of a few more things and head home." He said gently. "Oh, actually, can I get a drink before I go? If you wouldn't mind?"

"Of course. Your usual?" She asked.

"Yes, thank you." It wasn't even half way through the night and coffee was already going to be on the menu when he got home. He had at least a dozen disputes to settle, some businesses that needed a looking over and a few residents at the Estate were getting a little unruly.

Moments later Natalie walked back in with a glass of warmed blood that she placed on his desk. "Try not to stress too much, I know you're old but so far you've held off the wrinkles. You keep at it and they will appear without warning." She joked with a grin.

"There went your raise." He laughed back. "Thanks again and I'll try and keep the wrinkles at bay." She laughed and left him in the office, alone, to sort through paperwork. Sipping the blood, he shifted through the papers and did what needed to be done. Less than an hour later he was ready to close up his office here and head back to the Den where more paper work awaited.

Grabbing his keys and the now empty cup he was using, he stopped by the break room within the business and set the cup in the sink. Quietly, he snuck out the back door where his car was waiting.

Going on autopilot he made his way back out of town and to the fortress that he called home. His thoughts drifted to Kedah as he drove. She had survived a turn without the aid of her Sire, which was impressive, and then continued to survive on bagged blood, which was even more impressive.

It concerned him that she was out there alone, but he hoped she'd take his advice and stop by the Estate. That place was created for people just like her. People who needed a little extra help getting back on their own feet or for those that had nowhere else to go.

Getting side tracked, he came back to his own thoughts as he pulled onto the driveway, taking the road around back to the garage. As much as he liked everyone that worked and lived here, he really hoped everyone was somewhere else so that he could make his way to his office quickly and quietly.

Dashing in and up the first flight of stairs, he rounded the corner on the second floor and walked quickly into his office. Thankfully no one followed. Sighing in relief, he sat at his desk and opened his computer, prepared to spend hours responding to emails and making endless calls to his vampires throughout the state.

It was going to be a long night but before he even started it, he really needed to see about this new little vampire he encountered today. Miss Kedah, the survivor, was a mystery that he intended to discover before the night was done.

CHAPTER
two

"You aren't seriously going to go, are you? Kedah, there is NOTHING there. We've heard the tales of the Estate since we were old enough to listen. It's an actual class at the local college. We've lived in Briarberry all our life and every single person we know has gone to that place and has seen exactly nothing." Sadie shouted as she juggled her laptop in one hand and a bowl of candy in the other while walking to the couch.

Kedah smiled at her friend's concern as she poured blood into a mug and popped it into the microwave for a few seconds. Second to animal blood, cold blood, could make a person wish for death. "I am seriously considering it. He wasn't a threat to me, didn't turn me in for stealing, invited me back for what I needed, and was kinda hot. The least I can do is go and say thank you. Maybe I should bring flowers? Or a cookie bouquet."

"Are you really considering bringing cookies to a house full of vampires?" Sadie asked as she plopped down on the couch, setting the bowl of candy beside her and pulling up the internet on her computer.

"No, I guess not. I wish someone would send me cookies though." Sipping on her drink, she sighed and resisted the urge to throw back the entire mug like the largest shot ever. Instead, she sat down next to Sadie and peeked over at her computer.

"Tell you what, next birthday, I'll make you cookies. Lots of them. Then I will put sticks in them and BAM, cookie flower thing." Sadie smiled and laid her head on Kedah's shoulder. "I don't want you to go to this place because I don't want to lose you. What if you die, again? Or life there is better? That would be great for you, but not for me. I'm being selfish, but still."

Kedah finished off her drink and set it on the table. She smiled over at her friend. "Let's not think about the what-if's, okay? I'll take the week and think about it. And I promise I won't do anything without telling you first." She wanted to believe that, but it felt wrong. She was going to have to do this alone, and probably lie a lot on the way. Which sucked, majorly.

She trusted Sadie with her life. When Kedah crawled back to their house, neck torn out and muttering about a vampire attack, she quickly learned life would drastically change. Before Sadie could even call for help, her heart stopped beating and she died. Moments later fangs sprung out and Kedah took a breath with a heart that still wouldn't beat. Sadie never faltered as she jumped into action, saving her new life.

Her memories of the actual transition from human to vampire weren't clear, aside from a few things that really stood out. Pain, hunger, and more pain. Yet, somehow through the days of the transition, Sadie stood vigil over her. She moved her to the upstairs bathroom, blacked out the windows, stole blood from who knows where, and made sure she never hurt herself. If it were up to Kedah, Sadie would have made sainthood for her actions.

"Alright, enough emo dark brooding talk, let's find something trashy on Netflix and you can watch as I get sugar wasted." Sadie pulled up a random movie and they sat and watched for a while, laughing to tears at how bad the acting was and how poor the special effects were. It was late when the movie ended and Sadie all but stumbled to bed while Kedah sat on the couch trying to figure out what exactly she should do next. One night a week she had off work so she could take care of her needs, food wise. Now that that was all taken care of, she still had at least 6 hours before daylight broke and her bed called.

Turns out, if you start a show that has multiple seasons, you can kill several hours without even realizing it. Yawning, she shut the computer down and tossed it on the kitchen table, grabbed a bag of blood, nuked it, and wandered to her room in the basement. Funny how the basement in this house used to freak her out and now it was home. Karma was a fickle bitch sometimes. Just before shutting her eyes, she heard footsteps above her and knew Sadie was up and getting ready to go to work. With a sad thought of how much she missed the sun, Kedah shut her eyes and crashed for the day.

Darkness and death plagued her dreams. Blood filled every corner of her thoughts and screams echoed in the hallowed halls of her mind. Something was coming. It wanted her dead. Wanted her gone. So she ran. She ran as fast as her legs could go and still it wasn't fast enough to outrun the nightmare. She screamed, thrashed, and bit her way out of a struggle that had no end. Her heart, which was normally silent, beat wildly as blood began to pool on the surface of her skin. She scratched at it and scrubbed frantically but to no avail. It kept flowing and she screamed in such terror that when she awoke, she sat upright, sheets a tangled mess around her body, sobbing hysterically.

It was just a dream.

It was always just a dream.

Crap, she mumbled in between a hiccup and a sob. She laid back down, holding her arms in front of her face for inspection. Nothing. No trace of blood or nightmares. Same pale skin with a few lingering freckles that she had when she fell asleep this morning. Closing her eyes, she caught her breath before another sob took hold and tried to calm her emotions.

Nothing good ever came from dwelling on the emotions of a dream. At least that's what her parents tried to tell her when she was alive. It worked somedays; most days it didn't.

As long as she could remember, she'd dreamt of blood and death. She thought it was a premonition of her transition, but now that she turned and was still having them, maybe it was just fate with a constant warning. But, if fate was warning her, why was the nightmare getting worse. Some days she just laid in her bed awake, scared that this would be the day she couldn't claw her way out of her own mind. Scared that the night would prove more horrors than she could handle and maybe, just maybe she wouldn't even wake up after a day's sleep. People always said the mind was a scary place to be and she agreed. Hers was downright terrifying.

Reaching over to the nightstand, she grabbed her phone to check her messages. It wasn't like she really talked to anyone, aside from Sadie. She died after all. That tended to stop people from calling or texting. It was depressing really.

The memory of her funeral flashed forward in thought. That was devastating. They buried a body that wasn't hers. The official report was that it was too badly burned to really be identified. Only a tooth was discovered and used to identify it as Kedah. A tooth that was planted by her and Sadie, of course.

Vampires weren't real, after all. They were sparkly and drank from bottles of synthetic blood. They lived in books and the magic of digital effects. Yet, here she was with fangs that popped out like an uncomfortable boner of the mouth. Not that she used them anyways, because she had no idea how. No one ever taught her and she was too terrified to even try.

Fangs. Vampires. Jensen.

Kedah thought about her eventful evening and the new vampire that may hold the key to changing her life. At the very least he could teach her how to survive better than what she was doing now. Granted, she was surviving, but at some point she knew she'd have to move away from Sadie and this place. The no aging thing put a damper on staying put, or at least that's what she assumed.

A shrill alarm broke through her thoughts reminding her it was time to go to work. She'd found out that some low key places, like the local diner, hired under the table workers, with no questions. This was great for her because she could make some money, get out of the house, and feel like an almost normal person.

Quickly, she got out of bed and got dressed, tucked her phone in one pocket and part of her apron in the other, then wandered upstairs for her liquid breakfast. She really missed food and coffee. She told herself the blood was like drinking coffee with a little more of a bite. Somedays that motto worked. Somedays it didn't help in the slightest.

One bag down the hatch and she was ready to face the night.

The diner was within walking distance of the house, so getting to and from at late hours was not much of a challenge. No one ever seemed to bother her anyways. The air was clear and crisp, a hint of winter on the horizon. Shuffling into the back door, she waved to Cook as she slid her apron over her head and got to business. Ironically, he was the only cook at the Greasy Spoon and that's just what people called him. It made life easy for new hires, or so that was the response he'd give when asked why his name was also his job. To say he was mysterious would make light of how Cook presented himself.

Nights tended to be a steady wave of busy then dead as customers came and went with the passing hours. Despite the ebb and flow of customers, the dishes in the sink never really stopped, keeping her busy and leaving not much time to think.

Hours later Cook lightly tapped her shoulder to let her know it was time to go, handed her the night's pay, and waved her away without a word. He was a nice guy, quiet and large, but gave off a commanding personality that tended towards the do not fuck with me vibe. Anyone who tried almost instantly regretted it. He was definitely good to have on your side and not the other way around. "Bye." She said with a smile as she tucked the smallest part of her apron into her back pocket and slowly walked to the back door.

As she stepped out into the alley, letting the old metal door slam shut, she ran her tongue over her aching fangs and thought that maybe she was going to have to feed again. She really wished she knew exactly how much blood she needed daily to actually function. For now, it was like an epic game of roulette, hoping that each day she got just enough to not turn psycho.

"Hey, pretty girl." A gravelly voice called out. Tired, greasy, and hungry, she was completely unsocial and had no desire for any interactions of any kind. She just wanted her bed and a shower.

Ignoring the man, she continued down the alley, picking up her speed. In all honesty, she could probably just run past the man, but that would raise questions that she didn't know how to deal with.

"Hey. I'm talking to you. Where do you think you're going in such a hurry?" The man laughed deep in his throat, sending off a chill of a warning. Human or not, this wasn't anything she wanted to deal with.

"Just, let me pass. I have no money and nothing to give." Kedah muttered.

"It's not the money I'm after sweetheart." The man stepped out from the shadows he was hiding in, causing Kedah to come to a halt. He was the size of a boulder and smelled like a gutter. Covering her mouth, she took a step back, only to bump into another man she hadn't noticed.

"Aren't you a pretty little thing?" A breathy voice behind her said. He leaned down, his hot breath at her ear, and inhaled deeply. "Smells good too, boss."

She shuddered, she couldn't help it. Now what? She surveyed the man in front of her and behind, thinking if she couldn't run she could at least throw a punch or two. Maybe? Those men were really huge and maybe a punch wouldn't even phase them. But, she could try. "Just let me pass."

"Sure sweetheart," the man in front of her said with a toothy grin. "Right after you pay the price."

"I already told you, I don't have any money." She had a feeling she knew exactly what the price was, which wasn't money, but she'd keep at that angle as long as she could.

"And I told you, we don't want money. Hold her." Rough callused hands crashed down on her shoulders, holding her in place. The tingle of magic swept across her skin giving her the first awareness that the men weren't human. This was definitely problematic. She didn't even know much about her new species, let alone anything else that roamed around.

She began to struggle then, but the hands on her shoulders gripped tighter, threating to crush bone. She stopped and closed her eyes. Struggling was stupid. She should have just run, but since she didn't, her brain began to scramble for how she should get out of this situation.

Somewhere deep within, her anger stirred, her fangs elongated and her muscles tensed, making her fight or flight instinct want to fight. She hadn't a clue how, but be damned if she wasn't going to at least try.

Taking action, she lifted her knee forcefully, nailing the first guy in front of her in the crotch. As he crouched down in pain, she brought her knee up and connected it with his nose. "You Bitch," He howled in pain.

The guy who was holding her shoulders, let go with one hand and wrapped a muscled arm around her waist, hoisting her off the ground. Screaming, she kicked out wildly and tried to claw at the man's arms, desperate to be back on the pavement. "You're going to pay for that," he growled into her ear. Taking the opportunity, she reached back and dug her fingers into his eye socket.

Guy number two howled in pain and nearly dropped her before she was ripped out of his arms by guy one who was back on his feet. He threw her against the wall and she cried out on impact. Pinning her with one hand gripping her neck, he used the other to push her shirt up laying his hand on her bare skin. She screamed and struggled, his touch burning her skin. Her screams seemed to do nothing more than excite him as he pushed harder into her neck, causing her breaths to come in short desperate gasps.

Tears started to stream down her face as her brain tried to process what was about to happen.

This can't be happening, her mind pleaded with itself. One moment she was in a panic and the next she was utterly calm. Her control on her inner vampire snapped like a stretched out rubber band.

Suddenly stronger than she realized, she pushed against her attacker. Escaping his grasp, she immediately struck out, connecting with his nose. There was a loud crack and blood began to pour out.

Blood.

So much blood.

Zeroing in on the blood, her fangs throbbed and everything else around her slipped away. She was so thirsty. Without warning, she sprang and was on him, fangs ripping at his throat. As the copper tang of his blood soothed the ache and fire within her, his hands grabbed at her, trying to free her grip. Somewhere in the distance she heard a crashing noise and a moan, but didn't seem to care what it could be. All she cared about was the blood that she was after.

Closing her eyes, she savored the moment, suddenly feeling really alive for the first time. She never noticed that the man under her hold had stopped moving. Suddenly a pair of hands came from out of nowhere and yanked her away, dragging her unwillingly down the alley. She snapped at the person pulling her way. She thrashed and struck out. The hold on her never wavered and through her blood induced haze a voice started pushing through. "Kedah, hun. You gotta come back. Come on girl."

Come back? From what? She blinked several times. Flashes of what just happened replaying in her mind in confusing clips. She began to shake as she crumpled into a heap on the dirty alley ground.

"Kedah, you okay girl? Come on now, clear your head." The stranger's voice was soothing, soft, and commanding. Comforting. She obeyed, willing herself to calm as much as she thought she could.

Slowly, as if she was surfacing from the depths of a murky lake, her eyes began to focus and the stranger took shape. He was crouched down in front of her, more than an arm's length away. She looked at him and felt a small amount of relief. At least she knew him. Then she saw the blood covering her hands and began to shake again. "Did I kill him? Oh my god, is he dead?"

"Almost, but I got ya off of him in time. Neck's a mess, but it's nothing some stitches and a turtleneck can't hide. You coming back to reality, girl? I gotta good hold on your actions and I'd like to give ya control back of your own body. Ya think you're good to go?" He asked, his voice thick with a deep southern accent and years of smoking.

She didn't understand his comment until she tried to move and couldn't. Her mind was working. Her body wasn't. It was the oddest sensation, but somewhat comforting to know she wouldn't snap again. She wasn't sure she wanted control back.

Looking down at her hands, because she could at least move her eyes still, she saw the blood, and could feel it starting to dry on her skin. She had the sudden urge and desire to shower in bleach and boiling water.

The man who had dragged her back, and probably saved her life, was Cook from the diner. She was relieved until she realized that he must know what she was, and didn't seem phased by it. "How?"

"Ah girl, I am not as dumb as most think. And I am much older than most expect. Never you mind all that though, you okay for me to let you go now?" He stood up and stepped back, leaning against the wall and taking a long drag of a cigarette that suddenly appeared in his hand. Now that she could get a good look at him in a different light, she could tell he had some years on him and was wiser than he led on to be. There was definitely more to him than she knew.

"Yeah, I think I'm okay." She said and almost immediately a weight was lifted from her mind. The first thing she did was scrub her hands on her jeans. "How did you know to stop me? I can't. . . I don't know what happened."

"S'okay girl. I expected something like this would happen eventually. Being untrained and all that. Those guys had it coming. So I'm not sorry you tore into them like ya did." He took a last drag of his cigarette, dropping it with a sigh. "I called Jensen for a cleanup and to get those boys taken care of. He said to tell you to wait here and he'll take you somewhere safe to wash off. I'm going to leave the door cracked, you holler if you need me again, okay?"

"Okay." She muttered still confused with everything. "But, what happened to me? I don't understand."

"You're a vampire, girl. That's what happened. Do me a favor and wait for Jensen, okay? And I'll see ya tomorrow at work, ya? Oh, those guys won't bug ya, they're out cold." Cook smiled gently at her and walked back into the diner. He looked casual and cool, like this sort of thing happened daily. Like she didn't just almost kill a person and was now covered in his blood.

Too much was spinning around in her head, so she just sat, slumped against the wall, staring off into the distance, trying not to think at all. Some time had passed, she wasn't sure exactly how much, before a familiar voice called out to her. "Kedah. Can I come back to you? I've got two men handling the guys back here." The voice paused and she heard small murmurs and footsteps. "I'm going to walk towards you, okay?"

She couldn't understand why he was talking to her like a child until she remembered the last 15 minutes. She was almost a killer with blood drying on her clothes. She was a monster and he had every right to treat her as such.

"Kedah. I know you're still hungry. I've got bags of blood with me and I'm bringing them to you." Jensen's voice was slowly coming closer just as her stomach roared in hunger.

"Okay." She whimpered. She was so hungry and even the thought of Jensen made her look up at him like he was a tasty little snack. Which then made her stomach roll for other reasons.

"Close your eyes and open up. I need you to chug this." Jensen said as he stopped in front of her and held out a bag. "You're not going to hurt me. Once we get a few bags into your system you'll be you again. Those guys will be gone and nothing more than a distant memory."

Still feeling like she was on autopilot, she watched as he stabbed the bag open and greedily grabbed at it, closing her eyes and drinking it dry in seconds. She'd done this before, though she preferred to pour it out into a mug or cup. Beggars can't be choosers at this point. Three more bags later and she felt relativity better, albeit very tired.

"I'm sorry." She muttered as she raised her gaze to see Jensen squatting in front of her smiling.

"No worries. Blood lust happens without warning and has several triggers, most of which young vampires can't identify right away. I'm just surprised it hasn't happened before now. You're lucky Cook was around. Things could have been much worse." He stood and held out a hand, offering to help her up.

She took his hand and stood, groaning as her body protested the sudden change in status. Trying not to look down at her stained clothes and hands, she folded her arms into her body and looked around, noticing that they were the only two left in the alley. "Where did they take those men?"

"Away. A local pack will deal with them." He leaned against the wall and slid his hands into his front pockets, watching her.

Pack. Like wolves? Well, of course, she thought. If vampires were real, why not the rest of the supernatural creatures. "Do I need to give a statement, or anything?" She wanted them gone. Away. Never to be allowed back out with people. She didn't feel even the littlest amount of sorry for them. "What exactly were they? And what is Cook?"

"Werewolves. We've actually been looking for them for a while, so I owe you a thank you for tearing into them. They won't bother you again. And Cook, well, you'll have to ask him someday. He's a good guy, if that's the information you're after. He can be trusted." An air of mystery surrounded his words, but she didn't have the energy to push further.

"And you? Can you be trusted?" She asked.

"Yes and no. I, we, are vampires. Trust comes with time and knowledge and you don't know me. However, you really have no choice but to trust me right now. I could have turned you in last night, and I didn't. I cleaned up this mess, and I didn't have to." He commented.

"True. I guess a thanks is needed then." She pulled her arms closer into her body, suddenly aware of a chill creeping in. "Thank you."

Jensen shrugged out of his jacket and slowly held it out for her. She wrapped her body in it savoring the warmth of the body heat that still lingered. "Just promise me you'll stop by the Estate. Think about it, if I had wanted to hurt you, I'd have done it already. In one way or another.

26

The Den, as we sometimes call the Estate, can help. Briarberry Estate is known around here and the name gets long after saying it awhile. Plus humans, if they over hear us talking, won't understand it. Now, I have a safe house about a block from here, come on. We'll get you a shower and a change of clothes before you go home and scare Sadie."

Before Kedah could take a step she froze. She never mentioned her roommate, not that she had one nor her name. In fact, she hadn't mentioned anything about her personal life to him. "How do you know who my roommate is?"

"I make it a point to know who all the vampires are in this city and who they associate with. Since you came onto my radar last night, I did some research." He led the way down and out of the alley and she followed, seeing that she really had no other choice.

CHAPTER
three

The term, safe house, had her believing she was being led to a little place with a white picket fence and a cheery disposition. What she saw before her was anything but. It looked unsafe, to say the least, and that it should be on the set of the haunted mansion; the grass was knee high and dead in random patches. Windows were boarded up and broken, nothing had ever been repainted, and it basically screamed stay back. When Jensen opened the front gate leading to the house, Kedah took a giant step, in the opposite direction.

"I'm not going in there." There was no way that anything inside that house was safe or helpful. It was probably all just a trap.

Jensen stopped and turned towards her with a sly smile. "Oh yes, you are."

"Nope. I'm not." She argued.

"For God sakes Kedah, you are a vampire. You are what goes bump in the damn night. Get your ass up those stairs. Now." There was no amount of joking in his face and with a jerk of his head towards the house, he signaled for her to get her ass moving.

Despite her better judgment, and with a low growl in his direction, she put one foot in front of the other and walked carefully towards the door. The steps groaned as they cautiously made their way. He didn't knock, just took out a key and opened the door for her.

She expected to see dust and debris with decay and missing floorboards and holes in the walls. She expected wrong. Everything was clean and tidy and the furniture looked comfortable and inviting. She could see her reflection in the kitchen floor and absolutely nothing seemed out of place or off. "Not what I expected."

"Nor should you have. It's not meant to be welcoming to everyone. Just to those that need it and are invited, so to speak. Upstairs in the room to the left should be clothes and a shower. Take all the time you need. I have some calls to make, but I'll be here when you're done. Then I'll walk you home." He waved her towards the stairs and walked off towards the kitchen.

She took a moment to look around the house, admiring the art that hung on the walls, the carpet that blanketed the floor and the general appeal of the entire space. The inside was as safe as anything she'd ever seen and there was no threat that she could detect. Making her way upstairs, she turned into the room she was directed to and went straight for the dresser. To her complete surprise, it was fully stocked as was the closet, with clothes of all sizes and styles. Someone clearly spared no expense in the selection of goodies for others to use.

Leaving the doors to the closet open, she wandered over to the bathroom to take a quick shower. It was a simple bathroom but came fully stocked with all kinds of bathroom goodies. She couldn't help but wonder and imagine who needed to use the safe houses and who exactly funded and ran them.

Turning the water to hot, she stripped off her stained clothes, carefully stepping into the hot spray of water, groaning as it caressed her skin. Closing her eyes, she savored the moment, enjoying the feel of her muscles relaxing and her body unwinding.

When the water became chilled, she shut it off and wrapped herself in a towel. Moving to the closet she grabbed a pair of jeans, a simple black shirt, some under things and a pair of shoes.

Quickly getting dressed, she towel dried her hair and inspected herself in the mirror. The same person from the morning looked back at her, and yet, she felt completely different. Maybe she was finally embracing the fact that she was different.

Sighing, she tossed her old clothes in the trash, not needing that memory to follow her home.

Walking into the kitchen, she stopped and looked at Jensen. He was framed by a bay window that faced a shabby and over grown back yard. He was talking quietly on the phone, staring out into the predawn sky. Admittedly, he was beautiful standing there, looking more human than vampire. It was hard not to stare. He hung up his call, shoved his phone in his back pocket and turned to face her. "Feel better?"

"Much, thank you. What do I owe you for these?" She said gesturing to her body and the new clothes she wore.

"Think nothing of it." Jensen waved her over to the table where a mug was waiting for her. She took a whiff and groaned in delight. "I figured you needed some after the morning you had."

Since her turn she hadn't touched coffee, thinking it would come back up instead of staying down. She felt silly now, just standing there staring at the cup. "I can drink coffee?"

He laughed and picked up his mug, taking a sip, proving it was fine. "Have you not tried?"

Groaning, she held the mug to her face and inhaled the rich aroma. When she took her first sip she nearly cried. "Oh good god this is heaven."

"It's pretty standard stuff but it gets the job done. Please tell me you've at least eaten?" He asked, a little bit of shock showing on his face.

"I can eat?" She asked feeling flustered and ridiculous.

"Good lord, it's no wonder you went blood crazed on those weres this morning. You've damn near starved yourself." He shook his head with a sad look. "You have to eat, Kedah. In a few hundred years or so you won't have to eat much, but you still can to enjoy the evolving culinary world. Come on, let's get you breakfast. I'd wager a pretty good bet that you'll feel almost human with enough food and blood in your system."

The list of food she was going to get was miles long. She could eat. She felt like an idiot for not even trying but seriously, this was all new to her. She had some crazy notion that if she had food she'd be seriously sick and wanted to avoid that. "I'm a terrible vampire, aren't I?" She mused out loud. It seemed she fell into the Hollywood glamour of what a vampire should be without trying to figure out what she really was. How sad.

"I've met worse, but you're not winning any awards this year." He chuckled as he took her mug and put it in the sink. "Come, breakfast awaits." The caffeine was making its rounds in her system and she smiled in delight for the first time in months. "You'd fit in at the Den with ease."

"The Den?" She asked with curiosity.

"The business card I gave you, remember? The Den, also known as the Briarberry Estate. It's a bigger safe house than this, much bigger. It's a shake smaller than the Biltmore, if that helps the imagination. I'm not the one to explain it though, for that you need to just come by and see." Jensen started walking down the cracked sidewalk towards the closest restaurant.

"Okay. I'll come by. But, are you sure it's there? Seriously, we've been there dozens of times. I've never seen anything other than some very large briar bushes." She said, resigned. She was curious now, wanting to know more about this new world she had just entered.

"The Estate is warded to not show up to humans. You are not a human anymore, thus you will see it. Go to where the Estate used to be. Just watch. You'll see it. Sadie won't, unless we wish her to." He said.

"Warded? And why?" She questioned.

"Because she's human. You are not. Anyone not human can see past the wards while humans merely see the briar patch." He explained.

She still didn't understand. "What's a ward?"

"Magical shield of sorts." He stated. That still explained nothing to her. "Swing by sometime and I'll explain it to you and show you. Let's get some food for you, dawn is on its way."

The approaching dawn felt like an itch under her skin; a subtle warning to seek shelter. It wasn't like she died with the rising sun, but she got very tired very quickly. Which then begged the question she hadn't thought to ask until now. "I can't be out in the daylight, can I?"

"Yes and no." He replied.

"That was incredibly unhelpful." She shot at him. "Care to elaborate?"

"No." He said while opening the door for her. He waited patiently as she drooled over the menu and ordered enough to feed everyone in the restaurant. She was so hungry and thought for sure she'd never be able to eat enough to satisfy that hunger. She also ordered several large coffees because Sadie never drank straight coffee and she had a craving for it now. Grabbing her goodies with a grin, they left and walked back to her place.

Thank you didn't even begin to cover what she needed to say to him as they approached her house. He was basically saving her life. Just as she was about to open her mouth, the front door swung open and a very nerve racked Sadie was standing framed in the morning shadows. It looked like Mother hen was pissed. Kedah bit her lip and looked apologetic at Jensen.

He waved her off and smiled politely at Sadie. "Good morning, Sadie. I trust you are well?" He said with a grin. "Everything you're thinking isn't true so just calm your nerves." He turned back to Kedah and spoke softly. "You're in for a bad day when you walk in that door. Good luck. Oh and Kedah, do not tell her about the safe house or how to get to the other place. I will know if you have. I'm trusting you, as you trusted me. She may know about you, but it's dangerous to know about the rest of us. Lie to her, Kedah. If you want her to continue to live, you'll have to lie. Do you understand me?"

Knowing that he was right, and hating that she knew, she nodded and said her thanks. Not looking at Sadie, she hustled into the house as fast as she could. Sadie slammed the door behind her and followed her to the kitchen, watching as she dumped her food on the table. She was so going to eat before her darling roommate dug into her with 20 questions.

Jensen walked away from Kedah's little house in the city completely baffled as to how she had survived for months on stolen blood and no actual food. He'd known vampires who died from far less and yet, somehow, this girl survived. He just couldn't wrap his head around it.

Though her situation did pose an issue for him. If she survived, then who else might have? How many were out in his state with sires who bit and bailed trying to fend for themselves. That was a problem that was going to need to be addressed and soon. Last thing he needed was a horde of uncontrolled vampires running loose in Briarberry.

Running a hand down his face, he quickly made his way back to the safe house and double checked the locks. There hadn't been much in the way of break-ins in this area, but with a place such as this, one couldn't be too careful.

As he stood outside the gate, he looked down the long worn down road and tried to decide what he needed to do next. It had been a long time since he was calm for a moment, that it was almost unfamiliar territory.

Kedah was going to need more attention, in some form or another. The threat of vampires running loose around the city was going to need some serious attention. Things needed to be dealt with back at the Estate and the sun was rising soon, which meant he only had an hour or so before he needed to sleep.

He needed more coffee. Coffee was a guilty pleasure he had come into within the last 50 years, especially with the invention of instant coffee makers and flavors of every kind infused within the cup. The Greasy Spoon had the best in town, if you knew who to ask and what exactly to ask for. Smiling to himself, he headed down the old street, casually watching the morning begin to creep into the horizon and the sounds of the day beginning.

Making his way to the local diner, he walked around to the back and into the alley, the very one he just pulled Kedah from. Before he could even knock on the back door, Cook opened it and handed him a Styrofoam cup that had steam rising from the vents on the lid.

"Thank you." He said.

"Sure. You get Kedah squared away?" Cook asked, stepping into the alley and lighting up a smoke.

"I think so. Were you aware that she hadn't eaten solid food since her turn?" He asked.

"I thought that may be the case. Lucky she didn't die." His voice rumbled out and seemed to echo around the alley.

Jenson nodded as he took a long sip of coffee. "Have you seen any other kids running around here that are like her? No Sires present?"

"Nope." Cook said as he finished off his smoke and dropped it on the ground, putting a boot to it before turning and heading back into the kitchen.

Jensen knew that Cook wasn't much for talking, so it was constantly frustrating to hear short answers instead of revealing ones. Having a few minutes left before needing to make it home, he pulled out his phone, called for a ride, because he was sure the others he was with when Kedah had her incident had taken the jeep back, and walked over to the Book Nook, which neighbored the Greasy Spoon.

It wasn't currently open, as it was still pretty early in the morning, but he had a key and knew the owner well. Quickly disarming the alarm when he entered, he made his way to the back of the store and dropped into a large dusty brown leather wingback chair. It was well used and loved and in combination with his coffee, he forgot for just a moment that he was a vampire who held more responsibilities then any one person should.

Life never used to be this complicated, but as the years progressed and technology advanced, things steadily became more complicated and harder to manage. He was definitely due for a break; it was just a matter of when that break would come.

CHAPTER
four

Taking a bite of a biscuit, Kedah's stomach groaned in delight.

Sadie stood and watched quietly as she continued to carb load, washing everything down with not one but two cups of coffee. She didn't feel bad for her observer. Kedah was starving and had four months of food to catch up on.

"So, you can eat." Sadie muttered, more a statement than a question.

"You have no idea how good this is. I'd share, but no. Also, if you touch my food, I will bite you. I am not even kidding. It's been four months since I've eaten and I'm now totally invested in this." She finished off some hash browns and another cup of coffee before sitting back, happy and full. "You may speak now."

"Who the hell was that and what happened to your clothes?" Sadie blurted out, sounding like she had been holding that in for hours.

"Long story." She muttered trying to come up with a clever way to explain the morning.

"Spill it." Sadie demanded. "Now."

"Don't you have to head out soon? It's nearly seven and if you don't leave soon you'll be late for work." She asked, stalling.

"I'll call in with a heart attack. Boss owes me a few hours give or take for coming in at random times anyways. Spill it Kedah, now." Sadie crossed her arms over her chest. She wasn't going to move an inch without something to tide her over about the morning events.

"I got attacked outside the diner. I went vampire crazy. Tore one guy's throat out and gouged out another's eye. The cook at the diner pulled me back. Jensen, the guy I was walking with, cleaned up the mess, gave me clothes to change into and told me I could drink coffee and eat." She knew she'd catch hell from her best friend and was ready for it. Hell, if the situation was reversed she'd be freaking out. However, that was all she was going to tell because she was not going against Jensen.

"Are you serious?" Sadie gasped out as she stood up and began to pace the kitchen, her face a mixture of worry, concern and amusement. "You could have been killed, again!"

"Believe me, I am very aware of that. I thought I was going to die for good. But then something snapped and I defended myself. Not well, mind you, but well enough to get the point across." Kedah stood up and tossed her trash into the bin and leaned against the sink.

"Fine. You're fine. You'll freak out later, you always do. If you think this is no big deal, then fine, I'll accept that. But under no circumstances are you to not tell me who that hottie with you was. Was that THE Jensen?" Sadie questioned. "Also, does he make it a habit of carrying woman's clothes around, because I'm not going to lie, that's a little on the creepy side."

"Yes, that was Jensen and no on the clothes. He sent for them." She smiled. "I told you he was cute, but totally unavailable." She looked at her friend, who was clearly worried about her, and hated how much she had to scoot around the truth when talking to her. "You. Go to work. I'm fine. I need to sleep. Dawn is here and my eyes are refusing to stay open." If she didn't get down to her room soon she was liable to fall asleep on the floor, sleep took hold that quickly sometimes.

"I want you to check in when you get to work and when you leave." Sadie asked. "Please." Grabbing her coat and purse, Sadie walked over to stand directly in front of Kedah. "I love you. I really don't want to lose you, permanently."

Kedah shook her head and hugged her friend. "I love you too. I'll keep you posted." Sadie hugged her back and left for work, shutting and locking the door. Kedah gathered up her leftovers, threw them into the fridge and wandered downstairs. Stripping off her clothes, she climbed into bed, ready to sleep off the events of the morning.

Almost as soon as her head dropped onto her pillow, she was out, dead to the day, entering the realm of restless nightmares.

As the nightmares took hold of her unconscious mind, she tossed and turned, moaning in silent agony. She frantically reached out to take hold of reality but it avoided her grasp. Blood pooled at her feet, dripping from her fingers and fangs. She screamed soundlessly for a resolution that didn't appear. When her body finally gave into the fear, she awoke gasping for breath.

Another nightmare. More blood. More desperation. There was something new this time. Something positive. A small spark of willingness to live, despite the feel of death taking hold.

She needed a vampire psychologist because this was getting out of hand.

Glancing at her phone for the time, she sighed heavily at the knowledge she still had a few hours till dusk and was stuck down in her room.

A good soak in her tub was exactly what she needed, she thought. Rolling herself out of bed, landing with a thud on all fours, she slowly got to two feet and made her way to the bathroom. Turning music on, she ran the water and submerged her tired body. Within moments the hot water soaked into her skin and began working to calm her nerves.

As she began to relax, the events from the morning bubbled to the surface and the breakdown that Sadie predicted began to flow. She cried for what those men could have done. Cried for her reaction to fear, then cried harder when she remembered what she did. She cried for her transition and the life she lost. She cried until her tears dried up and her sobbing subsided. Then a strange numbness took hold.

Vampires were supposed to be magical, strong, and fearless creatures. And yet, here she was, sobbing from fear, having a panic attack in her bathtub, unable to face her new reality. A reality that she hadn't a single clue about.

She missed her family. Her parents had been devastated to hear of her "death". Although she assumed any parent would be, it seemed to her that hers took it harder than expected. Maybe because there was not much of a body to bury? Or because they never really understood what had happened? Any way she played it out, it stung her deeper than she ever could have realized. Sadie kept in touch with them, and passed along news of what they were up to, but it almost hurt worse to hear that their life had continued while hers had stalled out.

The glamorous life of a vampire was a joke. She wasn't laughing.

She missed being social. Sadie was great, but she worked and was human, and though she tried her best to understand and be compassionate, it just wasn't the same. She missed late night movies and lunch dates at the local Mexican restaurant. She missed skiing in the winter and hanging out at the lake in the summer.

Fear kept her mostly at home. She worked to have a little money, but that was it. She feared going out because she didn't want to risk running into anyone she might have known. How awkward would that be? She'd move, but how would she do anything? It was all terribly confusing.

Frustrated, she closed her eyes and sunk her body under the water enjoying the peacefulness that the silence brought. Her senses were always on high alert now and submerging herself gave her a few moments of complete silence. It was bliss. Until her phone ringing cut through the stillness. Resurfacing, she grabbed it and answered. "Hello?"

"Kedah?" A gruff southern voice asked.

"Uh, yeah. And this is?" She asked, more than a little concerned. She was supposed to be dead, after all, and new callers weren't supposed to happen.

"It's Cook. Listen, I got someone to cover you tonight. So, you have places to go, ya? People you need to go see?" Well, wasn't he on top of things this evening? He seemed to know more about her than she did and that made her just a little wary. She'd be asking questions the next time she was in.

"Are you sure? I need the money and where exactly should I be going?" She said cautiously. Jensen said he could be trusted, but she was still leery.

"I'll give you the money you'd make tonight if you promise to go to the Den." She heard him sigh loudly before covering the phone with his hand and barking out a few orders. "Girl, you need some help and that's the place that will help ya. I promise you, nothing bad will happen there. You need to move on and be who you are. A diner is no place for the likes of you. I'll miss ya but you're better than this."

"I can't take your money, Cook, but I promise to go. However, I'll be at work tomorrow, so don't cover my shift. Okay?" Well, at least she now had plans for the night. Nerves coiled in her stomach but it was probably just as well. She needed to just rip the band aid off this, as they say.

"We'll see. Call me on this number if you need me?" He hung up. She looked at her phone to make sure he really had just hung up, and thought he was such a strange man. We'll see, he said? What in the crap was that supposed to mean? Grabbing a towel, she dried off, and got dressed. Her reflection caught her gaze in the mirror and she stopped.

She had always loved her looks but most commented that she wasn't overly special. Green eyes that flaked brown in the summer. Light brown hair that occasionally got confused and had a few strands of red or blonde that pushed through. She'd always been a healthy size eight and never thought it as a bad thing. She was beautifully average. A tiny part of her was disappointed that after she turned she didn't end up like Barbie with fangs, but mostly she was good with staying the same. Her skin was paler, no more sun to kiss it, and her teeth sharper, but still just as beautifully average as before.

Smiling at herself, she braced for the day. Simple ponytail and a dab of makeup and she was ready. Except that the sun was still up enough to cause her some amount of issues. But, she thought, would it? She actually didn't know.

No time like the present to see. Sliding her feet into some flops she carefully made her way to the first floor, nerves fluttering again. What was the worst thing that could happen? Burst into flames, she thought grimly, if that legend was even true.

Peeking out her door, like the cowardly lion she was, she watched rays of sunshine gleam through the curtains. Despite the nerves, the light brought a small tear to her eye because she never thought she'd see it again. She missed laying out and reading.

Taking a deep breath, she took timid steps, drifting carefully towards the windows. With the drapes closed all she had to do was reach out and open them.

It was that simple or that deadly.

It gave her some comfort that she knew exactly what she would see the moment she drew back the curtains. She knew where the neighbors would be and exactly what the oak in the front yard would look like. Little old lady Moore would be sitting in her rocker by the window of her house, watching her soaps. No one would be paying attention to the vampire in the dark, tempting fate with the light.

Holding her breath, she grabbed the curtain and jerked it back, letting the light touch her face and arms for the first time in four months. She imagined, just for a second, that the light touched her skin in kindness and warmth.

Then the smell of burning flesh rose and she screamed in terror as her skin began to bubble. Letting go of the curtain she dropped to the floor, hustled away from the window, curled into a ball, and cried as the burn began to sizzle on her skin. She literally felt like she was on fire, though no flames were present. The very thought of moving another muscle had her cringing, thinking it may cause more damage than it was worth.

She was angry and so disappointed. When she finally calmed herself for a moment, she realized that the burns weren't as bad as she expected. She'd not be sun tanning anytime soon, but she wasn't covered in flames either.

Cringing, she gathered herself up and crawled back to her dungeon, sprawling out on the cold ground, enjoying the dark on her skin. She had a few choice words for Jensen and his cryptic message of what daylight could do to her.

After a few minutes of her staring at her ceiling, which really needed to be repainted, she noted, she felt the ache in her skin ease as a new one arose. Her stomach clenched and her fangs elongated. Oh great, she was hungry again. Carefully sitting up, she studied the marks on her arm and decided to avoid mirrors for the night. She had no desire to see what her face resembled.

She needed to get back upstairs and get to the kitchen for blood. And a cheeseburger if one was in the fridge.

Climbing the stairs, once again, avoiding the windows, she scurried to the kitchen. Grabbing a mug from the cupboard and a few bags of blood from the fridge, she gingerly walked to the microwave to nuke the blood before dumping it into her mug. Whatever plastic the blood was kept in was surprisingly microwavable. Throwing it back quickly, she grimaced at the taste but immediately felt better. Tossing the bags in the trash, she put the mug in the sink and checked out the fridge for something to eat. Not seeing anything that screamed at her, she closed the door and slumped into a chair, feeling utterly defeated.

Time seemed to skip around as she sat there; speeding up then slowing down. She totally zoned out. Without realizing how long she had been sitting, she nearly jumped out of her chair when the front door opened and Sadie walked in. She dropped her bags at the door then froze when she realized that Kedah was in the kitchen.

"I tried to see if I could withstand the sun." Kedah murmured, answering Sadie's unasked question. "Bad news is no, I cannot. Good news is, now I know. I also know what burning flesh smells like. It's not a good smell." She tried to smile and make a joke out of it all, but Sadie wasn't having it.

"You tried to go outside? Are you kidding me?" Sadie exclaimed.

"Nope, not kidding. And I didn't try to go outside, just opened the curtains. It hurt like a son of a bitch and I won't do it again. Lesson learned." She said, still trying to make light of the situation. Sadie just looked at her with her eyes wide and mouth open.

"Why?" Sadie finally asked.

"Why not?" She said with a shrug. "I don't know what I can and cannot do and no one will tell me. So, live and learn I guess."

"You guess? I... wow. I don't even know what to say." Sadie looked a combination of pissed and hurt and a little bit offended. She could understand her concern, but it was misplaced.

She didn't want to get mad at her roommate, but maybe this was the excuse she needed to duck out without Sadie asking 20 questions. "Look, I'm fine. Okay? I did use up all the blood I had so I'm going to go get more and hang out around there a bit. I got called out of work today, so don't wait up. And yes, I'll have my phone on me." Kedah stood and grabbed her phone off the table, shoving it into her pocket along with a few dollars she had in her wallet on the counter.

Sadie looked a little taken back by her straight forward attitude but stepped out of her way as she made her way to the door. "Yeah, okay. Be safe."

Kedah didn't want to look back at her so she waved and left. Lying to her best friend wasn't ideal but it seemed necessary. This was the person who saved her life and has bent over backwards to help her. But, she made a promise and she didn't want Sadie's life to be in danger. If a lie kept her from dying, then she'd continue that lie forever. It was the least she could do.

Autumn was coming and the air smelled of falling leaves, baked goods and a hint of coffee. The sidewalks were bowed and cracked and in desperate need of a little TLC, she noted, as she walked the path she'd walked for years on end. The city still bustled around her, despite the feeling that she had stalled, and she felt everything around her should have stalled out as well. She stopped, why didn't they?

Taking the business card from her pocket, she traced the name with her thumb and grinned shyly. Maybe she'd finally find a place where life went on; went on with her moving to their beat and her own, a beat that was so obviously different than the world around her.

CHAPTER
five

Hitting up the app on her phone for a ride, she waited patiently, while continuing to watch the people around her. Once inside the car, which smelled only slightly better than her last ride, she sent it in the direction of the Estate, with only a small grunt from her driver. Kids go there all the time, for various reasons, so it probably wasn't a shock to him to be driving out that way anymore. She still didn't understand how it could be hidden to one group of people and not another, but she guessed she was either going to be happily surprised or epically disappointed. A few miles outside the city the car stopped aside an old wire fence that had chunks missing and was rusting. She sighed, got out, paid the man, and walked into the chill of the night, wishing she would have grabbed a jacket. Rubbing her arms to keep warm, she listened as the car drove off and then headed off down the worn out dirt road.

She never had been the praying type, but she prayed that something was here, because if not she'd look like an idiot. An idiot that would have to call for a ride home. The further she walked the more she felt like something was off. Something magical was near, at least that's what she thought she was feeling. Stopping where the magic felt the strongest, she looked into deserted briar bushes, not sure what she should be expecting. It looked the same as it always had, except it was dark now, so that added to the eerie effect of the entire situation.

As she stood there, staring at nothing but an old briar bush field, the air began to wave and shift, morphing into shapes and structures. A haze began to push against her, like it was searching for something. She wasn't uncomfortable, but wasn't comfortable either. Suddenly, the magic burst past her revealing a giant wrought iron gate and a solid brick wall on either side going on for as far as she could see.

She turned towards the road, making sure nothing else had appeared, and turned back, dumbfounded.

Timidly, she reached over to the call box that had also just appeared, and pushed the button. "Yes." A voice clipped.

"Uh," She stammered, still more than a little confused. "I got this card from Jensen. Is he here?"

"Name?" The man behind the box asked.

"Kedah." She responded.

"Hang on." He said.

"To what?" She muttered before slapping a palm over her mouth. Sarcasm was her natural defense against the unknown, and most of the time it got her in trouble.

While she was waiting for, whatever, she peeked through the gate, trying to get a glimpse of something, anything, to give an indication of what she was headed into. All she could see was the outline of some trees and darkness. Ominous.

Her nerves were shot and the longer she waited the worse the scenario playing in her head became. Was she headed into a nest of vampires? Was this Jensen's house and he wanted her for other reasons? Could she be walking to her death? She really had nothing to lose, but a gruesome ending to the already tragic start to her immortality wasn't ideal.

A sharp click of a lock broke the silence, followed by the metal gate sliding open, stopping with just enough room for her to scoot in. "Go in and follow the path to the main house. They are expecting you. Do not deviate from the path or you will be shot."

"Okie dokie." She nervously muttered as she stepped into the gate and listened as it slammed shut behind her. No turning back now. Taking a moment to let her eyes adjust, she began to walk the path, hoping to not get shot in the process.

The moon shone down between the trees, casting shadows and giving her a hint of what the grounds looked like. Amongst the darkness, it looked a little ancient and wild. In the daylight, this place was probably magical. As she continued to walk, noises began to become clearer. Just muffled sounds, like people talking and laughing. A car in the distance starting up. The smell of a wood burning fire floated through the air. There was also the smallest hint of chlorine, which was terribly weird.

Another few hundred feet and she came to a stop, looking up at the largest house she'd ever seen, in person. The higher she looked the bigger the place got. It seemed to spread in every direction. "Dear. God." She muttered as she took the steps to an old front door. Before she could knock, the door swung open and she was waved inside.

"Kedah right?" When she nodded, the man continued. "Follow me." The guy was dressed in jeans, a graphic tee and boat shoes. Utterly casual and completely out of place for what she would have expected for this place. He gave off a very frat house type vibe.

She walked in and immediately tripped over her own feet because that's what she did. Humiliate and embarrass herself at every opportunity. It came naturally. The man caught her arm and nodded slightly, asking if she was okay. She muttered a thank you and followed him into a sitting room that was bigger than the first floor of her old house. "Wait here. Someone will be here to help you in a few moments. Do you need anything?"

"No. Thanks, though." She said with a smile.

Getting fidgety, she began to look around the room, taking in the furniture and decorations, the attention to detail that was right down to the trim. She hadn't realized she was no longer alone until someone tapped her on the shoulder. She squealed in surprise as she fumbled to turn around. Her face flushed as she came face to face with the most well-built example of male she'd ever seen. He was strikingly tall and thick with muscles that stretched under his perfectly shaped jeans and casual shirt, a cocky smile caressing his face.

"Jesus, you scare easy." He laughed. His laugh rang out through the room and it sent a small sliver of warning through her. This man, as hot as he was, was dangerous, and he knew it. He kept a lazy smile on his face as his gaze swept down her body before catching her eye again.

Jensen was dangerous because he was an older and a wiser vampire, she understood that. But this man was a walking danger sign, and she felt completely drawn to him. No reasoning as to why, just that she was. It was in her very nature to attract trouble of any kind, so of course she would be instantly attracted to him.

"Let's have a look and see who dragged you here." He said with a grin and held out his hand. It took her a good minute before she realized he wanted to see the card. She dug it out of her pocket and handed it over. "Jensen. Of course."

"Is he here?" She asked.

"Maybe." He shrugged.

"Maybe? Maybe yes or maybe no. Maybe you don't know. Help me out here." She questioned.

"Maybe." He jested and she flushed with annoyance. Good looking, he may be, but damn annoying he was proving to be more.

"Exactly what do you need? Or are you here to just annoy me?" She asked, her voice starting to go a pitch higher on her. Naturally, when she became upset or in unfamiliar territory, a shield went up and she got overly angry and sometimes aggressive. It was almost as if she needed to prove she wasn't as scared or pissed off as she really was.

"Mostly to annoy you, is it working?" He commented while she shot him her best evil glare. "It is, good. I'm your personal welcoming committee."

"My what? Really?" She looked him up and down, noting the casualness of his demeanor and the nonchalant attitude. Not a chance he actually worked for Jensen.

"Did I stutter?" He asked.

"If it's all the same, I'll just wait for Jensen. Could you go get him?" She asked, having had about enough of this guy and doing everything within her power to stay calmer then she wanted to be.

"Probably. But my so called job," he actually used air quotes saying that, "is to tell you where you are. Sit." The guy pointed to the couch, which she took one look at and shook her head.

"No."

"Feisty." He purred and she shuddered. "Fine. So here is the quick rundown on the Briarberry Estate, or as us paranormals like to call it, The Den." The guy laughed at himself and crossed his arms over the huge expanse of his chest, leaning against the door frame like he was posing for an art class. "This Estate is merely a front for what lies beneath and beyond. This place is for all you poor souls who have been abandoned, lost, forgotten, and rejected."

Alright, this guy was so done. She already felt like a horrible vampire, this guy was just making it worse. "I don't mean to be rude, but you're a bit of an asshole. You know that right?" She shifted her weight between each foot, fidgeting with her hands. This jerk surely didn't belong here and couldn't have anything to do with Jensen. If he did, she got the way wrong impression of the head vampire.

"Aw, thanks." He said with a grin. "Now, back to what I was saying. The rules state that you aren't a prisoner, you can come and go as you please, but we'll be watching and if we don't like where you're going, we'll bring you home. Yeah?" He questioned, then continued on quickly, leaving her no room to speak. "House has rules, you'll get them in the six-thousand-page welcome packet that'll be in your cell, er, room. Mostly standard stuff like no stealing, biting, killing. And really, you're a vampire, I think, so no unauthorized biting on the grounds. Cafeteria has awesome little bags of liquid nourishment for you to have. Bite somewhere else. Okay? Good. Killing, seriously, don't do it. It's usually me that has to clean it up and I hate it. Puts me in a bad mood." She had no idea if he was telling the truth or not, and that was a little frightening. He was smug, laughed at himself, cocky.

"A bad mood? Well we wouldn't want that, now would be." She shifted her eyes around the room, trying to find something else to look at, but was drawn back to the man in front of her.

"No, you really wouldn't." He agreed. "Now, the puppies have their own cottages in the back and sometimes use the basement floors for their time of the month." He started to explain again.

She blinked several times as her brain spun out of control at his statement. Surely he didn't mean actual puppies. "Wait, puppies? Werewolves?"

"Yes, I said that. Puppies. Keep up, lass. Anyways, gets noisy as hell in here during a full moon, with the howling of the pups and the chanting of the witches, so most people choose to leave for the night. Or invest in very good ear buds. Or have very loud sex. My personal favorite is to go the latter route, so look me up if the full moon gets to ya." He winked at her, and did a leisurely look of her body.

"Witches?" She asked, trying to distract his eyes. "And, also, I am so not having sex with you."

"Come on Kedah, keep up. And never say never, sugar, you don't really mean that. Sex is always an option." He was, by far, the cockiest person she had ever met. He continued talking as if nothing that was said was off point. "Everything you ever read is based on some amount of truth. Those things that go bump in the night, I'm related to. You are now too. Everything else, as real as the carpet you're threatening to wear a hole in with all that shifting." He nodded to the floor under her feet where a small path was beginning to form. She stopped moving at once.

"Alright, I think that does it. Questions, comments, concerns? Never mind, I don't really care. Jensen knows you're here and I'm sure he will want to chat as soon as he can break free of whatever boring meeting or call he's occupied with." He pulled a phone from his pocket, looked down, laughed loudly and put the phone back. "Oh, I think there is a library here somewhere. I know there is a pool and gym and a track. Cafeteria is so-so, so I'd suggest you make friends with the local restaurants."

She felt like her brain was going to explode. It was way too much information to handle at once. There was no way this place was actually legit. And the cost? Was she going to have to sell her soul to live here? "I don't have the money to pay for all this." Nothing was ever free, right?

"Does it look like we're hurting for money?" He began to walk the room, touching books and paintings, looking bored and distracted. He stopped and looked back at her. "Jensen, I'm sure, will explain."

She just stood there staring at him. "Who exactly are you?"

"Oh, did I not say?" He laughed. "Sorry, oh wait, no I'm really not." He winked at her and stood to his full height, putting his hands in his back pockets. "I'm sure someone will tell you who they think I am. I look forward to hearing what tales they weave about me. Believe none of it, or all of it. I really couldn't care less." He turned his head sharply and smiled brightly. "Aw look, Jensen is just in time to miss me. See ya around vampire." The guy turned sharply on his heel and left the room without another word.

She looked at the stairs and just as Mr. Mystery had said, Jensen was descending them. He quickly crossed the entry way and smiled when he came closer. Stopping suddenly, he scanned the room and the adjoining rooms. "Doran beat me to you, didn't he?"

"Doran? Is that his name?" She asked.

He sighed heavily and shook his head. "Yes, and he's a piece of work. Sorry about him. What did he tell you?"

"Well," she paused, thinking of the right words to say. "Basically, The Den, is for the supernatural and caters to their every need so that they are not lonely or lost. Give or take."

"You wrapped up his entire speech into one sentence. Impressive. Don't tell him I said that though, he'll get cranky." Jensen laughed.

"That wasn't him cranky? Geeze." She smiled. She was comfortable with Jensen now, and it felt nice to finally relax a little. It was nice to know that Doran wasn't just an ass to her.

"Well, welcome. I'm glad you decided to come. First off this isn't my place, not exactly. You'll meet the founder of the Briarberry Estate another day. She's around, but not too much." Jensen held out his hand towards the stairs, signaling her to follow him.

"In case you were wondering, I am the vampire who is in charge of all the others here and basically our entire state. Before you ask, I am very old, and no, I won't tell you just how old. You can come to me for anything you need and yes, I will teach you what you need to know to be a functioning vampire. At the very least, I will teach you how to feed properly, what you can and cannot do, and where you can and cannot go." He stopped at the foot of the stairs and looked over at her. "How'd the sun tanning go?"

She blushed, remembering she probably still looked a tad burnt. "You could have warned me. That was awful." She said in a grumpy tone.

"I could of, your right. But I wanted to see how far you'd go to make discoveries on your own. Welcome to the undead Kedah, where the rules of the human world no longer apply." He led her up the grand stair case, stopping on the second, of three floors she could see, and led her down a long hallway.

"Exactly how big is this place?" She wondered out loud, choosing to avoid the subjects of the sun and the new rules she needed to play by.

"The main house is three floors high with several levels of basement. There are a dozen or so houses located throughout the back of the property. We're on several hundred or so acres of land that contains a forest, several small streams, and plenty of paranormals."

"That's incredible." She said in awe.

"It's quite the operation." He opened a door and gestured for her to go in. "Come into my office so we can get the boring stuff out of the way." She followed him into the office and stopped to take it all in. The walls were a neutral tan color, the furniture normal and inviting, and very thick oak colored curtains were pulled back from the window. Instead of sitting right away, she went to the window and looked out over the grounds. The view was unbelievable.

Jensen stepped up beside her to gaze out. "Our Matron has put a lot of effort into making this place an escape from the hell of our long pasts. It's a far cry from when I was turned and even farther cry from where others have come from." He turned and motioned for her to sit, again. "Sit, please."

Kedah walked to the chair across from his desk and sat down, enjoying the soft plushness of its cushions. He walked around the desk and pulled out a manila envelope, sliding it to her. "This is everything about who we are. What our rules are and what we do here. Basically, if you want to, you can move in and live with us. You'd be safe and taken care of. Of course, we'd ask that you work to help out. We have jobs here within the estate or you can work off the property in one of our outside endeavors."

"Like the blood bank." She asked. She noted that Jensen seemed very methodical and imagined he'd have to be to keep order in a place such as this. Everything had to have its rightful place or the whole thing could come crumbling down.

"Yes, like the blood bank. We really won't be offended if you chose not to stay here, and of course you'll be allowed to come and go as you please. But you should really read and review what this says and consider your options. In ten years, your friends will look older. People at the diner will recognize that you've not aged. At some point you may run into a problem that may require the attention of others. That's what I'm here for. I wasn't joking when I said that you can get blood from the blood bank, as much as you need. You need to keep yourself nourished or things like the alley will happen again, and next time I won't be so forgiving."

She swallowed hard and looked up at him. "So forgiving?" Guess it was time to get real about this new world she was in.

"You don't think that we'd allow a rogue vampire to just go around attacking people and get away with it? Those guys deserved what they got and you were clueless as to what was happening. That was your free pass, but you won't get another. The general public doesn't need to know about us or any of the people here. Vampires, weres, shifters, witches, and fae all live under the watchful eye of each other and one tiny mistake can be devastating." He was deadly serious and she couldn't help but be a little terrified.

She was suddenly very uncomfortable. There was a lot more to this then she expected or had even considered. "Well, you certainly know how to make a day go from intriguing to terrifying in under a minute."

"It's a talent I have perfected over the years." He smiled and reached across the desk to touch her hand. "I want what's best for you. But I also want what's best for our community. I will do anything for my people, to protect them and to protect the humans from them. Understood?"

"Oh perfectly." She muttered.

"I will be your friend, but I will be the Master of the vampires in this area first. So consider me a friend or foe, but choose that wisely. I've been around a long time and know more than a few tricks." She had no doubt about that.

"Yeah, I got it. Basically, don't fuck up." Her tone was harsher than she meant it to be, her nerves playing tricks with her verbal responses, but he didn't seem to be worried about it. She was probably a million times nicer than most people he met and dealt with.

"Precisely. Now, do you want to see the rest of the place or shall I have someone bring you home?" He asked.

As much as she wanted to see the place, she felt her decision should come from knowledge of the rules and not a desire to swim in the pool. Which was very tempting right now if she was being honest. "I'd like to go home. I do need to stop and get more blood though, my little sun incident sorta killed my supply."

"I imagine it did. I'll have a car brought around for you. They will take you to the blood bank and home." He stood and picked up the phone on his desk. He talked quickly and quietly and hung up just as fast. "Oh and Kedah, please remember. You can't tell Sadie about the existence of the Estate. I know that you may not want to lie to her, but you don't have a choice. It will kill her."

"You'll kill her, you mean?" She questioned.

"Probably not by my hand, but someone else's. She'll slip up and say the wrong thing and it will essentially sign her own death warrant. You have no idea how this world works, Kedah. It's not nearly as glamorous as people try to make it out to be." He waved his hand towards the door and Kedah got up, grabbed her information, and headed that way. Jensen walked her to the hallway and stopped. "Stairs are to your left, and the front door is right there. Someone will be waiting for you. You have my number, call me when you have made a decision."

She looked up at him and tried to find some sort of emotion on his face and got nothing but a pleasant smile. She sighed and said her thanks as she exited the room and almost ran to the stairs. She was a little scared, a little interested, and a whole lot of confused.

Stumbling down the steps, Kedah wasn't watching where she was going and ran right into Doran, who was sitting on the bottom step. Well not ran into him as much as she tripped over him and fell flat on her face.

CHAPTER
six

Sometimes Doran really hated being here in The Den. Maybe not being here, per se, but hated the arrangements he had made with the Matron who created this place. For him to stay here, without questions being asked, he had to do things like help Jensen with security around town and greet some of the local paranormals when they were invited.

As not many came in via the front door, he didn't have to do the latter often, but when he did, he tried to scare them off and overload them with information. Because he was an asshole and it was amusing to watch them all get flustered. Every single person he'd had the pleasure of being the first to greet, had gotten overwhelmed and their initial reactions usually showed who they truly were. So, in a sense, he was doing everyone a small favor by showing others true colors, instead of waiting on the person to decide when to flash those colors.

Kedah was no exception to the rule, however, there was something entirely different about her that when he walked away he had a feeling of regret, which is why he walked faster. She was freshly turned, under six months as far as he could tell, and utterly clueless about everything. He didn't need to be a mind reader to know that. She radiated wonder and excitement, but more than that radiated confusion, nerves, and general apprehension.

As he continued up the stairs and away from the girl, his mind kept drifting back to the parlor. She was a vampire and she was untouchable to him. His mind thought otherwise as it flashed into his subconscious; her emerald green eyes and chestnut brown hair that had a slight wave and curl to it at the tips. Her cheeks flushed with annoyance and frustrations and because it was such a sexy look on her, he kept baiting her. She responded every single time.

Shaking his thoughts away, he charged into his room and to the fridge where a beer was waiting. He needed to go ahead and just scrub her from his mind. Not even a one-night stand would be worth it with her. Vampires and he weren't good bed fellows, as they say, so a chance to have her in his bed would never come to pass.

Dropping to the couch, he grabbed the remote and started flipping stations to find something to distract his thoughts. Cracking open his beer, he kept changing stations, determined to find something on that could clear his mind. He grinned as he stopped on a reality show of the wives of a certain city. Call him crazy, most did anyways, but he loved this shit. It was his guilty pleasure; the reality shows like this. The drama and general bitching reminded him of days long ago when things were, surprisingly, simpler and yet sometimes more complicated. His family loved to argue and it became such a daily occurrence that now that he no longer heard it, he sometimes craved the crazy.

He'd been known, on occasion, to zap himself to those houses and stir the crazy pot just a little bit, if the drama was starting to lack and drift. Yes, he was messing with people's lives and yes, he really didn't care. It made them money and made him laugh, everyone won.

As he sat and watched the drama unfold, he briefly caught, from out in the hall, a bit of Jensen talking to Kedah as he led her to his office. It shouldn't have bothered him, because he was done with her, but it did. He found himself turning the volume down and listening harder to what they were saying. He'd even set his beer down so he wasn't distracted.

From what he caught, they weren't talking about anything important, or pertaining to him. He was surprised by this because he had been such a dick to her that he'd imagine she'd be complaining and Jensen would have to be apologizing. But, nothing.

He had the sudden desire to change that. He wanted her to talk about him, even if it wasn't anything good. And what could it hurt, to go down and bait her a little more. He could probably get another good laugh out of the entire encounter and he'd get to see her again.

Grabbing his beer, he downed it quickly, tossing it over his shoulder and almost making it into the trashcan. Leaving his room, he quickly jumped down the stairs and sat at the bottom of the steps, waiting for her to come back down. This was the only way out, so it was only a matter of a few minutes before she would be headed this way.

Perched on the bottom step, he picked at the carpet to waste time until he heard her leave Jensen's office and, by the sound of her quick steps, was trying to make a quick getaway. He'd just sit right where he was and make the getaway a little less quick, if he could help it.

He watched as she was utterly oblivious to anything other than herself and her thoughts, and started to laugh right as her legs stopped when they hit his unmoving body and she tumbled over, right onto her face.

Laughing loudly, he watched as she scrambled further away from him as she tried to get back to her feet. She looked like a frightened little kitten. He hated to use the word adorable, as it never graced his normal vocabulary, but she was every bit it. "Damn Kitten, walk much?"

She scowled at him and he smiled harder. It was hard to be mad at a kitten for the little hissing they may do. Despite her plea to look fierce. "You're a jerk, you know that?"

"I do know that, actually." He commented as he grabbed the folder she dropped and handed it over. She tried to pull it out from his hands but he held tight. With every pull he brought her closer and closer until she was only an inch from his body.

His body and all his senses flared to life with her that close. Things stirred deep within his body, so much so that he had to hide a gasp of surprise. Her face was flushed with irritation, her hair falling wildly about her face, and her breathing was hitched and uneven. Sexy. She was absolutely sexy and all he wanted to do was kiss her.

He was totally out of his fucking mind.

She was off limits.

He should have just forgotten about her and moved on.

As he looked down at her, watched her puzzled look continue to gaze on him he knew that forgetting her may be harder than he'd like. Something was drawing him to her and he was helpless to stop it. But he'd try, damn it. He would try because she would be bad news for him.

"Who are you?" She asked, her voice a little breathy. He closed his eyes and willed himself to not answer truthfully. That would take all the fun out of this, now wouldn't it? No one here knew who he was, though a good few were pretty close on their guesses.

"Who do you think I am?" He asked, snapping his eyes open and bore a look down at her.

"I think," she muttered, pausing to consider her answer. "That you're a bully. But what else, I don't even know."

"A bully, huh?" He laughed and shook his head, taking a step away from her, giving him more breathing room. "Probably pretty true." Before she could respond or even think about his answer, he took the stairs back to the second floor and back into his room before he took another breath.

She was definitely very bad news for him. And he wanted to be all over that bad news like flies on death. He was an idiot and time would prove it.

Scrambling down the front steps she hurried away from the estate, glad to finally be able to breathe easier. Something about Doran was causing an interesting reaction from her, one she'd have to explore later. Right now, she needed to just get home and sort out her thoughts. A very casual looking man was leaning against a simple gray jeep, smiling as she approached. "Jensen said you could use a lift. I'll swing you by the blood bank and then to your place. Cool?"

"That would be great, thanks." She said as she climbed into the passenger seat, closing her eyes as the man got in and began to drive off. Events of the night played on repeat, drilling into her brain every single detail she could remember. Everything Doran had said to her, everything Jensen had explained, and every tiny detail of the Estate. This is what her new life would be like, if she chose to move there.

As if she needed that reminder of her old life, her phone buzzed in with a message. Sadie had texted to say she was sorry about earlier and to be careful. Best friends were so great. She hated the idea of having to leave her, but somehow always knew that one day she'd have to move on. It was the logical thing, even if she hated it.

Kedah had no idea how to even make new nonhuman friends and that gave her a little anxiety. She loved being social, but getting to the social part was sometimes a little stressful for her. Did she ask them if they wanted to go out for drinks? Was there even a blood bar they could go to? She tried to tell her imagination to stop worrying, but it was taking its time circling all the 'what if's'. Everyone except Doran. He was his own piece of work. He wasn't a vampire, but she wasn't sure what he was. She knew he was hot, beyond hot if she was being honest, but also a total dick and totally off limits. Yet, somewhere in the back of her mind, something screamed out that he was familiar. Almost like she'd heard his name before or had seen someone that looked like him. She couldn't quite place it, but either way, he was a complication that she didn't need at the moment.

Even as she was putting Doran in the 'I'll-deal-with-him-later' box in her mind, she couldn't shake the feeling that somehow she knew him. Surely she'd have remembered a man of that size and that ego, but nothing was ringing a clear bell. She'd wager a bet that he was either going to be a constant annoyance for her or easily forgotten. Honestly, she'd go ahead and put money on the constant annoyance, because even though she'd tried several times already to just brush him off, he kept creeping back into her thoughts.

When they pulled up to the blood bank, the woman she'd met before was waiting with a cooler and a smile. Kedah rolled down the window so the woman could pass the cooler through for her. "Here you go, hun. I put our business card in there so you can call us directly when you need more. We're happy to help." She gave a reassuring smile and turned to leave, just as quickly as she appeared.

The driver then zipped off into traffic, driving fast and efficiently. Maybe a little too fast for her taste so when he came to a sudden stop, she all but fell out of the jeep and onto the sidewalk. Grabbing her things, she waved to the driver and said her thanks before he zipped back into traffic and away from her sight.

"Crap," she muttered as she patted her pockets searching for the key she knew she had forgotten. Grumbling to herself, she set down the cooler and made her way to the back of the house where a spare was kept hidden under one of several pots of dead plants. Neither she, nor Sadie, had a green thumb despite trying for years to grow anything. Not even weeds would grow for them. Once she set the pots back to their resting position of death, she made her way back to the door and entered.

The house was still and silent as she entered so she went straight for the fridge to put away her food supply. It didn't surprise her that Sadie was MIA, parties happened every night and social gatherings were almost as mandatory as going to class or showing up for work. Even after they had graduated college. At least for people in the mid to late twenties. It was a rite of passage and she missed it greatly.

Surely she didn't have to stay hidden. Or at least completely hidden. Her fear of the unknown kept her caged in the house, but it didn't have to. A hat and a pair of sunglasses, or her hair down and glasses, could change her appearance enough to be able to go out, right?

Decision made, she fumbled down to her room, where she went on a hunt for a hat and sun glasses. She had to search a little harder than normal to find these items as they seemed to be missing, so a pair of fake glasses would work just fine. Grabbing more cash and her keys, she headed for the kitchen for a little snack before she left. It had come to her attention that she needed way more blood intake than she had been getting in the past. Who knew?

This would be the first time since her turn that she ventured out on her own to do something normal. It felt good. Felt right. Hiding like she had been doing was slowly driving her crazy. Seeing as how she seemed to already walk that ledge most days.

After leaving the house and locking up, she walked along the sidewalk and began to notice that others walked the streets. Not others as in humans, but others as in non-humans. Swallowing back the instant panic and fear she felt, she tried to look at life with different eyes. More knowledgeable ones. There was no point in being terrified of what she now was a part of. Magic filled the air and she could pick out non humans as they passed, going about their everyday lives. How had she missed this all the years she'd lived here? They all looked more than normal and it was only the brush of magic that really gave them away. It seemed to be a strange and brand new world, one she was finally seeing for the first time.

Half way to the local theater she realized she was being followed. Not wanting to stop and alert the person who was following her, she continued to walk while thinking of her options. Either she was being paranoid and she wasn't actually being followed or she was and that probably wasn't good. A dark magic, one that seemed to cling to her bones, brushed past, answering her previous question. Whoever this was, wasn't selling cookies, of that she was sure.

She really wished she'd saved the number to someone in the Estate, just in case this went as south as she thought it might.

Stopping abruptly, she whirled around and stood directly in their way. She was not moving aside from her rapid breathing, standing her ground with a fake bout of confidence. Those that were following her, there was two of them, approached slowly, definitely not selling anything she wanted by their looks alone.

"Kedah right?" The larger of the two asked. His hair was buzzed and his face was set solid and ridged. He was handsome, in a very dangerous way. She should be running, but something kept her where she was.

"Depends. You are?" She asked carefully. It was probably a bad sign they knew her name.

"Max. This is James." He said as he gestured with his head to the man that stood beside him, equal in height and build.

"So, you know who I am, but I don't know you. Can I help you?" Kedah's skin began to tingle, giving her the feeling that something was crawling into her through her pores. She resisted the urge to scratch, despite the fact that now she had a major case of the heebs.

"Come with us." Max demanded.

Her response was on the tip of her tongue but never made it out of her mouth. She wanted to say no, to run, but her legs acted without her permission, following the men. She tried to stop herself from moving, even tried to open her mouth to scream, but nothing happened. It was like someone had reached into her mind, took the controls from her, and was now steering without her permission.

They walked in silence, turning down dark streets and across abandoned lots until she was well and truly lost. Which, was a little shocking since she grew up in this town and ideally knew it inside and out. But, she was lost anyways and a warehouse, that had been abandoned dozens of years ago, was their final destination. She briefly wondered when her last tetanus shot was and whether or not that even mattered anymore, as she looked around at the rust and decay that surrounded her.

"Sit." Max ordered, as he shoved a chair into the back on her knee's, forcing her to sit. Grabbing a chair for himself, he swung it around and positioned himself directly in front of her. "You figure out who we are yet?"

Initially she hadn't a clue. Not until she really thought about it. What she knew of vampire legends, and how her blood seemed to suddenly call to his, had her breath hitch and her face flush with anger. This had to be her Sire. The single person who was responsible for ending her life. The man who cared nothing of her until the very moment something good might come of her immortality. Just. Fucking. Great.

"Oh good, you remember, don't you? I can see the hate in your eyes. Perfect." Max leaned forward, his elbows resting on his knees as he looked deeper into her, like he was studying every reaction she wanted to make but couldn't. "Let's have a little chat, shall we?"

Still unable to talk, she continued to stare at her Sire, and hoped that whatever it was he wanted to talk about was milder than where her imagination was going. Because she and her imagination were currently not seeing 'eye to eye'.

"I'm sure you have a ton of questions, so let me start by saying just how much I don't care. I made you for one purpose and it's time to serve it. I will admit that you are very pretty, a little plain, but pretty, and I was shocked to see how well you survived after the turn. Most don't. Maybe after you've done what I need, I won't kill you." Max mused with a laugh. James smiled, his fangs playing peek-a-boo, sending chills down her spine.

The thought of these two coming any closer than they already were made her insides turn to acid.

"I saw that Jensen has finally found you and you have paid a little visit to the Briarberry Estate, or The Den, whatever you people like to call it. I'm going to need you to go ahead and accept that invite to live there. Once in, I am going to need the layout of the place, the grounds, and who all resides there." Max commanded casually.

She moved her eyes to look at him, then at James, wishing she could spit in his face. Something inside her head released and suddenly she could talk but not move. The first words out of her mouth maybe weren't the smartest. "Hell. No."

Without hesitation, James balled up his fist and punched her square in the jaw. An involuntary moan escaped her lips as blood began to pool in her cheek and stars dotted her vison. Through squinted eyes, she watched as James sat back, looking clearly pleased with himself and watched as Max did nothing but smile.

"You're cute, but not too bright." Max commented. "What you fail to realize is that you do not have a choice but to do what I ask. I am your Sire. Your blood flows because of mine. It will always respond to me and me alone." He grabbed at her jaw and forced her to look at him. He studied her face for a moment and released her.

Beyond anything she could understand, she could hear the truth in his words and wanted to be sick. This was not how her new life was supposed to start. This wasn't how anything was supposed to go. She couldn't be a spy, she was a terrible liar, and was totally sure she'd be killed for even trying.

"Oh, I almost forgot." Max nodded to James, who pulled out his phone, swiped a few times, smiled, and held it out for her to see. "A little insurance." There in the photo before her were her parents, walking down the road by their home, staring off into the distance. Not a care in the world and not a clue they were being watched.

They meant to use her family as their insurance policy. "Don't," she choked out. "Please."

"It's all up to you, now isn't it? Do what we ask, everyone stays relatively happy. Don't do what we ask, and we kill mom and dad. Slowly." Max explained, deadly calm. "So, we clear?"

She nodded as they both stood and loomed over her. Neither spoke, and yet the unspoken words rang clear, she was their bitch and there wasn't a damn thing that she could do about it.

Before the thought of how exactly she was going to get out of this current situation, a knife appeared in James hand. That hand swung down, handle first, and bashed her in the temple.

Lights out.

CHAPTER
seven

Awareness shot through her body, causing her to jerk upright. She had no idea where she was but at least, she was happy to note, she had control of her body again. Her last conscience thought was how badly it was going to hurt to get her temple smashed in. It was exactly as bad as she expected it to be.

Her head throbbed and her stomach rolled. Something smelled awful and everything was dark. But not nighttime dark, because her skin itched with daylight.

Feeling around her surroundings, she noticed all kinds of textures and shapes, but nothing stood out specifically. It did seem that the walls surrounding her were metal as was whatever was shielding her from the sun above her. When her eyes adjusted further she still couldn't make sense of the vast array of randomness surrounding her.

A loud thud landed on top of the metal above her, scaring her to an even straighter sitting position, in which she promptly smacked her head and laid back down just as fast. Moaning loudly, she brought her hand to her head and cussed silently as she felt a trickle of blood.

"Kedah." She winced at the instant recognition of the voice calling her name. Goody, this day was getting better and better.

"Doran," she responded reluctantly.

"Kitten. Would you care to explain what you are doing in a garbage can?" He inquired smugly.

"Is that where I am?" She muttered. "That explains the smell."

"But it doesn't explain why you're in there. In broad daylight." He questioned, sounding like he may be choking back a laugh.

She didn't reply right away, because she wasn't sure what to say. Did she tell him what happened and see if he could help her? No, she thought. He definitely seemed the type of person to not help someone out unless it benefited him, and she couldn't see how this would benefit him in the slightest. She needed to lie, but no amount of quick thinking brought a lie that sounded like something probable. She was a terrible liar after all. So, avoiding the question would have to do.

"How did you find me?" She asked.

"Someone named Sadie called the blood bank demanding, and I'm quoting here, the immediate release of her best friend. I'm told she went on and on about how kidnapping was bad and threatened everyone with wooden stakes. Jensen is pissed, obviously, but I found the whole thing amusing as hell. I will say that this Sadie chick got quite creative with her words. I like the lass." Doran chuckled as he began to swing his legs with a steady tap, tap on the side of the trashcan.

Crap, she thought. Sadie. She probably called a dozen times and when there was no answer called the blood bank. She must have found the cooler with the business card. "Sadie didn't mean any harm." She said with a loud sigh. "But still, how did you find me here?"

"How did you get here?" He retorted.

"I fell and hit my head." She lied. Badly.

Doran snorted and kicked the metal wall hard, causing it to ring and her head to pound. "No, you didn't."

"Well someone hit my head." She groaned. "I ran into some creeps who didn't like me saying no to them. They hit me in the head with the butt of a knife and dumped me here. Apparently."

"So, let me get this straight." He laughed. "You're a vampire. Fangs, fast, and deadly, and you let someone basically jump you and stuff you into a trash can."

"Yes. I suck at being a vampire." She muttered.

"I'm aware." He laughed.

"Seriously, I know you're an asshole, but don't you think you can just check the attitude for a few minutes. I'm already lying in a trashcan filled with god knows what and have a huge knot and cut on my head. I'm humiliated, injured, and probably in deep shit with more than one person. Isn't that enough?" She yelled out in frustration.

A deep laugh filled the air and she resisted the urge to bury her head, only because she had no idea what exactly she'd bury it in. "So, you comfortable in there or do you want me to get you out?"

"It's daylight, you idiot. I can't leave." She shot back.

"Sure you can. You just have to say the magic word." She heard rustling around and then saw his face as he peeked in, making sure no light got near her. "Oh gods, that smell is rank. And I've been in the streets of medieval London. This may be worse. You are so not going back to the Den like this. That smell will stick to everything."

She growled at him and backed herself against the side of the can. "Can you really get me out of here, without killing me or covering my body in third degree burns?"

He gave her a look, one that asked if she seriously had asked that question, and shook his head. "Of course I can. I just want to hear you ask me."

"How did you say you found me again?" She questioned, still skeptical.

"I didn't. Now, my offer only stands for another moment, the smell is really starting to make my skin crawl, and that is not an easy task." He grumbled.

"Doran, can you please get me out of this god awful trashcan?" No sooner had the words come out of her mouth, did he reach out and grab her hand and they were suddenly standing in her basement bedroom. The lights flared on and she had to blink back the spots that appeared in front of her eyes. "How the hell did you do that?"

"Dunno." Doran said with a shrug. "Nice digs. What are you, like, 16?"

She gaped at him as he surveyed her room with a few quick glances. "You know damn well I am not 16."

"Well your taste in decorations would suggest otherwise. Is that really a tie-dye blanket?" He laughed and held it up. To be fair, she'd had it since middle school and it reminded her of her human years. It was sentimental.

"Put it down, Doran. Don't touch my stuff." She demanded as she swiped it from his hand and tossed it back on the bed. He grinned at her and took a step back waving a hand in front of his face.

"You really smell awful. Go shower, we have places to be." He laughed while scrunching his face up in mock disgust.

"Wait, what? Where do we need to be?" She questioned

"I told you, places. Come on." He shook his head then stopped with a smile, like he just then remembered something important. "Oh, Jensen has Sadie and from what I last heard, she was getting mouthy."

"He has Sadie? What for?" She shrieked as she grabbed a towel and headed into the bathroom. Flipping the water on high, she slammed the door, stripped down, and shoved her clothes into the trash bin. At the rate she was destroying clothes, she was going to need a better job just to afford a wardrobe.

"She was threatening his vampires. He took it personally and snatched her up. She's probably okay. Maybe. I was just told to go find you and bring you back."

Kedah scrambled to the shower, groaning as the water scored her skin, taking away the lingering smell of god knows what that had hitched a ride home. Jensen having Sadie was anything but a good thing. She knew he wasn't a personal fan of humans, despite trying to protect them. Plus, he had warned her that Sadie wasn't to be involved in their world. And what did Sadie do? Dive right in. What a fucking mess.

Distracted by her thoughts, she forgot about the open wound on her forehead and when she leaned back she howled in pain as water began to flush out the cut.

"What's wrong?" Doran demanded, as he burst into the bathroom.

She probably should have cared that Doran was suddenly in the bathroom with her, but at that very moment, she was trying to ignore the stupidity of her low pain tolerance. At some point, she was really going to need to man up and suck it up with pain. This wasn't the first wound she'd have and it sure wasn't going to be her last. "Open wound meets water. Not a great combo." She grumbled. Then a thought occurred to her. "Why hasn't that healed yet?" Wasn't she supposed to heal quickly?

Doran muttered to himself as he stepped back to the door. "You haven't fed. You can't heal if you don't feed. Where do you keep your blood?"

She couldn't help but notice the sudden tension in his voice. She could have mistaken it for concern, if she thought he would be concerned for her. But that didn't fit his personality at all. "Upstairs, in the fridge in the kitchen."

"That's a dumb place for it. Guess you all don't get company much." He muttered as he left the bathroom.

Rolling her eyes, she quickly washed her hair, twice, and washed her body, twice. The smell was awful, and Doran was right, it was clingy. However, with some determination and elbow grease, she was fairly sure the smell had left, or was masked enough to be socially acceptable. Shutting off the water, she opened the shower, peeking out to make sure Doran was nowhere in sight, and grabbed her towel off the counter, wrapping it around herself. Her head throbbed and for a brief moment she wondered if pain meds would be able to help. With her luck, that would be a no, but she had to remember to ask at some point.

Opening the door to her room and shuddering involuntarily as the cold air hit her, she looked around for Doran, and when he wasn't to be found, she made her way to her dresser and began digging around for clean clothes.

From somewhere behind her, Doran cleared his throat while chuckling as she nearly jumped right out of her towel. "You really are a pretty crappy vampire, Kitten. How did you not sense me?"

Maybe because she didn't want to, she thought. Looking into her dresser mirror, she could see that he was laying on her bed, back propped against her headboard, ankles crossed, and the latest issue of Cosmo in his hands. Blushing, she rushed to grab her clothes, dashing back to the bathroom. Once the door was shut she leaned her head against it, and then cringed as she yet again forgot about the bruise that was there.

"Hey Kedah. Have you tried anything on page 32? I'm always looking for something new to try. Opinion?" She heard him call out to her. He was having a good laugh; she was not. She groaned and got dressed quickly. Running her fingers through her hair she pulled on a head band and called it the best she could do. Her headache was getting worse and all she really wanted to do was curl up in her bed and sleep for the next week.

Doran hadn't moved as she exited the bathroom. He lay casually and comfortable on her bed, the magazine he was reading, open, while a grin crossed his face. "So, page 32?" He smirked.

Kedah beat back a blush and shook her head. "No, no, and no some more. I have no need to know about your sex life and you have no need to know about mine."

"You don't have a sex life." He said as he tossed the magazine to the side and jumped off the bed.

"You can't even begin to know that." She commented, not even sure why she was baiting into this conversation.

"Oh believe me, I know." He grinned again and walked up closer to her. Standing less than an inch away from her body, she could feel her breathing start to quicken and if her heart could race, it would have. "Your face is pale, you okay?"

She had forgotten all about the pain she had just felt and decided to not mention it. "I'm a vampire, aren't I always pale?"

As he leaned in closer, his scent swirled around her, consuming her. It was a delicious mix of musky earth and cedar. Manly. As she looked up into his eyes, eyes that were boring into her, and noted the specks of green that dotted the chestnut brown of his eye color. His eyes

71

continued to stare into hers, as if they were searching for something, something she couldn't even begin to imagine. The corner of his lip twitched, like he wanted to say something but held it back. She, on the other hand, couldn't complete a coherent thought, even if she had wanted to. His body being so near to her had rendered her motionless and defenseless. He leaned in, just a little closer, like he was going to kiss her, and so help her, she was going to let him. Closing her eyes, she waited.

"We need to go. And at some point, you and I are going to have a long conversation about your lack of sex life." His words were merely a whisper and she was so caught up in the moment that it took longer than it should have to get what he had just said. Her eyes shot open as he stood abruptly, took her hand, and instantly relocated them to Jensen's office.

Flushed and unsteady on her feet, she stepped away from him only to bump into another solid body. Sharply she turned and grimaced at a very unhappy looking Jensen, who was studying the two of them with a blank look across his face.

"About fucking time you got here. Christ what did you do, stop at the great pyramids on your way here?" He bit out in anger.

"Yeah, then we went to Rome and toured the coliseum." Doran shot at him, clearly irritated. "Chill the fuck out Jensen and remember who you are talking to." Anger and an unspoken tension laced his every word. They both stood glaring at each other before Jensen gave a slight nod and turned his attention back to her. "Kitten needed a shower because she was playing in the trashcan and smelled a little worse than death." Doran amended to the silent question that hung in the air.

"What the hell were you doing in a trashcan?" Jensen demanded.

CHAPTER
eight

Kedah was having just about enough of everyone treating her like a child and talking like she wasn't even there. It's not like she chose to be dumped there nor could she tell them why she was there. Damned if you do and damned if you don't kind of situation. But the talking like she wasn't there was going to stop, right now. "I was knitting a fucking sweater. That's what I was doing in the trashcan." She exclaimed.

All bodies stopped moving and turned to stare at her. Doran smiled and Jensen made no move while Sadie, whom Kedah hadn't seen until now, let out a wail of laughter. Everyone ignored her and kept staring at Kedah. "What?"

"You have some explaining to do. I don't like being called and threatened. I don't like sending out my men to find a little vampire who is seemingly attracted to trouble, and I do NOT like being lied to." Jensen snapped, clearly done with the situation already.

Sadie wisely shut her mouth while Kedah's mind whirled with possible answers. She'd stick as close to the truth as possible and hoped her ability to lie got better the more she had to. She hated it, but wouldn't be held responsible for her parent's death. Even if there was a small chance that Jensen, and maybe even Doran could help.

"Oh seriously. I can't control Sadie's actions." She started in, hating to throw her best friend under the bus, but would if it saved lives. "But to be fair, she was just worried about me. No one else was and she had to have had no idea she would be taken so seriously. As for me, I was basically jumped. They wanted something. I said no and got busted in the head for my troubles. They must have dumped me in the trashcan. Next thing I know is Doran zapping me from the trash to my house to shower and then zapped here." She turned to Doran and put her hands on her hips. "How did you get me to my house and here anyways?"

He shrugged with a grin and plopped down on a sofa, crossing his arms behind his head.

Jensen paced the floor for a moment before stopping in front of Sadie. He placed two fingers on her temple and she suddenly froze, her body going limp and her head dropping.

Kedah screamed and rushed to her side. "What did you just do?" She demanded. She lifted her friends face in her hands, but Sadie's eyes were shut and her breathing was steady.

"She's asleep and I was making a point." He lectured. "You really have no idea about what we can do and how dangerous we can be. Your friend, calling my people and making threats, could have gotten herself killed, without a second thought. It was only because you're so new and your circumstances are so unique that I am allowing her to live. But let me be perfectly clear, if it happens again, I will kill her and I will not hesitate to do so. Do you understand me?" Jensen's voice remained calm but the threat lingered in every word.

There was no doubt that Sadie's life was on the line and that from now on they would have to tread lightly. "I got it." She declared, standing a little straighter while facing Jensen. "I'll move in, if for nothing else than to save her. What she doesn't know can't hurt her right?"

"Oh what she doesn't know can and will hurt or kill her." Doran said with a chuckle from the couch. She turned to him and scowled. His input wasn't welcomed. "Calm down Kitten. You'll get those adorable blue panties in a wad."

She hissed at him, actually curled her lip back and hissed, before turning back to Sadie and Jensen. Something about Doran got her anger boiling and yet, when she looked at him, she had the urge to crawl all over him. Looking at him, he had her swooning but the moment he opened his mouth, she wanted to smack him. It was probably wise to resist both urges, as nothing good would come of either at the moment. "Tomorrow," she said to Jensen, then looked down at her best friend. "I need tonight with Sadie. I have to explain."

Jensen looked at her for a moment and nodded. "Lies Kedah. Tell them well. She cannot know about this place, not even just a little bit. The less she knows about this world, the better. Any kind of knowledge can get her killed. Do you understand that? Truly understand?"

"Yeah, I got it. Lie to my best friend. Lie to the only person who saved my life. Y'all are a bunch of jerks, you know that, right?" She scoffed, not even mad that her southern accent slipped out.

"Yes." Jensen and Doran said together.

She just shook her head and sunk down onto her knees next to Sadie. She was tired, confused, and suddenly very hungry. As if reading her mind, Doran shouted a heads up and tossed her several bags of blood, without even looking over the couch to see his aim. He didn't need to though; they fell right into her lap. Ripping into a bag, she sucked it back quickly, following suit with the second bag. Her headache and irritation ebbed slightly and as she placed the empty bags on an end table, she looked up at Jensen, who was grinning. "What?"

He shook his head. "Nothing. Everything. Doran will take you and Sadie home and I'll send a car for you at 8 PM tomorrow."

"I never said I'd take them home." Doran remarked with a playful whine.

"Just shut up and take them home. It'll take you two seconds." Jensen ordered. She briefly looked between the two, knowing that Doran was not one to be ordered around, and then watched as he accepted it, without so much as a bat of an eye.

Doran groaned, almost as if his body didn't like the change in position, as he stood up and walked over to her and Sadie. Sadie was asleep, still, and Kedah looked up at him with a tired look. "Thanks for the blood."

"Well someone has to look out for you, being that you're a terrible vampire and all that." He said with a grin. "Sadie is not winning in that department today either."

"Is Sadie going to be okay?" She asked, to no one in particular.

"She'll wake up as soon as you get home." Jensen said.

"Fine. Take us home." Kedah muttered. Everything was such a mess and it was only going to get worse. She looked up at Doran who stood not moving and rolled her eyes with a sigh. "Please, take us home."

"There, that wasn't so hard. You youngins have no respect for your elders." He reached down, and grabbed her and Sadie's hands and within a moment they were back in Kedah's room. Sadie was laying on Kedah's bed and she and Doran were standing in the middle of the room.

As she looked up at him, she couldn't help but gaze into his eyes, drawn back to their uniqueness. They were beautiful, and the closer she looked, the more she realized they were just like hers, only opposite in color.

Carefully he reached out and brushed back a strand of hair that had fallen into her face. His hand lingered a moment on her skin, as if he was unsure of whether his touch was welcome or not. But before she could lean into the touch, he dropped his hand back to his side, never taking his eyes off of her.

"So, thanks for the lift home." She whispered, not sure what this moment was or where it was headed.

He crossed his arms over his chest, standing taller and stepping back. The moment was clearly over. "Sure."

"I guess I'll be seeing you around then?" She questioned shyly.

"Yeah, I guess. Just, try to stay out of the trash. I'm not doing that again." His smile absorbed the sudden awkwardness that was lingering in the air.

She shook her head with a grin. "I make no promises." Then he was gone, leaving no trace that he was ever there. Just to be sure, she did a quick sweep of the room, not seeing him anywhere.

"That must be a really neat trick to have." She muttered as she walked over to the bed and stood by her friend. With a sudden jolt, Sadie jumped up, mouth open, ready to yell, but stopped when she saw where she was. She dropped back down onto the bed. "What the hell happened?"

Kedah jumped up on the bed and sat at her friend's feet. "Jensen knocked you out."

"How? Did he bite me? Because if he bit me I'm going to. . ." Sadie began, but Kedah interrupted the thought before it could finish.

"You're going to what, Sadie? Kick his ass? Stake him? I really don't think so and I really don't think it's a good idea to keep saying stuff like that. It almost got you killed."

Sadie sat up and crossed her legs under her, looking up at her best friend with a frown. "He wasn't going to kill me."

"Yes, he was. It's only because of me and my fucked up situation that saved your ass. Any other person, calling and threating the lives of his vampires, would have died instantly." She warned.

"I'm sorry, I was just worried. And scared." Sadie's face fell and Kedah felt bad for her, and felt bad for what she was going to have to say, or not say, to make this move happen.

"Thanks." She took a deep breath, preparing for the upcoming change in topic. "We gotta talk."

"You're leaving, aren't you? They have brain washed you into thinking I'm going to kill you and are making you leave. Right?" She said with a sly grin, letting Kedah know she was only a little serious.

"First off, stop reading those books so much and for the love of god, stop watching so many movies about vampires. They don't have close to anything right." She lied. Some of it was close to the truth, but most was not.

She grinned. "So you don't sparkle?"

"Only if I were wearing last year's Halloween costume." She laughed as she remembered the memory fondly. "I gotta go though, and deep in your heart, you knew I would have to at some point."

Sadie frowned and shook her head. She didn't look happy but at least she wasn't looking completely surprised. "You sure?"

"I am. And really, I suck so badly at being a vampire. It's pretty much a sad thing all around, actually. Where I'm moving, I'm going to learn the ropes and work and stuff. It'll be fine. I promise." She held out her arms for a hug and Sadie hesitated for only a moment before hugging her back.

They sat like that for a few minutes, letting memories from the past wash over them. Sadie sniffed back a few tears and sat back. "Where are you going? Can I visit?"

"No, you can't." She watched as Sadie's face completely dropped and felt horrible. "I can't tell you where I'm going, but I'll have my phone with me. You can call or text anytime. Please don't ask me for more than that right now, okay? Trust me."

"I'm going to raise so much hell later though, you know that right? When I'm allowed to, I will be the thorn in everyone's side." Kedah was absolutely sure of that. "Jensen's on my list." Sadie muttered.

"I wouldn't expect anything less." Kedah laughed and knew that if and when Sadie could get back ahold of Jensen, he was in for a surprise. If there was nothing else that Sadie was good it, it was being an absolute badger to people who made it on her list. Some never even had a chance to get off the list and her bestie still bugged them.

"So, changing the subject. What is up with the hottie, Doran? You two were shooting sparks at each other like the freaking Fourth of July." Sadie fanned herself and grinned widely.

"I have no idea what you are talking about. He's a dick, seriously." She teased, but not really wanting to open that can of ugly worms at the moment.

"Oh of that I have no doubts, but whatever sparked between the two of you was hot, like sizzling hot, and heavy. You have GOT to get on that boat, honey. Soon." Sadie said with a giggle.

"Not happening. Not ever." She shot back.

"Whatever. Something is totally going to happen between the two of you and I demand all the deets. Seriously. All of them. Every last one." Sadie smirked.

"Sure, like I'd give you anything less. Now, come on. I need to pack a few bags. I'm not sure what all I can bring, so I'll start with the basics." They both rose from the bed, hugged again, and started emptying drawers into bags she had around the room, as well as a few bags that Sadie went and grabbed from the upstairs.

Thinking about it, she had no idea what to pack. So, for now, clothes would have to do. She could always come back for more. If she got to stay. Assuming she didn't screw everything up more than she probably already had. Vampire life was complicated.

After several hours of packing and talking, with a break for coffee and ice cream, she sent Sadie off to bed so she could nap. Sadie's schedule was all kinds of mixed up and selfishly, she needed sleep too and needed a drink. The bruise on her head had finally gone away, but her hunger lingered and her fangs were poking at her bottom lip. It was a good thing Doran had given her the two bags when he did, she needed them more then she wanted to admit to.

After another two bags, she crawled into bed and sighed closing her eyes, hoping the stillness of sleep took hold and wasn't interrupted. The last thing she needed was a nightmare laced sleep before her new life began.

CHAPTER
nine

Kedah was having her first day of dreamless sleep. It was so peaceful that when a foreign noise entered, she just simply ignored it. It wasn't until it kept going, being ever so persistent, that she finally searched out blindly to figure out what it was. Grabbing her phone, which she realized was making all the noise, she answered it. "Hello."

"About time you answered the fucking phone." A voice bellowed. Her foggy mind thought the voice sounded like someone she should remember, but as she just woke up nothing was coming to her just yet.

"Who's this?" She murmured.

"It's the goddamn Easter bunny." The voice growled. Her brain clicked, causing her to sit straight up.

"Then I hope like hell you're bringing me a shit ton of chocolate for waking me this early in the day." She muttered, knowing that was probably not the wisest thing to say to the person on the other end of the line.

"Do I need to remind you of who I am, Kedah?" He asked.

"No. What do you want? And thanks, by the way, the trashcan was a nice touch." She said.

He laughed a sick and hated laugh, one that makes the skin crawl and she shuddered involuntarily. "Did you make contact with Jensen yet?"

"It's been less than 24 hours since we last spoke, what do you think?" She snapped while hiding a yawn.

"I think your answer better be yes."

She blew out a frustrated breath and sighed. "Yes, I talked to Jensen. I'm moving in tonight. Can I go back to bed now?"

"I'll call in a few days." And that ended the call. She held out her phone, looked to make sure the call had ended, and groaned as she fell back into her pillow. What in the hell was she going to do about her Sire? Whatever it was that he wanted from her, and from the Estate, would probably get her killed. Yippee.

Sighing in frustration, she rose and stumbled to the bathroom to take care of needs and to pack up last minute items. It was only three in the afternoon, which she discovered when she looked back at her phone. That left her damn near five hours to waste.

It almost felt like she was going off to college for the first time. Her nerves were a mess and her stomach was threating to evict everything she'd eaten, ever. Grabbing toiletries by the handful, she threw the rest of her stuff into a travel bag, and chucked it over with the rest of her stuff. Memories, both good and bad, haunted this place. Maybe a change in scenery was a good thing.

Noticing the envelope Jensen had given her, still unopened, she guessed now was as good a time as any to see what it had to say. She realized now that she had completely forgotten about it yesterday and felt a little bad about that, but not too much.

Grabbing the envelope, she plopped back down on her bed and pulled out the paper, flipping through the pages quickly before actually reading it. It looked to be basic stuff, with the added vampire bite to it. No biting anyone on the premises unless it's consented. No killing. She giggled at that, but then, someone had probably killed for the rule to be there. It was the whole be careful the coffee is hot in the cup thing, for the undead.

Mostly it was a lot about common sense and what they expect of the people living within the walls of the Briarberry Estate. The lady that started the place worked very hard to establish a place where any creature, be you fairy or vampire, were or shifter, even witches and warlocks, could live away from the eye of nosy neighbors and irritating humans.

Everyone worked within the Estate or in one of the outside venues. That paid for each person's room and board and food and facilities. They also got a pay check which was a pretty sweet deal. The whole thing felt very self-sustaining which made sense, since they wanted to be as far from human eyes as they could be, while working within the realm of humanity.

Every group of people that lived within the walls had a leader to report to, who was ultimately in charge of their specific group. Jensen was obviously in charge of the vamps, and he happens to be the appointed leader of all the vamps in the great state of North Carolina, not just Briarberry. He also had taken on the role of leader of the Estate, or so she had gotten the general feel of when she was there.

The weres had a pack master as did the shifters. The fairies had a princess who was in charge and the witches and warlocks had a head priestess that was also in charge. It all seemed like everyone got along for the most part, but she was willing to bet that with this diverse of a group some conflicts still arose.

Funny, she thought, there was no specific mention of Doran. Because she looked. Twice. He seemed like a little bit of a big deal and expected to find out why. Or at the very least who he was in charge of, because he certainly wasn't someone who tended towards following others. She loved a good mystery and it seemed like she stumbled onto a good one with him.

The Estate itself sounded like anyone, including her could make a decent life for themselves there. That was the point of the place. For those that couldn't find a niche in the real world, could find one there. It was either a fairytale come true or a nightmare waiting to happen.

Pulling her from her reading, her phone buzzed with a text letting her know that Sadie had ordered pizza and it was on the way. Nothing said safe travels and happy trails like greasy cheese and pepperoni goodness.

Shoving the papers into her backpack, she tossed the pack at her other luggage and ran upstairs to be greeted by the smell of sizzling spicy pepperoni on thin crust happiness "Smells like heaven in here."

"I'm glad you figured out you can actually eat." Sadie said with a smile and held out the open pizza box. Kedah grabbed a slice and sat down at their little kitchen table, taking a huge bite of her food and moaning happily. It was as good as she remembered it to be, maybe even better. "You all set?" Sadie asked as she sat down across from her.

"Yeah," She said over a mouth full of food. "I mean, I don't know what all I can bring, so I'm just bringing clothes and will get more things later if I can. I can't figure out if this is a place that I will stay forever or just like a halfway house. Like a place for me to crash until I don't suck at being a vampire and can get out on my own. Who knows really?"

"Tell me that's pizza I smell. You guys really shouldn't have." Doran said with a smile as he walked into the kitchen. "How did you know this was my favorite?" He said, stopping to stare at the girls with the open pizza box, a smile touching the corners of his mouth.

Sadie raised a brow at Kedah before turning her attention to Doran. "First off, no one invited you. Shouldn't you have to actually be invited in here? And what are the odds that its Kedah's favorite too?"

Kedah nearly choked on her pizza before Doran gave her a hearty slap on the back.

"Easy there Kitten, don't die before the fun begins." He grabbed a slice of pizza and plopped down on the counter, taking up more space than either girl thought possible.

"Not that I don't adore looking at you, because believe me, I do, but why exactly are you here?" Sadie questioned. She looked over at Kedah, smiled wider, and then looked back at Doran.

"I was bored and smelled the pizza, so I thought I'd come in and get a free dinner." He responded casually, like there was nothing odd about him just walking in and helping himself to dinner.

"Seriously?" Kedah asked.

"That, or I'm your welcome wagon, again, and I'm here to cart you off to your new life, like the dead being brought to their grave." He said while taking a bite of his pizza. "Um, this is so good." He moaned.

"That was a terrible analogy." Kedah muttered.

"Really? I thought it fitting. You are dead. You are coming to live with us fine folk. Probably permanently, so it's like a grave. Dead being brought to their grave. See?" He chuckled.

"You are a witty one, aren't you?" Sadie grinned.

"Lass, you have no idea." Doran said while looking directly at Kedah. She flushed and turned her head while taking another slice of pizza, hoping Sadie hadn't seen her face. The kick she received under the table proved otherwise.

The three of them made idle chat for a while, finishing off the box of pizza and two bags of chips. Two pints of ice cream later and everyone was full and happy. Doran was actually being civil, if not even just a little bit friendly, which was unusual from the casual encounters she had had with him in the past. Far be it for her to complain, though. It was nice to have company and be herself. She even had blood in one of her favorite mugs and no one even batted an eye. That mug, along with several others, seemed to be a running amusement between her and Sadie. Every time they saw one that was cute or had something relevant to them, they bought it. Which was why several were packed in her luggage and several more would be making their way to her new home, whenever she was settled.

"Time to get going." Doran suddenly said as he jumped off the counter and made his way to the basement door. "I am assuming you didn't pack light?"

"You know what they say about assuming, right?" He shot her a look and she grinned. "I did. Mostly clothes. I wasn't sure what to bring." Kedah replied as she led the way to her room for the last time.

"Less is more as they say. I'll take these out. I'm sure you two want to get all lovey and crying with your good byes and I don't really want to see that. Unless you're going to make out. Are you going to make out?" He asked as he gathered her bags in his arms with no effort.

"Making out is reserved for morning hours only, sorry you missed it." Sadie laughed.

Doran pouted and left the house, leaving the two best friends staring at each other.

"Let's just not with the good bye, okay? You want to meet later in the week for coffee?" Kedah said, holding back tears that were threating to fall.

"Sounds good." Sadie said with a sniff. She pulled Kedah in close and hugged her tight. "You seriously need to get on the Doran wagon girl. And I expect full details when we meet." They both laughed and waved bye as Kedah headed out of the house, only to stop mid step and stare at the car waiting for her.

The car, if even that small of a word could describe it, was gun metal black, smooth as a river stone and looked utterly out of place parked on the street in such a small town. It sat so low to the ground that Kedah was sure one pothole would total it right out. It was beautiful, sexy, and dangerous.

Speaking of dangerous, Doran shut the trunk and turned to her, smiling like a boy with his favorite toy. "I grabbed the least flashy car I had."

Kedah picked her jaw up from the ground and walked to the car, afraid to even breathe on it. "This is the least flashy car you had? What exactly is it, aside from expensive."

"I'm hurt you don't know what this is." He gasped in mock horror.

"No you're not." She argued.

Doran opened the passenger door for her and she slide into the black bucket seat, afraid to touch the seat belt. He flashed himself into the driver's seat, adjusted the rearview mirror and started the engine. "Listen to her purr." He closed his eyes and looked like he may need a moment, alone. "This, Kitten, is a 2016 Maserati GranTurismo."

She was actually stunned that an object such as this could cause such a smile to cross his face. She knew that boys, and some girls, absolutely loved their vehicles and he seemed to be no exception. She shuddered to think what would happen if it ever got scratched or dinged. Worlds would probably collapse. Atlantis would rise and sink again.

"Seatbelt." He advised with a nod of his head.

"Seriously?" She asked.

He turned to face her, his gaze sweeping her body, lazily. Slowly, he reached across her body to take hold of the belt. His body was brushing against hers, his scent filling every inch of the car. Her breath hitched and she licked her suddenly dry lips as she watched him slowly bring the belt over her lap, lightly trailing his fingers over her legs, clicking it in place. He didn't move his head as he continued to look at her, his eyes searching hers for every inch of her soul that she had to bare. He leaned in, his lips brushing her cheek before stopping right at her ear. His breath was hot on her skin and she thought that if he didn't act soon, she was going to pass out from the closeness and the tension that was riding the air. "Safety first." He whispered before pulling completely away, leaving her cold and confused. "So, ready to go?" he asked, straightening himself behind the wheel. "Oh wait, I should call Jensen and let him know not to send someone."

Still stunned stupid by his closeness, it took her a minute to understand what he just said. "Wait, what? He doesn't know you're here?"

"Nope." He boasted with a grin. He grabbed his phone from his pocket before throwing the car into drive and darting off down the road. "Sup slacker. I've got Kedah and we're headed your way. Don't you yell at me; I'm doing you a favor. Yes, she's safe. No, I won't kill her before she gets there. Yes, she can hear every word I'm saying. And what do you mean did I take your Maserati? What kind of person am I?" He laughed and threw the phone onto the dash.

"This is Jensen's car?" She balked, holding onto the 'oh shit' handle like her life depended on it.

"Oh what, this thing? Please. Jensen only thinks it's his. I've had sex in it far more times than he has. It's practically mine. You know the old adage, if you lick it it's yours. Same rules apply." He continued to speed down the road, disobeying every law she knew and probably some she didn't. She felt sick but resisted the urge. The bill to clean the interior of the car was probably more than she even wanted to know.

She also thought it was wise to not even comment on the sex thing. She didn't want to know. Though her imagination did wonder exactly how that worked as the car was awfully small for such adventures.

Slowly, after a few tense moments, she let go of the 'oh shit' handle, thanks to the steady rhythm of the soft back roads calming her nerves. Doran remained quiet, which was either good or bad. She hadn't decided yet. He didn't seem the type to remain silent for long.

The combination of the silence and the lull of the car, combined with the purr of the engine, began to rock her to sleep. She closed her eyes, thinking it was safe for just a few minutes to rest her eyes.

CHAPTER
ten

"Wake up sunshine, we're home." Doran exclaimed as he slammed on the brakes a little too cheerfully. Her body jerked forward, catching on her seatbelt, her head snapping up as her eyes shot open.

"It's come to my attention that I really think I hate you." She muttered as she fumbled for her seat belt, swung the door open, and all but fell out of the car.

"Nah, you love me. You just don't know it yet." He grinned at her and got her bags out of the trunk. "However, just as a sign of good faith I'll drag this up to your apartment. Ya?"

"You know where I'm living already? Before me?" She asked as she stood and looked up at the building in front of her. There was a good chance she'd never get used to the sheer size of the place.

"Of course I do." He admitted.

Easier than humanly possible, he scooped up her bags and took the stairs two at a time, dashing into the Estate without her. Trying to hurry after, she grabbed her pack and flung it on her back as she chased after him through the front door.

Jensen met her right inside the door and she had to skid to a halt, to not run into him. She briefly looked for Doran, but when she couldn't find him, she focused back on Jensen. "Someone looks excited to see their apartment."

She was, but didn't have the heart to tell him she was chasing after Doran with her stuff. He looked like he wanted to be the person to show her around, and far be it for her to stop him.

"This place is incredible." She said in awe, as she paused and really looked around at the parlor.

"Isn't it?" Jensen replied. "And you've not even seen the place in all her glory."

"You know," She said casually, still glancing around at everything. "This feels more like a college dorm than a building filled with apartments for the paranormal."

"We get that a lot. And in a way, I guess, it is like a dorm. Except, our rooms are nicer, our food is better, you don't have to take classes you don't want to take and we keep the frat boys locked in cages in the basement." Jensen grinned.

She stopped and raised a brow at him, not sure whether to believe him or not, He was another hard one to read, but she supposed that ability came with time and practice, both of which he'd probably had.

"I'm kidding, only the willing are kept in the basement. Maybe a few unwilling, but that's not really a today conversation. Come on." He led her through the front of the house, some of which she'd already seen, most of which she hadn't.

They walked toward the back and pushed through a door that entered into a spacious kitchen. It was a good bit larger than the diner she worked in and seemed to sport all the new and best gadgets and appliances. One would be inspired to actually cook if this is what they had to work with. Almost.

Jensen walked to the far corner where a large metal door stood, typed in a code on the keypad and swung open with a hiss. He motioned for her to go first and as she stepped in she looked around with wide eyes. "This is our food source. One thing we ask is that if you take from the vein, to not do it on the grounds, unless it's consented. It should always be consented, for that matter. There is plenty here and you'll get your own code to get whatever you need whenever you need it."

"That's a whole lotta blood." She blurted, still looking at all the bags, hanging neatly in their own separate coolers. "Is it different blood in different coolers?"

"Different types, yes. Type A and B and so on. You'll learn what tastes best over the years. Some people just don't care but some of us do."

"That's so weird." She said while still trying to take in the actual size of the cooler and the amount of blood it held.

"Says the one who was stealing blood up until a few nights ago." Jensen remarked.

"Uh, better that than murder don't you think?" She retorted.

"I'd prefer it because if murder was involved I'd have to eliminate you." He shot back, in the nicest possible tone one could have when threating your very life.

"Well, now that that's out of the way." Kedah said nervously.

"I don't mean to scare, but I do mean to enforce. Things are going to be very different for you now, more so than you can even imagine. Vampires, we live by a different code. We don't like what you're doing, you don't live anymore. It's that simple." He said.

"Right, I mean, I get it. At least, I'm sure I will get it." She muttered, turning to exit the giant cooler that suddenly felt a hell of a lot smaller than when she walked in. Her mind had drifted to her Sire and what he was going to ask her to do. She was terrified. Scared and terrified and alone.

She was so screwed.

"Something on your mind?" Jensen's voice broke through her inner monologue and she tried to brush off her thoughts.

"Nah, just taking it all in."

He studied her for a moment before guiding her out of the kitchen.

She may not have noticed her actions, but Jensen did. He had had hundreds of years of practicing the art of reading people, right down to the smallest detail. The slight jerk of her movements and her eyes darting from thing to thing answered one major question he had. She was hiding something. She was so young, so new, that just about anything could be bothering her and it wasn't his place to get it out of her until she was ready. He just hoped it wasn't anything overly complicated or life threating. "Come on then, I'll show you around a bit." He said as he waved her forward into the dining room.

Idly he droned on talking about the kitchen and when meals were served, if people were interested. There was even a section of the kitchen that anyone could use to make their own meals, if they wanted to. He asked if she was any good at cooking, and laughed when she recited the number for several local pizzerias and a local Chinese shop. That was all the cooking she'd ever done. Personally, he wasn't a good cook either, but that was because he hadn't had a need for several hundred years.

Continuing around the first floor, he showed her where intake was and where they did paper work for people living in the house. Paper work was anything from applications to work in the house or out, to orders for certain products and services. It was a lot of work that came in and out and most days the women who worked it needed more help than was ever given. She also made sure people were placed in areas where they would cause the least amount of problems. Vampires on the same floor as werewolves always ended in blood shed, just as certain as some fey couldn't be kept in the same area either.

Doran had reported to him that Kedah was pretty simple, kind of clumsy, adorable, and quiet, so it was decided that she be placed in the main house on the second floor. Strangely, Jensen recalled, he had also suggested, recently, that she was to be near where he stayed. He thought it was odd, but wasn't going to argue. If anyone was going to look after Kedah, Doran would be the one to do it.

He continued the tour, stopping at one of the bay windows to point out across the grounds where the cabins in the back were and where the outdoor recreation facilities were. He rolled his eyes as he saw the Weres were out playing Rugby and knew in an instant he'd lost Kedah to them.

"Oh God. Is that a bunch of guys playing football out there? In kilts?" She exclaimed as she drew closer to the window.

Sighing, he shook his head with a small grin. "It's Rugby, and yes. Though I wouldn't interrupt right now, they get pretty violent with the game." The boys got down right bloody most games, but it kept their aggressions at bay, so no one really cared.

"Oh I am so going to cheerleader that later." She laughed.

He smiled and kept his thoughts to himself. Most of the weres didn't like vampires and usually ignored or intimidated them if they approached. That was one lesson she was going to have to learn on her own, and he wouldn't mind watching it when it went down. There was going to be a lot of things she was going to have to learn and unlearn.

She was definitely proving to be an interesting case for him and honestly he couldn't remember if he ever had met someone like her in his few hundred years as a leader. It was amazing that she even survived the turn, let alone lived with a human and drank nothing but stolen blood. He couldn't even imagine the amount of control she must have. If she could survive this long, it also begged the question of, could there be others out there like her? If so, how in the world was he going to track them down?

Another problem for another day. He'd add it to the list of things he needed to figure out.

"Come on, let's get you settled." He said and took her arm to guide her away from the windows. She let out a huff and allowed herself to be led away, making promises to herself under her breathe to revisit later.

Leading her upstairs, he watched as her eyes continued to wander, taking everything in. It really was a grand place to live, being the most favorite of the places he'd lived in his lifetime. It was very reminiscent of the years past, the castles that were bustling with staff and people, working together as a huge coexisting family. Those days were long lost to history and to the memories of a select few who were there, but they tried within the Estate to bring some of that back.

"The second floor is yours that you share with a few other people and also with my office. My living quarters are elsewhere. We put you in the main house but at any time you can move if you feel you need to. We have three floors here, several basement floors and a fair number of houses out back." He pulled a key out of his pocket and handed it to Kedah. "There you go, you're right here."

She took the key and hesitated at the door, looking unsure. "Who else is on this floor with me?"

He thought he probably shouldn't tell her who exactly was on the floor, not knowing how she would react, so he kept his answer vague. "You'll meet them soon, I'm sure."

She gave him a look that was a little suspicious, but put the key in the door and went in without another word. He had given her one of the smaller rooms, because she was single and really didn't seem like she needed much. Her expression though, was totally worth bringing her here. It had been far too long since he'd seen true excitement and wonder in someone's eyes.

There was something so, well, magical, about seeing someone excited for the first time. Whether it's a new friend, a new object, or a new living situation, that feeling of newness and awe could never be repeated. It left a stain in the air, in the room and in the building that was delightful and warm. And in a world where things were almost always bad, tragic, or hurtful, having this one moment of pure joy was a gift.

"Holy crap." He heard her mutter as she stepped into the apartment and took it all in. She turned slowly, looking everywhere all at once. He never thought of the apartments as much, but when you didn't have much to begin with, he supposed this was more than expected.

He had to remind himself, every now and again, that when he became a vampire, life was very different. People didn't generally have much so suddenly becoming something else and having nothing wasn't much of a shock. Kedah had probably lost almost everything, save for what Sadie could do for her.

These apartments came furnished with the basics, mainly because they found that people trying to move things such as beds and couches in and out tended to attract attention. There was a bedroom set with a bed, dresser and nightstand. A couch and TV in the living room. Lastly there was a small kitchen table and two chairs in the kitchen. Rooms where vampires would be staying had black out curtains on every window and a mini fridge dedicated just for blood. Residents could replace anything they wanted and could fill their apartments with whatever as well. It was their home and they were all encouraged to make it as such.

"This is amazing. I mean, this is just so much. I had no idea. I don't even know what to say. I'm rambling." She shook her head and smiled.

Jensen just grinned and nodded. "You are welcome. We try our best to take care of our own. If you need anything let us know. In the meantime, make yourself at home, because you are home. Once you start working and making your own money, you're welcome to decorate, paint, and do whatever you like to the place. It's yours for however long you choose. We have much more to go over, but I'll leave you for the night to unpack and hang out. Feel free to look around the grounds too, just don't wander away. Doran will probably complain loudly if I have to send him on another rescue mission."

"And we wouldn't want that." She muttered.

Jensen opted to ignore that comment all together. "Oh and there is a phone book, of sorts, on the counter by the house phone. It's got numbers to everyone important. Just like a hotel, you just enter in a room number to get someone's room. Most people don't use the phones often, cell phones being all the rage now." He said and took a step into the hallway. "Also, one more thing, please be thinking about where you want to work so we can get you set up and started soon."

She laughed and stepped over to the door to shut it when he left. "Got it, no to kitchen duty. I'll let you know later tonight or tomorrow if I think of anything."

"Sure. And go down to intake so we can get some general information for our records too. That has to be done tonight. Okay?" She nodded at him and waved as he backed out and back to his office.

With Kedah taken care of, he had a whole nights work still ahead and needed to get started before more time slipped away. Some days being a leader was rewarding. Most days it was just tiring and tedious.

After dropping off Kedah's meager amount of things in her room, Doran wandered to his and found himself pacing. He was surprised by how little she had, but guessed he really shouldn't have been. After all, she died and her roommate probably had only a small amount of time to save what she could from her old life. He felt, bad, he guessed. It was a new feeling for him so he couldn't be sure.

Then, in the car, as he brought her to the Estate he'd almost kissed her and was kicking himself in the ass for not actually doing it. Nothing was stopping him but himself, which was another new feeling for him. What had gotten into him? He could be a flirt, yes he absolutely could, but this wasn't flirting. This was something brand new and it made his stomach cramp.

There seemed to be an unrelenting attraction that he couldn't shake. When he was near her he almost immediately let his guard down and it felt like the most natural thing to do. Hanging out with her and Sadie, eating and joking around was something he was sure he'd never done in his entire existence, and he enjoyed the hell out of it.

Sure, he had friends, but thinking back, he never just chilled with them. They probably went on a few killing sprees, and had a few nights where the alcohol flowed and the women were plenty, but nothing more than that. Kedah was changing him and he wasn't sure if he should like it or be worried.

It came as no surprise that his body went on full alert the moment he felt that she was across the hall in her apartment. It took every bit of his godlike strength to not walk out of his door and through hers. He was that drawn to her.

The main reason he stayed put, aside from raising unnecessary suspicion in Jensen, was that he never told Kedah that he was also in residence on her hall. He wasn't sure of her reaction, so he kept it to himself. And yes, he was absolutely listening to what she and Jensen were saying because one, the door was open and two, being a god did have its advantages.

Another good reason for not going over to her just yet; if he stepped foot in her apartment, he wasn't going to be in full control of his actions. He was either going to be a total ass, like normal, or he was going to push her against the wall and kiss the hell out of her. It was an either or situation at this point.

His thousands of years of control came crumbling down the moment he felt her presence within the walls of the Estate. Never had he had to focus so damn hard to keep his hands to himself and it was trying on his patience. It was a completely unnatural feeling.

Something in his vast array of useless knowledge screamed that he knew what was happening when Kedah was around. Something from a long time ago was pushing its way forward, to the forefront of his mind, and he was helpless to stop it. Could she be his soulmate? That would explain nearly everything that was happening.

The more time he spent around her, or within the same walls as her, the more his brain pushed at the soulmate thing. If she was his, then he'd not be able to keep to himself much longer. Neither would she for that matter. He had exactly zero experience with soulmates; being that he always thought he'd never have one. He always believed that since it hadn't happened in thousands of years that he wasn't entitled to one. It was an accepted punishment that he'd long since given in to. Plus, she was a vampire, the one species he could kill by merely being himself.

His attraction to her came straight out of left field and the more he tried to ignore it the harder it kept pushing back.

This was never going to work and it very well might kill him.

Growling to himself, he grabbed his phone, headphones, and a water bottle and stormed out of his room, intending to hit the gym hard, and for hours. To sweat until he wanted to pass out, then crash for the day. That seemed the only option he had given that his other option for passing the time wasn't a go, yet.

That's what he intended to do, until he left his room without looking up and came face to face with Kedah, who struck him absolutely speechless and stupid.

"Oh crap. Is that why Jensen avoided answering my question on who lived here? Because you, of all people, live across the hall from me?" She said in an amused panic, her cheeks suddenly flushing brightly.

The flush on her cheeks sped his heart and he shoved his hands into his pockets to keep them still. Of all the reactions she could have had to finding out they were neighbors, he supposed this wasn't the worst. He needed a distraction.

Something or someone.

Nothing showed. Fuck.

"Doran, hey. I'm talking to you." She snapped her fingers in front of his face, snapping his attention back to the thing he was trying to avoid. Her.

He took a deep breath and put on the most neutral face he owned. "Of course I live here, Kitten. Someone has to make sure you don't fall down the stairs or attack the neighbors." He was an Idiot. Insults would only fuel her anger, but he couldn't help it. She was, for lack of a better or manlier word, precious when upset.

Kedah's jaw dropped as she crossed her arms over her chest. "I would never attack anyone! How dare you accuse me of that?"

He shrugged and smiled. "But you didn't admit to falling down the stairs. See? I'm a hero before it even happens." Baiting her really was too much fun. He should stop. Really, he should. He just couldn't help it.

"I don't even know what to say to that." She muttered.

"That seems to be a common occurrence with me. Anyways, I'm hitting the gym before I crash. See ya, Kitten." He needed to ghost out quickly. But since he wasn't supposed to zap within the Estate walls, unless it was an emergency, he needed to turn tail and run.

Despite the attempt at leaving her behind, she lit up and spoke with a happy flair to her voice. "I haven't seen the gym yet. Will you take me there? You know, so I don't fall down the stairs on my way."

He smiled, he couldn't help it. Of course she'd use his words against him. Of fucking course. "Oh sure, I love babysitting."

"Great. Let me grab my bag." She ducked into her room, grabbed a bag and was out and locking her door in a flash. "Let's go."

Kedah looked so excited to be exploring, that not even an asshole could deny her. So he didn't. It had been so long since he just stopped and saw new wonders through others eyes. When you live as many years as he had, things just weren't new anymore and in some way he'd seen and done everything there was to do. Twice. Maybe three or more times. So, he thought, he really shouldn't mind showing her around. Except that he really should be avoiding her.

They took the stairs down to the first floor, a natural silence settling between them. He'd have assumed their walking in an uncomfortable silence would be awkward, but this was far from it. He casually glanced in her direction several times and watched as she looked around the place in fascination and excitement, two emotions that he himself hadn't experienced in a very long time. Turning down several halls and going down another flight of stairs, they entered the gym. He wanted to stay, but his body demanded that he go and be distracted before he could say something else that was stupid and idiotic. Eyeing the treadmill, he trailed off, leaving Kedah to stop and stare at the vastness of the place.

If he was being honest, it was a pretty sweet set up. All the latest and greatest in workout equipment. A mat for sparing, a track for walking, a hot tub and sauna, and a lap pool. It was the best set up he'd seen since the days of the first Olympics, and that was saying something both in the set up and the fact that he could remember the first Olympics.

Once he found the machine he wanted and the workout settings were set, he spared a glance at Kedah who was still standing at the door, looking around with her jaw dropped. She was cute, sexy, and going to be the biggest amount of trouble to walk into his life since he left his family in the heavens.

CHAPTER
eleven

Anyone would have stopped in their tracks at the sight of this place and Kedah was no exception. The gym was beyond massive. It was the kind of place that people paid hundreds of dollars a month just to use for an hour a day. It had everything one could imagine. Weights, tracks, pool, hot tub, sauna, equipment that she didn't even know what they did, treadmills, stair climbers, and mats.

Of course all that was great, but it was the pool that drew her gaze in. Forgetting about Doran, she casually walked to the water, bending down to dip her hand in. Having grown up with the smell of chlorine permanently on her skin, she honestly never thought that after she turned she'd ever swim again. She wasn't even going to lie about how excited she was to get back in the water and stretch her muscles.

Chatter from a distance caught her off guard and brought her attention to the front of the gym where a group of the biggest guys she had ever seen were walking in, laughing and punching at each other. Her eyes gazed upon each person and instant alarms rang. These guys were solid, walking, trouble. She had no idea how she knew, but she did. Call it vampire instinct but she immediately knew she needed to be anywhere but here.

Frantically she looked around for Doran, seeking out a distraction or help. He was running on the treadmill, sweat marking his shirt with proof of his continued workout. He looked to be fully committed to the task at hand and probably was too far in the zone to help.

She was totally, momentarily, distracted. His lean muscles straining with each step while his hair sat wildly framing a face. A face that was utterly concentrated on the task at hand. She couldn't help but to stare at him. Only when the voices of the men got louder did she remember why she was searching him out to begin with.

Quietly, she stood up from the pool side and started to make her way over to the treadmill, only to run into a wall of men, blocking her way. "Well, what have we got here?" A voice rumbled out like thunder. Oh man, she really shouldn't be here.

"I'm sorry, I didn't mean to run into you." She mumbled apologetically, looking for a gap to duck through. As she looked up at the wall now blocking her way, her eyes just couldn't take in the sheer size of the men. They were huge and terrifying.

But, as they were terrifying, she was supposed to be equally so. She was a vampire, as everyone kept reminding her, and she could do this. Hopefully.

The group of four began to circle her, like wolves on prey. Which, now that she thought about it, they probably were, wolves that is. Their bodies formed a solid wall, one that she couldn't seem to see past. They'd be on the verge of hot if they weren't looking at her like she was dinner, while smiling. Something in their faces said we're actually not that bad while their body position and demeanor said, do not fuck with us. She didn't understand it at all.

"Is that a," one of the wolves said as he inhaled deeply, "vampire I smell? And she's scared? What an interesting surprise."

"Look at her, she's nearly trembling. Are you sure she's a vampire?" Another gruff voice laughed out.

She tried to keep her fear in check, but imagined they could smell it either way. Surely they wouldn't risk hurting her inside the Estate walls. Maybe? They really were huge men. No book had ever done justice to the sheer size of them as they surrounded her. Standing shoulder to shoulder and at least a foot taller than her, they looked down with a grin that suggested the thoughts in their minds weren't PG or pleasant.

"She's definitely a vampire." One of them grunted. "The smell is revolting."

"Well you don't smell like roses either." She shot at him.

"HA!" They laughed, a sound that clapped like thunder around her.

"What's your name little vampire." The one who stood a little more relaxed than the rest asked. If she had to guess, he was the leader of the group.

"Kedah." She answered. "Yours?"

He looked at her with a curious gaze. "Aidan. I'm the leader of the pack on these grounds. These are my boys Zane, Luke, and Cooper."

She nodded to them and returned her gaze to Aiden. He was the leader so she'd talk to him, no one else. He'd have to have the final say in almost anything. At least that's what she hoped. "Uh, well, Aidan, it's nice to meet you. But I'll be on my way now."

"Oh I don't think so. See, we don't like vampires and we certainly don't like newly turned ones. They tend to be crazed and out of control, thinking they can take on the world." Cooper grumbled, attempting to make himself just a little bigger. It reminded her of a peacock fluffing his feathers. She almost laughed but resisted.

"Good thing I am far from normal then, huh. No world domination thoughts here." She said, still locking gazes with Aiden. "Okay guys, really, I should go."

"I dunno, I've never met a non-typical vamp." Zane said with a sly smile.

"Nor I." Cooper agreed.

Aiden remained silent.

As a group they took a step sideways, forcing her to move with them. A few more steps and they were standing with their backs at the lap pool. Well, she thought with a smile, at least she could swim if they decided to chuck her into the water.

Where in the hell was Doran?

Gathering what little courage she had left in her and leaning on the fact that she is a vampire and supposed to be tough, she stood straighter and looked up at Aidan. "Look, I'm new and haven't had a chance to learn boundaries and such yet. However, I do know that I am allowed to be here as much as you, so please, get the fuck outta my way so that I can leave you to your workout."

There. Consequences be damned.

All four boys looked at each other and for a moment she was sure she was either about to get wet or get hit. Then one by one, each burst into laughter and stepped away from her.

She totally just got hazed by the local werewolves, didn't she? Of course she did. Why wouldn't she? She took a deep breath and resisted the urge to reach out and smack each of them. They were far too big to be even thinking of playing that game. But it was so tempting.

"You said your name was Kedah?" Aidan asked as the other three wandered off to various places in the gym.

Still in a little bit of shock that she wasn't actually going to get her ass handed to her, she nodded.

"You took out a few rogues that we've been hunting for a while. I'm impressed." He said with a nod.

"Ah, well, that wasn't intentional. Believe me." She said shyly.

"You just move in here?" He asked, thankfully changing the subject.

"Yeah, like 2 hours ago."

"Good. Jensen told me a little bit about you. You've a bit more badass in you than you think. What you've survived, most couldn't." He said, clearly as surprised as she was.

She blushed and shook her head. "I'm just here to learn to survive and not screw things up. I'm really not that special."

"Seriously?" He asked, shocked. "Come here." He ordered and she followed. It intrigued her that someone who was at least six times her size would think that she, of all people, could be anything more than just a survivor. She didn't feel like a super hero, more the sidekick to life that seemed to be handing her a shit deal.

They walked over to the weight benches and he pointed to a 50 pound weight. "Lift it."

"What?" She asked stunned. Clearly he'd lost his mind on the four second walk to the bench.

"Lift that weight." He commanded. "With one hand."

"You're kidding?" She had always thought that vampires had added strength, but never felt any different after her transition. She just assumed it skipped her.

He rose to his full height and crossed his arms over the expanse of his chest. He was intimidating. A little hot, but mostly intimidating. "Does it look like I'm kidding?"

Nope, he was most certainly not. She shook her head, dropped her bag at the bench and walked over to the weights. Looking down she mumbled to herself and reached for it. Without any bit of effort, she lifted the thing right off the bench. She hardly strained. Her eyes got wide and she turned to look at Aidan, who had a grin on his face. "Grab the other weight, in the other hand."

She did. She stood in front of a werewolf, holding 50 pound weights in each hand and felt, powerful. She felt like she could do anything. She could be anything. She finally felt it.

"You are not nothing, Kedah. You will never be nothing. Whatever you were as human, you aren't as a vampire. The next time I see you being a sissy or not standing up for yourself, I'm going to kick your ass. And trust, I will." Aidan threw her a wink and smiled. "Now, the boys in my pack are usually dicks, so just be cautious. Vampires and weres aren't known for being overly friendly, but as you helped us out, accident or not, we owe you. Yeah?"

The steady rhythm of his feet as they hit the tread calmed his frayed nerves. Sweat dripped down his face in hot streaks and as each bead fell from his face it was like a sliver of tension gone. Thirty more minutes of this and he'd be back to himself. Irritated at everyone and bored to tears.

Immortality did have its downfalls some days.

But then, he knew boredom was irrelevant if Kedah was near. She tended to cling to his mind no matter how hard he tried to unhinge her. Without even needing to look up from his treadmill he knew where she was. Could feel her presence like a tether that was tied between them. Moving when she moved.

As he was completely distracted, despite trying not to be, he damn near tripped when he felt that the wolves had descended into the gym. Shit. Just fucking great. He pulled the emergency stop and jumped off the machine grabbing his water. He turned, intending to find Kedah, and nearly tripped, again, when he saw where she was.

Of course she'd be wedged between Aidan and his crew. Of fucking course she would be. Why? Because either she truly attracted trouble like she took a breath or they were looking to haze the newbie. Either way, if he went in being all nosy and heroic she'd hate it. So instead of doing what he wanted, he held back and watched.

He watched as she held her ground, telling those pups to get out of her way and go away. That a girl, he thought with a satisfied grin. There's the warrior coming out of her.

Continuing to watch as three of them moved away, paying him no attention, which was smart, he carefully looked at Aidan talking quietly to Kedah. He didn't like her being so close to him, and that irritated the shit out of him. For fucks sake he had been fine for thousands of years then suddenly this little kitten of a vampire walks in and it's everything he can do to not be around her 24/7.

Fate, those bitches, had a twisted sense of humor that he never understood. Someday he was going to have a very long and very overdue chat with them, though not a lot of talking would be involved.

But as frustrated as he was at the Fates, a deeper part of him was weary and lonely. Knowing that she may hold the key to fixing that, gave him the warm and fuzzies that people always talked about. He'd deny the feeling ever existed, if asked, but for now, it was a small comfort until he knew for sure what was going on.

Kedah and Aidan were on the move, heading for the weight benches when he decided to follow, staying back far enough that neither noticed his movements. He couldn't hear what was going on but when she picked up a 50-pound weight, his interest was piqued. Another weight in the other hand and she was beaming with pride. Her smile literally lighting up the entire gym.

Now he felt like a dick, because some wolf could make her smile like that and he couldn't. All he ever did was make her feel like shit. And now he felt like a shit.

As he moved forward, he overheard the pep talk that Aiden was giving Kedah and it made him feel, uneasy. Aiden almost never made friends outside his pack and yet it seemed he'd taken a special interest in Kedah.

She looked up at Aiden and gave him the most genuine, beautiful smile that caused his heart to lurch. Which was stupid because, well, it just was. Damn it these new feelings were going to drive him nuts. Was he jealous of the wolf? Hell, fucking, yes he was. That smile should be for him, not a playboy wolf who was good with his words.

"Damn. You got a little super kitten hiding in there, don't you?" He said, cutting through their conversation and interrupting the moment that should have been his.

"Apparently," she shot at him and he winced at the venom in her voice, "at least someone here is nice and thinks I'm more than just a pair of clumsy fangs to entertain the masses." Oh god, that was not a good tone and not a good reaction.

He gave a nervous laugh and held up his hands in defeat. "I meant no disrespect."

"Oh sure. I'm so sure you didn't." Danger, his subconscious screamed. Red flag. His mind fogged and thoughts were stalling. He had no idea what to say to make things better. He looked over at Aidan, who was smiling like the wolf he was, not budging an inch to help. It was a damn shame he didn't have a dog toy on him. Or silver.

"Whoa, Kitten. I was just coming to say how impressed I was. Don't get your panties in a twist." Christ, what was up with his mouth speaking before he could think?

"Get my panties in a twist? What are you, like, ten? And don't call me Kitten." She growled.

He looked back over at Aidan and tried again. "Wolf."

"Oh no. I'm not in this. It looks like the two of you have unresolved issues and I'm enjoying the show." Aiden muttered, taking another step back.

Now what. His brain, completely rebelling and taking her side, kept throwing up warnings that his mouth was choosing to ignore. "Maybe you should get wolf boy to help teach you what to do with those weights. Counter balance those falls. Maybe you won't end up in a trash can again, asking for my help to get out."

What in the name of all that rules hell was his mouth doing? What in the actual shit was he saying?

Her mouth dropped open, then closed, as her eyes got wide. Aidan, in probably the wisest move he'd made that day, stepped back another foot from her. Her eyes, her beautiful emerald green eyes flashed red and he could see that her fangs had descended.

Just fucking great.

Being that she was still so new as a vampire, she wouldn't have the slightest idea how to control her rage if she got too angry. He knew that when vampires got overly stimulated, and couldn't control their actions, natural instinct took over. Eyes bled to red, fangs out, muscles full strengthened, and they'd fight until they were tired or subdued. He was going to have to restrain her, and she was going to hate him for it. Not to mention it was going to be pretty painful for him. Even though she wasn't fully aware of it, she would be damn strong when she needed to be.

Worse yet, if she went for someone's throat, it absolutely couldn't be his. Not because he was worried she'd kill him, she couldn't. He could kill her. His blood was poison to vampires, for reasons he still wasn't aware of. It had something to do with his being born in the heavens and her being born of hell. His best guess was it was something like getting air in your blood stream. Deadly to anyone.

"You need me to take care of this?" Aidan muttered quietly. "Or are you just going to stand there and make things worse?"

"Shut up." He grunted, trying to think of something semi clever to say or do for her.

"Better do something quick then. She's going to snap any minute and if she hurts anyone you know she's going to put the blame right on you." Damn if he wasn't right though, she will blame him for her actions. She had every right to, too. It was his fault this time.

"Seriously wolf. Shut up." He really needed to think, to focus, and Aiden wasn't helping.

"You think I don't know what's going on between the two of you?" He commented, changing the subject to an even worse one. "She doesn't know, does she?"

Doran kept his gaze leveled with Kedah's, watching her every move, waiting for her to jump. So as much as he wanted to turn to his side and punch the wolf in the face, he couldn't. "I don't know what you're talking about."

"Oh this is how you're going to play this? Alright. I'm out." And he was. Ghosting himself out as quietly and quickly as a wolf could. Fucking puppies.

The world suddenly shifted to a haze of scarlet and the only thing she focused on was her anger and the vein in the neck of the person in front of her.

The tip of her fangs dug into her bottom lip and the sensation of pain and the taste of blood sent her skin tingling. She was so hungry.

"Kedah," a whisper of a voice called out. "You're going to have to calm down."

Calm down? She couldn't really understand the command. Her brain and actions felt like they were being controlled by something else entirely. There wouldn't be any calming down.

"Kedah you cannot go after my vein. It will kill you." The whispered voice demanded. Kill her? Blood was life, and she needed it. Why would it kill her? She needed it. Craved it. It was calling to her. Commanding her.

Acting on impulse, and pure adrenaline, she launched herself into the air, zeroing in on the vein she wanted. The moment she was about to sink her fangs into flesh, strong arms wrapped around her waist and tossed her off. She flew through the air and landed with a grunt several feet away.

Springing to her feet in a crouching position, she hissed at the intruder, heard muffled voices, and jumped after her prey once more. Again, she was caught and tossed off. This time she landed hard on the floor, the jarring sensation bringing a moment of clarity.

Images and sounds began to shift into place. People took form. She was sure Doran was there. Someone else too.

Her gut feeling was that she was mad, but she couldn't remember why. Anger and rage cloaked her thoughts and only a few coherent things pushed through. Her stomach roared in hunger and her fangs ached.

"Kedah." The whispered voice spoke again. It sounded like static to her. "Stop." More static. "Please."

"I can't." She ground out over the echo of her hungered thoughts. "Hungry." An animalistic urge propelled her forward, only to be slammed into a wall of body. Something grabbed her, forcefully flipping her body so that her fangs faced away from where they wanted to be. She was suddenly being held tightly against her will and the animal within bucked wildly in protest.

Her body ached and burned with the need to fight and feed. Since she was being denied the very thing she craved, she fought with every bit of strength she possessed. She thrashed out, kicked wildly, threw her head back and jerked her body in every direction imaginable.

Minutes dragged on as her body continued to struggle against the hold of the person restraining her. She fought with everything she had, mentally and physically. The panic her body felt lasted for what seemed like damn near forever until her everything just gave up, dropping her numbly against the person behind her.

For several minutes her body tingled with unawareness before she gasped loudly and swallowed a shuddering breath.

"Welcome back." A voice rumbled from behind her.

Her throat felt like sandpaper and her stomach burned. "I need to feed."

"Yeah. You think?" Doran's voice was muffled, she thought, because his head was resting on her back. His arms were still wrapped tightly around her body, which she was grateful for as she wasn't ready to be released just yet. A bag of blood suddenly appeared in her line of sight and with zero hesitation she punctured the bag with her fangs and drank it dry. Four more bags later and she felt the last of her tensions ease.

"Anyone care to explain what the hell just happened?" Jensen's voice rang out. Very loudly. Very clearly. "All Aiden would tell me is that shit hit the fan. I could gather that much."

"That about sums it up." Doran muttered sounding more tired and reserved than she'd ever heard from him. She hadn't known him long, but did know enough to say this wasn't his normal.

"Kedah," Jensen asked of her, bringing her focus to him.

"I have no idea what happened." One minute she was crazy irritated then next everything was hazy and confusing. Then she went numb and woke up.

Jensen made an inhuman noise of frustration and got down to her level, so that when she cracked her eyes she was staring at a very unhappy face. "This cannot happen in this house. I will not allow it."

She wanted to roll her eyes. Of course he wouldn't allow it. She could have killed someone. She was very aware of this. "Okay."

Jensen looked at her a moment longer before standing up and backing away. Her head leaned up to follow him and she felt Doran's do the same. They both watched him leave in silence.

"I am in so much trouble, aren't I?" She muttered as she dropped her head forward.

"Probably not." He replied with a groan.

"How can you say that?" She said with a sad sigh. "I could have killed someone. I probably hurt you. Didn't I?" His body was still wrapped tightly around hers and she thought for a moment that it may be because he couldn't move it yet. Did she really hurt him? She couldn't remember what she did but since her body felt like it ran a marathon, through a herd of gorillas, she couldn't help but wonder what he must have felt like.

"Yes." He groaned into her back, moving his head so his cheek rested on her shoulder. It was an intimate position that felt anything but awkward.

"Please don't sugar coat it on my behalf." She sighed as she leaned her head back onto his.

"Wouldn't dream of it, Kitten." Slowly he uncurled his body from around hers and she felt the absence of his body like all the heat had been sucked out of her. She wanted him back, but would never dare to admit it. It was an unusual feeling and she decided to just chalk it up to the after effects of the panic attack she just had.

A shadow looming overhead brought her attention up to see Aiden staring down with a grin.

"Wolf." Doran cautioned in warning.

"Just came to see if the pretty little vampire needed any help." Aiden mused. The look he gave her and probably the look he was giving Doran made her feel like she'd missed something important. She probably should know what but didn't have the energy to ask. Later though, she was so digging into that.

"Back off, wolf. I got it." Doran warned.

"Kedah?" Aidan asked again, ignoring Doran.

"I'm fine Aidan, thanks." She said politely. She was pretty sure she was okay. Just needed a shower. And a nap. Maybe some ice on her muscles. Some food too. Ice cream would be a major win in her books.

"Right. So I watched Jensen leave here, deadly quiet. That is never a good look on him." Aiden's wolfy grin was cute but a little annoying at the current moment. She was right, though, Jensen was so mad at her. Great.

"Oh believe me, I'm aware." Doran gently placed his hand on her shoulder and hefted himself up off the ground. He groaned and his body groaned louder. It was not a comforting sound.

He stepped in front of her and held out a hand, lifting her to her feet with ease. That's when she got a good look at his face. His nose was broken, possibly a cheek was busted, and his lip was cut. She gasped and put both hands over her mouth.

"I take it I look as bad as I feel?" He tried to smile but winced instead.

"I did that?" She stuttered as she reached out with a shaking hand to gently touch his cheek. Oh god what had she done?

"Yeah but I'll be back to my devilish good looking self within hours." He shrugged and she grimaced, dropping her hand.

"How?" She wondered out loud.

"How what? How did it happen or how will I be back to my beautiful self by day?" He responded.

"Both?" She mused. She knew he wasn't a vampire so the quick healing of that was out. But what then was he to heal as quickly as a vampire? Or quicker.

"Anyone ever tell you, you have a damn hard head?" He commented, changing the subject.

"You're the first." She remarked.

"Well you do. And I'll be fine. Trust me." He said with a small grin.

Despite him being an ass and this being basically his fault, she trusted he would be okay. But that didn't make her feel any less bad about it.

"Come on, I'll take you up to your room to rest." He held out a hand and she took it, feeling the warmth of him creep up her arm. She needed that warmth. It was an anchor that was holding down her emotions from becoming overwhelming.

CHAPTER
twelve

Doran's hand rested on the small of Kedah's back as they began to walk, slowly, back to the stairs and to the second floor. They were both silent and thankfully so were the halls, aside from a few people who were standing at the stairs, talking to themselves. They didn't look up at them for more than a second before going back to their conversations which was a little bit of a blessing as she was in no mood to say an official hi to anyone new.

Continuing to the second floor, Doran stopped outside her door and they both stood there, a little awkward. Something different was happening between them, she just wasn't sure what.

It was obvious he cared about her more then he led her to believe, merely because he took a beating on her behalf. He didn't have to restrain her and go along for that brutal ride, yet he did without a single word of complaint.

She wouldn't deny an attraction, but she wouldn't go so far as to declare it out loud. She was still trying to get ahold of all this vampire business and didn't need complications thrown into the mix, because that is exactly what he would be. A huge, incredibly sexy, complication.

She did know that right now, this complication was the only thing keeping her from totally losing her shit. She wasn't sure why, or how, but the mere force of him near her seemed to tell her things weren't all that bad. Even if he was probably the cause of her losing it earlier. None of this made any sense.

Maybe, she could crash on his couch. If he had one. Or, you know, wherever he let her. At this point she'd take a pallet on the floor if that's what was offered. "I, uh, I don't really want to be alone. Do you have a couch I can crash on? Or do I need to worry about you damaging my virtue?"

He cocked a brow and shook his head with a little smile. He took her hand, led her to his door, and opened it without ever touching the handle. It looked like zapping places wasn't his only talent.

Not too sure what she was expecting of his apartment, she was pleasantly surprised when she walked in. Soft dark carpet covered most of the floors, the walls were a neutral tan and modern looking furniture adorned the living room and kitchen. It was inviting and warm. A complete contrast to his normal personality.

"You need anything to eat or drink?" He offered as he kicked off his shoes, tossed his phone on the table beside the door, and headed to the kitchen. She followed, dropping her bag by the front door, kicking off her shoes, and heading after him.

"I think I'm good, thanks." She said as she watched him down a bottle of water from the fridge, reaching for a second.

"Sit." He commanded, pointing to a chair.

She did, because she had no energy to fight it. The moment her butt hit the chair, her body grew weary and all she really wanted to do was sleep. Then she wanted a Vampire for Dummies book to figure out how to actually be a damn vampire. Crossing her arms on the table, she dropped her forehead to her arm and closed her eyes. There was so much she didn't know and she was beginning to feel a little hopeless.

Being the undead was starting to suck more than it was worth. The books and movies had it so wrong and it was crazy stupid how much they missed.

"Here." The sound of a water bottle and something else being placed on the table in front of her was so loud she cringed. "You need to drink that and eat the other. I don't care what order you do it, but both need to be gone before you leave this table. You look like the dead." His voice was soft but commanding.

She ignored the command. "I'm already dead. I can't die again."

She heard a chair groan as he plopped down and felt a hand under her chin, lifting her face. "I promise to not be an ass here, in this apartment, if you promise to stop being so damn hard on yourself." Lifting her head all the way up and straightening her body, she looked at him, his serious face, his determined gaze, and noted an almost complete change in his demeanor. What do you know, the big bad Doran did have a heart. How intriguing.

It may not last, she accepted that, but for now she'd take what he was giving. "Okay." Tentatively she opened the protein bar, a brand she'd never heard of, and took a bite. It wasn't half bad and she was suddenly hungry enough that she inhaled the rest of it, chasing it down with the bottle of water.

"Better?" He asked.

"Yeah, thanks." Sitting at the table, now full for the moment, she felt sleepy but wasn't ready to crash just yet. Rising from her chair she did a quick inventory of the apartment, noticing it was sparsely decorated and nothing personal was present. Sure it was furnished, and nicely, but there was nothing personal about it. No pictures or knickknacks anywhere to show who Doran was and where he'd come from. Nothing she could use to help her identify who he was.

She was mildly disappointed, but that just meant she'd have to dig a little deeper later.

Sighing, she plopped herself down on the couch, sinking into the soft cushions, and rested her head on the arm, closing her eyes. What a day. Seriously. It would be her luck that the moment she decided to move into the Estate she'd run into the local werewolves, almost get into a fight, slip into an anger-induced blood rage and nearly kill Doran. She was winning all over this place.

She never heard Doran move, but felt him sit on the other side of the couch, not making a single bit of noise or attempting to talk to her. Which was nice as she had no idea what to say. How do you say thank you to someone who essentially saved your life and allowed you to inadvertently kick their ass? Thank you seemed insignificant, to say the least.

Opening her eyes, she peered over at him while he stretched out his legs and crossed his arms under his head. At some point he'd cleaned off the blood from his face and the swelling had gone down. He was healing faster than she expected. The question of what he was floated through her head again, but she knew that if she asked, he'd ignore her or change the subject. She'd find out though, somehow.

He looked incredibly peaceful laid out like he was. Like nothing in the world could hurt him. Something about him drove her nuts while simultaneously keeping her calm. It was the oddest sensation. She'd been attracted to guys before, dated, had boyfriends, had sex and yet when she was with Doran, everything was completely different. None of her previous feelings could compare to what she felt with him.

Right now she just wanted to be held and made to believe she'd survive another day.

She'd been so independent for so long that it was second nature to take care of herself. But now, with Doran, she wanted him to tell her she was doing okay. That she didn't suck too badly. It was silly, though, she never needed a guy's opinion to matter to her. Doran just felt, different.

She looked at him and longed to have him reach out and accept her. And as if she willed it, his eyes popped open and he held out his arm in an invitation, one she didn't even consider denying. "Come here, Kitten." He said sleepily and she went, crawling across the couch, to rest her body against his, her head on his chest.

For all the good being immortal was, it never seemed to dull physical pain. It only made healing faster. His face hurt. His body hurt. Muscles in his arms and legs burned like he'd been back in the gladiator pit fighting for hours on end. Kedah was a hell of a lot stronger than she realized and he really had to struggle to keep her restrained.

And he'd do it a thousand times again if he needed to.

Why? He had not a damn clue except that it was the right thing to do.

And that drove him fucking nuts.

He had never worried about doing what was right before because he was a god and could do whatever he wanted. Right or wrong. It never mattered and never crossed his thought patterns. He just did. Just existed.

Now, now he wondered what a certain tiny kitten would think if he did something and wondered what she thought of him. He hated it. If this is how humans existed daily, it was a wonder they even lived to be adults.

The biggest issue is that he really didn't understand why this woman, of all the people he'd met over the years, was suddenly changing his way of thinking. A way of thinking he rather enjoyed because it was not complicated.

He knew why, though. Or, rather, he thought he knew why. However, the concept had been long forgotten, just like his past and his people. People that were no longer worshiped, save a few that still practiced the old ways. The time of the gods and ancient practices were long gone.

Except, was it? He'd been so far removed from them, for so many years, that it wouldn't be a surprise if old traditions and customs slowly became reality again without him realizing.

After all, he was once a god of the old time. A god long forgotten and forsaken, but a god none the less. He still retained a good amount of god like powers, and of course, his immortality. But it had been so many years since he'd thought about his brothers and sisters. Kedah showing up and his sudden ability to really care about her proved that maybe they hadn't forgotten about him.

Despite being forsaken from the kingdom from which he dwelled for many thousands of years, and cast down to live as an immortal

mortal, could he be gifted with a soulmate? Could he, he who thought he'd never have that treasure, have finally found his Anam Cara?

This was either a blessing or going to be an epic disaster. It was still too early to tell which way that was going to go.

Closing his eyes, resigned to enjoy this moment for what it was, he felt his body begin to loosen and relax. His body was using a hell of a lot of energy trying to heal and what he really needed was a solid few hours of sleep. Absently he began to run his fingers through her hair, loving the feel of it as it caressed his skin. He never imagined an action as simple as this could be so soothing.

He was starting to doze when he realized he really should go to his bed. But he didn't want to go alone. What were the odds she'd join him? "Kedah." He muttered.

"Hmm." She grumbled.

"Come on Kitten, the bed's more comfortable than this old couch." He suggested, still running his fingers through her hair. She must have been enjoying the action as well because she slowly moved her head with the movement of his fingers.

"I'm not having sex with you Doran." She muttered, still cuddled into his side.

He hadn't even considered having sex, but now, now he couldn't get the image out of his head. And it was totally worth it. "That's not what I was asking." He said with a smile, knowing that he wasn't going to actually suggest it. He, for once, wanted to go to his bed to do nothing more than sleep. His body demanded it.

"Just making it clear." She lifted her head and looked up at him as he looked down and grinned. She was utterly adorable.

"It's clear. Come on, if I sleep here I'll end up more sore then I already am. Make me feel better and take a side and get some rest as well." He stood up, feeling the tension in his body return, and reached for her hand, pulling her up and towards his room. Her eyes never really opened as she stumbled, following him, and falling face first onto his bed. He stopped and smiled down at her thinking she really did look perfect in his bed. Maybe if she were a little more comfortable, and not hanging half off, but still, perfect.

"This bed is like a fluffy cloud of heaven." Her muffled voice said with a relaxed sigh. He tried not to laugh, and failed.

"You need something to sleep in?" Surely she didn't want to sleep in what she was wearing and he knew without even asking she wouldn't sleep naked with him around. Which begged the question, what did he have for her to wear? Quickly, while she was still processing the request, he jumped over to his closet, found a pair of sweats for himself, changed, and peeked his head back out for her answer.

"Please," She answered.

Ducking back into his closet he scrambled to find something for her. A pair of boxers and an old shirt was the best he had. The boxers were clean at least as he usually went without, but the shirt was questionable. He gave it a quick sniff, smelled nothing suspicious and came out to find Kedah sitting sleepily on the bed. He handed her the things and pointed to the bathroom so she could change in private.

She wandered away and within a moment came back dressed in his clothes. The sight took his breath away. She was stunning, even in an old questionable shirt and boxers that almost doubled as pants. "Which side do you sleep on?" She asked.

He smiled and shook his head to himself. Of course she wouldn't want to inconvenience him. Little did she know though, he very rarely slept in this bed anyways and hadn't ever preferred a side as a favorite. "Just get comfortable Kedah, I'm fine wherever."

And she did without thinking twice. She crawled into the bed, positioned pillows under her head and in her arms to hug, and started to drift within moments. He carefully laid on the other side, his back flat and arms crossed under his head. Taking a last look to make sure she was okay, he shut his eyes and felt his body going completely slack while sleep took its hold.

Sometime later he felt the bed shift and a warm body snuggled up to his side. Opening his eyes in alarm, he looked over into Kedah's sleepy face and grinned. She smiled softly at him and laid her head on his shoulder, bringing her body to the length of his.

Carefully, he stretched out his arm and wrapped it around her, holding her close. Some part of her must have known that the touch from another could aid in healing or, some part of her was also drawn to him in the way he was drawn to her. He hoped for the latter but thought it was probably just the body seeking comfort in touch.

With care, he tried to push the blanket from under them and after a few minutes of struggle, got it and pulled it over their bodies. Kedah was already back asleep and he knew it would only be seconds before he joined her.

Not in over a thousand years had he shared his bed with another person. And even back then, there wasn't a whole lot of sleeping going on. He'd had many lovers, but never here in his own bed, and never that wanted to just sleep. Things were suddenly different and it was taking him by complete surprise. Turning his body to the side, so he could face her, he tucked a piece of hair from her face behind her ear and resisted the urge to lay his lips gently on her forehead. He had no idea how she would react to that display of affection.

Closing his eyes, he drifted off to sleep with the sounds of her soft breathing at his side and the feel of her body pressed into his. A man could get used to this feeling, even if it became nothing more than a distant memory.

CHAPTER
thirteen

Somewhere in the distance someone was shouting and knocking hard on something, but Doran was too far gone into sleep to be damned to answer. He hoped that by ignoring it, they would go away and go to hell. He was too comfortable to move, or to be bothered.

"Doran, someone is calling for you outside your door." A sleepy voice muttered through a tangle of hair. Eyes still closed, she turned her body into his, pushing herself flush against him. Her face tucked into the space between his neck and shoulder. Yeah… he was totally going to kill whoever it was that was knocking at the door right now. He did not have any intention of moving.

Reaching out telepathically, he felt the person at the doors anger and urgency, and rolled his eyes. Of course it would be Jensen to interrupt with something he was sure was work related. He didn't have a choice but to go and see what was up. Carefully, he peeled his body away from Kedah's, happy to notice that all his aches and pains were gone and he felt back to himself again. He smiled and watched as she sleepily reached out and pulled a pillow to her side, replacing him.

If Jensen didn't have something life threating to share with the class, Doran was sure he'd do bodily harm to the vampire. With slow and sleep heavy steps, he shuffled to the door and opened it, giving Jensen a glare. "What?"

"Am I interrupting something?" Jensen asked as he took in Doran's sleep ridden hair and lack of normal clothing.

"Yes. What do you need?" He growled.

"We have a situation that requires your attention." Jensen stated, looking pleased with himself that he had, in fact, interrupted something.

"What kind of situation?" Doran asked scrubbing his face with his hand, waking himself up.

"The kind that needs you to swoop in on your fucking broom and take care of some annoying little shit that's causing problems for me." Yikes, Jensen was having rogue problems, again. They were getting feisty, brave, and coming out of the woodwork daily. Just fucking great.

"Specific." He sighed heavily, knowing he'd have to go, but didn't really want to. He felt when Kedah woke, probably hearing them talk, and prayed she stayed put. Jensen would have a field day with this, and he was not ready to dance with those questions. He listened as her quiet footsteps came to the door and felt her hand at his side as she peered around him to see the visitor at the door. Damn.

"Oh hey, Jensen." She said sleepily.

Jensen's reaction was just about priceless. His eyes got wide and you could see the struggle he had to not open and close his mouth. He looked at Doran, looked at Kedah, who was still sporting his clothes, looked back at Doran, then grinned. "Well that I didn't expect."

"Brilliant. I'm going to grab some clothes. Kedah," he said as he turned to head back to his room, "coffee is on the counter. Have whatever you want." Neutrality was key at the moment. Face neutral, actions neutral, he needed to give nothing away as to what was going on with her, because he really needed to avoid that conversation. Aiden may already know, but he trusted the wolf to keep that information silent. Jensen would not.

He watched as Kedah wandered off to the kitchen as he went to his room, grabbing clothes and shutting himself in the bathroom. After a quick shower, he changed and was back out to the living room before coffee was even done brewing. He didn't trust Jensen to not say anything stupid. He trusted himself even less, but he wasn't worried about him, he was worried about how others would react.

Kedah was standing at the counter, coffee mug in hand, staring at the machine like she was waiting on a best friend. It looked like he was going to start loving coffee again. It always just held the caffeine he needed, but now, now he'd enjoy the company more than the coffee itself. "You cool here?" He asked her while putting on his boots.

She looked over and grinned. "Seriously? I'm in my mid 20's and have been taking care of myself for years. Yes, I think I'm fine here. But, you don't have any breakables in the house, do you? In case the strippers get rowdy?" She said with sarcasm dripping from every word. In that moment he knew she was his soulmate. By that comment alone, he knew. He had to believe it.

"Just, no strippers in my room and stay away from the channels in the 900's." Turning back to Jensen with a stupid smile on his face he waved him out and followed. "Let's go."

When they were clear of the room, Jensen let in. "You know I have to ask what's going on, right? Because, damn, you moved quickly." He quipped with a grin.

He resisted the urge to backhand the man. He'd known Jensen a long time, nearly half a century, and knew he wouldn't be able to resist the urge to poke at him. Normally, he'd laugh and say that he moved in so no one else would, or something stupid to that extent. With Kedah, she was different. And nothing happened. Not that he needed to actually explain that to anyone. "I have not a fucking response to that." He muttered in a tone that clearly stated the subject was closed. "Drop it."

Jensen smiled but didn't say anything else as they walked into his office, shutting the door behind them. Doran sat down on a chair in front of Jensen's desk while Jensen leaned against the side. "So, what's going on?"

"We have a group out patrolling and one of Max's rogues decided to ambush." Doran watched as Jensen pushed his glasses back up on his face and pinched the bridge of his nose in frustration. Sometimes he felt bad for the man, with all the new problems that were arising among all the old shit that kept coming.

"The problem with these damn rogues is that they are starved and starved tend to do reckless damage. We have him cornered, but could use some strength." Jensen continued as he sighed, like it was a great deal of work to ask for help, when Doran knew otherwise. Their arrangement benefited him a great deal and he really never hesitated to ask for him to zap himself into various places to rescue or kidnap.

Truthfully, he enjoyed the work most days. It gave him something to do, something to use his powers with, and sometimes they let him kill people, which helped reduce stress.

"Yeah alright, where are they?" Most days he'd zap in and out and be done, but today, today he wanted nothing to do with the rogues. These new ones were feisty and fought, hard. He liked a fight, but he liked hanging out with his company back in his room more. However, because Jensen had promised to keep him a secret and to field any questions in regards to him while allowing him residence, he did what was asked.

"Back alley behind the blood bank. The rogue was trying to break in through the side door, though he wasn't having much luck. Couple of our day shifters caught wind of the noise and went to investigate. I'm actually surprised there was only one of them. Max is either getting careless or we're missing something." Jensen explained.

Shouldn't be too hard then, he thought. "What do you want me to do with the rogue?"

"Bring him below. And we need him alive." Jensen said, giving him a look he knew all too well.

"If I must." Kill one rogue that was needed alive and no one ever trusted you again. How unfair was that?

With just a quick thought he was outside, blinking to adjust to the sudden change from dark to light. He brought himself a block away from the rogue because sometimes in the confusion of people randomly showing up, the wrong person gets shot. It happened only once, before he learned to not come in as a surprise unless it was a life or death situation.

The idiot he was currently on the hunt for was going to pay for ruining the perfectly good sleep session he had going on.

Walking quietly and quickly, he turned the corner to the back alley of the blood bank and could see the shifters in the distance. Their trademark dark green shirts with The Den's logo on the back was a beacon and warning to paranormals while humans were none the wiser. As he studied the shifters, with their backs turned to him, he could see in their shadows the rogue, who was hunched on his knees, blood dripping on the pavement below. The situation was too still. Too calm.

The biggest issue they seemed to face with these rogues, was that they were from Max's line, and combined with something else, allowed them to partially day walk. And wasn't that a fucking thing. Starving, half crazed, bloodthirsty vampires that could go out in the day as long as they stayed to the shadows and didn't hit direct sunlight. That limited the number of people who could patrol during the day for Jensen and upped the ante for Max.

Adding to the problem, none of Jensen's men and women had been able to find any information as to how Max was creating these hybrids and that just pissed everyone off even more.

Jensen could go out during the day, he was old enough, but couldn't be out long enough to handle this shit alone. Which was where he came in. Like the angel of death, he'd duck in, grab his prey and ghost out.

Most of the time.

The past few outings hadn't gone as planned and that was starting to wear even on his immortal amount of patience.

So back to the issue at hand, something really wasn't fucking right. The shifters hadn't turned to greet him or acknowledged he was there. They always said something, and silence was a clear indicator that shit was off.

It always happened that when he wasn't looking for a fight, a fight was looking for him.

His skin began to buzz with magic the exact moment that two vampires dropped from the windows above him, landing with a loud thud on either side of his position. Apparently these guys had missed the lecture on stealth.

He smiled with a deadly intent while putting his hands up in the air, mock surrendering. "What's up gentlemen?"

They attacked in unison with a ruthlessness that only a starving rogue would have.

If they wanted to dance, who was he to disappoint.

"You fuckers are going to regret this." He muttered as he jerked back from one that sent a sloppy kick in his direction. He swept out his leg, kicking out the legs of the attacker to his left and laying him flat on his back with a noisy grunt.

The guy to his right managed a shot to his kidney, causing him to swear in several languages before he punched the rogue in the nose so hard he flew back against the brick wall, crumpling to a moaning heap.

Lefty was up and moving, fangs out, inches from his neck before he reached out with his hand and put a vice grip around the guy's throat, raising him off the ground, feet dangling. His fingers were clawing at Doran's arm, creating several gashes that bled and burned. "You are so going to pay for messing up my day, asshole." He growled out.

Squeezing hard on Lefty's neck, he flipped his wrist and a loud crack sounded as the dangler went limp in his hand. A broken neck didn't mean death, but it would slow him the fuck down for a good hour or more. If they were lucky.

Dropping the now unconscious vampire to the pavement, he turned in time to catch number one back on his feet with one leg swinging out, catching him in the face. A deafening crunch sounded and Doran knew his cheek was broken, again. "Damnit that just healed." He bit out as he threw a kick, hitting the rogue in the chest sending him flying. The bastard slammed into the wall so hard that he merely crumpled to the ground, going lights completely out.

Two down and one to go, he thought. Hell, his arm was on fire and his cheek was throbbing. Someone was going to pay for this, and his sights were currently on the vampire at the end of the alley, who still hadn't moved

He approached quietly, and at the sight of the shifters still breathing he let himself feel a small amount of comfort.

"Stop." The rogue on the ground spat out. "I'll snap their necks if you take one more step."

Ah, the little shit was old enough to have mastered a bit of mind control. All Doran needed was a brief moment of hesitation and he could flash behind the rogue, grab him, and dump him in a cell, all before the asshole realized what was going down. "I'm stopped."

"Back up." The rogue demanded. He was bleeding and down, probably with a few broken limbs, which made Doran smile. At least the boys got in a few blows before being mind-fucked.

"No." Doran grunted in response. "This is how this is going to play out. You listening?" He paused for a moment, giving the asshole time to really listen. "Because I am not in a good mood right now." He stood still, watching closely for his moment to strike. "You interrupted one of the best days I have had in a thousand years and for that, you are going to go fucking down. So, no. I'm not backing up. Drop the shifters, without hurting them, and we'll play. You and me."

He watched the rogue for that moment while he was considering the offer. The moment he saw it, the brief moment of hesitation or doubt, shit would go down.

There it was, the littlest of twitch while his eyes shifted away for less than a second.

Go time.

With little effort, he flashed behind the rogue, grabbed him by the neck, flashed to the basement of the Estate, dumped him in a cell, and then flashed back to the alley.

The shifters were on all fours, coughing and gasping for air, but alive. They waved him off so he went to scoop up the other two rogues, depositing them in the cell with their friend. He flashed back to the shifters once more before calling it a day.

"You boys need a lift?" He asked.

They stood and shook their heads. "We're fine." Another round of coughing begged to differ on that opinion, but Doran was going to let it go. They were big boys and could handle themselves. "Damn they're getting sneaky. I had no idea those other two were even there." One of the shifters muttered while brushing off his clothes.

"I noticed. You sure you good?" He asked, visually doing a check of their bodies making sure no one had been bitten or was seriously hurt. He may be a dick to most, and regularly called an asshole, but he did care. Even if he never outwardly showed it.

"Yeah. We're good." One of them said.

"Good. Make sure you report what's doing to Jensen." He suggested.

"Unlike some people in this alley, we do actually know how to do our job." One of them smirked. Yep, they were fine.

"Sue me." He flashed himself to the basement to check on the rogues. Jensen was already there, standing outside the cell, just staring. Probably reading their thoughts by the look of blankness of everyone's faces. "Check it out. Three for the price of one." He said, breaking the tension and Jensen's concentration. "You're welcome."

"What the hell happened? The shifters said there was only one and he was contained." Jensen demanded, still locking gazes with the three rogues.

"Two were waiting in hiding. They're getting creative. And this one," he pointed to the one slumped in the corner, "is old enough to control minds. He had your boys mind locked when I got there."

"So I gathered." Jensen looked over at him and noticed his cheek and arm. He took a cautious step back. "You're bleeding."

"Really," he drawled out slowly. "I hadn't noticed. I'll refrain from dripping on you." He said sarcastically.

"I didn't survive for hundreds of years to be taken down by you, and an accidental poisoning. Go lick your wounds in your own room. I'm sure Kedah's worried." Jensen said with a sly smile. He was going to play this Kedah card until Doran snapped, which may happen sooner than later.

"Don't." He growled in a warning. "Don't go there."

Jensen tilted his head and raised a brow, clearly intrigued, because of course, he'd forgotten to remain neutral. "Fine."

He scowled at him one last time, looked over at the rogues and ghosted himself back to his room. Normally he wasn't supposed to zap himself from place to place within the walls of the Estate, but he was in pain and annoyed. Jensen could bite him if he was mad.

Once back in his room, he cussed under his breath as the pain began to spread and walked quickly to the bathroom before Kedah got a glimpse of him. Last thing he needed was to hear her worry, even though it would be nice to be taken care of for once in his life.

Doran hadn't been gone long, maybe 20 minutes or so. So it was a bit of a surprise to her when he was suddenly in the apartment, cussing under breath as he stormed to the bathroom. She nearly dropped her second cup of coffee as she scrambled off the couch and hurried to the bathroom door, knocking gently. "Doran? You okay?"

She heard the water running, him hissing in pain, and tried again. What in the world could he have done in the short time he was gone? "Doran?"

The door clicked open and his face appeared, causing her to gasp and step back. "Be a doll and grab the med kit that's under the sink in the kitchen."

She hurried off, grabbed the red bag that was under the sink and rushed back to the bathroom. Opening the door, she stopped dead in her tracks, watching the blood flow from his arm and mix with the water from the faucet. His arm looked like something had chewed on it and his face was so swollen there was no way he could see out of his right eye.

Her fangs popped out and her eyes got wide. There was so much blood and her natural instinct was to not waste it. She really tried to not drift to those thoughts. It was just so much blood.

Doran sharply turned his attention to her and cautioned urgently, "Do not even think about it, Kedah. My blood's poison. Block that thought or get the hell out. Now."

She did. Somehow, she swallowed back the lust that was churning in the pit of her stomach and focused on the injury's at hand. "What happened?"

"Rogue attacked. It's not as much blood as it seems, it's the water making it look bad. I just need to stitch it up and I'll be fine. Can you grab out a needle pack and scissors from the bag?" He was focused on washing out the cuts in the sink, as she hurriedly grabbed out what he needed.

"I can stitch it for you." She mumbled as she got closer, eyes wide at seeing the muscles in his arm, something you should never have to see, ever.

"That'd be great. Doing it myself is a bitch and I can only see outta one eye. What you people have against my pretty face is beyond me but the next person that breaks any bone in my face dies. Slowly." He muttered, more to himself than to her. Which was fine as she was still staring at his mangled arm, trying to remember if she could in fact, stitch it up.

"Uh, noted." She said, trying to keep her cool and her fangs in check. It was a good thing she took a few medic classes in college, but remembering them was going to be a bitch. It seemed like a lifetime ago.

At one point in her life she was going to be a paramedic but the thought of dealing with death on a daily basis made her upset and it was recommended by the school's psychologist that she find something else to major in. Now she was the dead. So that worked out well.

Shoving thoughts aside, she pointed to the toilet and motioned for him to sit. "Can I ruin one of these towels?"

"You'd be surprised at how well the people here can get blood out of absolutely anything. So sure, stain away." He muttered.

"I'm assuming you're going to pull the man card and not let me shoot you with anything to numb the arm?" She asked as she knelt in front of him.

"Just do it. I'll be fine." He placed his arm as flat as possible on his leg and held her gaze as she nodded. Opening the sterile pack, she grabbed the needle with the scissors, got to the middle of the biggest cut and went to work. Amazingly, even though it had been years since she had done this, it wasn't too hard to remember what to do. And what do you know, he was the perfect patient. Didn't flinch or make a sound, though his face was etched with a fine line of sweat which was probably pain induced.

Sixteen stitches later and with all three gashes closed, she wiped the area off with an alcohol pad and stood up, admiring her work. Not bad at all. Actually, she was pretty impressed.

Doran gazed down at her work and nodded to her in thanks. Standing up, he threw away the trash and put the needles and such in a bin that was under the sink. A bin that wasn't empty which, begged the question, of just how often did he need to stitch himself back together.

She watched as he wandered to the kitchen and grabbed a frozen bag of corn from the freezer, then walked to the couch and dropped down, placing the frozen veggies on his face. "So, what happened?"

"A lotta shit you don't want to know about." He answered.

"Meaning?" She did not just stitch up his arm and resist the urge to lick the blood clean, although according to him it would have killed her, to have him blow her off. That wasn't going to fly anymore. She was thrown into this world and it was about time someone started to fill in the gaps for her. "Tell me."

Carefully removing the corn from his face, he sat up and looked her in the eyes, his face showing no emotion. "You have been here all of one day. You sure you want to get into the politics of all this? Because once you know, you're in."

"That sounds mildly threatening." She commented.

"You'd know if I were to threaten you, Kitten. This is just the truth of the world you live in now. You have your safe little bubble around you. It protects you. But once you know what really is out there, your bubble will pop and it won't go up again."

He was playing neutral but she could see the emotions in his eyes. He was worried for her. She knew she lived in a jaded world and she knew it wasn't how things actually went down. However, she wasn't stupid or as naïve as everyone thought and there was no time like the present to jump head first into the vampire world. Someone had to give a little and since Doran was here, he was tagged in for the job.

She grabbed the corn from his hand and dropped it back on his face. "Don't move that again." She said. "Now, spill it. You said you wouldn't be an ass here in your apartment, and if you're going to go back on your word we can take this up outside the door."

Groaning, he held the corn in place and made no move to remove himself from the couch. In fact, it seemed to her that he was stretching himself out to get comfortable, much like he did that morning. Irritated, she sat down with force on the other side of the couch, turning her body to face his, waiting.

"I won't say we're at war, because I have fought in more wars than your history books can recount. But, disputes, for lack of a better term, happen often enough that we have to always be one step ahead of everyone else. That being said, we have a group of people that regularly go out on patrol to make sure nothing is out of place. Humans on one side, non-humans on the other."

"You see, humans, as you may remember, are awfully stupid and tend to attack at things they don't know. If the littlest thing is questioned, and no answers can be found right away, it's automatically bad or evil. Humans have a lot of fucking growing up to do and sadly, in my lifetime, haven't even come close. In fact, most days I feel they are regressing in thoughts and actions.

"At one point in the history of man, the unknown was worshiped and respected. Life was simpler. Fuller. Life had more meaning." He shook his head in an action that looked like he was shaking off a distant memory. His eyes were focused on the past and she dared not interrupt.

"Anyways, humans are idiots and can't handle things that are uniquely different. Well, most humans at least. There is always those few that can handle it but it's the others that ruin the party. Which is where some of us come in. There is a whole side of politics that I won't get into, but bringing it down to the level it's at here, is we keep things civil and calm. There is a rogue vampire whose sole purpose in his undead life is to cause chaos. He enjoys preying on humans, making them pay for past aggressions that most hadn't even known existed. This vampire is in league with several other species who also hold onto grudges way too long."

"Jensen, myself, and a handful of others job is to not allow this ass of a vampire to ruin things that some of us have worked so hard to maintain. Secrecy is key. We have patrols out night and day ensuring that humans remain ignorant and non-humans remain in the shadows." He sat up, still holding the corn to his face, and looked over at her, again giving no emotion off at all. He had apparently perfected the art of his resting neutral face.

She took a deep breath and let it out slowly. It was a lot to process and yet, it made a lot of sense. The past was littered with examples of humans doing disastrous things because they didn't understand something. Naturally those that weren't fully human, would want to take steps to keep themselves hidden else a war would breakout.

Now she understood why Jensen was so adamant about Sadie not knowing more about their world than she already knew. Sadie may be trust worthy, but if she was captured, there was no way a mere human could withstand the strength and force of a non-human. She'd crack almost instantly.

"Can I take this shit off my face now?" He asked in a light joking tone.

Smiling, she reached over and grabbed the bag, setting it on the end table. "So, that's a lot to swallow."

"That's what she said." He responded immediately and with a huge grin.

"You keep making references that you're older than sin and yet, most of the time when you open your mouth a child comes out." She commented with a laugh. She truly believed he was as old as he claimed, but man, it seemed that the older men got the more they reverted back to their childish ways. Guess that transcended through species as well.

"It's more fun that way." He shrugged and sat up, turning his body to face hers.

"So, what happened today?"

"One of the baby rogues got a little too feisty. On a scale of kitten scratch to dragon slaying, this was probably just a step above a kitten." He shrugged.

"You have a broken cheek and 16 stitches in one arm. That's not a kitten scratch." She muttered. She would totally have to remember to ask if he'd actually seen and/or slayed a dragon. That was going to be yet another conversation for another time.

"Kitten, you have no idea the torture and injury I've dealt with. I've broken every bone in my body, at least twice." He said, and by the look on his face, he was utterly serious.

"You're joking?" She blurted.

He cocked a brow. "Am I?"

Shaking her head to clear the mental image that popped in uninvited, she stood up and paced, something she did when she was nervous or thinking hard about something. "So, who is the vampire that's causing the issues around here?"

"His name is Max." Doran stated.

Kedah tripped over her own foot and fell face first into the ground, barely catching herself with her hands. Oh crap. Oh no.

Doran jumped up and over to her in a flash, helping her back up to vertical. But the wave of panic that struck her made her think she might be better off on the ground. Her head spun and her stomach began to roll. "What the hell was that?" He asked.

"Sorry, I tripped." He didn't believe her by the look she was getting. "I, uh, think I have heard that name before."

"You better hope you haven't. He's ruthless as hell and will stop at nothing to seek out and destroy anything he puts his mind to." Doran took her elbow and led her back to the couch, where they sat back down, only Kedah knew she wasn't going to stay much longer. She needed air. Space. Time to think. To reevaluate.

Snapping fingers came into her line of sight and she blinked several times, shaking her head, realizing she'd spaced out. "Yo, Kitten. What the hell?"

"Uh," she stammered. "You need to clean those stitches out with a wash cloth. I can take them out tomorrow if you're body hasn't already pushed them out."

He looked at her with a slight confusion and nodded. "I know."

"Okay, well, this has been fun, but I need to get back to my room. I told Sadie I'd call and I need to pick a job or something, according to Jensen." She stood and quickly grabbed her bag and was out the door before he could call her back. She looked over her shoulder as she used her key to open her door and watched him watch her with curiosity written all over his face.

Shit. She was in so much trouble. What were the odds that this Max was also her Sire?

Odds were probably great, actually.

CHAPTER
fourteen

The most wanted vampire in the state, causing an insane amount of problems, was her Sire, or at least she thought he was. With his previous actions, she wouldn't doubt it. What she could do about it was a whole different chapter in the shitty book she was currently living. Shit.

Throwing her bag towards her room, she grabbed her phone and sat down on the couch, wondering what in the world she should do. Who should she even talk to about this? There was not a chance in a rainy hell that there were two Max's running around so that left her with a huge mess of a problem and not a soul to talk to about it. Jensen would probably just kill her and Doran, well, she had no idea but it wouldn't be good.

There had to be someone outside the Estate that she could talk to. Oh, she thought as the lightbulb went off. Cook, from the Diner. He may know something as he seemed to know more about this world than she did. Which, should have concerned her, but right now, it may be just the blessing she needed.

After a quick call to the Diner and a meeting set, she scrambled to her bedroom for a change of clothes. It was probably bad taste to go out seeking help wearing the clothes of the man she had just woken up in bed with and then stitched back together, plus, threw a bag of corn on his head. Man, her day had gone from great to weird to shitty in a blink of an eye.

Life as an immortal was sure to be interesting, of that she was certain.

Trying to follow the emotional roller coaster that was Doran may be what sends her to an early grave. Not to even get her started on how she felt about him. There were moments where she wanted to wear him like a graphic tee and there were times she wanted to strangle him with that same shirt. She hardly knew him but it seemed that he could get under her skin like they'd been friends and lovers for decades.

He was old, though he looked no older than late 20's early 30's, but wasn't a vampire. She was sure he wasn't a wolf either, given his distaste for Aiden and his pack. But then, what did that leave? She could safely say she had no idea.

Leaving thoughts of him aside, now she needed to figure out how to leave the Estate without much notice. If it was possible.

Walking towards the kitchen she picked up the phone list for the house and what do you know, a driving service. Awesome. After a quick call and saving the number, she was set to go. That was far easier than she expected it to be. They truly did cater to all needs here.

Quickly, as a second thought, she grabbed a few bags of blood, nuked them and downed them. She was still trying to keep ahead of any cravings that may happen and the last thing she needed was to go crazy, again, and have to get help from some random person, assuming she didn't kill them.

Sighing, she grabbed some cash, her keys, phone and a hell of a lot of courage, she left the room, locked up, and prayed to whoever was listening that none of her neighbors were out and chatty. Doran's door was shut and everything was quiet, thankfully. She did wonder, briefly, if it wasn't just her and Doran, plus Jensen's office on this floor alone, but thought probably not. It was odd she hadn't seen much of anyone else.

Hurrying down the stairs, she dashed out the front door where, a car was already waiting. After being polite and thanking the man for the ride and telling him where she wanted to go, they traveled in silence into town. She was dropped off at the front of the old diner and promised to call when she needed to come back. That, or she'd just hail an Uber if needed.

A bubble of panic turned in her stomach as she made her way to the side entrance and past where her first incident happened. Where her perfect little hidden life crashed and events spiraled out of control. Momentarily lost in that thought, she hadn't realized that Cook was already at the open door, waiting for her.

When she looked up, she jumped in surprise while Cook just smiled and waved her in. "It's good to see you, girl. You look healthier."

"Uh, thanks?" She thought she looked fine before, but maybe not.

"Give me ten and I can take a break. Got a few orders I need to grill out. Yeah?" He grunted and hobbled back to the grill, flipping pancakes and cracking eggs, going on with life as if there wasn't a vampire standing in the back of the kitchen. But then, he must have known what she was when he hired her.

"Sure. You need me to do anything?" She asked, hoping for something to do because standing there thinking wasn't good for her health.

He pointed to the sink where a mound of dishes was threatening to take over the counter. She grimaced but thought the distraction was overdue and honestly welcomed. Grabbing an apron, she tied it on and got to work, enjoying the feeling of being useful and productive. Instead of helpless and clumsy.

Maybe she needed to just do dishes at the Estate. Work with her hands. Be out of harm's way, for the most part. Honestly though, if she was being true to herself, she liked the idea of patrolling the city. The idea that maybe she could help to prevent what happened to her, from happening to anyone else. Those men, whoever they were, were recklessly destroying lives for a purpose that more than likely wasn't valid or moral. If she could just break away from Max somehow, and maybe learn how to be a little more badass, then that job would be ideal. If not, well, she'd work in the office or do dishes.

Lost in her inner monologue, she hadn't noticed that Cook had come over and was leaning against the counter, just watching. He cleared his throat and she snapped her head to the side, smiling. "You're lost in some deep thought there, girl."

"Yeah I was, sorry." Wiping her hands on her apron she took it off and hung it next to the sink.

Following him outside, she waited as he took a pack of smokes out of his pocket, tapped it on the heel of his hand a few times, grabbed one and lit it with a deep inhale. "So, what's on your mind?"

Time to just rip the Band-Aid off and go for gold, she grimaced. "Is there any way to break the connection between Sire and child in the vamp world? I mean, would you know? You seemed like you may know more than me, which isn't saying much as I know just about nothing."

Cook looked her up and down and took a few drags before answering. "Yes. Whether or not you're up for it is another story. It's painful. Painful and uncertain."

"I survived the turn, didn't I? Pain worse than that?" She grunted. Seeing as that was the worst pain, ever, she surely hoped nothing was worse than that.

"You did, and this will be exactly that same pain." Cook commented.

"Oh great." She mumbled. "What do I have to do?"

"You have to replace the blood in your system with that of another Sire. Best if that vampire is older than your Sire, blood will be stronger then, more magic. He, or she, will have to drain you to near death, then give you their blood."

"And that will work? For sure?" She questioned. Because to her, it sounded awful and incredibly hard to accomplish.

"Nothing is ever 100% but, it should do the trick." He commented.

Kedah groaned as her small problem just became bigger, when she realized she knew exactly one other vampire. One. And he was out of the question. Closing her eyes and rubbing her temples, she felt her first immortal headache brewing and it was a winner.

"Can I ask ya something?" Cook drawled.

"Sure." She muttered.

"You in trouble?" Cook took another smoke out of his pack and lit it up. He must be something immortal to be able to smoke like that and not have died already.

That was a tricky question to answer. She wasn't in too much trouble, yet, but it could escalate quickly. "Maybe. But I think I can handle it."

He shook his head with a sad smile. "Not alone you can't. I've been around a few years and have learned a thing or two. Alone is never the way to handle anything. Others will be far less upset with you if you ask for help, even if the situation is shitty, than if you try and go at it alone and end up worse off."

Well, there was that, she thought. Still, stubborn as she was, she was going to try and handle this on her own before asking anyone else to get involved. "Sure Cook, thanks."

"Oh and Kedah, one more thing, girl. The man with the long history, the hidden history. You know him and you need to trust him. Despite anything he tells you, as farfetched as it may seem, trust it." Cook took a last drag of his smoke, dropped it on the ground, snuffing it out with his boot. He ducked back into the diner and was gone before she even had time to process what he had just said.

Well, she was a vampire who ideally could live forever, which would make for a very long history. Everyone she knew, aside from Sadie, could have hundreds if not thousands of years of history under their belts. So that narrowed it down to, what, a lot? Only two she knew on a first name basis, but neither could be who Cook spoke of. Could they? She really didn't even have the time to ponder that. There were more important things she needed to worry about currently.

So, armed with this new knowledge, and nothing to do with it, what was she going to do with the rest of her night? She didn't want to go home because she didn't want to deal with the people there. Unfortunately, she did need to unpack and despite not wanting to go back, she probably should anyways.

Groaning to herself, she pulled out her phone and dialed for a ride. At some point, and soon, she was going to need to figure out a way to get her own car. This calling for a ride all the time was bound to get old quickly.

Making her way out of the alley, she stood against the front of the Greasy Spoons, the neon lights casting shadows across the street, and looked out into the town. This was her home and it was an unsettling feeling to know that a madman was running the alleys and streets causing as much hell as possible.

It was even more unsettling to know she had a direct connection to him. Something was going to have to give soon or she was going to lose her damn mind, or her life, whichever came first.

CHAPTER
fifteen

Aiden cursed as two shifters came back from patrol a little more than scuffed up. Though it wasn't exactly his duty to take care of those shifters, he tended to watch over them anyways.

"What the hell happened to you two?" He demanded as the men sat on an exam table in the estates tiny medical clinic. They each had cuts and abrasions covering any piece of skin not covered by clothes, which meant there was a good possibility of more that were hidden.

Carson, the larger of the two men scowled at Aiden, who just raised a brow back at him. In the hierarchy of species, technically Aiden was at the top, though he didn't pull that card unless absolutely necessary.

"Max's creatures are getting more erratic and harder to contain. The one we thought we had, was old enough to have practiced mind control of a varying degree." Dan, the other shifter, said as he moved an icepack away from his face with a wince.

Carson nodded to Dan, but offered no other explanation, which Aiden expected. Carson wasn't much of a talker. Something had happened that brought him to the estate that was bad enough that he chose not to speak. Only Jensen knew what had happened, and he wasn't telling, nor was anyone asking. Carson would tell his story when he was ready and the nice thing about everyone here within these walls, is that not a one of them would push him to talk before that.

"Shit." Aiden grumbled. Max was stepping up his game and not a single one of them seemed to be able to get a step up on him. And now with these attacks in the daylight, things were only going to get worse. It was entirely possible that humans would be involved sooner rather than later, and that's when shit really would hit the fan.

"Pretty much." Dan said. "Do you need anything from us?"

"Just your report to Jensen as soon as possible." Aiden said.

"Yeah we got it. Doran said the same thing before he ghosted out." Dan muttered.

Aiden rolled his eyes but didn't respond. Doran was his own creature, and a difficult one at that. However, if he was there, then that was probably the only reason these shifters lived. Doran was that good. No one should ever mention that to him, his ego would expand to larger than the property they lived on, but it was the truth.

"You boys should shift into your animal forms and let those wounds heal. I'd imagine your necks will be stiff for a bit, but you'll be fine." He said and watched as the two men nodded in agreement and jumped off the table. Both left quietly and both were limping.

Aiden dropped his head for a moment and took a deep breath. This was only the beginning of whatever was coming and it felt bad. Bad enough that he felt like his body would never lose the nervous edge that was creeping in.

Shaking his head, trying to clear out his thoughts, he turned sharply and left the medical room. If things were going to get worse, they should think about training some of the staff and residents to deal with injuries. He made a mental note to mention that next time he was around Jensen, because if anyone in this place could get that ball rolling, it was him.

Fuck, this was going to be a mess and he needed to not think about it. There was nothing he could do currently, so a distraction was definitely needed.

Just as he left the room, which was on the first floor, he cut to the left and made his way to the back of the house, thinking some exercise on all fours was needed. He hadn't run in a while, and his wolf was calling. Fortunately, a better distraction just walked in through the garage and he smiled as he placed himself directly in her path. His wolf could wait a few more hours.

True to Kedah's nature, or of what he'd noticed so far, she ran right into him, shrieking and scrambling back as an apology left her lips. "Sorry! So sorry." She muttered as she looked up at him. "Oh, Aiden, right?"

He smiled as he looked down at her. "The one and only."

"Oh, hey. It's good to see you. What are you doing here?" She stumbled over her words, looking adorable and nervous. He watched as she glanced around, probably looking for his pack mates.

"They're not here." Aiden said with a grin.

"Oh good. They are a little scary," she said honestly and he couldn't help but laugh. She was right, they were, and mean as hell most days. They weren't exactly vampire friendly, but to be fair, they weren't actually people friendly either.

"That they are, and just a fair warning, if you see them and I am not with you, or them, turn the other way. They won't attack you, but they won't be nice either." He warned.

"Noted," she muttered, still looking nervously around.

"Where are you headed to?" He asked, changing the subject. As he watched her reactions to things, and listened to her words, he felt a soft spot growing for her. Nothing like the attraction that he felt Doran had for her, but something a little milder. She just had that persona that needed to be protected. Not that she couldn't do it herself, he was sure she could, but that she just needed a few extra eyes watching out for her. Nudging her in the right direction so she could accomplish things on her own.

"I, uh, I don't know, actually. I just got in from town and don't have plans." She said, starting to look a little less nervous.

"Good. Come on." He said as he walked past her and towards the back of the house.

"Where are we going?" She wondered out loud.

"Outside." He answered.

"I haven't been out back yet." She said with some excitement.

"I figured. Come on, let's explore." He said with a grin.

She scrambled up to him, and walked silently as they passed through the back door and onto the well-manicured back lawn.

The property extended well beyond what either of them could see, although he had hunted every inch of the land, and knew it well. The immediate backyard was enormous and housed an array of activities for whatever you craved. Directly in front of them was a garden that was laid out into a maze that was nearly an acre long. In the spring it was a wonder to see.

To the left of where they were standing was an Olympic size pool complete with diving boards on the far end. The pool didn't get too much use, which was a shame, but he remembered the way Kedah had been looking at the small one inside and figured she'd enjoy it. "Look."

"Holy crap." She exclaimed as she rushed over to take a closer look. He watched as she walked the length of the pool, looking like a swimmer who was being called home. There was history in the way she moved by the water and in her eyes as she gazed down the lanes.

There was also something endearing about the way she seemed to look at anything new. She held excitement and wonder and after the death and darkness that this place mostly brought in, it was a nice change. "You can use this whenever you want. There's a tennis court and a basketball court past the garden. Trails go all around the property but it's probably a wise idea to not go walking alone. Too many things go hunting at night and in the thrill of the hunt, it's hard to tell the difference between friend and foe."

She looked back over at him, her eyes wide. "Well, that's a little terrifying."

"It was meant to be." He said with a grin.

"So, when does Rugby pick back up?" She asked, changing the subject with a cheeky smirk.

"Ah, you saw that did you?" He laughed and put his hands on his hips as he walked the few steps back to where she stood.

"Are you kidding? How could I have missed it?" She exclaimed happily.

"No set schedule, but mostly when aggressions need to be released in a safe-ish manner. We're wolves, so fights are common and contact sports even more so." They actually could use another game or two sometime soon. Tension was everywhere and he knew a brawl could break out at any point.

She actually stuck out her lip and pouted. "Poo."

He laughed and shook his head. "You're going to be a riot around here; of that I can already tell. Tell you what, you promise to go back to the gym and get in the pool or do something for you, and I promise to invite you to the next game. Deal?"

She jumped up and clapped her hands. "Deal!"

"Come on little vampire, the sun's not far off and you probably should eat and get to bed." He gestured back to the estate and she followed close behind. Though he couldn't see her, he could feel her gaze as it continued to search the grounds and building, always discovering.

Not many really young people, of any species, came into the Estate, and it was refreshing to watch her see things through younger eyes. He wasn't that old, but did have a few years on her. Give or take 50 or so if he guessed her age correctly. Jensen had at least a thousand on her and who knew about Doran. Everyone here tended to be older than the building itself or close to it.

Stepping inside, he made his way to the stairs and paused, watching as she started up. "I don't need to walk you to your room, do I?"

She smiled and shook her head. "No, I think I can manage." She went to turn to leave, but paused and turned back to him. "Thank you. I think you're probably the first person in this place to treat me as normal. To show me things I might like and not assume I'm as clueless as I feel.

Thank you for that." And if that wasn't the sweetest thing, she then decided to step forward and hug him. She wrapped her arms around his waist and hugged him like one would a very dear friend.

Growing up as a wolf, he'd never known a truly loving family. At least not his family, which was why he was now living as far away from them as possible. But, if he had had that loving family, Kedah would have been that sister he wished he could have known. He hugged her back and smiled to himself.

"Alright little vampire, get your cute little butt up to your room. Unpack. Make yourself at home. Crash for the day. I'm sure I'll see you around and when I do, I'll introduce you to some residents." He gave her a little squeeze and stepped away, still smiling.

"That sounds great, thanks!" She said happily and all but ran up the stairs to the second floor. That was probably a smart place to have put her, he thought, as Jenson worked from that floor and could watch out for her easier. Although, Doran was also on that floor, which would prove interesting for the both of them. Something was going on with the two of them, something big, he just wasn't sure if they were going to end up killing or loving each other.

He walked away from the stairs with one small laugh for himself. Whatever was going on with the two of them, when Doran saw her next and could smell Aiden all over her, he was going to pitch a fit and it would totally be worth it to see. He lived to irritate the man, and this would definitely hit the mark.

CHAPTER
sixteen

Doran hadn't seen Kedah since she stumbled out of his room and left in a hurry. Not that he was watching, but he was, and saw her leave the estate in a blur of motion. He debated following her, but thought better of it. First off, he wasn't exactly a stalker, most days. Second, she'd kick his ass if she knew he was following her. So, despite the fact that his body wanted to chase her down, he resisted and went to bed.

Rest was restless, but it always was. This night though, he was plagued with the memories of Kedah's sleepy yawns and unruly hair. Plagued with her scent that seemed to be clinging to everything in his apartment. And like the idiot he was turning into, he was craving her presence. But, instead of going to find her, he remained at home, trying to sleep. He tossed and turned, angering his stitches and irritating the bruises on his body.

At some point he drifted off into a few hours of sleep and when he woke, he felt mildly better. At least his body was no longer screaming at him with every movement. Groaning, he dragged himself from his bed and into the kitchen where he had a choice of coffee or beer. Normally beer would win, no matter the time of day, but for some reason, today, he opted for coffee.

Once a cup was made, he leaned against the counter, staring at his door. Some part of him was hoping she'd come knocking, but a bigger part knew that she probably wouldn't.

Maybe he should take her out.

His immediate thought to that idea was no, no he shouldn't. But, maybe she'd be okay with it. Or maybe he was turning into a sap, again. He just couldn't figure out why when it came to Kedah, he suddenly became a teenage boy. It was driving him fucking nuts.

Fuck it. He decided to just go over and bug her, and see where that would lead. It was what he was best at, after all. Maybe they'd go out or maybe they would stay in. His list of maybes was too long to not try and see a result of some sort.

Swallowing back the last of his coffee, he set the cup back under the machine and took off to his room to find clean pants and a shirt. He never cared before what he looked like or what he wore but be damned if he didn't care just a little today.

Once satisfied he looked decent, he headed for the door. No one was really out and about yet, so he managed to make it the ten steps it took to get to Kedah's apartment without bumping into anyone. Before knocking, he paused to get a feel for if she was even awake, and by the sounds of it, she definitely was.

Banging on the door a few times, he waited only a brief second before she swung the door open with a smile. The first thing that stuck him, aside from the fact she was in nothing but a towel, was the distinct smell of wolf on and around her. He wanted to be pissed and get mad, but swallowed that down, because she probably wouldn't have understood. "You forgot your clothes, Kitten."

She smiled and shook her head, opening the door wider. "Did I? Hadn't noticed. What's up?"

Fuck him because all he wanted to do was rip off that towel. Crossing his arms over his chest, hiding a scowl as he irritated his stitches, he grinned trying to get his emotions in check. "Just seeing what you were up to and why you smell like a wolf."

"You can really smell Aiden on me? Seriously? I thought you guys were just giving each other shit about that." She said, looking only a little confused.

"No Kitten, you smell like a wolf." He said, still trying not to be mad at her. Aiden on the other hand may eat some shit later.

"Good thing I was about to shower. Do come in so you can make sure I don't smell like a wolf after." She said sarcastically. He smiled and walked into the apartment while she shut the door and locked it.

She walked over to her bathroom, while he stayed in the living room. He wanted to follow her, but wisely kept his feet planted on the carpet. "By the way, Aiden and I hung out last night, which would be where the smell came from. I'll just be a few in the shower, if you don't mind waiting."

Aiden was going to get his ass kicked later, there was no question at this point. "Course not Kitten. Good thing I'm here, just in case you fall in the shower or something." God he could be such a dick sometimes. The worst thing about it is that he never knew what his mouth was saying before he said it.

"Yes," she said dryly. "Good thing." She ducked into the bathroom and he heard the shower water start to run.

As he waited, he looked around her apartment, noting she'd done close to nothing to actually move in. To be fair, she'd not been healthy long enough to actually be able to do much, even still, there was almost nothing personal. Until he noticed a picture that stood on the nightstand aside her bed. Curiously, he walked to it and stopped dead when he was close enough.

To anyone else, it was nothing more than a rundown gray stone castle nestled between overgrown trees and weeds. The rolling highlands in the background blanketed the ground in lush green tones and the sky was a heavenly blue.

To him, this was so much more and it shook him right to the soul to see it here in her room. "Hey." He said, keeping his voice neutral and calm. "What's this picture of?"

He knew, but wanted to know her take. Needed to know what it meant to her.

She peeked her head out of the bathroom and smiled, looking at the picture he was pointing to. He could only see her head and bare shoulders and had to really restrain himself from picturing what else was behind that bathroom door. Nothing good could come of those thoughts right now.

"Oh, that. It's just a castle I visited when I was in Scotland and I just fell in love. It's silly, the whole reason, but I love it. Isn't it cool?" She beamed a smile at him and went back into the bathroom, shutting the door.

"Oh come on now, you can't leave it at that. Tell me the story, lass." He asked, letting his native tongue slip for added support. It almost always worked to get the ladies talking. For some reason, everyone loved a Scot.

She exited the bathroom with a towel wrapped around her head, jeans that hugged all the right curves, and a shirt that hung loosely over her chest. She looked damn sexy walking barefoot over to him, picking up the picture and smiling a genuine smile. He hadn't seen that often on her and wished she'd do it more. Her smile lit the room. "It's silly. Everyone always called me a hopeless romantic. You'll just poke fun at me."

No, he probably wouldn't, because he knew what that place meant. He knew, almost without a doubt, what she saw there. He just wanted to hear her words. Her story. "Kitten, I've lived a long time, I'm sure I've heard far worse. Come on, let's hear it."

She looked at him and smiled again, causing him to ache to reach out and cup her face in his palm. To hold that smile as his own. He put his hands in his pockets instead. "You're from Scotland, aren't you? I hear your accent come through every once in a while."

She was stalling and doing a good job of it too. He'd answer her questions because it was the only way she'd tell him her story. "Aye. I am. I call it home every now and then." More like every day but that was his treasure to have, no one else's.

"Do you know this place then? The tour we were on took us out into the highlands for a few hours. They said they didn't do that often and not a lot of people got this far as it was so remote." She said, a gleam in her eye twinkled as he watched the memories of the land flash into her head.

He understood that feeling, had it regularly when he thought of home. "I may. Tell me your story, Kedah. I promise not to say an ill word of it."

She sighed loudly and let the towel fall from her head, her brown locks falling in wild waves around her face. "Fine. But if you make fun of me, I'm going to punch you in the kidney." She laughed as she held the picture close, like a treasure she wasn't willing to let go.

"It was beautiful, stunning really, set against the backdrop of the rolling Highlands. And the history behind the castle must have been amazing, though when I tried to research it I didn't come up with anything. Anyways, when we were there I could have sworn I saw someone in the window of one of the rooms on the second floor. Off in the corner." She held out the picture and pointed to the far corner of the castle. "There. And if you look, hard, you can see him in this picture. The image isn't as clear here, but in my mind I can see every detail." He carefully took the picture and looked where she had pointed.

Sure enough, there was the silhouette of a highlander. It was light, almost looking like a trick of the eye, but it was certainly there.

"When we were there, I swear he was there too. A highlander of old. Bare chested wearing only a kilt, he was looking out the window with a sort of longing about him. A sadness really. I always imagined, and don't you dare laugh, that he was looking for a lost love. He just looked so hopeful and I fantasized that he would find her one day. Through the sands of time, she would come and they would live in that castle, happy and in love." She set the picture back on the nightstand and turned towards him, her smile still brightening her features.

"None of the other students saw him, they all said I had been reading too much. But the guides said that I may have seen a ghost from the past. They said that ghosts walk the Highlands, always protecting their lands. They believed me, at least. Or they indulged my fantasy. Either way, when I got home and looked through my pictures, I could picture that man in the castle. I keep it as a reminder of my trip, which was magical to say the least, and to maybe carry on his love. Like, by me keeping the picture, keeps his hopes alive that she will come."

He was speechless for a moment. Maybe two. She had no idea how close she was to the actual truth. Aye, he knew that castle. It was one of his own, on his property that stretched across the Highlands for endless miles. That man, the one she'd seen and continued to hope for, was him. He remembered that day clearly, as if it had only just happened.

He was home, just milling around, looking for something to do when he was drawn to this particular place. Traveling in only his kilt, something he did when alone, he zapped to the house and stood watch as dozens of high schoolers wandered around, gossiping about the unkempt property and fallen trees. Not a one of them truly had any idea of the history they were standing on.

No one except one girl. One who looked up at the castle with an awe that he couldn't help but stare at her. Her face, now he knew it was none other than Kedah herself, was transfixed with wonder and it gave him some hope that maybe good people of the old ways were still out there.

Looking at her now, he could see that youthful innocence in her eyes. The same eyes that looked up into his castle believing in fairy tales. How he'd not seen it before was beyond him. He should have made the connection the moment she stumbled into the Estate for the first time, but somehow missed it.

"You're not speaking. You must think I'm totally hopeless." She said as she ran a brush through her hair and put it up. He wished she'd keep it down, it was so lovely framing her face.

No, he didn't think she was hopeless. He thought that maybe she was the one he was looking for. The one person whom he'd waited for, for thousands of years. Soulmates tended to be attracted to the same places, almost as if their very souls knew that's where the other would be.

"No, kitten. I dinnae think your hopeless. I think you're absolutely right. The guides were right too. The ghosts of ancient warriors that used to frequent those lands continue to watch over them. Making their rounds. The Highlands are a magical land, one never knows just what's going on and what has been." He knew, mostly. Had known for thousands of years.

He could remember when the people lived in meager huts, worshiping the gods for their daily needs. Remembered when they discovered how to build stronger homes and lived in manors and castles. Remembered a time when dozens of families lived together as a village, living off the land in a peaceful and mild existence. He remembered it all.

He looked over at Kedah again, lost in his own thought, and watched as she studied his reactions. His current mood. She stepped closer to him, her body being as close as it ever had to his, while they were awake. Every bit of him could feel her presence and if he wasn't careful he could drown in her essence.

"You know, now that I really look at you, you have that same look about you. The longing. Like you're waiting for something or someone." She stepped even closer to him, their bodies brushing. She reached up and placed her palm on his cheek, her skin soft and warm. He spared the moment to close his eyes and lean into her hand, allowing this one moment to be humble. He could offer her that, at the very least.

"What is your story Doran? What are you longing for?" She whispered to him.

You. He wanted to say. I've been waiting for you for a long time. But, he couldn't tell her, not yet. Not until he was sure. Absolutely sure. Instead, he'd stretch the truth, because he was scared of rejection. Opening his eyes, he placed a hand over hers, holding her to his cheek, savoring the moment of tenderness they shared. "Aye, lass. I long to not be so tired anymore."

"I don't understand." Her face was soft, her voice holding the innocence and truth of someone young and of someone who believes in fairytales that he'd long since given up on.

Smiling, he took her hand off his face but held onto it for just a moment longer. He promised himself in that moment that someday soon he'd tell her of the castle. Of souls that searched heaven and hell and thousands of years for each other.

"You don't need to understand, Kitten. Someday you will, but not today." He said with a soft smile.

"Doran, you are such a mystery." She brought his hand to her mouth and laid the lightest of kisses on his knuckles. She dropped his hand with a smile and turned to walk towards her kitchen, leaving him speechless, again.

She had kissed him. Her lips briefly touched his skin and all he could do was stand there, in her bedroom, like a fucking idiot. He was an idiot, because any other man would have chased after her, and yet here he was, frozen in place.

The inevitable pull of what a soulmate must feel like tugged at his being and the ancient word for soulmate, Anam Cara, drifted into his thoughts. As the words banged into his skull, he felt the exact moment that his eyes began to swirl and change color. Without even looking in a mirror he knew. The pain would only be temporary. Both of their eye colors were merging, becoming one. The eyes were the windows to the soul and now theirs were destined to be together. He'd finally found her, and it was just in the nick of time. Because, if he was being honest, he was tired. Tired of holding it all in and not being able to have that one person who could turn his tiredness into a renewed sense of living.

CHAPTER
seventeen

It was a little odd to have Doran in her room and sharing the story of the castle, but it was even odder to see that for the first time, he looked human. He looked as if he truly was as tired as he stated, and yet it didn't make any amount of sense to her.

Opening the fridge, she grabbed a few bags of blood and popped them in the microwave. At least she was getting used to feeding herself on a regular basis and really could feel the difference. No wonder Jensen was amazed that she hadn't died from starving herself. As she watched the blood circle in the microwave, a pain flared to life within her eyes and she shut them hard, bringing the heels of her palms to her closed lids.

Groaning, she tried to close her eyes tighter as the pain surged through her eyes, then was completely gone. It felt almost like a migraine was coming on, but that couldn't be because she wasn't human anymore. Did vampires even get migraines because if so, that would suck so badly. Standing up, she opened her eyes slowly, waiting for the pain to return, and when it didn't, she shrugged and finished getting her drink ready. That was really weird and hopefully wasn't some weird sign that she was getting a vampire illness of some sort.

"Kitten, I gotta go." Doran said abruptly. She looked over at him, slightly confused, and nodded. He already had the door open and one foot was on its way out.

"Uh, well, okay then. Thanks for the chat. And not making fun of me." She said, watching as he smiled slightly back at her.

"No worries. I'll run into you later." He muttered, then winked at her with a half-smile and left.

It was the oddest thing. She really thought something was happening, that a connection was being made, and he bailed. "Men," she groaned. Dumping her warm blood into a mug, she sipped it gently and looked on at the door.

Doran was going to drive her nuts and she just wasn't sure what to make of it. Shaking her head, she cleared him from her thoughts and tried to think of what she was going to do for the evening. Unpacking was done until she could get the rest of her things from Sadie. Doran had skipped out for the evening. Jensen was probably not the type of person to just hang out.

Aiden was probably around somewhere, but who knew where exactly. Plus, he probably had friends and better things to do than hang out with a little vampire, as he liked to call her. Though she wasn't mad at the name, because truthfully it was endearing.

That left her with not a single person to bug, unless she wanted to go into town, which was looking like her only option. Sighing as she finished her blood, she set the cup aside, and called for a ride, again promising herself she really needed to get a car. Maybe if she kept saying that promise every time she needed a ride, it would become a reality soon.

Sliding her feet into sandals and grabbing her things from the counter, she followed the same path as before, finding her way down and out of the Estate a little easier this time. The car ride into town was filled with idle chatter and quiet conversation, both of them being polite but not overly so. She really needed to make it a point to get to know more people around her new home

Her ride dropped her off a block from Sadie's place, which was fine as she enjoyed the walking. Stepping up her pace, she found her old place with the lights off and the front door not only locked but dead bolted. Sadie must have been already asleep, what a bummer.

Sitting on the porch steps, she looked around at the other houses and thought for sure she'd be missing this place a lot more than she was. It wasn't home anymore; it hadn't been for a few months now. She couldn't just go out whenever she wanted and chat with the neighbors, or ride a bike down the street. No, now she lived in fear that someone would recognize her and a new version of hell would break open as old wounds surfaced. Not to mention the whole supposed to be dead thing that was bound to freak anyone out.

Sighing, she stood and began walking in no particular direction. When her phone rang with an unknown number, her heart sank. This is not what she wanted for her evening. "Hello?

"Coffee shop. 15 minutes. Corner of Main and Sutter." The phone went dead.

Well, fuck, there went the evening, and not in a productive manner at all.

At least she knew she was going into this meeting none the wiser about the Estate, or the people within its protected walls. She couldn't give up information she didn't have. That didn't stop her from still being terrified because Max didn't like being disappointed and with her, he was bound to be very disappointed.

Exactly what Max could do to her, being her Sire, she still wasn't sure. She wished she knew if he could read her thoughts or just get her to answer questions truthfully. More like a compulsion than an actual mind read. If that was the case, she may be able to hold onto a few precious secrets, as long as he didn't ask the right questions.

New vampires really should be given a how to and what's what book when first turned. It would solve so many issues she currently had. Maybe that's what she'd do, she thought, trying to distract herself. There had to be a demand for some sort of how to guide. There was no way she was the only newly turned vampire that was as in the dark as she was. So after everything simmered down, and she was still alive, she'd write a damn book on how to actually be a creature of the night.

So lost in her thoughts, she completely panicked when the control of her body slipped from her mind. She had made it to the coffee shop without noticing plus was unaware of the vampires that were lurking by.

After coming to an abrupt halt, a bag was jerked over her head, someone grabbed her elbow, and they began to move again.

The smell of coffee was rich in the air and despite her current circumstances, she could have used a cup. The caffeine would go a long way to help her now frayed nerves.

Ungracefully, her capturers shoved her into a vehicle where she managed to tuck her legs into her body before the door slammed shut. Moments later, the vehicle shot off into the road, throwing her unrestrained body into the car wall. Twenty minutes of bumps and turns that rattled her brain, they came to a sudden stop. Desperate for a calm moment or a deep breath, she struggled to sit before hearing the door being thrown open. Gasping for air, she groaned as almost nothing made its way through the bag that still covered her head. Someone grabbed at her legs, forcing her out of the car, and straight onto her face. The ground was unsteady, as much as she was, and the two didn't make a good combination

Someone muttered under their breath and grabbed her by the shoulder, lifting her back to her feet, digging their nails into her skin in the process.

They walked and turned, walked and turned, which made her dizzy and it literally felt like they were doing nothing more than walking in pointless circles. Which, they may have been, just to try and get her lost. It worked. She had no idea where she was as the bag was yanked off her head.

Tall stalks of dried out corn stood surrounding her and stretched for as far as she could see. Oh, great, they took her to the set of every horror movie ever made. That made her feel wonderful.

The stars were clouded out and visibility was down to a minimum, even with vampire vison. Neither leaving nor staying boded well for her. If she had any control of her movements she wasn't sure what actions to even take. This whole being captured business was new to her.

Someone grabbed at her wrists, jerking them behind her body and slapped something around them, something that burned so badly tears sprung to her eyes and a scream caught in her throat. Cuffs? Cuffs that felt like tiny spikes were sticking out and burrowing into her skin while fire bloomed in her veins.

"That's silver on you so I would suggest you move as little as possible." Max's voice thundered around her as he stepped out from the stalks like a wrath in the night.

No shit, she thought. Her Sire released the control of her body and the first thing she did was tremble from the pain of the silver. That only made things worse.

"Here's how this is going to go. I'll ask questions and you'll be compelled to answer truthfully. I will know the minute you try and lie, so don't." Max stood perfectly still and yet it felt like he was surrounding her, smothering her.

"Fine." She quipped, irritated about almost everything in regards to the situation.

"Do you know any of the codes to get into the fences that surround the perimeter of the Estate?" He asked.

Codes? What codes? As far as she could tell there weren't any gates that required codes for her to come and go. However, that didn't mean much as she hadn't been there in good terms long enough to truly figure that out. When she wasn't being tortured, she was going to have to ask about it. Or, second thought, maybe not so Max wouldn't know. So, off to an easy start as that answer was easy to give. "No."

Clearly he didn't like that answer by the jerk of his head. "What about any of the codes in the Estate?"

Again, easy. "No."

Taking a deep breath, Max began to move, slowly circling her like a predator. "What floor is Jensen's office on?"

Well, damn. She tried to form the wrong answer in her mind and it literally wouldn't. Crap. "Second." If she couldn't lie, then she damn sure was going to only say the minimal amount of information required.

"Where on the second floor?" He asked, still slowly circling her.

She bit her lip and tried to refuse to answer. A sharp pain shot through her body, like the silver had somehow jumped to her blood and was everywhere and nowhere. She dropped to her knees, which jarred the actual silver at her wrists and this time she couldn't stop the scream that escaped. Her arms were on fire and she could smell her blood as it dripped from her fingertips.

Looking up at Max, through the tears in her eyes, she mumbled. "Go through the front door, up the stairs, take a left, follow the hall to the back and it's the last door on the left."

"What floor are you on?" He asked.

"Second."

"Anyone else on that floor?"

"Yes."

"Who?"

Damnit. "Doran, and others I don't know yet."

"Who's Doran?" Interesting that he didn't know who Doran was, but she would put money on that changing soon.

"Resident asshole." Truth, again. And all she wanted to say on the matter. She felt it this time, when his mind pressed into hers, digging for the truth in her words. He must have felt enough to leave it be because he pulled out and took another slow circle around her, staying quiet.

Her wrists burned and her legs were cramping. The muscles in her shoulders were twitching at being at an unusual angle and for the love of everything her damn nose needed to be itched. She was either going to pass out or fall over. Her body hadn't decided which yet.

"How did you get out in town if you don't have the access codes to come and go as you please?" He demanded, stopping to stand over her.

She tried, yet again, to not answer. Slivers of ice and fire burned through her skin as she fell to her side, screaming in pain. At this point, the cuffs were tearing into the bone and she literally wanted to just die. Nothing could be worse than this. It really couldn't get worse.

A dusty boot prodded at her chin, forcing her to turn her head and look up at Max, who was smiling down at her, his fangs on display. "How?"

"I have to call for a ride. They take me anywhere I want to go and then bring me home." Tears began to fall freely. The cruelness of the person in front of her was unlike anything she'd ever imagined. He was cold and unemotional and exactly the embodiment of evil that she could have pictured.

"Good girl." He looked down at her and as she looked back at him she caught a glimpse of his black soulless eyes. She shivered at the sight. His smile a warning that he enjoyed the pain of others at any expense.

In that moment of staring into the blackness that was her fate, she vowed to herself to no longer be helpless. Whatever it took, even if it was her death, she would not go down without a fight. She needed to get out of this mess so that she could do what needed to be done to take this asshole out of the world. He was done breathing her air.

"Alright my little lovely, that's all for now. I expect you'll be a little more willing to cooperate the next time we speak. Maybe more information for me? Yes?" He toed at her chin, reminding her he was there and that he was absolutely in charge.

"Go to hell, Max." She spat out.

"Oh sweetheart, don't you know?" He squatted down and took her face in his hand, forcing her gaze to meet his. "I own the place and made the devil himself my bitch." Dropping her head onto the ground, he spun on his heal and was gone before she could even blink. Closing her eyes, she counted to twenty, forwards and backwards, before letting herself break into a silent sob. Crying without actually moving one's body was a challenge, and she managed it for a full minute before a sob racked her whole body and a scream tore from her lips as the silver dug further into the bones of her wrist.

CHAPTER
eighteen

His eyes had finally stopped hurting but his arm burned like the fires of hell. And he would know, he'd played unwillingly in those fires. Stitched or not, it hurt like his own personal demon. Of all the stupid things that could render a fallen god completely useless it was a few vampire scratches. And to add insult to injury, the little vampire that stitched him up, all he wanted was to feel her nails scratching at his skin, but in a far more pleasant way than the last scratches that he acquired. He would suffer those wounds with a stupid grin all over his face.

His sudden need to be near Kedah, to be close to her and feel her presence fill the room had him on edge. He had never known that the desires of finding one's soulmate were so strong and when nothing could be done about those desires, it tipped the scale to insanity. He needed to go home, to his actual home. To breathe in the air of his ancestors and let it cleanse his body.

Closing his eyes, he imagined the rolling hills of his homeland, how they seemed to go on forever, the green of the grass and the blue of the sky, like a beacon, calling to him. Everyone had long since migrated from these lands in favor of bigger cities and towns, leaving behind dusty villages and empty manors. Leaving the lands with no more noise than the echoes of times long forgotten.

This was home.

Taking a big breath, he inhaled the deep rich air of the Highlands and let its natural calm caress his lungs and bring him the peace he'd been needing for the past few days.

Having put himself directly outside his place, he took powerful determined strides up the old stone stairs to the residence that he kept in the hills, safely tucked away from anything or anyone.

Entering his manor, he passed through an empty kitchen that had never been updated. The hearth still stood in the center wall, wide enough to roast a whole stag while cooking for a family and staff of at least 50. He was sure if he dug through some of the cabinets and drawers, kitchen utensils and things from the past could still be found. He had no desire to cook, so those things remained as a constant reminder of where he'd come from.

The stairs leading from the kitchen brought him to the second floor, which he'd converted to a large bedroom. This was where he'd kept his treasured memories of the past. The manor was so secluded that virtually no one would stumble on it, but if they did the place was so warded it would look like nothing more than a rundown pile of old rocks and weeds.

He took no chances in safe guarding the things that meant the most to him.

Treasures and memories littered the walls and every space of the room, filling the corners with echoes of pasts long gone, but not forgotten. His bed sat in the corner, adorned with sheets and comforters that were almost never made. Why bother, it wasn't like he ever brought anyone here, ever.

Except maybe, maybe now he'd like to bring Kedah. To show he wasn't a cold hearted bastard like he pretended to be. But then, maybe he'd been one for so long that changing was an impossibility.

Wandering around the room, shaking off the thoughts of the person he came here to forget, he reached out and touched objects as he passed, letting the memories of those times ground him. Remind him. Leave an impression on him.

Lying down on his bed, he closed his eyes and let the past wash over him, filling him with moments in time that made him who he was today. Thousands of years on earth gave one an unlimited supply of the good and the bad. The times of sorrow and times of joy. In a blink he was a gladiator. Another blink and he worked with his hands to help build the pyramids. To a tavern owner in the times of weary travelers and curious adventures. To now when technology was changing daily and he was just enjoying the ride, waiting for the next big adventure to show itself to him.

Everything that could be done had been. The rhythm of the earth continued to beat and he continued to ride the waves of time, drifting from here to there like a piece of wood lost at sea. It never had much meaning to him. Not until now.

Now he had the possibility to suddenly not be alone in his travels. Someone to create new memories with. To capture the essence of what life truly meant and to create moments with someone who could love him, and with whom he could love endlessly. Because despite being a dick to most, hated by many, and an all-around piece of work, he wanted what everyone wanted. A soulmate to share his life with. He had convinced himself long ago that he was never destined to have one as a punishment for falling from the heavens, but maybe he was wrong.

So, he tried to resist her. Tried his absolute fucking hardest. Because even though he knew she may be his soulmate, nothing in his life had ever been as cut and dry as that. The other shoe was bound to fall at some point. Yet, a small part of him hoped, prayed even, that maybe he could have a sliver of happiness.

Even here, thousands of miles away from where she was, his mind still wandered to what she might be doing behind her closed door. Was she tucked into her couch, wearing his clothes still, coffee in one hand and remote in the other? What was she watching? Some trashy reality show or some sci-fi fantasy thriller?

For fucks sake, he had never bothered to care about anyone this much and it was a combination of dreadful annoyance and awe. He had no idea what he was even doing half the times he was around her. His mouth tended to speak words he never agreed to say and his mind was a muddled disaster.

Damn, he was a mess.

Rolling off the bed he walked to the window, leaned against the frame and looked out at the lands that stretched further than any eye, human or not could see. The hills rolled and twisted, turned into forests and merged into streams. He knew every inch of it. Where the hunt was the best. Where the biggest fish could be caught. Which side of the forest had the best trees to climb and what fields had the best flowers in the spring.

Over the many years he'd called this place home, he only added a few modern things. More out of pleasure than anything else. He had an ATV and snow mobile, because why the hell not? They made traveling easier and a hundred times more fun. He'd built a forge in the back of the manor. From time to time he would go out and pound on some metal, twisting it and making it into things like swords and rings, chalices and dirks. That was a hobby from his past and a part of his godhood that he never could shake, nor did he want to. It was incredibly stress relieving.

His bed was new, because the technology in bed making had come a long way from feathers stuffed in a sack. Anyone that wanted to continue to sleep on that crap was just dumb in his opinion.

He thought about adding a bathroom with running water, but had no need in the past. If the future played out like he thought it might, he may need to bring the place into the present. At least in a few areas. Indoor plumbing and electricity seemed the most important.

I'm turning into a goddamn girl, he thought. Groaning, and rubbing his face with his palm, he pushed away from the window and took another glance around his place. This would always be his home and he hoped that whoever was destined to be with him, understood that and accepted it. He'd be extremely hard pressed to leave the land he was once worshiped on.

Out of nowhere his head began to ache and an echo from the distance drifted into his thoughts. Clear as day, he knew Kedah was in trouble. He wasn't sure how he knew but he did. And gods help him, he was going to rush back and see what had happened.

He couldn't leave that girl for a minute before trouble was knocking down her door.

In a blink he was in his room at the Estate, pushing his way out his door and pounding on hers. "Kedah? You in there?" No answer. "Kedah? If you don't answer, I'm coming in, and I don't give a damn if your naked or not." He shouted and still got no response. With a quick thought of his mind, he unlocked the door and stepped in. Searching the place came up empty. No Kedah. No phone or keys. When had she left?

Letting himself relax a moment, reaching out with his senses, he felt around the Estate, instantly knowing she was nowhere on the grounds. Growling in frustration, he zapped himself to the basement where Jensen was, still working on the new arrivals.

Jensen jerked his head at the sudden arrival and motioned for Doran to follow him away from the earshot of others. "What's wrong?"

"Do you know where Kedah went?" Doran demanded.

"I know she left an hour ago, took a car into town." Jensen didn't appear to be amused by this sudden intrusion and it showed all over his face and voice.

"She didn't say where?" He pressed, ignoring the tension.

"No. Why? It's not like you to be concerned about anyone, let alone a new vampire." Jensen asked, and rightfully so. This wasn't his normal attitude towards others.

"She's in trouble. And, no, I'm not explaining how I know." Doran muttered. His mind was shifting through all the places he'd known Kedah to go. Her old house and the Diner was all he was aware of because, for god's sake, he'd only known the girl for less than a week and was already on rescue attempt two.

"Fine. We can track her phone in security. I'll get a request out." Jensen said while pulling out his phone. "You know, we're going through an awful lot of trouble for one small, young, and mildly insignificant little vampire. You, especially, are going way out of your way for this one."

"I'm not explaining this right now." He grumbled. He really wasn't in the mood to be bantered about having a possible life mate who was so young, so vampire, and attracted to so much trouble. However, the trouble thing would explain why she was possibly destined to be with him. He was always trouble. "Text me when you hear something, please. I'm going to her house and the diner. This all may be nothing, and I'm merely just now starting to lose my damn mind, but if not, at least I'll feel better knowing she's safe."

"I'm pretty sure you are the oldest here and as they say, the mind is the first thing to go." Jensen quipped.

"Ha, ha." Doran said before blinking out of the basement and into the house that Kedah and Sadie had shared. In hind sight, that was probably a bad move as humans, he tended to forget, got a little spooked when something unnatural occurred, like, flashing into a house unexpectedly.

Sadie screamed with the passion of a child at a horror house and had the lungs to back it up. He didn't have time to deal with her and did something he normally avoided. With a wave of his hand her voice cut out and she stood in silence, looking more pissed then terrified. But as he took a step away, to look around, she ran at him, holding the first thing she could grab, which was a fucking lamp. Jesus.

"Stop." He commanded, and fortunately for her, she listened. "I am not here to hurt you. Have you seen Kedah?" He gave her her voice back, trusting she got the point.

She stood still and looked at him with a curious expression. "No, why? And what in the hell did you just do to my voice?"

"I stopped your screaming, it was making my ears bleed." Doran implied. "I think Kedah's in trouble. You sure she hasn't been here?"

"Nope. We were supposed to meet tomorrow for coffee. I haven't seen her since she left. What kind of trouble? What did you do to her?" Sadie crossed her arms over her chest, which was difficult with the lamp still in her possession, and gave him a once over look, the one that said she'd attempt murder if her friend was hurt. He wanted to laugh, but didn't. He was still eyeing the lamp in her hand and the damage it could cause. He still had injuries that were healing and didn't need reopening.

"Me?" He feigned in mock horror. He really didn't have time for this. "Nothing. I'm a damn saint when it comes to her." Which, wasn't exactly true.

"Not what she said." She shot at him.

"Don't care what she said. Where would she go, if not here?"

Sadie gave him another look and stood her ground, not saying a word. He moved so quickly that she didn't have time to blink before he was right in front of her, staring down at her wide eyes, a not so pleasant grin on his face. "Look, little girl. I do not play games. Not yours, not anyone's. I'm being nice and if you want it to stay that way, you'll answer the fucking question."

The perfume of fear poured off her and he smiled a little wider. He'd made his point, good. "Check the diner and talk to the cook. If she's not there, check the theater and the library. Then the park in midtown." She took a shaking step back, but held her gaze with his. Smart girl. "You think she's okay?"

"Probably. Knowing her, she just fell down a flight of stairs, again." He muttered, almost certain that she was not okay. Not with the sudden fear he felt. He nodded at Sadie and zapped himself out of there before she could start in on 20 questions.

He knew the cook at the diner, everyone that wasn't human did. He had been around for a long time, maybe longer then Doran had. He was most definitely a god, but from what pantheon, even he didn't know. This decade he was a short order cook, doing the dirty work most would leave for someone else. However, he always said it added character to a person to humble themselves down a few levels. Doran disagreed, whole heartily.

It really shouldn't have surprised him that Cook was waiting the moment Doran appeared behind the diner. Cook, or Charles to most immortals, was always about ten steps ahead of everyone else, whether they knew it or not.

"You see Kedah tonight?" Doran asked, knowing Charles was never one for small talk.

"Nope." Charles drawled.

"Do you, by chance, know where she may be?" He questioned.

Charles shook his head, taking a drag on a smoke. "Nope."

"Are you going to give me anything I can fucking use to find her?" He wondered out loud.

"Nope." Charles grunted, again, as he dropped the butt of his smoke and put it out with his boot. He nodded at Doran and went back into the diner, leaving Doran frustrated. The old man was lying, but why? What could he benefit from that and what trouble was Kedah in that she needed to be lied for. There was starting to feel like much more to her than anyone realized, and that was unnerving.

A wave of panic and fear washed over him and he looked around frantically. Kedah really needed to be found, like, ten minutes ago.

His phone buzzing in his pocket brought his attention back to the present. "You found her?"

"She's not picking up calls, but her phone is on and active and has been located in a field outside town. Damn near in the exact middle of it too." Jensen said from the other line. "She didn't get there by accident."

He snorted and hung up the phone, ghosting out to the only known fields outside town. Of course she didn't get there by accident, but how she ended up there was the question of the hour. Dead corn stalks surrounded him, high and foreboding. He was almost tall enough to see over it, but almost wasn't good enough here. Not a single breath of wind stirred the air, giving the scene before him an eerie glow. If tiny children began to emerge from the corn stalks, he was quitting his job and moving back to his castle. Fuck this crap.

Inhaling deeply, he calmed himself enough to get a good sense of where she was and hated the fact that he could tell immediately that she was scared and there was too much blood in the air. He took off in a dead run, dodging husks and leaves, running as fast as the field would allow. Once close, he came to a stop abruptly, being cautious in making sure they were alone and this wasn't an ambush of any kind.

171

Even if they weren't alone, the sound of her quiet cry was enough to make his feet move, without even a second thought. Once he had her, he could zap them home in a blink, assuming there were no complications.

The very site of her caused a hitch in his breath. She wasn't moving, but she was breathing. "Kedah." He could feel no one else around, yet the lingering smell of vampires was in the air. She hadn't been alone at first.

He watched as she painfully moved her head to his direction, a tear sliding out when she saw him. "I can't move. I tried, but I can't. Something is on my wrists and it burns every time I move."

Her voice was raw and laced with pain. He could see the tips of her fangs poking out and her eyes were red from crying. She didn't look like she was going to lose control but that had never stopped new vampires like her from doing just that. Most have lost control over less. She had earlier in the gym.

"Hey, Kitten. You good here?" He tapped at his own head hoping she'd understand. It killed him to not rush over to her, but if she took just one drop of his blood, she'd die. And that, that would kill him. "You're not going to go for my vein, right?"

"I'm fine. Just please, get it off. Something is digging into the bone." She sobbed painfully. His path set before her last words were spoken, he knelt beside her to see what was going on with her wrists.

She was bound with the nastiest set of silver cuffs he'd ever seen. And that was saying a lot because gods could be the nastiest people and they never came up with something this bad, that he knew of. Fucking hell.

Doran had put silver on and removed silver from many species, but never in his life had he regretted it as much as he was about to regret taking it off her. It was going to hurt, a lot. "Bad news, Kitten. This is some nasty silver and I need to remove it before I can take you home."

"Can you just, I don't know, kick me in the head first?" She asked with a groan.

What in the hell was she asking? Why would he. . . oh. She didn't want to stay awake any longer. "I'll try and get these off quickly. Okay?"

"Sure." Doubt laced her voice and he felt another twinge of guilt. He was going to have to break the cuffs and that would require him to get both hands on each one as he snapped them in half. There was no way around causing her more pain.

"I'm going to roll you to your stomach so I have a better angle to work with. Okay? Then I'm going to straddle your back to pin you down, to help you not move so much. Keep your head to the side so you can breathe. And Kedah?" He said in a soft voice.

"What?" She asked.

"I'm sorry Kitten. This is going to hurt." Once she nodded at him, his movements were quick and precise. He rolled her to her stomach, trying to ignore the cry that pierced the eerie silence of the night. Straddling her back, he took a hold of one cuff, snapping it, then repeating the action with the other. He tossed the cuffs as far away from the both of them as possible and rolled off Kedah, turning her over and gathering her up in his arms.

Her wrists were so raw that he could actually see the bone. These were definitely not normal silver cuffs. She was too young to even have withstood the smallest amount of silver and those cuffs were damn near solid. Who in the hell had she gotten herself mixed up with? Carefully resting her in his lap, he stripped off his shirt, tore it in two, and wrapped the pieces around each of her bloody wrists. She bit back a cry as the fabric rested into the wounds. He really couldn't do much more out here and he really needed to get her home.

She needed to feed. She needed rest. And for Christ's sake, she needed a fucking bubble wrapped around her so tightly that she couldn't leave the damn Estate. She had a serious knack for finding even the tiniest bit of trouble.

Zapping them back to his apartment, he laid her on his bed and sent a quick message to Jensen letting him know she'd been found and he needed to be here, now. As he waited for a reply, he scrambled to his medical kit and prayed the bottle he was looking for was still there.

No bigger than the size of a gas station energy shot, these little bottles could save a person's life if silver poisoning occurred. Everyone always had one in their rooms or on their person at all times. It worked for pretty much any paranormal creature and he even thought it may work for humans, although the likelihood of them getting silver poisoning was far less than anyone living in the Den.

Found it. "Here." He muttered as he handed her a small bottle of a very black looking liquid. "Kitten, you need to try and drink this down." Nicknamed AGR, this was a concoction of activated charcoal, blood, and something called Calcium EDTA. Mainly, the last ingredient attached itself to the silver in a person's bloodstream and flushed it out.

The side effects were mild, aside from the burning of the silver and the compound fighting and the need to pee more times in the next 24 hours then she thought possible. That was the only way the AGR pushed the silver out of a person's system, and that was far less painful then suffering with the silver inside oneself.

This small dose was meant for small amounts of silver poisoning, which she was beyond. It would help, but she'd require two injections into the thigh to really flush everything out. It would burn like hell, but she'd be alive.

With a shaking hand, she took the bottle and grimaced. "What in the hell is this?"

"I'll explain later, for now, it'll save your life." He said. Her face was beginning to pale into a grayish color, which was a direct effect of the silver in her blood.

"Bottoms up." She muttered as she brought the bottle to her lips and took it back. Her face turned another shade of pale as she tried to hold the liquid down.

"I think I'm going to be sick." She warned as she rolled to her side and hung her head off the bed, throwing up the contents of her stomach. Thankful for quick reflexes, Doran got a waste basket under her in time and felt like hell as he watched her puke. He rubbed her back and told her it was going to be okay and prayed that that was true.

Jensen needed to hustle.

CHAPTER
nineteen

Kedah had never felt so sick in her entire life, human or not. Throwing up in general was terrible, as a vampire, it was worse. Her throat burned, her mouth was on fire, her nose stung, and her eyes watered. Every time she thought about what her wrists must look like, she threw up all over again. She was probably going to die for real this time.

While her head was dangled over the side of the bed, Doran kept rubbing her back, telling her it was okay and it was probably best to get it all out of her system. He was being incredibly supportive and nice, and if she felt better she'd ask why. But as she felt like dying, and he was being nice, she was almost convinced it was the end. What a fucking way to go.

Apparently, vampires could, in fact, go into shock. Her body began to quake and a chill crept into her bones.

Another round of the dry heaves had her 100% done with it all. The next time she got sick she was totally convinced that pieces of her stomach were going to make a very nasty appearance.

She wasn't even sure she could move from where she dangled off the bed. Doran, bless his old stubborn heart, carefully lifted her back onto the bed and laid her head onto a pillow. Everything hurt.

"I think she's got silver poisoning." Doran said to someone who had entered the room while she was emptying the contents of her stomach. She could see his shoes, but no real idea whom they belonged too.

"Of course she does. Far be it for her to just have a small reaction to silver. She's damn lucky she hasn't died yet." Oh, it was Jensen who was here and he seemed less than pleased. She did agree on the dying thing. Why hadn't she keeled over yet? "She needs more than bag blood at this point."

"I know." Doran said quietly.

"I'll make a quick call and see if I can't get someone up here. Maybe one of the pack mates will volunteer. I also need to make a quick stop to my office." Jensen's voice faded in and out, as she fought to remain in the present. She really wanted to know what was going on, but at the same time she wanted to give up. The moment she gave up, she was afraid she'd fall asleep and this time not wake up. Her body hurt that badly.

She really just wanted to sleep or to take a really long bath. Either would be welcomed. And a cure. A cure to whatever was making her feel like she was lying in a pit of fire would also be nice.

"Call Aiden, he'll help her." Doran muttered in a voice that held a little bit of sadness and defeat. Aiden? She thought, hoping she heard him correctly. He didn't like him, like, at all.

God, she was going to puke again, she thought as she managed to move her head to the side and prayed she was aiming for the trashcan.

"He's an alpha. You going to be cool with that?" She heard Jensen ask.

"I don't have a good god damn choice, do I?" He bit out. Yikes. "She doesn't have a choice either at this point."

Jensen stayed silent and stepped away from them, making the call and probably running to his office. A moment later, or minutes, she couldn't tell, he came back and knelt down to be at her eye level, after Doran had put her back up onto the bed in a vertical position. "You're getting a crash course in how to feed off a person in just a moment. At this point, it's learn to feed or die, so I need you to nod your head that you understand me."

She knew she felt like death but fuck if it wasn't worse to hear Jensen actually tell her she was going to kick it if she didn't do something. Nodding seemed like such hard work, but she did it anyways, knowing that the consequences would be hell if she didn't. Jensen was a good man, well vampire man, but he was clear and to the point with absolutely zero fucks to give about how others took his commands and thoughts. It's what probably made him a great leader. So she thought it best to just go ahead and agree with him.

"One more thing." He held up a full syringe of something strange. First she was dying. Then she was going to live if she fed off someone. Now, a needle? Her insides turned to stone as she cringed and tried to move in the opposite direction. "This will push the silver out of your system faster. Its more concentrated than the stuff you took earlier."

She didn't mind the needle; it was what was in it that was the issue. However, she hoped and prayed that at this point things could only get better and not worse, so what the hell. It still looked suspicious and it was an unnatural gray color that wasn't comforting. "Where?" She groaned, praying it would be somewhere not to embarrassing.

"Upper thigh." He said as he prepped the needle, bleeding out the excess air.

There went the not so embarrassing part. At least she had on cute panties. Truth be told though; she wasn't sure she had the actual strength to pull down her jeans. So, cue the embarrassment level to even higher as she realized she needed to ask someone to pull her pants off. Hopefully everyone could be the adult they pretended to be for just a few minutes more.

Blushing, she looked up at Doran, hoping she didn't have to actually say aloud what she needed from him. She nodded her head slightly to her pants and watched as he blushed, which any other time would have been adorable, when he understood what she was asking. Honestly he shouldn't be more embarrassed than she, but his face told a different story.

Quickly, with warm shaking hands, he undid the button of her jeans, unzipped the zipper and ever so carefully slid them down far enough that her upper thigh was exposed. She was blushing so hard her ears were red. So were his.

Without prompting, Jensen leaned forward and drove the needle in, pushing the liquid into her system. She winced and moaned as the liquid entered her body and took back all the times she ever told people to just suck it up while getting a shot. Whatever was in that needle felt thick, was ice cold and it made her feel like hell.

As soon as Jensen was done, Doran wiggled her pants back up over her butt, not bothering to do them back up as she probably would be changing soon anyways.

As the liquid from the needle moved further into her system to battle the silver that was already there, her head began to pound as her stomach rolled and her muscles tightened. Her body was fighting against itself and she felt like she was drowning in a silver lined hell.

Jensen stood and left her while she concentrated on not totally dying. Her body was slowly eating at itself and the pain was past the point of oh-my-god and now she was just numb, which probably wasn't any better. God, she was so tired. So sleepy.

Doran must have sensed her fading and got up on the bed. He sat with his back against the wall, bringing her limp body up against his, forcing her to sit up rather than lay down, which was what she was on her way to do until he stopped her.

She groaned and tried to force herself back down, but seemed to be completely at the mercy of his hold, which was unyielding. "Nope, you're going to sit. No sleeping."

If she could have growled at him, she would have. It just took too much effort.

"Eesh Kedah, you look like hell." Aiden's voice sang out from somewhere in the room. He sounded amused and she couldn't figure out why. Not until the grip on her body tightened.

Of all the times for Doran to get jealous, he chose now? What in the hell? There was nothing going on with them. Oh, this really wasn't going to go well.

"You," Aiden said, pointing to Doran. "Out. You're not going to want to be here for this."

Doran growled and held her tighter. This sudden possessiveness was a nice gesture, but needed to stop. Aiden was a friend and was here to help, possibly even save her life. Doran couldn't do it, or so she was made to understand, which meant he held no sway in the decision. At the same time, she felt like him being with her was the right thing, like he was meant to stay at her side. "No," she croaked. "I don't want him to go."

Jensen shook his head but remained silent. It was Aiden who crouched down to look at her. "Yeah, I know you don't. Here's the deal though, you're going to have to feed from me and he's really not going to like it. So much so, he may get violent. It won't be totally his fault, but it'll happen."

She didn't understand the why's of what Aiden was saying but heard the truth in his words. If she survived this, a few people in the Estate were going to have to answer a good number of questions, and no wasn't going to be an option. "I don't want anyone to get hurt." She responded.

"Good." He stood and placed a strong hand on Doran's arm. His muscles tensed, but he said nothing. "Doran?"

Carefully he moved himself out from behind her, leaving her cold and alone. He took her hands in his and looked down at her, his eyes blazing with fire. "I'll be right outside the door."

She nodded and he turned to leave, his steps heavy and slow.

Another wave of nausea flooded her system, and she closed her eyes, trying to not lose her stomach again.

Aiden got down to her level and spoke quietly. "Here's how this is going to go. You need to feed from the vein, it's the only way to heal you quickly. Bag blood is good but fresh is always better. The silver that bound your wrists got into your blood. Silver poisoning my friend, and you have a nasty case of it. There is no real cure but we can flush it out if we can get to you quick enough, and I think you'll be just fine. So, I'm going to get behind you, much like Doran just was. This way, I can hold you down as you feed from my wrist, which will protect my vital organs. I'll let you know when you've had enough."

The way he put it made it sound logical and fairly easy. The way her imagination made it out to be was messy, deadly and slightly chaotic.

"Trust your instinct, Kedah. Your body knows how to feed itself. Your fangs know where they need to go." Jensen said as he stood just a little closer to the both of them. She wanted to tell him her instincts were terrible and had nearly gotten her killed several times, but didn't have the energy to open her mouth.

Well, she thought, time to party. She nodded at both of them, then everything seemed to go into slow motion. Aiden gracefully got behind her, holding her body tightly to his. He then put his wrist directly in front of her mouth. Somehow it was already nicked and a tiny drop of blood welled, causing her fangs to descend and throb.

She struck without thinking. As her fangs pierced his skin, his blood pooled in her mouth, coating her throat and eased the burning sensation in the pit of her stomach. Getting her arms free she grabbed onto his wrist, holding it steady and close as she took giant pulls from his vein.

Instantly her body awoke and her eyes rolled, a moan escaping her throat. She took several more pulls before he pulled his arm back away from her, being gentle but firm, and held onto her body for just a moment longer.

It took just a second for her brain to process that she wasn't feeding anymore and even though she still felt hungry and her fangs still itched to pierce skin, she knew she'd taken enough. Feeding from Aiden was as easy as promised and she cursed silently at the stupidity of not having done this sooner.

"How are you feeling?" Jensen asked, stepping into her line of sight.

"Better." She croaked. "Tired." Embarrassed that she couldn't have done that on her own, but she wasn't owning to that verbally. At least she no longer felt like she was dying.

"No doubt." Jensen commented. "You seem to have a knack for finding trouble."

"So it seems. Sorry." She mumbled.

Aiden moved his body away from hers and stood. "Well, this has been fun. I'm going to let grump back in so he doesn't break down the door or put a hole in the floor. And Kedah," he said as he turned back to face her. "I'm going to teach you how to defend yourself and throw a damn punch. None of this finding trouble shit is going to go down again." He winked at her and walked to the door, opening it as Doran all but fell through.

Heavens knows she really needed to know how to throw a punch, so the idea of learning from Aiden was thrilling. Finally, a way to learn how to be less of a comic and more of a threat. Well, that was the hope, anyways.

As the adrenaline of the past few minutes began to fade, she yawned loudly and sleepily blinked her eyes. Doran and Jensen talked quietly before Jensen left and Doran went to another room in the apartment. She listened as he rummaged in the kitchen a moment and briefly saw him go into his closet.

He came over to the bed and handed her the items, sitting down carefully beside her. "Drink. Change. You need to rest and not a soul is going to even think about bothering either of us until we wake up on our own."

"So, I'm staying here?" She curiously asked. She wanted to because she felt comfortable here. But his emotions were so all over the place that she felt like a case of whiplash was coming on. And people thought women were confusing.

"Yes." He seemed tired and conflicted, but she was too tired to even try and iron that out. Later, when she was rested, she'd attack it. Now, now she just wanted to go back to sleep and pray that tomorrow was a better day.

Before she moved though, she gazed at his features, noticing that she could see both his beautiful brown eyes now that the swelling in his face had gone down. His stitches looked angry and painful, and she thought it was weird they hadn't healed. "That doesn't look much better."

"It's fine. Vampire scratches don't agree with me." He stood and ducked into his closet, coming out with pajama pants in hand. "I'm going to jump in the shower real quick."

"Okay." She said, feeling suddenly a little out of place. She uncapped the water and took a swig, letting its coolness caress the inside of her mouth and throat, smothering the last of the burn. She downed the bottle moments later and stood, taking off her shoes and putting them in the corner of the room. She already felt better, which was a step up from feeling like she was going to die at any moment. As she placed her shoes down, she caught sight of her wrists and the bandages made from Doran's shirt. She probably couldn't get too much of an infection, but she still thought a fresh and proper bandage would aid in the healing.

The medical bag she needed was probably still in the bathroom where a very naked Doran was now taking a shower. She quickly shook away that image that barged into her thoughts, however nice it may have been. They could both be adults about this, right? Maybe? She was already a flush shade darker thinking about it. She knocked anyways.

"What?" Doran called out.

She poked her head into the bathroom, letting the steam of the shower fill her lungs. "I need to bandage my wrists up and the supplies are in there with you. Can I come in real quick and grab them?"

Cue the silence. "Hang on."

"Uh, I'm already sorta in here. Stay there, I'll just grab the bag." She said, but didn't move.

The water cut off but there was no movement from behind the shower curtain. "Grab me a towel. Please?"

Nope. Her brain said. "Yep." Her mouth responded. Traitor. She grabbed a towel from the rack and opened the curtain a bit to hand it in.

Totally not regretting the little glimpse of skin she saw. All the right curves in all the right places. She blushed harder.

Backing up to the door, she watched as he exited the shower, damp hair falling in his face, and towel now firmly secured low on his hips. Really low.

She couldn't help it, really, she just couldn't. Her gaze traced every single inch of exposed skin. Damp from the shower, it was a sight worth seeing. The definition of his abs was almost illegal.

He stood in front of her and both of them froze, awkwardly. Finally, Doran cleared his throat and found the bag of medical supplies, setting it on the sink. "You want to shower first?" He asked, his voice a few octaves lower than his normal. God that was sexy.

A shower was probably a good idea, she thought. A nice cold shower was probably a great idea. In her own shower. In another room. In another state if that could be managed. "Yeah, I'll just go over to my place and take a quick one."

"No go. You are not leaving this apartment until you are one hundred percent healed." He shook his head and handed her a clean towel. Then walked out the door and shut it. "Let me know when you're done and I'll bandage your wrists."

Okay then. Quickly she shed her clothes, careful to not bump her arms, and got in the shower. Stepping under the spray, she moaned in delight as the water caressed her sore tired muscles. That was until the water seeped into the bandages and burned the gashes on her wrists. She muffled a scream while carefully taking the bandages off.

They looked as bad as she expected, but at least she couldn't see the bone anymore. She could tell that the blood had helped speed up the healing a bit, which was pretty handy to know. Carefully she washed her hair and body then let water run through her wounds, cleaning them out the best she could.

Shutting off the water, she dried off and wrapped the towel around her body, just now remembering that she left the clothes in the bedroom. Oh well. She sat on the toilet and called out to Doran, who must have been right at the door, as she wasn't even done saying his name and he was there.

He stopped short and his hungry gaze took in her body. From the very top of her head to the tip of her toes, he silently ate her up and it was the sexiest thing to watch, ever. She blushed and bit at her lip, not knowing what else to do in that moment. Being a vampire was new. Feeding was new. Getting hit on by an emotionally unstable immortal, was also very new.

Clearing his throat several times, he got the bandages from the sink and set to work. His gentle hands took hers and slowly he looked over the wounds with an inspecting gaze. "I don't think stitches will help at this point. So I'm just going to spray them with an antiseptic and put a bandage over each. And yes, antiseptic is needed, you may be immortal and undead, but if you don't clean that out it'll get infected and cause more hell. Okay?"

"Yeah," she said softy. She held her arms steady and tried not to wince when he sprayed the antiseptic. It burned like crazy, but she bet it was better than how badly an infection would feel. Closing her eyes, she kept still as his gentle touch wrapped both wrists swiftly and carefully.

"I put your clothes on the sink." He muttered as he stood up and backed away from her.

"Well, technically, they are your clothes." She said with a grin, trying to break a little of the tension that was slicing the air.

He laughed a little and smiled. "And they look a hell of a lot better on you than they do me."

She smiled as he shut the door. After she was dressed she wandered out to the bedroom, smiling to see that Doran was already there, on top of the covers, reading a book. There really wasn't anything sexier than a man barely dressed, lying in bed, and reading. She had no intention of having sex with him, but if he kept up doing what he was doing currently, she'd be tempted to suggest it.

Her steps faltered a moment before she caught herself and climbed into the little slice of heaven that was his bed. At some point she really needed to see what it was made of and where she could buy one for herself. She was officially spoiled now.

Lying on her side, snuggled under the blankets, she looked at Doran and sleepily smiled up at him. What the hell, they were adults and he looked cold. She could fix that, at least. "Come on. Lay with me and help me forget that I nearly died today. Please?"

"I thought you'd never ask." He moaned out as he scrambled under the covers, throwing his book aside. He gently pulled her body to his and she could feel his body completely relax. "Rest easy Kedah."

"Rest easy, Doran." She said with a sigh as she relaxed into a deep and restful sleep.

CHAPTER
twenty

There was no doubt in Jensen's mind that Kedah had gotten herself mixed up in something she shouldn't be mixed up in. Something had to have happened from when he found her in the blood bank to when she finally showed up at the Estate. Whatever it was, it had to have been something that attracted an unwanted amount of trouble for her because in all his years he'd never met anyone who could stumble into trouble like she could. Let alone a vampire who didn't understand their very nature.

How she survived this long was a complete mystery to him. It seemed she was an odd combination of good and bad luck, wrapped into a cute little clumsy package.

Vampires he could deal with. Weres and shifters he could deal with. Most paranormals he could handle. Doran's unusual reaction to Kedah was driving him nuts because it was about as far from his normal personality as he could get. He'd known the man for years and years and had never seen him act this way. Doran was the only reason that he hadn't sent Kedah on her way. Or to be honest, he'd just have killed her because of all the unknowns she possessed. She seemed to be unnecessary trouble, but since he needed Doran, he'd deal with her as best he could.

Doran was an asshole by trade. It was what he was best at. That, and helping with the security teams in certain areas. But mostly, he just stuck around, annoying people. Jensen suspected, and had for a long time, that Doran was a god, fallen or bored. He did help, and was damn good at what little help he gave. Good enough that no one questioned about him and just accepted that he was there. Along came Kedah and her secrets and Doran seemed to have lost all control of his actions and mouth. Any other time and situation, it would be amusing to watch. Right now, it was just frustrating.

So, he left her to recover with Doran and wandered to his office to check on the never ending list of things requiring his attention. Truthfully, he hated the politics of his position, but he was good at it. The journey to get to the position of leader that he held was mostly bloody and nonpolitical, so it was a nice change, even if it was a slow one.

Humans, in general, weren't anywhere near ready to accept paranormals. Every day they proved that by the constant bickering and non-acceptance between themselves. Very small differences between fellow humans caused the biggest disputes. If paranormals were thrown into the mix, an unimaginable hell would break out.

The Estate was founded as a safe place to go, no matter what species you were. To live without worry or fear of human interference. A lot of the residents were without a place among their own people as well, so they made it work here. Plus, without the interference of humans and their ways, they could handle para issues the way they needed to be handled. Which, most of the time, wasn't anything that humans would ever agree to.

Over the years, as the Estate grew, it became more than just a safe house. It still housed those that needed it but it also doubled as a local command center. Himself, as well as other leaders within the Estate worked together to deploy out security to monitor the surrounding areas. They worked with local and state-wide packs and covens to make sure things continued to run smoothly for all the para's in the area.

Having everyone deploy and meet from one location kept the hassle of things down to a minimum.

He was, however, the only leader, out of the ones located at the Estate that actually held a higher position. He was the head of the state for all vampires residing here. Knowing the Matron of this place, and having helped bring the vision of this place to light, he was allowed a permanent residence and office here. Plus, he loved it here. It was quiet, out of the way, comfortable, and self-sustaining.

Despite their best efforts to continue to keep the peace, there is always that one person who feels the need to cause trouble. Every few decades, one of them would cause more hell than the rest and become more of an issue. Max Vaughn was this decade's leading asshole. He was ruthless, cunning, and gave little to no shits about humans, or most of his own people. All he was after was power and didn't care how he got it. It was a deadly combination of strong will, arrogance and power among others that led to the Estate security on high alert. Max's biggest power play were the humans, and how far he could push at them until they finally broke through and realized they were not alone. Jensen could not allow that.

Max's end game, as far as he could tell or had gotten intel about, was to take his position as head of the vampires in this state, so that he could move forward and take over the country. World domination by bloodshed and fear. Max was the thorn in everyone's side that needed to be removed, if they could ever get to him. The problem is he was so well hidden that no one could ever locate him. If they could, the issue could be solved quickly. As it is, they were still very much in the dark.

Jensen sighed as he entered his study, frustrated and tired. Once he was sitting at his desk, he looked up at the only personal painting in the room and wished with everything he had that the woman in the painting could be here with him. The love that shone in her eyes, the warmth in her smile and the slight blush in her cheeks reminded him of a happier time in his life. He could still feel her hand resting on his shoulder when nights were long and problems were plenty. She was always assuring him that all would be well and that he was so much loved.

She was his one true love. His soul mate that he was lucky enough to find early in his immortal years. He loved her so much and so hard that when she was killed it completely broke him. The story of her death was never something he liked to revisit, and maybe one day he would, but what he held onto the most were her words. They were the reason he continued the never-ending job of trying to maintain peace. It was why he worked to make sure everyone felt they had a place in this world and that they were protected.

"Even the darkness can love. You just have to show it how." Those were the words whispered with her last breath and were the very words he continued to live by. She showed him how to love, even in his darkest moments, and he would spend a lifetime repaying that debt. It was the least he could do.

Shaking off the memories, he looked back at his computer and checked his email while playing any phone messages that had come in. Nothing overly exciting or urgent was needed so he decided to go back down to the basement and try his luck with the rogues one more time. They'd die, maybe not today, but they would. It was his hope that they gave up any piece of information they could use to find Max before they met the sun, but if not, they couldn't be let back out to do more of Max's dirty work.

Taking the stairs in the back, he descended to the basement, his mind focusing on the task at hand. The three prisoners were in a vampire proof cell, ankles chained with silver, looking as close to death as they could without actually becoming ash.

He felt bad for them, slightly. They had never chosen this path, never wanted to put their lives in this direction, but the call of the Sire was strong and unbreakable and they had to do what was told of them. Which was why they had to be killed. The bond was damn near impossible to break and because of that it was a danger to everyone.

"Anyone feel like talking yet?" He casually asked as he pulled up a chair and sat outside the cell.

A round of go to hell's echoed within the cell walls and Jensen smiled as he sat and let them stir inside the cell for a few minutes. Quiet usually helped to unnerve most, as they never knew what to expect of it. Grabbing a set of spikes from a table outside the cell, he stood and waved open the cell door, stepping in. Casually he walked up to the vampire that was the oldest, and yet only months young, the one who could freeze minds, and shoved a spike into his shoulder securing him right up into the wall. There was no hesitation on his part.

The vampire screamed, the sound piercing the silence, making the other two vamps cower back. "I've got several more of these little treasures, lots of patience, and an unlimited amount of time right now. So, let's rethink our answer, yes?"

The spikes he possessed were solid silver, and though they burned his hands to touch them, they did a hell of a lot more damage when pushed into skin, muscle and bone. They were long enough to pierce through a body and anchor it to whatever surface was near. They were a gift from a very old friend and one of his most prized possessions.

"What do you want to know?" The new vampire muttered, defeated already. Pity.

"What's your name and how old are you?" Jensen calmly asked.

"Tat and I was turned 6 months ago." He answered.

"Well, Tat, you made a pretty bad judgment call by attacking one of my personal businesses. Then you attacked my people." He twirled one of the spikes in his hands, watching as Tat followed the movement carefully.

"What exactly do you want to know or are you going to stand there and play with your stick all day?" Tat muttered, but before the last word was out of his mouth, the spike was through his thigh and into the wall. Tat howled as the silver dug into muscle and bone.

"Who's your Sire, Tat?" Jensen asked, though he knew the answer. He just needed to hear it.

"Max." He spat out.

"Did Max tell you anything about his plans and why he was suddenly interested in going after my people and staff?" It wasn't a sudden thing; it had been picking up for months now. This latest wave of rogues were more aggressive and unfocused. It was unnerving and troubling.

Tat raised his head, blood dripping from his mouth. An eerie smile crossed his face as he spoke. "A war is coming and you can't stop it. He's made hundreds of new vampires and continues to keep them hidden. Starving. It's the perfect plan and you'll never be able to stop them."

The signs had pointed to something like this, Jensen had just hoped they were wrong. This was seriously bad news for the residents of the Estate and outside of it. Bad news for everyone, really. That many baby vampires released at once would level a city in a matter of one night. Bloodshed and destruction would be everywhere and there would be no way to keep that hidden and off of the humans' radar.

"Do you know where Max is keeping them?" He asked. It was a longshot as Max would have had no reason to disclose that to a newborn.

"You're just going to have to kill me now, because I won't say another fucking word." Jensen could taste the truth in his words and turned sharply, shoving the last spike into the vampire's heart, killing him instantly.

Max was increasingly becoming more of a pain in the ass and if he wasn't taken out soon, things were going to go from bad to shit storm worse. He was going to have to schedule meetings with every species within the city and inform them of what was going on. They could choose to help or step away, but they needed to at least be informed. And what a headache that would be.

Something of this magnitude could change the entire existence of everyone. One wrong move could trigger a domino effect that would out vampires and others alike. Mass panic and hunts of every nature would arise. Things would go to hell in a matter of a single moment. That was definitely not happening on his watch.

CHAPTER
twenty-one

Doran couldn't remember the last time he'd slept so solidly, if he ever had. Normally he was down for a few hours of tossing and turning before giving up and searching for some hell to raise.

As he slowly came back to reality, he couldn't resist the stupid grin on his face. The feeling of Kedah's body pressed into his was unlike anything he'd ever experienced. He dared not move and risk waking her, she was far too peaceful. Nestled into his arms, she fit perfectly, like a piece to a puzzle that he didn't know was missing. Closing his eyes again, he rested his head against hers, breathing her in, enjoying this moment of utter peace, the first he'd ever had.

She made a soft little noise, almost a whimper, which brought his eyes open and his attention to her. He raised his head to look down, noticing that her eyes were moving rapidly behind closed lids. At first he thought she was just dreaming, but when her movements got a little sharper, his concern grew.

Her head began to jerk back and forth and her arms and legs began to flail, like she was fighting an unknown force, or trying desperately to get away from one. Sweat began to bead on her skin as her movements quickened.

She looked terrified, her breathing quickened and her body showed clear signs of panic. He tried to gently shake her awake, but it did no good. Her panic seemed to be worsening. Scooping her up in his arms, he held her close and tight as she continued to fight and thrash. He tried to whisper to her, telling her she was okay, that she needed to wake, but nothing seemed to be getting through. She fought against him, desperate to get away from whatever was plaguing her nightmares.

"Come on, Kitten. Wake up for me." He pleaded for what felt like the hundredth time. This time, she came awake like a shot out of a cannon, eyes snapping open and mouth wide in a piercing scream. It took all his strength to not let her scramble away and it took another minute longer before she quieted herself and slumped back into his body.

"Sorry." She muttered.

"You're okay." He said, running a hand over her hair, smoothing it back down. "What got you so spooked?"

"Nightmare." She said. "I've had it all my life."

"All your life? Did you have one last time we slept together?" He asked, concern lacing his voice.

She looked at him for a long moment, then shook her head. "No, actually. I don't think I did."

He wished that made him feel better, but it didn't. "Tell me about the nightmares."

"I'm covered in blood and death is all around." She shuddered and turned her head into his chest, wrapping her arms around his body. Taking a deep breath, she tried to calm her nerves and was only mildly successful.

His mind did a little hiccup as he paused in dread. That wasn't a dream. It wasn't a nightmare either. It had been many years since he'd seen it happen but there was little doubt in his mind as to what she was experiencing.

It was a death omen and they never lied. It would come to pass, and there was nothing he or anyone could do to stop it. No one was ever sure why some people experienced them over others, but it was believed the more empathetic one was, the more in tune with death they could be. Even if it was their own death.

Fucking hell.

It was his luck that the woman he was slowly falling for, the one who was possibly his soulmate, was now plagued by a death omen. There wasn't a damn thing he could do about it either. Neither gods nor man could stop death when his hands were around your neck.

"Did they get worse after your turn?" He asked, curiously.

"A bit. More vivid. More blood." She said sleepily.

He didn't know what to say. Or, more accurately, he didn't know the right thing to say. Did he tell her about the omen or just let it pass for the time being? It was a damned if you do and damned if you don't situation and right now, he was just going to be damned if he didn't. She didn't need that knowledge bearing down on her daily. Not right now. Not if there was nothing to be done.

"What time is it?" She asked as she uncurled her body from his, stretching out the tension in her limbs. He tried not to obviously stare at the beauty that she was, but probably failed.

Grabbing for his phone, he peeked at the time and snorted a laugh. "Six in the evening. We slept for about 12 hours." That was definitely a record for him. "Oh," he muttered as he grabbed the thin black case from the bedside table. "Last one." he held up the needle and almost laughed at her initial reaction.

"Uh, first, I really have to pee. Like, I feel like I've never peed before in my life." She shot up and bolted for the bathroom barely shutting the door before he heard her sigh. He laughed, he couldn't help it. When she was finished he heard the water run, and the look of relief on her face when she slowly came back to the room was adorable.

"Sorry. That's a side effect of the AGR. The next 24 hours may be rough on your bladder." He said sympathetically.

"At least I'm not dead." She grinned and without warning dropped shorts to her ankle and stuck out her leg, flashing her thigh. "Come on, pick up your chin, I'm still wearing more than the models on the cover of swimsuit magazines."

He was speechless. Utterly. Her laugh managed to bring him back to reality, and he took a moment to admire the view she was offering. He just wished he was doing something entirely different with it. He wasn't sure where the Kedah from a few hours ago went, but he didn't care. This was too great to pass up.

Taking out the needle, he uncapped it and stuck it in her thigh with little warning. She sucked in a breath at the sudden action, but handled it better than last time. Once done, she pulled up the boxers while he walked the needle to the red bin in the bathroom.

"I'm starving." Kedah said with a smile as he walked back from the bathroom, feeling lazy and relaxed. Feeling comfortable.

He stopped and looked down at her smiling. She was simply adorable and sexy as hell in the morning, well, her new morning which was evening for most. Hair a mess. Eyes glossed over from sleep. He was going to lose the fight to not kiss those lips sooner than later.

You know what? Screw it.

He took a step closer to her and before he could chicken out, bent his head down, and when she looked up at him in surprise, he brushed his lips ever so gently against hers. She only hesitated a moment before placing hands on his hips, urging him closer. He pressed further into the kiss, his lips crushing hers in a demand that had been building for days.

His hands gently cupped her cheeks, while his lips kept exploring hers. She met every demand with a fierce need of her own. Her hands began to travel up his back, holding tight to his shoulder while her small frame pressed into his body.

He was completely lost in the moment. He didn't even care if he took another breath.

She broke away first, breathing heavily, but smiling up as she placed a hand on his cheek. She held his gaze for a moment before breaking contact and taking a step back. "Food sounds like heaven." She said, continuing to stretch her body as if nothing had just happened. Clearly she was into it, of that he was sure, so why the sudden change?

He wasn't going to question it, or what they had just done, and simply just enjoyed the moment for what it was. It would happen again, and soon if he had a say in it. Soon and often.

Moving away from her, he grabbed a shirt from his closet as they walked out of the room. "You want to change?" Not that he was objecting to her current outfit. Those boxers looked far better on her than on him. And that white shirt, that fit like a dress, but still managed to keep a sex appeal about her that he just couldn't ignore.

"Nah. I live here now, right? Might as well show my true colors sooner rather than later. I am 100% that girl that will stay in sweats, or whatever is comfortable, unless it's absolutely necessary to wear something else. And even then, it can be a fight to get me into something socially acceptable." She grabbed her phone, checked it really quickly, and set it back on the table. "Lead the way."

He was totally onboard with that train of thought and was thinking it really should be a rule somewhere, enforced daily. Grinning at the images that were running through his head, he led them from the apartment down the stairs to the main kitchen, on the first floor and helped her search for something to eat. Finding Cheerios, because who doesn't love those little circles of heaven, they grabbed bowls and milk and headed for the tables. Grabbing a seat that looked out a window onto the grounds, they sat and poured out cereal and milk, like a couple who'd done this a million times.

He watched as she ate silently, staring out the window, her eyes roaming over everything that there was to see. There was so much he needed to say to her, so much he wanted to say, and yet the time just wasn't right. But then, would it ever be?

As she looked out over the grounds, her thoughts drifted to the man sitting in front of her. That kiss they shared was possessive, from the both of them. It shocked her just how much she craved that. Of course every girl dreams of an attraction that was on the verge of magical, but the fierceness of what they had took her breath completely away. It was on a whole different level. All she could do when they broke apart was change the subject, because if either had mentioned it, there would be no stopping their energy's from colliding again.

She knew he wanted more, could feel his constant restraint. His eyes were always hungry for her. His hold on her protective. Sometimes when he spoke she heard a certain longing and desire, but it washed away quickly when he realized he wasn't being an asshole.

This had the potential to be something huge, but she couldn't afford to chase it just yet. She needed to deal with the Max thing and the figuring out her life thing. Jumping head first into a powerful relationship just wasn't what she needed at the moment. As much as she hated to admit that, once she went down that road with him, she'd not resurface for a long time and right now, she just couldn't dedicate the time.

"You seem to be thinking awfully hard over there. What's up?" Doran asked, cutting through her thoughts.

"Oh, nothing. Just thinking." She said behind a bite of cereal. He looked at her and raised a questioning brow. She just shook her head with a grin. "Oh crap, I need to pee again." God her bladder suddenly felt like a balloon about to pop.

Doran laughed, a deep from the gut laugh, and pointed towards the corner of the room where she hoped the bathroom was. Darting away from the table, she hurried to the room and was so ever grateful that it was, in fact, a bathroom. She also noted on her rushed run that a few other people, women who looked close to her age, sat in another corner to the room, talking and laughing. It was such a normal sight to catch that she almost stopped to stare. Almost. Her bladder disagreed with the business of stopping.

After doing her business and washing her hands, she walked back out and sat down across from Doran who was still grinning.

"Better?" He chuckled.

"You have no idea." She sighed happily. Who would have thought going pee could feel so good but when one's bladder is so full it could burst, relief was sensational.

She looked back over at the women and smiled as they caught her staring and waved, looking genuinely nice and inviting. She really was going to need to stay in residence long enough to explore the people more. She was about to say something to Doran, like if he knew the women or not, but was interrupted.

"Hello doll," a voice boomed from the other side of the kitchen. Kedah turned her head sharply and smiled as Aiden strode over to them, looking ever more the wolf than he did last time she saw him. He had a nights worth, well days' worth, of stubble on his face and his hair was a wild mess. Looks like they weren't the only ones just waking up for the night.

She could have sworn she heard Doran growl from beside her. Seriously, who growls at people? She ignored him.

Standing, she leaned over and gave the wolf a quick hug. "Aiden, it's good to see you. Thank you again for yesterday." She was raised in the south, which meant she hugged everyone, especially those that had a hand in saving your life. Doran, she noticed, was not happy. Oh well, she was still choosing to ignore that behavior.

"At least you don't look like hell anymore, so think nothing of it." He grabbed a chair, swung in around to their table, and plopped down with an audible thud.

"Wolf, I don't remember inviting you to this party." Doran noted with more than a little distain in his voice. She turned to glare at him, clearly indicating that he needed to chill or she'd make him. Whatever he saw in her face was enough to have him slump back.

"Simmer down, I'm not here for you." Aiden shot at Doran. He then turned back to her and grinned. "You though. I'm about to rock your world."

"Are you now?" She replied in a playful jest. She didn't need to look at Doran to know he was probably gaping at them. He'd live. She was enjoying a normal, playful conversation with a new friend and he could just go blow steam elsewhere.

"Talked to Jensen and we agreed that you need to learn to defend yourself, or at least try. No more nearly dying on us. We're going to hit the gym after you've eaten and see what looks good in those pretty little hands of yours." Aiden relaxed his arms on the back of the chair looking completely at home. If Kedah had had a brother, Aiden would have been him. There was just something about him that was brotherly and it was comforting.

"Why didn't Jensen talk to me about this?" Doran demanded.

"Check your phone dipshit. We tried. But, it seems like," he said as he slowly gazed between the two of them, "you were too busy."

Before Kedah could even think about her actions, her hand shot out and grabbed onto Doran's arm, which was tense and ready to swing. "No." She commanded, and to Doran's shock, he held back. "You," she pointed at Aiden. "Knock it off, you're just baiting him. We were sleeping. That's all. Okay?"

"Okay." Aiden chuckled. He passed a look to Doran that she didn't understand, but added it to the ever growing list of shit she needed to bring up with him at a later time.

"So, what exactly are you going to teach me?" She asked, changing the subject.

"Going to put a few different weapons in your hand and see what feels right. Trouble seems to follow you like a boy band groupie, so we'll be needing to put a halt to that. There's only so many times you can bleed out or take a silver bath before you start to go a little crazy. Oh speaking of, how's the AGR working?"

"Great. I feel back to normal aside from peeing more than I ever thought possible." She responded. It was true, she really felt great this morning and no longer felt like she was going to die. Whatever was in this AGR was totally worth the investment to make.

"I hear that's a pretty interesting side effect." He laughed.

"Better to be peeing for the next 24 hours than dead, I'd imagine." She jested.

He smiled and shook his head, stood sharply, and gave Doran another look that she couldn't identify. If those two ever went at it, she wasn't entirely sure who would win. "Check your phone." He looked back at her. "Gym. 30 minutes. Be prepared to sweat. Feed first." He then turned and left without another word.

"Y'all don't get along very well, do you?" She observed as she turned back to Doran.

"I don't get along with anyone very well." He pushed his food aside, picked up his coffee, and swallowed it back in one breath.

"You know; you really should stop being such a dick." She muttered. She was excited for this little training session and he was killing her high.

"What?" She asked, looking over at him as he broke into a grin.

He looked her over while standing and clearing the table. "Kitten has finally found her claws, hasn't she?"

"Oh shut up, Doran." She quickly helped him clear the table and dashed back upstairs to change. Or at the very least to put on a bra. Working out braless was a danger to everyone's health.

Pausing at her door, she grunted to herself, remembering that all her things were still over at Doran's. Turning to wait for him, she was shocked to see he was already in his door, both her keys and her phone in his hand. He held a sly grin and tossed both in her direction, which she missed, and cringed as they clattered to the ground. He ducked into his room, slamming the door before she could even shout a sarcastic thanks in his direction. Jerk.

Quickly grabbing her keys and phone, she unlocked the door and scrambled into her apartment that still looked sad and unlived in. Someday she'd make this place her home, hopefully. Grabbing the first thing she could find, she changed in record time, throwing her hair up and out of her face and lacing her tennis shoes. Thankful that she had remembered to pack them.

After getting dressed she dashed to the kitchen to grab a bag of blood. Foregoing the need to microwave it, which she regretted, she managed to choke it down and promised herself to never be in such a rush that she couldn't warm her blood. Cold was not okay, ever.

She quickly walked to the door, locked up, and skipped down the steps and towards the direction of the gym.

CHAPTER
twenty-two

Aiden paced around the gym wondering exactly how this mess of a training session was going to go. He liked Kedah. Hell, he thought for a vampire, she was pretty chill. But she was clumsy and uncoordinated and had the potential to hurt herself and others with a mere flick of her wrist. He was going to have to be damn careful.

Clumsy aside, Aiden could handle her. The likelihood that Kedah could do serious damage to herself, or him, at this point in her immortal life was minimal. What he was worried about handling was Doran. If he and Kedah were soulmates, which was probably accurate to say they were, Doran was going to have a knee jerk reaction to protect. Doran was going to have to fight that reaction and Aiden wasn't sure how well that was going to go.

Kedah was going to have to learn to fight her own battles, despite Doran feeling like he needed to fight them for her. She wouldn't ever allow it, Aiden was dead sure on that. So, this training session would prove a valuable learning lesson for Doran and Kedah. Aiden had faith in Kedah. His faith in Doran was not as strong.

Should be a fun day.

He really had never met a vampire who couldn't at least put up some amount of a fight if attacked. He wasn't sure if Kedah was just gentle by nature or had a shitty past and had refused violence, but either way, it ended today. It had to if she had any hope of surviving this new world of hers.

Her life was always going to be in danger. A threat always lurking. If she was going to live long enough to enjoy immortality, then she needed to learn how to throw a punch, or defend herself by any means and to get the hell out of harm's way.

At the very least, if she faltered in a fight, Doran would pick up the slack. Aiden had seen him fight firsthand and, adding the fieriness with which he'd protect a soulmate, there wasn't anyone that was likely to stand in his way.

Speaking of the devil, Doran strode into the gym, the air around him prickling with tension and magic. Aiden threw off some of his own magic and stood a little straighter. "Doran. Forgot your girlfriend, didn't you?" He shouldn't bait the man, he knew that, but it was just too easy sometimes.

"Wolf, she is not my girlfriend." He growled.

"Forgot your soulmate then?" Aiden jabbed. Doran shot him one of those if-looks-could-kill looks and he backed off. For the moment. "You're not going to get in my shit about doing this, are you? I'd hate to lay you out in front of Kedah." He then asked, because it needed to be said out loud.

"Wolf, I'd have you buried 60 feet under an ice cap crying for your momma before you could even think about laying me out, so please, don't even fucking start with me." Doran promised.

He should have stopped. He just couldn't help the words that slipped off his tongue. "I'm doing this as a favor, just like the favor of letting her take my vein. I almost said no, but then I remembered, you can't let her take yours, can you?"

His last words hadn't even left his mouth before a fist flew and realigned his jaw. The force of the punch jerked his body back, causing him to stumble before righting himself. Rubbing a hand over his face, he spit out blood and grinned. "Feel better?"

"Not in the slightest." Doran muttered as he walked over to a far wall and leaned against it, giving him a full view of the entire gym.

Aiden stretched out his stiff jaw and groaned. Fuck that man could pack a hell of a punch. Before he had time to even register another action, Kedah walked into the gym, looking cute and as far from deadly as possible. He laughed. He couldn't help it. He was probably going to get punched again, but fuck it, some things were worth a spot of violence.

"I hate to be the one to remind you of this, Kedah, but you do remember you're a vampire, right? Scary creature of the night. You have an image to uphold and this," he gestured to her body, "isn't helping." He said as she approached, wearing purple workout pants and a blue tank top. Little pink straps of a sports bra were peeking out. Not a single bit of black or kick ass written anywhere on her.

To be fair, if they could get her a little bit of training, the whole looking like a Girl Scout could work to her advantage. No one ever suspected the Girl Scout.

"I wasn't aware vampires were stereotyped into being deadly and scary." She remarked with a smile.

"Honey, vampires have been stereotyped since the dawn of time. It surpasses stereotype when it's nothing but the damn truth." He would continue to bait her to see what she was made of, plus it was amusing as hell to get her feathers ruffled.

Jensen wanted to know what, if anything, she could do to start defending herself, even if it was something as simple as getting her ass out of the situation in one piece. He was also convinced she was hiding something and he needed to know what it was and whether it would cause more problems in the future.

"So then, if that is the case," she began with a grin. "Am I to assume you're nothing more than a dog who likes to stick his head out the window and drink from a toilet bowl? Maybe lick his own balls when he's bored?" Oh damn, he thought as he choked back a laugh. Doran's burst of laughter echoed through the gym and he stood a little stunned by her retort. Girl had some balls after all.

"Touché." He grabbed a staff from a bin that held various training weapons and walked carefully towards her, watching her movements, her eyes, and the way she tracked him. Circling behind her, he smacked her ass with the staff and tried not to laugh as she screeched. "Get. Run. Five laps. Go."

Her mouth hung open so he whacked at her again, this time going for the back of her thighs. She jumped and took off running, mumbling something under her breath that may have made a sailor blush. Little Kedah wasn't as innocent as she was leading everyone to believe. She just needed the fire lit a little higher under her ass.

He watched her run around the gym, her technique showing she had some athletic background. That was at least a little helpful. When she was done running, he led her through some stretches and warmups, more out of habit for himself than for her.

So first up, he tossed her the staff and grabbed another for himself. She missed the toss and laughed as she scrambled to pick it up.

"You ever use one of these things?" Aiden asked as he slowly began to circle her.

"Doesn't everyone pick up a staff and swing it around in their spare time? I mean, I'm pretty sure I was Gabby in my past life." She claimed sarcastically as she kept her eyes on him and not the staff.

He laughed and struck out, cracking her on the arm. Not hard enough to break but hard enough to welt. "I hate to break the bad news, but your past life lied. There isn't a snowy chance in hell you were Gabby my friend."

She scowled at him and struck out widely, swinging with no rhyme or reason. He dodged and jumped out of her way, swinging his staff and landing a blow to her side. "Ow." She squawked.

"Kedah. Separate your arms shoulder length apart and watch my staff and my movements." He took a couple of careful steps in another slow circle around her, watching, waiting. She mimicked his movements and struck out, managing to actually hit his staff a few times before he snuck in a blow to her thigh while she was distracted.

After another ten minutes of a painful learning curve, it was evident this was not her thing. Just as well, he could see her hurting herself more than others with it. "Well," he said with a grin. "You're terrible at a staff."

"You're a shitty teacher, you know that." She shot at him.

"Correction. I'm a great teacher with a shitty bedside manner." He laughed as he collected the staffs and tossed them over to Doran, who could have caught it with ease. He chose not to, watching as they flew past, clanking to the ground.

Aiden rolled his eyes and focused back on Kedah. "Now, come here and punch me in the face."

"What?" She asked, astonished.

"Punch me in the face. Come on, give it a try." He was confident that she'd not be able to land a punch, however he knew that if she did, it would hurt.

Kedah's eyes were wide and she hesitated for a long moment. Finally, she took a few steps forward, balled up her fist, and threw a punch at his face. She was slow and sloppy and he had no issues catching her fist in one hand, applying pressure, then twisting her arm, flipping her body, laying her out.

She coughed a few times, took a huge breath and stayed right where she was. It was a pretty good bet that fighting hand to hand was going to be out of the question for her as well. Stepping over her body, putting one leg on each side, he knelt down and grinned

"You gotta do better than that." He laughed, right as she brought her legs up, nailing him in the family jewels. He howled in pain as Doran howled in laughter.

Aiden stood up and took a giant step back while she scrambled to her feet, trying not to look mortified. She stood ready to try and fight again, fists balled and feet separated. She was smart enough to know to hit where it counted, so at least she had that going for her.

"Better." He choked out in a struggled wheeze. "Just remember to pull that on something attacking you, not teaching you."

"You were attacking me!" She exclaimed while never dropping her guard. She was learning, well. He wasn't mad, but fuck he hurt now. "I have no idea what in the hell I am doing, and yet you still came at me!"

"Not attacking. Training." He corrected.

"I don't see the difference." She pointed out.

"Honey, I hope you never have to see the difference, but if you do, you come and let me know after you've clocked your attacker so hard in the balls he chokes on them." Aiden said with a lopsided grin.

She snorted and dropped her fists. "Fine. Are we done?"

"With hand to hand, yes. But, as much as this may pain me even more, no, we're not done. I'm about to put a damn gun in your hand and see how you do." She'd be fine because he was a good teacher, plus Doran was still lurking around. So yes, she'd be fine, but it didn't make the situation any less unnerving.

"Seriously?" She questioned. "I thought you were kidding."

"Nope. Come on, range is just beyond those doors." He said pointing to a set at the back of the gym.

"We have a gun range in the gym?" she asked.

"Yes."

"Whoa."

Aiden shook his head and started for the range, grabbing ear protection as they went in. Doran followed close behind. At least he was behaving, though at what personal cost Aiden couldn't even imagine. His control was either rock solid or he was losing his shit internally and when that seeped out things would get, interesting, for lack of a better word.

A gun cabinet lined the back wall of the range and was only accessible by fingerprint. Once scanned, the case unlocked and slid open, showing an array of weapons. Everything from several 9mm to AK 47's and some custom shit someone built in their spare time. He grabbed two 9mm's, a few boxes of ammo, and several target sheets. Doran reached behind him and grabbed a .45 with bullets and a target sheet, apparently joining in on the fun.

Locking up the case, Aiden walked over to Kedah, and handed her ear protection. "Have you ever shot a gun before?"

"Do I look like someone who would have ever shot a gun before?" The sarcasm dripping from her words made him smile. If anyone was paired perfectly for Doran, this was the girl. She'd drive him absolutely nuts and there wasn't anything he could do about it.

Aiden watched as her nerves spiked, noting she didn't really hide emotions well, and groaned inwardly. "Everyone should know how to at least handle one correctly. I'd imagine the world would be a shake safer if gun safety was taught to everyone and not held as something to be terrified of." He truly believed that too. As they say, knowledge is power.

"Well, I skipped that class so, let's get this over with." Her voice shook, but she stood strong. Guess that was a good sign, or as good as he was going to get.

"Ear protection." He stated, holding up the ear buds. "Always wear it in the range, no matter what you're shooting or how immortal you think you are." The sounds couldn't permanently hurt them, but it would ring like a bitch for hours.

She took them from his hand and put them around her neck, mimicking his actions.

"This is a 9mm. I'm going to show you how to make sure the chamber is clear. Then we're going to unload and load it. Check to see if the safety is on. Then we're going to do it again. And again. Until its second nature, like breathing." He explained.

"We're not going to actually shoot it?" She questioned.

"Yes, but safety first. Seriously. Even if you can't hit the backside of a barn, I need you to know how to disarm someone, and that means unloading the magazine and emptying the chamber. It may save your life or someone else's."

"Alright." She responded and he was glad she at least understood the need for safety.

"Okay, first thing we need to do is see if there is a round in the chamber. Watch." He held out the gun so she could see what he was doing. Holding the handgrip, he grabbed the slide and slid it back, moving the latch on the side to hold it in place. He looked down into the opening, to make sure it was clear. "See, nothing there. You try." He hit the release letting the slide go forward and handed her the gun, butt first.

Carefully, she held the gun like he showed her and slid back the slide, looking in to make sure nothing was there, and hitting the release to let the slide go forward. She did it several more times to make sure the idea of checking it was ingrained in her motions of handling a weapon.

"Always do this. I don't care if you're an expert sniper or a 10 year old mortal. Check it. You can use your pinky to feel in there too, if it's too dark to get a really good glimpse. Okay?' He asked.

"Got it." She said, handing him the gun, exactly the way he handed it to her.

"Good. Now, let's load it. You're going to take the magazine and almost slam it into the handle, making sure it's in place securely. Then pull back the slide and release. This action puts a bullet into the chamber. To release the magazine, you just hit the release button, and the magazine drops out. Then check the chamber like I showed you and the bullet that's in place will pop out." He demonstrated the action of putting the magazine in and taking it out, watching her to make sure she was still following him.

He handed over the 9mm and she did exactly as he showed her. Several times. He let her hold onto her gun as he grabbed his and loaded it. Making sure the safety was on, they set them down while he put a target on the track.

"You ready to shoot?" He asked. For this part, she was ready. He was almost confident nothing would go wrong, almost.

"Oh, sure. Let's do this." She said.

"It's not going to bite you and I promise you won't hurt yourself." He said with a smile. "Now, stand almost to the side, facing me. You right handed?" When she nodded he continued. "Left leg needs to be in front and legs shoulder width apart. Grip the gun in your right hand, making sure your pointer finger is resting aside the gun and not near the trigger. Your left hand grips around your right." He showed her with his actions then watched as she carefully did the same.

She began to shake with nerves. Like down to the bones shaking. It was so much that he couldn't let her shoot in her current state. "Doran." He muttered. Without another word, Doran came around the corner and stood behind Kedah, resting his hands on her hips, steading her instantly.

He watched as Kedah looked over her shoulder at Doran, conflicted with emotions. Poor girl had absolutely no idea what was going on and why her body was responding to his. Why her very soul was reacting to his. He almost felt bad enough to say something but knew that if the roles were reversed, Doran would sit back and do nothing. So, he too would sit back and say nothing.

"Alright. Now all you need to do is slide back the safety, look down your sights at the top, find the little red dot, aim the little red dot, and pull the trigger. Deep breaths. It'll kick back a bit. Oh and for the love of all the gods in heaven and hell, do not, I repeat, do not, close your eyes. You can close one to help you focus out of your better eye, if you need, but do not close both eyes." Too many times he'd seen people close both eyes out of fear and the bullets went flying in every direction. That's not what they needed right now.

Taking a deep breath, Kedah steadied herself and brought the gun up to her line of sight. Turning her head, she looked down the sights, flipped off the safety, moving her finger to the trigger. Letting out a deep breath, she fired, letting out a squeal in the process. Quickly she put the safety on and set the gun down.

"Whoa." She exclaimed happily. "I shot it!"

"You did. Now, pick that back up and unload the magazine into the target and we'll see how you did." He insisted, nodding at her in encouragement.

She looked back at Doran who smiled and nodded as she picked up her weapon and, after doing everything she was taught, began to fire off shots. He took that moment to step into the other booth and fire off a few shots of his own. Practice makes perfect, as they say.

When the echo of shots stopped, he went back into her booth as Doran was pulling back the target. It wasn't pretty but at least she hit the paper.

"Ugh, I didn't even hit the target." She groaned.

"But, you did hit the paper." Doran said softly. Aiden nodded his head in agreement.

"You did. However, I'll bet guns won't be your thing. Time to try something else." Aiden dropped the magazine out of his and watched Kedah do the same, making sure everything was clear and in the right position. He took a small comfort in knowing she could at least disarm a gun if needed. Taking the weapon from her, he walked everything back to the safe and locked it all up.

She then followed him through another set of doors into another range. Doran continued to remain silent, stepping off to the side and out of the way.

"I'm going to take a wild stab at this and say that you have never shot an arrow before."

"Nope. But it can't be harder than shooting a gun." She said.

"It can be, in different ways. It takes a little more strength. Come on, let's get you some gear." They walked over to the back wall where he handed her a standard bow and a quiver of arrows. Grabbing a set for himself, they walked back over to the booth where, instead of putting a target on a line, they had a target already set up on a bale of hay.

Aiden had every intention of teaching her how to shoot an arrow, but he paused. "Doran, you wanna get this? You're better with a bow, aren't you?" Something in his memory banks told him that at some point in Doran's life he'd been an archer. Plus, this gave Aiden a chance to sit back and watch Kedah. Study her.

"Sure." Doran said gruffly as he kicked himself off the wall, taking up his place beside Kedah.

"Oh goodie, grumpy is finally going to join the party." Kedah shot at him. Aiden smiled, because she was totally baiting him, just like he did. Something was up in her pretty little mind and he had every intention of letting it play out, right now if needed.

Without a word, Doran grabbed the bow, picked up an arrow and shot the target, dead center, before anyone could blink. "Now that I have your attention. I'm not going to be nearly as long winded as wolf boy was."

"You know he has a name, right?" Kedah asked, turning her focus to him. Aiden chuckled to himself and stood watch.

"Yeah. It's wolf boy. Now. Watch." He stood beside her and held his bow with his left hand. Grabbing an arrow with his right, he lined up the notch on the arrow with the string on the bow, holding his left arm straight out. Using two fingers on his right hand to hold the arrow in place, he pulled back on the arrow, taking the string with him. Lining up the arrow by his cheek, he let out a breath and let go, sending the arrow flying at its target, hitting the center, again.

"Damn Robin Hood." Kedah muttered. Aiden was impressed with the shot too, even if he wasn't going to admit it.

"I come from a time when guns weren't even invented yet. This was all we had." Doran stated.

"And I bet dinosaurs roamed the earth too. Bet those were a bitch to bring down with an arrow." She shot at him.

Aiden smiled and was actually a little sad that she didn't still have a gun in her hand. It looked like things were about to get amusing as hell and he was going to enjoy the fact that he wasn't involved in it.

"Dinosaurs were too chewy to eat." Doran said as he set his bow down and turned to face her.

"Ha ha." Kedah said. "What's your deal?"

"Don't know what you're talking about." Doran muttered, rubbing the back of his neck.

"Oh yes, you do. Your actions this morning after finding out that I was headed here after breakfast. Throwing my stuff at my door. Staying utterly silent this whole time. I mean, I get you have the outward appearance of an ass to keep up, but damn, this is pushing those limits to the max." Kedah crossed her arms over her chest and gave a look at Doran that would scare paint off walls.

Aiden was seriously going to enjoy this.

"This isn't the time for this conversation." Doran grunted.

"Oh don't stop on my account. I'm just here to make sure no one gets blood on the equipment." Aiden cut in with a smile.

Both Kedah and Doran shot him a look and he just smiled back. Neither of them were actually out for him so he was just going to step back and gather any information that may be shared in the heat of the moment.

"Why? Because I have access to a weapon or because we have an audience?" She asked.

"I'm not scared of you Kedah, and I couldn't give two shits about the wolf." Doran responded.

"Fine. So, what's up?" She demanded.

"I don't owe you an explanation." He shot at her.

She dropped her jaw then picked it up. "No, you're right. You don't owe me anything do you?"

Doran groaned and ran a hand down his face. "I don't know what you're wanting from me right now. What do you want me to say?"

"You know, I vowed years ago to not babysit the emotions of anyone. If you don't tell me what's wrong then I'm just going to leave it be and leave you be. From this evening when we woke up, together in your bed, I might add, to now, you're a completely different person." Kedah snapped.

"I'm more than very aware of where you woke up today, Kedah." Doran said, shooting Kedah one of those you've-got-to-be-kidding-me looks. He looked weary and conflicted and Aiden could only imagine how hard it had to have been for him to fight his very nature that was trying to take over. The bond and power of soulmates was a strong one, and even stronger with his because of age and who he was. If he was correct in thinking that Doran was a god.

"Oh my god, then why are you avoiding the question!" She said with a loud sigh. Aiden watched her carefully now, not needing another blood craze to take hold. Not here. Not when she was holding a bow and a full quiver of arrows.

"Because you wouldn't understand why. It's complicated."

"What's complicated?"

"Everything with you is complicated! You are. Your knack for finding trouble. Whatever it is that you're hiding from everyone. Your nightmares. Everything." Doran said. Interesting. He hadn't known that Doran was aware she was hiding something. He thought he was too distracted to know, unless Jensen had mentioned something.

"What in the hell are you talking about? Where did all this come from?" She said as she took a step back away from him. Aiden watched her face, her reactions, and it all confirmed one thing. Well the one thing he needed to know. She was hiding something and it scared her enough to not have confided in anyone.

"You know what? Fuck this, I'm out." Doran snapped as he started off for the door.

"Seriously?" She screeched.

He didn't look back as he left the range, slamming the door. Kedah just stood and looked out the door before turning back to stare at him.

"You know anything about this?" She demanded.

Aiden pushed off the wall and shook his head. "Nope. I'm just here for the training. Come on, let's shoot shit."

She looked him over before picking up the bow and trying to do exactly as Doran did. The first few dropped right off the string before she could even get forward momentum. When she finally got the string pulled back with the arrow and released it, the string snapped against her arm so hard she howled in pain and dropped the bow.

"That one almost hit the target." Aiden said, trying hard not to laugh.

"Can you even shoot one of these things?" She retorted. "I swear this thing hates me, too."

Aiden smiled as he picked up a bow, laced the arrow, pulled it back and let it fly, hitting the target's bullseye.

"Showoff." She whispered.

"You asked." He said with a shrug. "One last weapon to go. You ready?"

"Thank god, I am so done with the damn idiot bow." She groaned as she picked up her bow and his. Aiden walked down to the target, grabbing arrows as he went, grabbed the few on the target, and walked back, putting them in their quivers then away.

"You're not as innocent as you lead everyone to believe, are you?" He commented lightly.

"No, I am for the most part. It's a genetic flaw as my friends used to say. Always the nice clumsy kid. Blah, blah, blah." She explained.

"I believe it." He laughed. "Grab that rolled up thing over there follow me."

She grabbed the package and followed him to a long table set up along another booth. This one had a wall that looked like corkboard. "Knives?"

"Yep." Aiden said as he unrolled the parcel and grabbed a knife by the handle. "Harder than you'd think as you have to flick your wrist just right and arch the knife correctly to rotate it to land blade first. It's more a practice thing than anything else." He flicked the blade and it soared through the air, landing on the wall in a perfect shot. He really didn't have a lot of hope here, but it was the last thing to try. If she failed, he had no idea what they were going to do with her, aside from some serious general training.

"Okie dokie." Kedah grabbed a knife, held it by the blade, stood at the edge of the booth and let the knife fly, utterly surprising herself, and him, as it hit the board perfectly. "Holy shit." She muttered.

"Huh." Aiden said, clearly awestruck that she hit the wall the first go around. He handed her another blade and she hit the wall again. Three more knives later, all of them hitting home, and Kedah was beaming with pride. She almost glowed with how excited she was.

"Guess we found what you're good at huh?" Aiden said with a smile.

"I cannot believe I can throw knives! How cool is that? How totally random." She walked down to the wall, pulled all the knives out and walked back. Handing them back to Aiden.

"Guess we'll get Jensen to order you some throwing knives to keep on you whenever you go out. Just, try not to stab anyone that you know. Okay?"

"Like Doran?" She said with a sly grin.

"No, stab that bastard. It'll do him good. But anyone else you probably shouldn't." He said back, smiling with her. He really didn't care if she stabbed Doran and if she could pull it off, he'd like her even more.

"Ha." She snorted, then laughed again at her snort. "Why don't you like him?"

"He's annoying." Aiden said with a shrug. "You probably should go get some vampire food and shower. You stink." He had so much more he'd love to spill about Doran, but wouldn't, right now. Later was another story, though. If Doran didn't wise up before then.

Kedah gasped and shook her head. "I do not! But thanks, for all of this. Really. I know I am not an easy person to teach."

"I've taught worse. You did fine. You want to set up a time to meet and work on hand to hand stuff. Because, Kedah, like it or not, you're a vampire and you will continue to attract trouble. It's just the nature of things. You may want to know at least a little on how to handle yourself." He said to her. Truthfully, she really did need to step up her game. He liked her and wanted her to stay alive.

"Yeah, I'd like that. Thanks." Kedah said as she waved to him and headed out the door. Once Aiden was sure she was gone he sent out a message to Jensen.

"Kedah's damn good at knives. Get her shoe size and order her boots and knives. Arm sheaths too. Also, definitely hiding something. Doran suspects too. Will continue to ask questions."

Satisfied his message went through, he locked up the equipment and left the gym. He was in need of a shower and a hunt, in no particular order. The full moon was coming and he could hear its call singing in his veins.

CHAPTER
twenty-three

Kedah felt like a superhero. Not a vampire, even with her fangs doing a little peek-a-boo action, but a freaking superhero. With the high she was feeling, she could take on the whole world. Her and her awesome crazy knife throwing skills that came right out of left field and directly onto the target. Every. Single. Time.

This was the first real time since her becoming a vampire, that she could actually see a positive. She was stronger than before. She could be deadly. No more was she the awkward 26 year old human who had no idea what was going on in the world. Now, she could be a 26-year-old vampire who actually had a fighting chance at surviving. Maybe she wasn't such a disaster of a vampire after all, just a late bloomer.

That seemed to fit nicely; late bloomer. Wasn't that what most people in their 20's were like anyways? Late bloomers. Not young enough to rely on others to get things done and not quite old enough to know how to rely on themselves. Turning into a vampire complicated the hell out of things, but maybe she wasn't as lost as she thought. Maybe she'd finally break from the awkward stage of things.

As she made her way back to her room, she passed by Doran's room with a frown. If ever someone was going to continue to confuse her, she was sure it would be him. His reactions to situations were so extreme that she wasn't sure what side of him she'd see. Her emotions were probably similar, but she at least hid it well.

She was attracted to him. Who wouldn't be? Her hormones did a little happy dance every single time he walked by or bumped into her. But what she couldn't figure out was if her reaction was typical with her new heightened emotions and senses or if it was something else. Because let's face it, this was all new and she still had no idea what was going on with her new body.

What she really needed was a vampire girlfriend or mother, someone not male and who'd been alive as the undead long enough to be able to help her figure out what in the hell was going on. A fairy vampire godmother would be totally awesome right about now.

All this would be great to explore and figure out, assuming she could figure out a way to get out of the mess she was currently in with Max. From what she could tell, he had the ability to control her and make her do whatever he asked. Where that stopped she hadn't the slightest idea.

If she could sort that out, then she'd go after the Doran mess. Maybe she'd bug Aiden for answers, even though he was a wolf. He was a good guy and had done more for her than anyone else. Plus, he had hot friends, albeit very scary looking. Who could say no to that combination?

But first, she really needed a shower, which she realized she had been doing way more than before. Not that she had bad hygiene, but merely that she seemed to be sweating and getting into situations more now than ever before that required water to solve them. Once in her room, she stripped off her sweaty clothes, tossed them in a pile on the floor, and made her way to the bathroom. Twenty minutes later, plus a fresh and clean body, and she was ready to face the rest of the night. Training had taken a few hours, but not nearly enough to call it quits on the day.

Wrapping a towel around her body she went to her closet and pulled on jeans and a shirt before wandering over to check her phone. Sadie had called half a dozen times and left several messages. She sighed and called her back before she went postal and got them both in trouble. Again.

She also chose to ignore the several missed calls from an unknown number, because she really didn't want to deal with that shit storm right now.

"OMG, where in the hell have you been?" Her best friend yelled as she answered the phone on the first ring.

"The shower." She casually replied.

"For the past 20 some odd hours? Last I heard Doran was looking for you because you could be in trouble. What the hell happened?" Sadie demanded.

"Oh, that. Yeah. Sorry. No, everything is fine. I'm fine. You know me, I got a little lost and forgot my phone. No one had heard from me in a while and dawn was coming, so he was worried." She tried to remain as calm and collected as possible, hoping her friend wouldn't hear the lies in her voice. There was no need to worry her about the past.

Sadie snorted a laugh and sighed loudly. "You're lucky I know you and totally believe that. But why didn't you call me to tell me you were fine. Or hell, text me. Something would have been better than radio silence."

"Sorry, I was sleeping. I've had a long few days getting used to this place and crashed pretty hard." She was totally omitting the part about sleeping with Doran. That was a conversation for another day, because it would be a day long conversation.

"Hang on a sec, okay?" Kedah muttered as she held the phone to her shoulder with her ear and downed the two bags of blood she just nuked. Any bruising she may have had probably would go away now and she felt 100 times better. Funny how she never realized just how much she needed until she was getting it on a regular basis.

"Ew. Were you just eating while on the phone with me?" Sadie said in disgust.

"Yes. I had training just a bit ago and got my ass kicked. It was needed." Kedah replied.

"Training?"

"I'll explain over coffee. You wanna meet sometime soon?" Going out and away from the boys of the house sounded both like a brilliant idea and a bad one, but she missed her friend and needed the girl time.

"Yes ma'am. In an hour?"

"Sounds great. Our usual?" The usual had been a coffee shop in town that they had been going to before they even knew they liked coffee. It was tradition and it was perfect, and it was open super late. Which, now that she thinks about it, she wondered if it was open late to cater to the nocturnal in the area. Huh, wouldn't that make a whole lot of sense.

And, she'd totally go there, even if she had been kidnapped the day before at the very same location. What's the likelihood it would happen two days in a row? Her luck, it was probably good but she was willing to risk it.

"As if I'd change that in a million years." Sadie laughed.

"True that. See ya in a few."

"Bye sweetie."

"Bye." With that taken care of she called for a ride and had everything settled to go in 45 minutes. Now, all she needed to do was avoid everyone else before leaving and she'd be set.

Not even a minute passed before her phone rang and she jumped, startled. Unknown caller. Shit. "Hello?"

"We need to talk." Max demanded.

"Uh, I'm a little busy, can I get back to you?" She lied.

"No." He grunted.

"Well, I don't know anything more than I did 24 hours ago. I've been recovering from a nasty case of silver poisoning you so graciously gave me." She spat out.

"Good, the cuffs worked. Two o'clock. Book Nook on Main." He said then hung up. Shit.

Her phone binged as a picture message came through. She gasped at the image of a sniper looking down at her parents who were eating dinner in their home. *"Don't be late."* The message said.

That bastard was playing so dirty it made her skin itch. She had no doubt now that he would kill her parents, even if she did everything he asked. Damn it, now what she was going to do?

A knock at her door nearly caused her to jump out of her skin. What now, she thought to herself as she tripped over the carpet while scrambling to get the door. She fell onto all fours and groaned. Carefully she rose to her feet and dashed to the door. Thank god it wasn't Doran. "Yeah?"

"Kedah. You okay? I thought I heard a loud thud." Jensen asked with a half-smile. He knew, the jerk. He totally knew she just met the carpet and was going to make her say it out loud.

"Uh, yeah. Gravity, the bitch. What's up?" She asked, her nerves now causing her stomach to churn.

"Aiden said you did really well today. I wanted to come by and see if you truly were okay." Jensen asked as he walked into the room, semi uninvited. Her eyes widened a bit, but she shut the door and stood awkwardly beside the couch.

"Yeah. I mean, I survived. He didn't kick my butt too badly. I did well at throwing knives though. That was pretty cool. Everything else was pretty rough." She fidgeted with her hands, putting them in her pockets and then taking them out. Holding them in front of her, then behind.

Jensen watched her for a brief moment before looking back at her face. Anyone else may not have caught the pause, but he did. Of course he did. She was guilty and it showed.

"Aiden suggested we get you a pair of boots that have pockets for a few knives and maybe an arm sheath. Just so that you can have something on you when you leave the Estate. Would you wear that?" He asked.

She was speechless. Here she was hiding this epic secret and he was offering her a gift. Now she felt bad. Really bad. Given her situation though, they may come in handy, even if her guilt made her sick to accept them while keeping her secrets. "Yes! That would rock. Thank you."

"Alright, well, what size shoe are you?" He asked.

"Eight would be fine. Can I buy them?" She asked, feeling like she should at least offer.

"Think of it as a house warming present." He said with a smile. "So, I hear you're headed out tonight."

"Oh yeah. I was going to text you. Just coffee with Sadie. The coffee shop in town." She said quickly.

"You can come and go as you please, we told you that." Jensen said, but something in his voice held a tone that a 'but' was coming.

"But you do tend to attract trouble, or have thus far. We'd just like a starting point if something goes wrong. Okay?" He began to walk around the room, eyes roaming. Looking. Studying. "Do you want to get more things from your old place?"

"Uh, yeah I probably will at some point. I'll let you know when." She muttered, assuming she lived long enough to decorate.

He nodded. "I'll let you head out." As he walked to the door he turned to her and spoke. "Oh and Kedah."

"Yeah?"

"Everyone is entitled to their secrets. We all have them. However, if they jeopardize the safety of yourself or people around you, it never hurts to confide in someone." He walked out, closing the door behind him.

Now she felt worse than the gum on the bottom of someone's shoe.

If anyone else called or came to the door, at this moment, she was liable to have a heart attack.

Peeking out the door, praying for no more surprises, she saw the coast was clear and darted for the stairs. Everything was quiet and lonely, and for once she was ever so thankful that not a soul had a sudden interest in her whereabouts.

Her ride came not too much after she had gotten to the door and she rode in silence, thinking about what may happen. She really wanted to avoid Max. Either he would kill her this time or surely Jensen and Doran would think she was just too much trouble and let her die. There was always a small chance she could get out of the situation herself, but that was very minute.

Hopping out of the car, saying her thanks, she made her way up to the coffee shop. Dread began to seep into her bones, until a smiling face bounded towards her.

"Hey!" Sadie squeaked as she came in for a quick hug. "You look great! Aside from the fading bruise under your eye. Trip down some stairs into someone's fist again?" She laughed as she led her to their table.

"No stairs involved. Just a fist." Kedah said as she waved over the waitress and ordered her drink. After the fact she thought about the possibility of someone noticing her, but it was late enough that she should be okay. Well, she hoped so. She didn't happen to know the waitress, which was a good start to staying hidden in a small town.

"Seriously. A fist? As in someone actually hit you? Spill." Her best friend said as she crossed her legs under her, which meant she was getting comfortable and Kedah was in for a long conversation. More than one coffee may be on the menu tonight. "Wait." Sadie muttered as she leaned over and grabbed Kedah's face and peering closely. "When did your eyes change color?"

"What?" She asked, confused. Her eyes hadn't changed colors, had they? Was that even possible? Sadie pulled out her phone, got really close and snapped a picture, then showed her. She gasped. They had changed and instead of green with flakes of brown, they were now swirled to hazel. Why hadn't anyone else said anything because surely Doran saw this when he was gazing at her so intently earlier.

"So, you didn't know?" Sadie remarked.

"No." She muttered. "But I'll be inquiring when I get home." And she would. Straight to Doran. She was going to have a nice long conversation with the man as soon as she got back, whether he wanted to or not.

Changing the subject, she told Sadie about the training earlier and about everything she felt she could talk about. There was so much she couldn't say that she was beginning to understand why distance was needed between humans and paranormals. She didn't want to lose Sadie, but it looked like the distance was inevitable. It was a really sucky feeling to know you had to push someone away for their own safety.

Sadie filled her in about work and their friends. Boys and all of the normal human life stuff that she was used to hearing about. Sadly, Kedah found herself drifting. Not because she was bored with Sadie, but because the human side of things just didn't seem to mean much to her anymore. She wished that boys were the most she had to currently worry about, though one boy was at the top of her list.

When Sadie mentioned her parents, her attention returned to 100%. "You saw mom and dad?"

"Oh yeah." She started in sadly. "They were at the supermarket the other day. They looked really good hun. Not like totally happy and everything is perfect, but that they were adjusting and getting along. You know, what you've always wanted for them. They asked how I was doing and I had to pretend to be really sad, which wasn't too hard since you moved out and all, but it was odd. Have you seen them at all?" She asked.

"No." Kedah said quickly. "No, I wouldn't dare risk it. My luck I'd fall in front of them while spying and everything would go to hell."

Sadie giggled a moment. "Yeah, probably. Anyways, it's getting late and as I would love to stay here all night, I can't. I'm working early in the morning." She stood and stretched, yawning loudly.

"Ah yes, the weary soul of a working mortal." Kedah laughed. "Alright you. Come on, I'll walk you home."

"I don't know if that makes me feel safer or not." Sadie replied honestly. She looped her arm in Kedah's and walked out the door, cherishing a single moment of pure happiness in a world of insanity.

And for that moment, one single minute in an endless supply of minutes, nothing was wrong. Nothing hurt. No one was in danger. Evil didn't lurk around the corner. Things that went bump in the night were silent. As they walked and laughed, Kedah had a moment to feel human again. To feel like she belonged.

"You okay?" Sadie asked, turning to her concerned. "Kedah?"

"Sorry, yeah. I'm fine." She shook her head and forced a smiled.

Sadie didn't look convinced but said nothing. She leaned in and kissed her cheek, hugging her bye and went into their old place, safe and sound. Kedah stood outside for a moment, listening to the locks click into place, praying her friend would be alright. Her next stop could be her last. She hoped not, but her gut was singing a different tune.

CHAPTER
twenty-four

Kedah made her way back to the coffee shop and ordered another drink, preparing for what could be a very long night. Selfishly, she was making up for lost time in the caffeine department as well. It seems that caffeine was just as useful to vampires as humans and man how she missed it.

Her phone rang, causing her to nearly jump out of her seat, but smiled when she saw it was just Sadie. She really needed to bring her nerves into check soon or she was liable to keel over and die from a phone call. "Miss me already?"

"Totally. As I am usually clueless and sometimes should be blonde, I forgot that I have something here for you. Can you come back for just a sec?" Sadie's voice wavered just a moment, but that moment was enough for Kedah to know something was wrong.

"Sure." She said with a pause. "I'll be there in a few."

Kedah's heart dropped. No one other than Max would use others as a scare tactic to draw her out. Her options were, as she thought, close to zero and there was nothing else to do but to reverse her steps and go. She'd literally do anything to continue to protect Sadie and her parents. Even if it meant dying. For good this time.

Grabbing her coffee, because hello caffeine and priorities, she hurried out of the shop and down the old sidewalks. Her feet knew the path well and walked it on autopilot, while she drank back her drink. Quicker than she wanted, she was back at the house, knocking on the door. For the briefest of moments, she considered her options of being able to call Doran or Jensen, but the moment passed as dread and fear crept in. Her concern for her friend and family outweighed common sense and in the long run, that would be her undoing.

She stood waiting on the front step, and without a doubt felt her Sire within. Nothing good was going to come of tonight. Sadie tentatively opened the door and before she could speak, Kedah leaned in and hugged her tightly. "It's not your fault."

Sadie's eyes watered as she moved out of Kedah's way, letting her walk into the room where Max was suddenly in her face, smiling like a cat who caught a mouse. "Hello Kedah."

"I said I was going to meet you." She shot at him.

"Just wanted some insurance, that's all. Thank goodness you two made a very public display of going out. I was a little worried I'd have to chase you down." Max reached out and froze all her movements. Everything except her speech.

That's when everything happened so quickly that she didn't even have time to blink. One minute she was standing stock still and the next she heard the front door crash in, an arm grabbed her around the waist and she was in Doran's room, crumpling down to the floor. "Stay. Do not fucking move." He growled out and disappeared.

She didn't move. Not even to untuck her legs from the odd angle they landed.

He appeared again, face red with anger, fists balled at his sides.

"Get up." He demanded. She did, quickly.

Her mind was reeling and her mouth moved before she even had a chance to tell it not to. "Where's Sadie? Is she safe?"

Doran's eyes got wide, his expression was a mix of pissed, mad, worried, scared and relieved. "She's fine."

"Where is she?" She demanded, still trying to wrap her mind around what exactly had just happened.

"She's with Jensen." He ground out.

"With Jensen? Oh god, could you have picked a worse person to put her with? He hates her! He's, he's going to kill her!" She said in a panic. As she took a step forward, Doran's massive body blocked her exit and forced her to back track in order to not be crushed.

"Shit." Doran grunted in anger and frustration. "What in the actual fuck is going on, Kedah? Do not lie to me. I'll know and I am not in the mood."

Oh she got that much. "I can't," she said with a hitch in her voice. "Doran please, I can't tell you. He'll kill my parents. He'll kill Sadie. He'll kill you." When the first tear escaped, the rest followed freely.

Doran looked hurt as he gazed at her face, watching the tears fall to the ground, making no move to stop them or wipe them away. He took a deep breath and some of the anger he was harboring subsided. "Trust me Kitten, I am not an easy kill." He began to pace in front of her, moving in long determined strides.

Kedah dropped her head in regret as the tears continued to fall. The moment she found out who her Sire was and then found out that he was the one causing all kinds of hell in this state, she should have said something. She should have just asked for help. Instead, she dug a hole and hopped right in.

His pacing stopped and suddenly the air was still and calm. Nothing moved. No sound was made. She looked up to see Doran staring at her, concern in his eyes and all hints of anger slowing seeping away. "Kitten, whatever this is, you need to tell me. I can't help fix it unless I know what to fix."

Why would he even bother to try? She really couldn't understand, but believed that he may be genuine in his offer. Maybe she wasn't in as much trouble as she expected, or she was in more than she realized. Either way, this had to end. "Why do you call me Kitten?" She wondered out loud, changing the subject.

A small smile caressed his face softening his features. "Because kittens are small, young, and seem to be defenseless."

She grinned. "Yes and no."

"No, you're right. They have claws and sharp teeth and will go after anyone that gets in their way. I can see that in you. Your claws and sharp teeth are itching at the chance to prove themselves. You're like a little kitten that will grow to be a fierce cat one day, you only need to trust and have faith that it'll happen." Doran reached out and cupped her face in his hand, brushing away the last of her tears.

It was such a sweet gesture that she almost lost it all over again. "He'll kill them, Doran. He'll kill you. No one needs to die for me." She whimpered.

"No one is going to die Kedah. Not a one. You just have to tell me what's going on. Talk to me. Please." He looked at her and offered a small smile of courage. "Are you even aware of who that was back there?"

Well, here goes nothing. "Max Vaughn. He's my, uh, my Sire."

He stilled and dropped his hand away from her face. "I'm not struck speechless much but, damn. I thought you didn't know who your Sire was?"

"I didn't, at first. He found me right before I moved in here. I promise, I had no idea who he was until that point, and even then didn't know how bad he was. I swear it. I would have said something but he said he'd kill my parents and Sadie. He has people watching them and sends me pictures to prove it." She watched as he processed the information, standing still and thinking hard. She wished he'd say something but wasn't going to press the issue.

Running a hand through his hair he sighed loudly. "Well, I'll say this. If you're going to go big, you go the biggest. Christ Kedah. I've lived a very, very long time and haven't met anyone as ruthless as he, aside from a few Gods that I won't mention I know. And it's not because he has a huge body count, but because he's smart and has outsmarted everything and everyone."

230

That made her anger spike as the realization of what Max had done hit her. He had to of known how this was going to play out long before he even turned her. She was just a pawn. What a bastard. "It's not like I had a choice when he turned me, did I? He didn't even think I was going to make the transition, and since I did, well, here I am." All the anger for the entire situation was finally bubbling to the surface and she couldn't stop the emotions from pouring out. "I don't even know what to do, Doran. He can control me, make me do things. Make me tell him things. I had no idea a Sire could do that. I have no idea how to even be a damn vampire. Then you guys come along. He pops up making demands. My life flipped, again, just when I was getting the hang of the new life I was creating."

"I'm going to tear his fucking heart out." Doran said with a growl. Kedah shook her head and took a step forward, putting her hand up to stop his tantrum. He stopped immediately.

"You're going to kill the un-killable? You said it yourself, no one can find him. No one's been able to beat him." She stood nose to nose with him, breathing deep and resisting the urge to stop fighting and refocus their energy elsewhere. "How did you even find me?"

"I was following you." He said as his eyes trailed from her gaze to her lips, drinking her in. She shuddered involuntarily.

"Well at least you're honest. Why?" She demanded, though, if she thought about it, it didn't surprise her.

"Because you don't hide anxiety well and you talk in your sleep." He said as he returned his gaze to hers.

She gasped. Of course she talked in her damn sleep, why on earth would she not? She did it as a human and it got her in trouble more than once. "You didn't tell me I talked in my sleep."

"I didn't. You're right. I also didn't tell you that your anxiety rides on your face clear as day because I needed to know what trouble you had gotten yourself into." Doran said.

"Jerk." She muttered under her breath.

"I may be a jerk, but I'm still going to kill him, Kedah. I make that promise to you." He said in a deadly calm voice.

"No, you're not. You're not going to kill him and you don't owe me any promises." She retorted. Because he wasn't. With clarity she realized that she wanted the kill for herself and for all those that may have been lost to his evilness. She had never wanted to harm another person before, but now, now she wanted the kill to be hers.

"This is not up for debate. I will rip his heart out of his chest and I will make him choke on it while I laugh and piss on his grave." He said.

There was a mental image she was going to have to scrub from her memory. Mental image aside, his anger felt misplaced and pissed her off. Not once did he stop and think exactly what Max had done to her. "If anyone is going to kill him, it should be me. It's my life he fucked up. MY life he took without remorse or thought. My blood he drained from my helpless body while he sat back and laughed. My very essence he watched as it floated from my body, never to be reunited with my flesh. For fucks sake, Doran, he took my soul without thought and turned me into the damned, just because he wanted a fuck buddy who could do his bidding. Stop for a second and think how that makes me feel. How I should have reacted to all this? How would you?"

She watched as Doran stood still, not saying a word, the anger he was feeling written all over his face. He was thinking about her words, but was being a typical male and only focusing on one thing and not the bigger picture. It was sweet, actually, but not what she needed at this very moment. She sighed heavily. "I should have died, Doran. I wanted to. I did even still, up until about a handful of days ago. It's not nearly what I expected and having to have gone at it alone was terrifying. It's all his fault and I want him to pay."

Doran grinned at her, despite her seriousness of the current conversation. But at least he no longer looked like he was going on a murder spree. "You really are pretty terrible for a vampire," he said. "But Kedah,"

"What?"

"I have seen worse. What people forget to mention about life is that to be anything; it's a learning curve. Most of the time you only see the good and the accomplished. But to get to that point, you have to fall, get up, and fall again. You may have to kill and betray people. Life definitely sucks from time to time. Those shitty times are always outweighed by those few moments where time stops and magic happens. Things do get better or you die. It's just the way of things."

That was sadly non-motivating, but he was absolutely right. Of course he was right, he was old enough to have invented right and wrong. She wanted to laugh then burst into hysterical sobs. "Thank you." She said instead. "For rescuing me and the pep talk."

"My pleasure." He said with a smile.

"Really? You enjoyed this?" She muttered.

"It seems, that when it comes to you, it doesn't matter what I am doing, I'll enjoy it in the long run." He responded.

"Why is that?" She mused, hoping for once he'd answer.

"This isn't the right time to talk about it." Of course it wasn't. If they kept this up they were either going to kill each other or have the most mind blowing makeup sex known to man. She was hoping for the latter, but time would tell.

"What does that mean, Doran? Seriously." She stood and waited for an answer, a determined look on her face.

God damn, could she look any sexier standing there frustrated as hell, frazzled, and just, damn. After everything that just went down, the knowledge of who her Sire was and that she could have betrayed everything they'd worked so hard to protect here, he still wanted to push her up against the wall and claim those lips as his. He should be furious, but just couldn't find it in him to be.

He was done fighting it. "I promise to you, Kedah, that I will sit you down and explain everything. I just can't right now. Other things need to happen first and what I have to say will take your full attention." He took a step forward and brushed the hair out of her face. Staring down into her tearful eyes, ones that had blended just as his had, to match in a swirl of hazel. He was lost to her. She was his soulmate, which was no longer a question. The question now was when he told her, how would she feel about it? Because he'd love to sweep her off her feet and live happily ever after, but happily ever afters very rarely came without its share of bumps in the road. "Please."

"Fine. But, when I ask again, Doran, I'll be demanding an answer. After that, I won't bother." She was serious too, he could absolutely tell. If he let this opportunity slip away, she'd not give him another.

"Understood." He needed a distraction. At that moment his phone buzzed and he couldn't help but chuckle at the message on the screen. "We should go. Jensen just texted and asked if this human sitting in his office was dinner or was he obligated to let her live."

Kedah's eyes got wide. "Oh god, he wouldn't really hurt her, would he? Doran, we have to go get her."

"Calm yourself. He won't touch her. But we should go get her quickly. He tends to be less patient than me." He grabbed his stuff and led Kedah out the door.

"I find that hard to believe." She muttered as she rushed down the hall to Jensen's office.

He followed her at a slower pace, enjoying the view of her backside more than he should. Shaking his head to clear the new images that snuck in he promised himself some quality one on one time with her as soon as possible.

She stopped outside of Jensen's door and looked up, clearly confused as to whether or not she should just barge in. He made the decision for her and swung the door open, startling Sadie, who was tucked into the far corner of the couch. Jensen looked more annoyed than he had been in a long while. It was amusing as hell.

Kedah rushed in and went right to Sadie, checking her over to make sure she was okay. They cried and hugged, then talked quietly to each other. Doran went over to Jensen and spoke low, so neither of the ladies could hear.

"Why in the hell did you drop her off here? You know how I feel about humans in this house." Jensen asked, irritated.

"Well she was about to be killed by Max, as was Kedah." Doran offered up as an explanation.

"What?" Jensen asked.

"Max is Kedah's Sire. He was using her as bait."

"Shit." Jensen cursed.

"About what I said, although I may have been a little more colorful and loud about it."

"That's some serious shit, Doran. We can't have her here if he can follow her."

"Good news is, he can't follow anyone when I zap them out of his line of sight. Bad news is, he can absolutely control her if he's near her. That I saw firsthand."

"Aside from killing her, I don't know what to do about her then. We can't have him track her here. We're also going to have to start checking new vampires when they arise. If he turned her just to get intel, then there is no telling how many more are out there that he's using for god knows what." Jensen pinched the bridge of his nose and closed his eyes briefly.

"You can't kill her." Doran said.

"I know. When are you going to tell her she's your soulmate?" Jensen asked.

"Jesus, does everyone know?" He muttered.

"Pretty much everyone except for your soulmate at this point."

"When the time is right, I'll tell her."

"And when will that be? Is there ever a right time?" Jensen challenged.

"So what in the hell are we going to do now?" He said, changing the subject.

"Don't know. You should probably research something."

"Oh because I have the time for that."

"Just saying."

"I hate to interrupt whatever you have going on over there, but are my parents in danger?" Kedah asked.

"Fuck. Probably." Doran said. "Yes." Jensen answered.

"Go get them and take them and Sadie to the safe house. I'll be over shortly to explain some things and make sure guards are posted." Jensen stated as he rose and walked around his desk and approached Sadie.

"Hey," she said in a panic. "I'm not going to say anything. . . . " Jensen put a finger to her forehead and she slumped over, completely knocked out.

"She's fine." He said before Kedah had a chance to ask.

Kedah stood by her friend's body, protecting it. Doran watched as the warrior in her started to show. He knew in a past life she was fierce, loyal and determined. It was only a matter of time before that came forward in this life. He hoped like hell she lived long enough to see it happen. With Max looming overhead and her death omen, things weren't looking good. It broke his heart to know that she may actually be running out of time.

"Stand down, Kedah. Doran will make sure she's safe as well as your parents. Then you and I are going to talk." Jensen said.

He shot Jensen a look, but stayed silent. He could safely say that Jensen wouldn't kill her, because that would get the man killed, by him. But as she was in his domain, and under his authority, it was up to him to dish out whatever was necessary. This may not go well, he thought. Nodding to Jensen, he scooped up Sadie and left before either could say a word.

CHAPTER
twenty-five

"Drink?" Jensen asked as he walked over to the wall where he kept a hidden cooler. He loved his office for reasons just as this. Everything here was made to his particular preference, adding in a few unique things here and there.

"Yes, thanks." She said quietly. Grabbing a bag for himself and one for her, he shut the cooler and popped them into the microwave. Once nuked, he handed her the bag and poured his into a glass he kept on his desk.

He could drink out of the bag, sure, but why bother. If he was being honest, he could really use a vein at this point, especially with where this night was headed, but the bag would have to do. He'd call for someone later.

He watched Kedah down her bag, gently placing it on the edge of his desk when she finished. He noted, without much surprise, that her eye color had changed, blended with Doran's to create a beautiful hazel color. The hazel you'd see in shallow waters where rocks and vegetation blended into the sea. His eyes had once changed colors and blended with another's, but that was a very long time ago in a very distant memory.

It surprised him at the amount of control that Doran was exercising around her. In his shoes, Jensen would have already caved and had his soulmate in his arms.

He commended Doran on his ability to withhold the soulmate information, despite the willpower it must be taking. It just wasn't the right time to drop that bombshell on her. She had enough on her plate to deal with and throwing in a soulmate may tip the scales in the wrong direction. It may not and may be what pulls her through all this, but they had no way of knowing.

Now, he needed to think. What was he going to do with this delicate little young vampire in front of him? He had killed for much less but knew that wasn't the answer now. She never chose anything in this life and yet she thrived and survived so much. Despite making bad decisions she really was doing what she felt was best. Now it was his job to rewrite those decisions and do what was best for the Estate.

"Fill me in on everything. Leave nothing out." He leaned back in his chair, propping his feet up on the desk. Might as well get comfortable, this could be a long story to tell.

She looked around nervously, and began to talk. She told him how Max had found her right before she moved in. How he had total control over her, which wasn't a surprise as he sired several of his own children. How he had dumped her in the trashcan and cuffed her with silver. She talked about how he kept saying he would kill everyone she knew and loved. She made sure to mention she was so sorry every other sentence. This was all new and terrifying for her but sadly it was repetitive for him. He'd been down this road, or something similar to it before with others. The small complication in this was that she was Doran's soulmate and she was a damn strong survivor. He felt he owed her at least a little bit to try and fix this mess.

If this situation would have happened years ago, even just 100 years prior, he'd of just killed her and taken away the problem all together. It wouldn't have mattered, much, that she was someone's soulmate or if she carried the answer to world peace and salvation. For far too many years' brutality had been the answer to any problem. Times were changing, as they say. Or he was getting soft in his age. Both were a possibility.

With age comes the ability to read a situation as it develops. Being able to predict the ending and what led to it with only hearing one small detail. As Kedah began her story, he could watch it play out in his head. Watch as the situation went from bad to worse, and was almost certain, despite what they said or talked about tonight, it was going to get one step worse before it was over. This wasn't the first time someone has sired a child for evil purposes, he was a good example of that, and it wouldn't be the last. He was just sorry it happened to someone who seemed like they were a good person with a long human life ahead of her.

Being that she was Max's child she could be found, tracked and mind raped. Among other things certain vampires could do, depending on the line they originated from. He hated everything about this situation.

With the wards and security measures in place, they were safe from Max and his ability to find her and them, for the moment. Something had to be done, though, because one small slip up and hundreds of years that had been put into the Den could fall in an instant.

"I am so sorry, Jensen. I really am. I'll pack my stuff and leave tonight." She quietly stated.

He waved off her thought. He wasn't going to send her out alone and certainly Doran wouldn't allow it. He'd lose one of his most valuable soldiers if he booted her and that couldn't happen. Not with Max gearing up for a potential war. "You're not leaving, Kedah. Neither Doran nor I are that cold hearted, despite the rumors."

"Why? You have every reason to. All I do is attract trouble. As for Doran, I can't even begin to understand what his deal is. I'm sure you have killed for less than what I have brought down on you both." She commented, her voice barely a whisper.

"You're right, I have killed for less. And so has Doran. But, it's as simple as you are under my protection now and as such, I will protect.

Doran, well, that's his story to tell." And he better do it soon, Jensen thought.

"Of course it's his story to tell. His story that somehow involves me. Yet I'm clueless." She groaned in obvious frustration.

"Give it time." He answered to her frustrations. "You are young and have a lot more time than you realize."

"Sure." She muttered then looked at him. "Exactly how old are you?"

"Somewhere in the thousand range." He debated on whether to answer truthfully, and decided the truth was probably welcomed. His age didn't really matter in the grand scheme of things, but the fact he told her the truth would be what meant more.

"You're kidding?" She gawked.

"Nope. I'm one of the oldest here in the States." It was always possible that there were others here that were older, but he was pretty sure he'd have felt them if that were the case.

"So you're older then Max?" She inquired, a hopeful gleam in her eye. He didn't like that look. Not one bit.

"Yes." He answered cautiously. A distant memory floated forward into his thoughts, something he hadn't thought about in a long time. He wondered if he was paranoid or just over imagining things. He hoped he was, because where his train of thought was headed wasn't anywhere pleasant.

"Huh, good to know." She huffed.

"Why?" He questioned.

"Just something someone told me." She answered.

She knew. He had to wonder who she had asked about that little secret. Only a very few number of vampires knew that a Sire could be changed by one that was older, and even fewer cases of it working were on record.

Assuming she, and Doran, were interested in even attempting a Sire change, it could be a solution to part of the current problem. But again, who she may have learned this information from was circling his thoughts. It made no sense she knew of that, but not her very nature. "Can I ask a favor?"

"Sure." Kedah said as she finally sat down in one of the chairs by the desk.

"Could you please just stay here for the next few hours? I'll go talk to your parents and Sadie, make sure they know not to leave the house until its safe. I won't mention that you're alive and make sure Sadie remembers to keep her mouth shut. Then I need to look up a few things and after a day's sleep we should be able to make a little headway into this mess." He set his glass down and rose, signaling Kedah to do the same. He grabbed a bag from beside the door and handed it to her.

"What's this?" She asked as she peered into the bag, making a happy little noise at what she saw. While she was out and things were happening here, Aiden had gone out and gotten some boots plus a set of knives for her.

If she was going to leave again, which he had no doubt she would do, at least now she'd be armed. "Those should work out for you, but if not, we'll have one of the pack members go back out and replace whatever is needed. Try them on when you get back to your room and wear them for a while. Boots are hell to break in."

"Uh, thank you!" She exclaimed, looking shocked and thankful. Taking a step closer to him, she looked like she wanted to hug him, but stuck her hand out instead. Grinning, he took her hand and thought again of just how young she truly was.

"Just don't get yourself killed, okay?" He said on a sigh as she left the office. He didn't even make it back to his desk before Doran appeared.

Some days the fun just never stopped.

Jenson groaned but answered all Doran's questions before they were asked. "No, I didn't kill her. However, you may want to say something soon to her because she is about two seconds away from giving up on you. Her eyes have changed, in case you failed to notice."

"I saw." Doran said.

"Good. Do something about it." He remarked.

Doran scowled a little. "Everyone is in the safe house and a few shifters and witches are on watch. I zapped a very sleepy Sadie there and took the parents by car. Told them it was a national security issue." Doran smiled as Jensen groaned.

"National security issue, really Doran? What am I supposed to do with that?" He said, wishing he had a bottle of whisky in hand.

"Don't know, don't care. Is my job done?" Doran asked as he eyed the door.

"Yes, but Doran." He said. "Leave her alone. Seriously. Sit tight. I'm asking as your friend. Let her sleep in her own bed, gather her own thoughts. Too much has happened in a short amount of time. If you go in there now, she'll demand to know about what everyone is avoiding, then things will either get ten times worse, ten times more awkward, or you'll be so far down each other's throats that nothing will get done."

"And the problem with that last part is?" Doran said with a grin.

"Doran, please. Just let her be. Just this day." Jensen asked.

"Fine." Doran muttered. "Since I should steer clear of my place, do you need me to take you to the parents so you can work your mind magic and get back before dawn. I'd hate for the sun to burn you before I can." He said.

"Why do I keep you around? Truly?" Jensen mused.

"Because I look pretty." Doran reached out and grabbed Jensen's arm and then they were outside the safe house.

"Ten minutes." Jensen muttered as he waved to the guards, straightened out his suit jacket sleeve, and entered the house. It took a few lies and something about a list of names that had been leaked with Kedah's parents' names on it to convince them to stay put until someone came and got them. As lies went, he was pretty convincing, but to be fair, he'd had hundreds of years of practice. Sadie was awake but remained tight lipped about everything. She just sat with Kedah's mom, holding her hand and nodding when she needed to.

Sadie, he feared, was going to be a thorn in his side for a long time. She had that look of pure stubbornness about her. Smart as hell, but stubborn. And there was something else about her, something that he couldn't place. He couldn't spare a moment to explore that, but he would. Something about her drew his attention far more than any human should

Exactly ten minutes later, he exited the house and he and Doran went back to the Estate. Doran left him in the office and Jensen hoped he listened and just went home. Ideally he should have zapped himself back to his other home for a while because Kedah really did need some space for at least a day and she wasn't going to get it if he stayed local.

Looking around the office, he saw nothing urgent that needed him, so he picked up the phone and called for one of his favorite donor veins. She was local and fey and had full access to the Estate, even if she chose to live elsewhere. Fortunately she was close by tonight and sounded delighted to be joining him for a few hours. She was only about 20 minutes out, which was perfect for him.

Quietly he dropped down onto the couch, closing his eyes and savoring a rare moment of quiet.

A soft knock sounded and he waved the door open, cracking his eyes open to watch her stroll in with slow swinging steps.

He rose and greeted her with a kiss on the hand, no words needing to be exchanged. Leading her to the couch, he ran a hand down her cheek as he pulled her body close to his. He lowered her down onto her back closing his eyes as she ran her fingers through his hair and whispered into his ear. She was a sweet little thing, one of his personal favorites as of late, and as his fangs slid out, and pieced her throat, a delicate sigh left both of them.

CHAPTER
twenty-six

As soon as Kedah got back to her apartment, she kicked off her shoes and put on her new boots. They weren't as heavy as she expected and were surprisingly comfortable. Opening the package of knives, she slipped two of them in each boot and was happy to see that they were completely hidden. When she stood, she confirmed the knives were hidden and smiled widely. It was like her own little badass secret. Satisfied, she walked back to her room and carefully put the knives away in her dresser, promising herself she'd go get a proper case or safe later.

Now what, she thought as she looked around her dark and quiet room. Ever since she ran into Jensen at the blood bank her life had been nonstop. To be still for a moment was, odd. She didn't know what to do.

She wasn't hungry. Dawn was still an hour or so away, so sleep wasn't an option just yet. The gym sounded like a bad idea. A walk around the grounds sounded great but also a bad idea. She didn't need Max finding her because she wanted to take a walk.

What she wanted was too see Doran. To talk to him. To ask him what he meant about everything, but didn't feel like opening that conversation. He really was more emotionally unstable than most teenagers she'd known, herself included. He came off as the guy that gave you the best sex of your life and then left you with a cold coffee in the morning. Yet, neither of those things had happened, and truthfully, she was a little disappointed. Because seriously, he was tipping the scales on the looks. Did that make her shallow? Yes. Did she care? Only a little.

Never once had he even made a move on her aside from that one kiss. And lord, that kiss, she'd like an encore of that, please.

She wanted to either push him down the stairs or wrap her body around his, and sooner rather than later, she was going to have to pick one. Or he was going to have to decide for her because this game between them was officially old news and she was done with it.

Groaning with indecisiveness, she changed back into Doran's boxers and shirt, mainly because she wasn't sure where her regular jammies were. She somehow managed to keep the boots on, which was an impressive feat in itself. They were comfortable, but Jensen was right, they needed to be broken in. Plopping down on the couch, she flipped channels trying to find something mind numbing to kill time with.

A knock at the door sounded, causing her to jump in surprise. Opening the door, she smiled as Doran stood on the other side, a laugh trying not to escape his lips.

"Nice outfit." He said with a lazy smile.

"I thought so. I wasn't expecting company." She replied, trying to keep herself neutral. She bet she looked like an idiot and yet, the smile on his face showed otherwise.

"At some point I'm probably going to need those boxers back, you know." He said with a grin.

"No you won't, you don't wear them normally." She said, leaning against the frame of the door.

"You noticed?" He asked, his cheeks flushing. She hadn't before but you could put money on her noticing now.

"Tag was still on them when you gave them to me." She commented with a grin.

He looked positively embarrassed. It was adorable. "Ah, well. I just wanted to stop by and say that your parents and Sadie are safe. They seem like nice folks."

At the mere mention of her parents, Kedah's mind flashed in images and feelings that were hard to ignore. She could still hear them cheer at every meet and competition she ever participated in. She could still feel their arms wrapped around her in comforting hugs when things didn't go right. She could close her eyes and picture every detail of them and her wonderful life. When she first died, bringing those things back to the surface hurt, but now it was more a comfort

"Sorry, I didn't mean to bring up bad memories." He muttered, bringing her back to reality.

"No, it's fine. They are great people. Both of them. I'm glad you got to meet them. I'm glad they are okay. Sadie keeps me posted on them from time to time. She said that they are finally adjusting to life without me. I just wish I could tell them I'm okay." She said wearily.

"I'm sorry. I never had parents to care about, but I can see the pain in your eyes and understand that loss." Doran said softly.

"You never had parents? Like you never knew them?" She questioned. What an odd thing to say.

"Never had them. Pretty much born into existence via good luck and fortune, or whatever. Long story. Another day." Clearly he wanted to drop the subject, which made her want to open it up wider. But she wouldn't. Not today, at least.

"Well, on that note, I should probably go and crash. It's been a long few days and I'm beat." She said, trying to change the subject quickly. It made her uncomfortable that he was momentarily so open, like he was revealing a piece of his soul. She didn't know what to do with that. That, and she really just wanted to kiss the sadness from his face, and that was a no go right now.

"Yeah I have some shit to do, or should do but I'm avoiding." He looked down her body again, slowly, a hunger growing in his expression. If he reached out to her she would be lost. Completely. "Those the boots Jensen had someone get for you?"

"They are. Aren't they badass? I have two knives in each. Oh yeah," she remembered. "You didn't see me throwing. You stormed off in a temper tantrum."

He grunted. "Aiden texted and told me about it."

"Well, someday I'll have to show you." She said proudly.

"As long as it's not at me, I'm game. Oh, and the boots look great, especially with the boxers. Right on the verge of sexy." He said, that blush dusting his cheeks again.

"Cute but deadly is my new look." She grinned.

"It'll suit you well. Get some rest, Kitten." He said.

"Thanks, you too." She muttered as she watched him turn away and head back to his room. Before he stepped in through the door he turned back to her.

"Oh and if you have another nightmare, I'm right here if you need me."

"Been dealing with them alone for years, Doran. But thanks. I'll keep you in mind." She said waving him off and shutting the door. Her response felt harsh, but it was the truth. She'd been dealing with them her whole life; his presence didn't make too much of a difference now. Except that waking terrified next to a strong body had brought her to calm quicker than ever before.

Rolling her eyes at herself, she took off the boots and set them by the door, then wandered to her room, crawling under the covers. Her bed wasn't as comfortable as Doran's but it was so much better than the last one she slept in, so it took little to no time for the rising sun to lure her into sleep.

Sometime later, her skin began to burn, like a thousand tiny fires had suddenly sprung to life covering her body. The fire spread into her veins, under her skin, into her stomach. She screamed and wanted to desperately shake it off, to drink water, to do something to put out the burn. She couldn't move, though. Her arms lay limp at her sides and her legs felt like they were encased in cement.

Her head began to throb and her eyes stung with tears that couldn't fall. The sharp smell of blood filled her nose and her fangs itched. Sweat was dripping down the sides of her face and onto her shoulders, each drop feeling like acid on her skin.

Screaming, she tried to move, tried to break free, but was hit with a complete inability to do so. Blood began to cloud her vision, bathing everything around her in a haze of crimson. The overwhelming feeling of death circled her, caressed her, weighing her down like a hot wet blanket. She couldn't breathe.

If she could just die, the pain would stop. But, something was stopping death, not letting him do his job. It was almost as if something was shielding her. In one last effort to break free, she thrashed her arms out and pierced through the invisibility that was holding her down, waking tangled in her sheets, a thin layer of sweat covering her body. Breathing deeply, she tried to quickly gain control of herself before someone came running into her room, thinking she was being murdered in her sleep.

With unsteady feet, she got out of bed and went to her fridge, finding a bag of blood, nuking it, and downing it quickly. That helped, a lot. A nice hot shower would help too. She wandered to her bathroom, flipped the water on scalding and took the longest shower on record.

After she was dressed, she searched around for her phone to find the time. That's when she saw the text that was sent an hour ago. Unknown number. With shaking hands, she pulled it up.

"*Since you seem to have forgotten that you belong to me, and have somehow managed to hide your family from me, I'm improvising.*" There was a picture of at least half a dozen people, blindfolded, kneeling on the ground, bleeding from the neck where it looked like someone bit into each of them. She couldn't stop the tears that broke from the dam, cascading down her cheeks. "*They aren't dead yet, but will be shortly if you don't get to the location we spoke about yesterday. You have 2 hours. Be alone.*"

Oh god, she moaned as she took off to her room for socks, then back out to quickly lace up her new boots. There was no question as to what she had to do, whether it meant her life or not. She was going, no ifs, ands or buts. Pride, being the fickle bitch that she is, spoke loudly and once again, she listened, and did not call for help. Even though she knew damn well that at least Doran would come in less than a heartbeat.

Checking her phone, she panicked seeing that she had just under an hour to get herself into town. Somehow, she needed to slip past Doran and Jensen, all the residents of the Den and get into town, despite promising to stay put. This was her fight and she was going to do anything to make sure she fought it. Stupid or not, this was going to end tonight.

Thinking quickly, she realized there had to be a garage for all the vehicles that everyone owned and used, which meant that would be the place to get a car to leave with. Ducking out of her room, she headed for the stairs inching down as quietly as possible. She managed to sneak to the first floor and started checking doors, looking for the garage, the one she'd only been in once before. She breathed a sigh of relief when she finally opened the right door, revealing an impressive looking garage with vehicles of all kinds. The garage door already open.

Maybe someone was looking out for her after all.

Glancing around, she took a moment to appreciate the array of vehicles that were parked within. Pretty much anything expensive looked to be making its home there as well as a row of solid black vehicles in various sizes. A few black jeeps lined the entrance of the garage, she guessed they must be the general property of the Den, and headed towards them. Black was a safe color and despite the idea of taking something flashy being appealing, if she lived through this, she didn't want to be killed for stealing a car worth more than the property itself.

Quietly she ducked around the cars until she could peek into the driver's side window and let out a silent breath as she noticed that keys were in the ignition. Because, who, but her, would be stealing a car in a place like this. The moment she let her guard down, a tap on her shoulder caused her to nearly pass out.

"Shit." She yelped and spun around.

"Can I help you?" The man asked.

"I need to borrow the car. I'll bring it back, later. Promise." She stammered.

"I can take you wherever you need to go. Just let me check in first." He said with a friendly smile.

No go. She felt really bad for what she was about to do, and hoped that she didn't actually hurt the guy. Balling up her fist, she nailed him quickly in the face, sending him flying back, slumping down onto the floor. "Oh god, I am so sorry." She muttered as she pulled the man's body to the wall putting him in a sitting position.

She ran over to the jeep, jumped into the driver's side, started the engine and was out before she could truly regret what she just did. She was sorry and promised herself she'd apologize if given the opportunity.

Finding her way out of the grounds wasn't as hard as she expected. Getting back would probably be hell. She'd worry about that later.

It did seem odd to her, the peace she felt as she rushed off to save those strangers' lives. If this was her end, then she'd be at peace with it. She'd miss Sadie, a lot. She'd miss Aiden and his wolfy ways. Hell, she never even got to play Rugby with him and the boys like she wanted. She'd miss Jensen and was sad he'd be disappointed in her.

She'd really miss Doran. For some reason, she was really starting to like the idiot. Okay, to be truthful, like was a bit of an understatement. She probably loved him, but wasn't willing to say the 'L' word just yet. His presence was calming and she really could have gotten used to him being around, being a pain in the ass and all that.

She'd really miss not getting to explore more of his kisses and his warm touch.

CHAPTER
twenty-seven

A strange numbness engulfed Kedah as she threw the jeep into park and took off for the bookstore. She knew Max was beyond the point of pissed, because Jensen and Doran had broken from his norm and no doubt that made him uncomfortable. He was a man who was used to getting his own way and when he didn't, everyone paid dearly.

A quick check on her phone showed that she had about 30 minutes to spare and yet she made her steps just a little quicker. The moment she was in visual range of the bookstore, a familiar control slipped into her thoughts and took over. She came to a stop just as an arm came flying out of the dark, punching her in the gut, sending her forward onto all fours, coughing and wheezing.

"You so didn't have to do that." She choked out. "I was coming willingly and alone."

"Yeah well, boss is pissed. When he gets pissed he sends us out and we don't play nice." The voice in the dark said. Someone grabbed her hair, lifting her back to her feet and pulled her into an alley. Another punch to the gut and she was down again, trying not to puke up shards of her own stomach. A bag was yet again forced over her head, blocking out the world.

Someone then jerked her to her feet and forced her to start walking. Some distance went by, at this point she couldn't be sure of just how much before she was stopped and held still. The sound of screeching tires filled her ears while the smell of burning rubber rushed into the bag she was breathing from.

Trying not to choke on the fumes, she felt hands begin to push at her body, forcing her to stumble into a van that seemed to have no seats, at least she hadn't hit any yet. Still blinded by the bag over her face, she took small breaths and willed her eyes to stay tear free while someone took her wrists and slapped silver cuffs on them. The cuffs immediately dug into her skin and the accompanied sob that followed was out of her control.

Well this was going well, she thought to herself.

Rough hands began to frisk her body, taking her phone, keys and the small amount of cash she had. They missed the knives in the boots completely. That was something at least.

The trip to wherever they were headed was bumpy, rough, and lasted damn near forever. The driver was taking extra care to jerk the car as hard as possible at every turn and managed to hit every single pothole on the roads. The silver cuffs continued to burn and dig their way into her skin. It didn't burn nearly as bad as before, so she was either getting used to it or the AGR was still in her system. That, in itself, would be a small miracle. If she did make it out of this, leather cuffs for her wrists were going to become a permanent addition to her new wardrobe.

Closing her eyes against the pain, she thought of all the people she loved and cared for. All that she would miss now that she had chosen to embrace the vampire within and not just hide the years away. She pictured Doran, the first time she had ever met him. Dressed in jeans that should have been illegal with a shirt that stretched across the width of his chest. His hair was messy and his feet were bare. She smiled as the image smiled back at her, thinking that was what she'd miss the most.

Inevitably the van came to a stop, someone un-cuffed her, and shoved her out of the vehicle where she lost her footing on the ground and went face first into cement, possibly breaking or spraining something in her body. Thank god, at this point, she was a vampire because as a human she'd have died already. As it was now, she'd heal as soon as she could get some blood in her. Assuming she made it long enough.

Someone grabbed her under her arms and hauled her up to her feet, forcing her forward while re-cuffing her hands behind her back. A few more minutes of stumbling and tripping, walking in what felt like circles, mixed with a random straight line, before someone pushed her into a hard metal chair. After some painful maneuvering, her arms were settled behind the back of the chair, removing her ability to move. The bag was ripped off her head and she took a deep breath, only to choke on the smell of rotting flesh and stale blood.

Death rode the air here like a warning, one she wanted to ignore but couldn't.

"Kedah." Max said from somewhere in the darkness.

"Max." She said coolly.

"I don't like traitors, Kedah." Even though she couldn't see his body, it felt as if he was speaking from every inch of the room.

"I don't think I personally betrayed you, Max. I think others found out and thwarted your plans. You can't hold that against me." She knew otherwise, but it was worth a shot.

"Oh yes, I can." Max came out of the shadows dressed in black leather pants, a tight black shirt and gloves. She was confused for a moment by the gloves until she saw what was in his hands. Silver chains. Lots of them. Too many of them.

"See, Kedah. You really are worth nothing to me. Disposable even. I was just going to use you for information then kill you. It really was a very simple plan. But then, you had to go and get people to like you. To look after you. I watched you for a few weeks before turning you. You really aren't that likable of a person. You are nothing." Max walked slowing around her twirling the chains around his hands. She paled and stayed as still as possible. His words stung but not as much as that silver would.

He stopped suddenly and took a chain out of the pile around his arms. Kneeling down, he jerked up her pant leg, exposing skin. With a quick flick of his wrist the chain wrapped itself around her flesh. She screamed in pain as the silver burrowed into her skin.

"I really don't like it when my plans backfire on me. It leaves a bad taste in my mouth. You can understand that, can't you Kedah?" He quickly shifted to her other leg, exposing the skin and sinking the silver in, smiling as a scream left her lips. She tried to stop it, but just couldn't.

Kedah watched behind tear soaked eyes as Max stood and began to circle her again. The pain in her body was damn near blinding and she found herself blinking several times to stay focused. Everything felt like it was on fire. But, through the cloud of pain that had enveloped her, she continued to focus on one thing. Those people in the text and what happened to them. She had to know.

"What about those people?" She bit out. "I came on time. You can let them go."

He laughed. A deep, from the gut laugh of a person who was mentally so unstable they should be locked away forever. He looked over at his second in command, James, and nodded once. James smiled a fangy grin and pushed a button. The wall in front of her slide open to reveal the people from the photo.

All of them were missing their heads. She swallowed a scream of horror. The heads weren't actually missing. They were laying by their bodies, faces frozen in terror.

Everything within her suddenly went completely numb. She was horrified. Not because of the scene in front of her, though that helped. She was horrified that someone could be so cruel. Doran had warned her of Max's wickedness but hearing about it and witnessing it were two completely different things.

She wanted to scream. Wanted to weep and cry for those people who would never breathe again. But no tears would come and no sounds left her lips. Even the pain in her wrists and legs was nonexistent as she continued to stare at the bodies.

She looked at them for a long while, memorizing every feature of every person. Their eye color, hair color, skin color. Their expressions and body size. Every little detail would be etched into her memory because their deaths were her fault. It was her fault they died because she chose to live.

That's when her vision turned red and a hunger swept through her veins like a wildfire in a desert plain.

"Now, now, Kedah, we'll have none of that in my home." Max drawled out as his mind took ahold of hers and everything within her froze. She could do nothing but look at those people in front of her and listen to the echoes of boots on the ground.

"If it makes you feel any better, they all died quickly and only screamed a little. But oh," he moaned in delight. "Their screams were like a soft lullaby to my ears. A lullaby that soothed the soul. I'll sleep with such ease when the day breaks." He knelt down in front of her, blocking her vision of the strangers and smiled, flashing his fangs. "Have you ever had blood tainted with fear? It's like a hundred-year-old whiskey that hits the tongue smoothly and flows with ease down your throat. There is nothing finer."

He calmly grabbed another chain, flicking it hard and letting it wrap around her upper arm, burning its way into her flesh. The other arm was wrapped just as quickly before he stood up and signaled for James to close the wall. She didn't scream, didn't cry, just watched as the door shut, blocking the bodies from her sight. She could still see each and every one of them.

"I think I'll go have a drink and let all this silver work its magic." He stated as he turned on his heel and left, leaving her alone, covered in silver, and utterly defeated.

The moment he left, the controls he had over her released but she feared moving even a millimeter of her body. Everything was on fire and all the chains were securing themselves to her muscles, like little leeches of death.

A small part of her begged for death. It begged for her to open her mouth and beg for the final blow to be taken. A bigger part of her bit her tongue and kept quiet because it wanted revenge. It wanted to make sure that no one else died at the hands of this monster. He wasn't a man or a vampire. He was a monster and he needed to be put down.

She needed to escape. However, she had no idea how to even start that train of thought. Her current state had her absolutely frozen in place. Maybe if she could get to her knives, she could start to dig the silver out. She always felt marginally better after the silver was away from her body. But, she couldn't get to the knives, they were too far away.

Closing her eyes, she let her head fall to her chest and cried out as that small movement jostled all her chains, sending waves of pain through her body. At some point soon she was probably going to puke. Or pass out. Most likely both. Hopefully not at the same time.

Think, she demanded of herself. You need to think. Push past the pain and focus on something else. Anything else.

Concentrating, she thought of the only person who seemed to be at the edge of all her thoughts. Doran. She needed to borrow his strength. She needed him to zap himself here and get her out. The very thought of Doran caused a sensation to wash over her, giving her the sudden feeling of leaving her body. Suddenly an image of Doran appeared directly in front of her. He was pacing in Jensen's office, looking like a caged tiger ready to strike. She had to hand it to her mind for keeping the details of this illusion spot on.

With a sharp turn, Doran looked towards her like he was looking at a ghost. Wait, could he see her? Was she already dead and didn't know it? That would suck. "Doran?"

"Kedah?" He asked cautiously.

"Kedah? Where?" Jensen asked but was quickly waved off by Doran. He stepped closer to her and reached out, putting a hand right through her body.

"Am I dead?" She asked, still not entirely sure what was going on.

"No." Doran said with confidence. Well, at least he was sure. She still wasn't.

"I need help." She asked softly, hoping that whatever illusion this was, it at least got her message to him.

"Okay. Can you tell me where you are?" He asked.

"I don't know. A warehouse, maybe? There is a lot of blood. Death is everywhere." She let tears fall as she spoke. "He said he wouldn't kill them if I came. There were six of them but they are all dead now. I came and they died. I can see the color of their eyes, Doran. Their voiceless screams are echoing inside my head. I killed them all."

"Kitten, you didn't kill them." Doran said softly. "Can you do me a favor?"

"Maybe. There's a lot of blood, here. Everything is red and bloody. I smell it. I can taste it in the air." She was starting to lose the illusion and starting to lose her grip on reality. There seemed to be blood seeping in through the walls. Oh god, her body began to quake violently.

"I need you to stay alive for me. Okay? Hang in there and stay alive. I'm coming for you. I'll find you." He promised and she only hoped that whatever this was, it was the truth.

"I'll try." She stuttered through chattering teeth that shook with the quaking of her body. The image of him faded and the cold metal walls surrounded her once more.

She knew what this was. This was her nightmares coming to pass, and this time she wouldn't wake. She was sure of it. This time death was coming for her and no one could stop him.

Did she allow death to take her or would she try and hold on to the hope that somehow she had spoken to Doran and he was coming. He said he'd find her. He promised. She wanted to believe him, but death's argument was a strong one. It promised rest from her troubles.

Kedah closed her eyes and Doran's voice whispered in. "Kitten, hang on. I'm coming. Just, hang on." Okay, she thought. She could hang on, for just a little while longer.

CHAPTER
twenty-eight

Doran awoke with such a jolt that he damn near jumped out of bed and ran for the door. What exactly he was about to go after, he hadn't a clue, but something was definitely wrong. His sleep was already crap so this added onto it just made things a hell of a lot worse.

Kedah. It had to be. She was in trouble. Or about to be. For fuck's sake he couldn't leave that girl a minute before she was off dancing with the devil.

He actually thought about praying that it wasn't Max, in relation to Kedah, but that's all this could be. He and Jensen had taken away Max's leverage over her so naturally he'd go full force after her.

Zapping himself to her room, he looked around and saw a wet towel on the floor, an unmade bed and her keys and phone gone. Her new boots were gone too, which was a small comfort in an ocean of dread.

Not even caring about the no-drop-in-unannounced rule that was in place, Doran zapped to Jensen's office, where to his credit, Jensen merely just looked up and said nothing.

"Kedah's gone." He said.

"I'm aware. She knocked out a driver and stole a jeep." Jensen turned his laptop and Doran watched as she took off in complete panic.

He had a moment to be semi impressed by her actions before remembering she was out facing Max, alone.

"She's in serious trouble." He said as he began to pace.

"From who? Me or you? Or an outside source?" Jensen asked, remaining calm.

"I don't give a damn that she left but I do give a damn that her life is in danger. Max has her. I'd bet my life on it." He wasn't normally one to lose his cool, in public or in private. He'd lived too long to have anything get to him to that extent. But this, this was Kedah and she was frantic. She was in pain, lots of pain, and terrified and he was feeling every bit of it.

"We don't have a single idea as to where he could have taken her. I've never taken her blood nor am I her master so I can't track her. Can you?" Jensen asked as he pulled out his phone and began typing quietly, probably putting everyone on alert.

"Maybe. She's terrified and I may be able to follow that." He wanted to yell and hit something. But before he could lash out, something odd washed over his body and throughout the room. A presence was here. A projection. He turned sharply to see Kedah standing in the corner, looking around confused and disorientated. "Kedah?"

Jensen stood quickly and looked around, saying her name. Doran waved him off and focused on the girl in front of him. He wouldn't be able to tell how badly she was hurt, not in a projection, but maybe he could get her to try and tell them a location.

"Am I dead?" She asked and almost immediately Doran could safely say no, she wasn't.

Projections weren't the dead talking, but most of the time they were very close to death's whisper. She didn't have a lot of time. "No."

"I need help." She said softly and his heart completely broke.

He'd do anything for her. He just needed to know where she was. "Okay. Can you tell me where you are?"

"I don't know. A warehouse, maybe? There is a lot of blood. Death everywhere." She started to cry as she spoke and he almost couldn't handle it. "He said he wouldn't kill them if I came. There were six of them but they are all dead now. I came and they died. I can see the color of their eyes, Doran. Their voiceless screams are echoing in my head. I killed them."

Shit. No one like her should ever have to face death like that alone. There was such an innocence about her, an innocence that was now lost. That pissed him off. No one should have taken that from her. Not a fucking person. "Kitten, you didn't kill them." He said, not that he thought it helped any. "Can you do me a favor?" He asked quietly.

"Maybe. There's a lot of blood. Everything is red and bloody. I smell it. I can taste in in the air." Her image started to fade and he knew he had mere moments left.

"I need you to stay alive for me. Okay? Hang in there and stay alive. I'm coming for you. I'll find you." I need to tell you you're my soulmate, he thought quietly. There was so much he needed to do and now he may have officially run out of time. The death omen was grabbing hold of her. It was only a matter of time now. No longer did she have days or even years. She was down to minutes, maybe hours. He had to stop it somehow.

"I'll try." She whispered and was gone. Closing his eyes, he fought back a wave of anger and fear and tried to get a grip. He needed to be level headed in order to actually find her.

When he opened his eyes, Jensen was right there with a worried look on his face. "What the hell just went down?"

"Death projection, I think. She's terrified and in a warehouse somewhere. She said there was a lot of blood and death. So maybe a warehouse that used to be a slaughterhouse? Or by a cemetery?" Doran started to rack his brain thinking of the area and all the abandoned buildings within a 50-mile radius. There were too many to narrow down on his own.

"Okay. I put everyone out looking. All feelers are out and a few favors are called in. We'll find her." Jensen said and managed to keep the other thought hidden. They'd find her, but whether she was already dead was a whole different story.

"Phones on me. Call the minute you have something." Doran muttered as he zapped himself out to the town. He needed to try and pick up a line on her fear. If he could find the place she was nabbed from, maybe he could follow it. What he needed and hated to admit it, was one of the wolves.

Five minutes and he'd call Aiden.

His panic tripled as he took off in a dead run.

Jensen sent out another wave of messages stating that if anyone knew anything that may help they needed to call. He also sent Aiden a message asking for a little help from the pack to sniff out their wayward vampire.

She really had the worst luck with things. He'd known people from time to time who attracted the wrong person or thing but this girl, she just attracted everything. Like a moth to a flame as they say. Normally he'd not have gone through this trouble. But, she was Doran's soulmate and those were damn rare.

His phone buzzed in his hand. "Hello?"

"Jensen, its Charles." A voice grunted from the other line.

"Charles, it's good to hear from you old friend. What can I do for you?" Charles was a very old friend; one he'd known for almost his entire thousand years of life. No one really knew who he was, or what for that matter, but he was always reliable and always trustworthy.

"Kedah's in trouble, and you're going to have to do something you have never done." Charles said. Charles could see the future, people and places, mostly things beyond his control. He also only shared such information if he thought you were a worthy friend or it benefited himself in some way or another.

"And that would be?" Jensen inquired, his interest piqued.

"You're going to have to become her Sire." Charles stated.

Jensen paused and took a deep breath. He was afraid something like this was coming, even though he really hoped it wouldn't. "I've

261

never had to do that before and the one time I witnessed it, it went very wrong. Scary wrong. You sure Charles?"

"Have I ever been wrong?" Charles asked.

Not that he had ever been aware of. "No, old friend, you have not. Do you happen to know where she is?" Wouldn't that be nice if he did, Jensen thought?

"That I can't see. I'll be at the Estate in a few hours, you'll have her by then. I'll take care of Doran." Charles was on top of his vision tonight, which was good news for everyone involved.

"You sure? He's pretty old." Jensen asked. To this day he'd not seen anyone that could take on Doran. Now that they were dealing with his soulmate, it would be even more of a challenge.

"I'm older." And with that Charles hung up, leaving Jensen none the wiser on Kedah's location and semi dreading what was going to have to be done when she was found. At least he knew she was alive.

He knew how to change a young vampire's Sire, but it wasn't a pleasant thing to be done. Adding to the complication of things was Doran, who would literally die to protect his soulmate. Jensen was going to have to kill Kedah, for this to work. And to think he had just thought that things weren't complicated enough.

It's going to be a painfully long night.

An even longer week if things didn't go the way they needed to.

It was possible, despite popular belief, for vampires to experience headaches and one was brewing up nice and strong, just for him. Perfect timing.

Grabbing a bag of blood from his hidden cooler, he skipped the niceties and just downed the thing, hoping it would help ease the ache. When his phone rang again, he debated on not answering it but thought better. He was, after all, the leader of the vampires in this state and was always on call for his people.

This just better be something he could handle because if it wasn't, he was going to hang up. "Yes?"

"Think we have something boss," one of the Estate security said.

"Really?" Jensen asked in surprise.

"Yeah. Newly turned and very chatty. Wants to live and whatever. Says he'll make a deal." The guard said.

Jensen laughed and shook his head. "We'll see about that deal. Where are you?"

"Downtown. Old bus station." Came the reply.

"I'll be there in a few minutes." He hung up and dialed Doran. "Got a lead. Come and get me." Not even a second after he spoke the last words did Doran appear in the office.

"Where?" He grunted.

"Old bus station downtown." Jensen said as Doran reached out and grabbed his arm, sending them through space and time to their destination in less than the time it took to breathe deeply.

The guard looked startled for a moment, but regained composure when he saw the look on Doran's face. Jensen decided to just let him have at the new vamp, because it wasn't like he could actually stop him.

Doran took two steps and grabbed the vampire by the throat, hoisting him high into the air and slamming him against a pillar. "Where is she?"

The vampire clawed at Doran's arms, struggled to breathe and frantically looked around for help. No one moved. "Deal?" He croaked.

"Vampire you're lucky I'm not ripping open your stomach and using your intestines as a noose. . . Where. Is. The. Girl?" Doran demanded.

The young vampire's eyes got wide as he grabbed onto Doran's wrists, trying to loosen his hold. "I don't know about a girl, but Max keeps people at an old warehouse on the other side of town. If you're looking for someone, try there."

Doran crushed the young vampire's neck and dropped him to the ground, turning to face Jensen. He hated to play interference but Doran really needed to take a moment before rushing in, guns blazing. Far more harm could come of that, and they all knew it. He just needed to be reminded.

"Wait. Just a moment. Please." Jensen asked while he waved to the guards to take the vamp back to the Estate for the time being. A crushed neck would hurt like hell but it wouldn't actually kill the vampire. Aside from beheading, fire, or a really bad case of silver poisoning, not much else would kill them.

"I know you want to go rushing in there, but we need an idea of what's got to happen. We have no idea the condition she's in or how many of Max's people are there." Reasoning with Doran was like trying to talk sense into a toddler. Once their mind was made it, it was set it stone and unmoving.

"You figure out what you need to do. I'm going to zap myself in there, look for Kedah, get her and bring her home. It's that fucking simple." Doran stated.

It wasn't going to be that simple but it seemed his friend was beyond reason at this point. And to be honest, if the roles were reversed, he'd couldn't say he'd be any different.

"Fine. Will you just let me get some people ready to go so that they aren't too far behind you?" Jensen asked as he was taking out his phone to make a call.

"You have five minutes. I'll be right back." Jensen watched as Doran disappeared and put his phone to his ear, calling his head of security. Talking quickly, he made plans for a group of ten to leave now so that they would arrive around the same time Doran did. Hopefully.

When Doran flashed back into the bus station he was dressed much the same, aside from the blade that was strapped to his back. The handle was made of black ivory and the blade was forged by Doran himself. It hummed with power and the runes that were etched onto the blade glowed. He was not fucking around tonight, which was good news for Kedah and bad for those that got in his way. That blade would decapitate in mere seconds, leaving nothing alive in its wake.

Jensen nodded to his friend and watched as he disappeared, hoping it wouldn't be the last time he saw him. Because if Doran lost Kedah, he'd snap and disappear. No question about it. She was supposed to live long enough to get back to the Estate. After that, it was up in the air for all possible outcomes.

When one of the Estate jeeps pulled up, he jumped in and took off into the night, hoping to secure one of Max's hideouts and save the life of a new family member.

CHAPTER
twenty-nine

Doran tried to flash himself into the warehouse, but hit an invisible wall and was thrown back a few hundred feet. Well fuck, he muttered. Someone had warded the place, and warded it well. There went his initial element of surprise. As much as he wanted to just go in guns blazing, he wanted nothing more than to get Kedah and get out. Jensen's people could do a sweep of the place when they got here.

Crouching low, he scanned the outside of the building noting where the guards were and what their movements were like. Everything was pretty standard and the guards looked far too young to put up much of a fight. He guessed they were there more as a show of force, which was great for him. Easier prey.

Running quickly, he grabbed the first guard, snapped his neck and dropped him into some nearby bushes. He quietly snuck up to the next guard and did the same, hoping Jensen's people got here before they woke and started to heal.

He could have killed them, a swift slice of his blade and they'd drop. Forever. However, in honor of stealth and quickness, he felt less blood was better. Blood tended to attract things and the less things around the more productive he'd be.

Stretching his senses out, he felt around inside the warehouse to get a good idea on how many vampires he'd have to deal with and where they were. Surprisingly, there was a lot more living creatures than he was expecting. Granted, a lot of them felt close to death and wouldn't be a bother, but it was far more than anyone realized. Jensen was going to have his hands full. The guards he could feel, or those that were more alive, per se, were few and far between. Max was either cocky or sloppy, it didn't matter which, because it was good news for his rescue operation.

His heart lurched and his legs moved, propelling him forward into the building at a pace no human or vampire could track. He'd found Kedah.

Zipping through the halls and avoiding guards, he continued to track Kedah until he ran into a locked door. Beyond smelled of blood and death, exactly as she described. Sadness and fear also laced the air giving Doran an acrid taste in his mouth.

She was just beyond these doors and he felt genuine fear for the first time in thousands of years. Fear of what he would see. Fear that his time with her was cut so short that he never got to even live to know her better.

Screw fear. He was terrified.

Cracking the door open, he saw nothing more than Kedah sitting on a metal chair, in the center of the room, her head hanging down with her hair loose around her face. He could see silver chains around her arms and legs, digging into her flesh, leaving trails of blood that dripped slowly to the cold metal floor.

No guards were stationed around and the smell of death was stronger here. Closer. He hated it. Hated it for her. "Kedah." He asked cautiously.

He watched her, looking for a reaction. His heart sank when she didn't move a muscle. He took a step closer to her, keeping an eye on her and one on their surroundings. "Kitten?"

She let out a small sound and tried to lift her head, but didn't get much further than a small nod.

Doran hurried to her, kneeling down carefully lifting her head in his hands. She opened her eyes and tried to smile. "Hey." She whispered.

"Ah, Kitten. What happened?" He choked out, resisting the urge to have a breakdown right then and there.

"He said he wouldn't kill them if I came. I couldn't help it. I wanted to save their lives." Her eyes teared up and she groaned. "They died anyways. He killed them all. Why?"

"I don't know, Kedah. I can't answer for him." He wiped the tears from her eyes and looked down at the chains. They needed to come off, and when they did, it was going to hurt like hell. "I need to get this stuff off of you and get you out of here. Okay?"

"Cuffs first. Poison in them. I can feel bone, again." She muttered. Doran looked behind her and cussed as he saw the cuffs had dug in further than before, bone and muscle visibly shredded. He'd seen a lot of gruesome things in his time, but this was by far the worst. It may have been because of his connection with her, but he was sick at the sight of her injuries.

Max was going to die for this. He was going to be killed and brought back a thousand times until he begged for death, and even then Doran was going to have to get creative on his punishment. He'd suffer for what was done here. There was no doubt about that.

"Try and hold still, Kitten. I'm going to have to break these, just like before." He said as he got behind her and as quickly as he could, snapped off both cuffs, trying to ignore the cry she gave as the silver brushed her battered skin. He should have brought blood with him because she was going to need a lot of it.

He was surprised she wasn't blood crazed yet with how much she had lost. It was probably only a matter of time at this point before she lost control. Although, she also may be beyond that point, which would be a really bad sign.

He needed to hurry, time was the enemy almost as much as those in the building. Either she would run out of time or they would. Neither was favorable. All he needed to do was get outside the wards with her and he could be back at the Estate before anyone could yell no. Then she could get all the help she needed.

"Kitten, I need to get all this silver off of you before I can move you. I need to do it quickly, we don't have much time before Jensen's people move in and we need to get the hell out. Okay?" He hated that he was going to have to yank this shit off of her, but it was better off than on.

"Yeah. Just, quickly." She whimpered.

He needed something for her to bite on so her screams wouldn't be a beacon for people to follow. Last thing they needed was company that wasn't wanted. Whipping off his belt, he stuck it in her mouth with a silent apology. "You're going to need to bite this. I'll go fast."

She nodded and bit down. Taking a deep breath, he steadied himself and reached for the first chain on her arm. The bastard had used chains that were just bigger versions of the cuffs. Every piece of the chain had spikes that hooked into the skin and wedged itself in, causing pain with even the smallest of movements.

Carefully with a quick jerk he pulled and unraveled the first chain, pulling off pieces of skin as she screamed into the leather belt. Not pausing he shifted to the other side and did the same thing, his entire body jerking in grief as Kedah continued to scream in pain. Dropping down, he grabbed at both chains, one on each leg, and yanked.

Kedah screamed as the last of the silver left her body and sagged forward, falling into Doran. He carefully held her up on the chair, taking a look at everything, making sure nothing remained that shouldn't be there. With the silver at least off her skin, she wouldn't be in so much pain, but she'd lost so much blood and the silver was working its way further into her system. They really didn't have much time.

"Alright kitten, let's get outta here. I can't take us home until we're out of the warehouse, so I'll carry you. Okay?" He said as he scooped her up in his arms.

"No." She muttered and carefully stretched her legs to the ground." I need to walk out."

That was the exact moment that he fell completely in love with her.

Silver was no fucking joke. Seriously. The pain it caused couldn't be compared to anything she could even imagine.

Pure. Hell.

As Doran pulled off the chains she could feel her flesh fall away and held back tears as her body slowly began to fall apart. Maybe it was her imagination but either way, it hurt like a son of a bitch. Everything hurt. Her eyelids hurt. Her toes hurt. Her skin was on fire. Her bones felt brittle and she wasn't sure there was any actual blood left in her body.

"Alright kitten, let's get outta here. I can't take us home until we're out of the warehouse, so I'll carry you. Okay?" Doran asked. As much as the idea sounded like heaven to her, she shook her head.

"No. I need to walk out." And she did. She wanted to walk out past those that died for her. To show strength to those that no longer had any. She may collapse and die the minute she stopped moving, but by god she was not going to let Max win this. Not today. Not this moment.

"Alright." Doran said as he wrapped an arm around her waist and helped her to her feet. At first she couldn't stand. Being vertical was nothing but a joke for her body. Her head spun and everything in the room got dark before coming back into focus. Another moment longer and she put pressure on her feet determined to move on her own power.

Her willpower, plus a whole lot of fear, kicked up a notch when footsteps could be heard in the distance.

Alright legs, she thought. Get with the program. As the footsteps slowly got louder, adrenaline replaced fear, and began to pump through her. Walking suddenly becoming easier. It was painful, but now that the silver was gone, it was manageable.

"We need to go, Kedah. Come on." Doran said as he started for the door, pulling her body with his, her feet working faster than they wanted to. As they reached the door that Doran came in through, a door at the back of the room opened and James walked in, freezing mid step when he saw the two of them.

"Where the fuck did you come from?" James demanded as he reached for his gun.

"Your nightmare, asshole." Doran said as he reached for his blade.

Kedah got to hers faster. Reaching down for her blades, she palmed one, stood straight and let it fly in a perfect arc, nailing James directly in the eye. Without stopping, she grabbed another blade and took out James's other eye.

Standing up straighter, she pushed away from Doran, to stand on her own. "That's for all those lives you helped take." She reached into her other boot, took out a knife and threw it into his neck, right into the vein. He howled in pain and dropped to the ground, unable to see and bleeding out. "That one was from me, you dick. I hope Max sees your failures and hangs you by your balls from the ceiling."

She turned back to Doran, looking up at his face and was surprised to see a grin that stretched from ear to ear. "What?"

"Oh nothing, just holy shit on that throwing technique. Damn, lass. Also, please remind me to never, ever, get on your bad side again. I like my balls right where they are, thank you very much." He said while wrapping an arm around her side and kissing the top of her head.

She smiled and leaned her head against his chest, taking a deep breath and trying to focus. Her strength was slipping but the approval from Doran was fuel to at least get out of this god forsaken hellhole of a place.

"Come on, Kitten. Jensen and his people will be here soon." He gathered her close as they exited the building to the sounds of shouts and gunfire. Jensen was already here. Good. Once out in the open, Kedah took a deep breath, inhaling the night air, letting it fill her. She was suddenly so very tired.

"I think I'm going to pass out now." She mumbled as her eyes rolled back and her body went completely limp.

Blissfully, everything went dark, silent, and numb.

CHAPTER
thirty

"Fuck." Doran muttered as he caught Kedah before she hit the ground. Out of the corner of his eye, right before he zapped them home, he saw Jensen come running, waving his hands for him to stop. This better be damn important.

"I need to come with you." Jensen said as he strapped two blades into his shoulder holsters, stopping directly in front of him.

"Why?" Doran demanded.

"Charles called." He answered.

Fortunately, that actually answered the why question and without any hesitation he grabbed onto Jensen's arm and zapped them back to his room within the Estate.

"My office." Jensen said as he left the room and headed for his office, which thankfully was right down the hall. Doran followed, still holding tight to an unconscious Kedah. Once in the office, he went straight for the couch, laying her carefully down. At least she was still breathing. For the moment.

"We need blood, lots of it. And another round of AGR injections." He muttered to Jensen, hoping he was already opening up his stash in the wall for her. When he turned, he saw that Jensen was leaning against the edge of his desk, Charles next to him.

"No." Charles said.

"What the fuck do you mean no? She is dying. She needs blood. Someone call a host of donors and get their asses in here. Now." He demanded.

"No." Charles said again, staying calm as he approached Doran. Doran stood to his full height, letting his arms rest at his sides, ready for a fight.

"I'm not asking again, Charles. What the fuck do you mean, no?" He demanded.

"Do you trust me?" Charles simply asked.

No. Yes. Sometimes? Damnit. "I've no reason to not trust you, except you're giving me a pretty good one right now by interfering. The longer we wait the more likely it will be that she can't recover." He was angry and starting to yell, probably scaring all of the residents in the house as his voice boomed off the walls and echoed down the hall.

Doran, not understanding, clenched his fists a few times and took a step back. He watched as Charles took out a small packet from his pocket and cracked it open, waving it under Kedah's nose.

"Step back. NOW." Charles was never a man of many words and in his current appearance, you'd expect nothing less. Overweight and dirty, he was the cook at the local diner who smoked too much and smelled stale and greasy. Yet most days he gave off more of the 'don't-fuck-with-me' vibe than Doran did.

Kedah's eyes shot open and she coughed, causing her wounds to open and blood to start seeping out. Doran held himself very still because if he moved, he'd have run down Charles and done something he'd probably regret later. Charles sat her up on the couch in a swift move and reached out, taking her jaw forcefully in his hand. "Girl? You hearing me?"

She blinked several times and it looked like she was struggling really hard to focus on the person in front of her. She finally got her eyes open and looked at him, nodding as she recognized him.

"You remember what we talked about a few days ago? The question you asked of me?" Charles asked.

Doran had no idea what in the hell was going on. What did she ask him? And when?

She nodded her head and a little voice whispered out, "I remember."

"Buckle up then girl, because shit's about to get worse before it can get better. You stay strong in there." He tapped her head. "Stay strong and I expect to see you in a few days helping me wash some dishes. Yeah?"

She nodded her head again and closed her eyes, her body swaying as it struggled to stay upright.

"What does that even mean?" Doran demanded. No one answered him.

Everything in the room was silent and still, like they were all quietly awaiting death to appear.

Just as he was about to give up and go back to her, Charles dropped his hand away from Kedah, backing up. Before she could fall, Jensen swooped in and took her jaw in his hand, holding her back in an upright position.

"Kedah? You ready?" Jensen asked in a quiet voice. When she nodded her head, not opening her eyes back up, he shook his head and held her head up a little higher. "I need you to answer me if you are. Not just nod your head." Jensen's voice was strong and determined. Magic began to fill the air.

"Someone has exactly two seconds to answer me on what in the hell is about to go down before I start breaking shit." Doran growled out. Charles took a step closer to him and placed a firm hand on his shoulder, gripping tight.

Kedah cocked her lip up in a little smile and managed to open her eyes. "Let's do this." She whispered.

"Charles, you have Doran?" Jensen asked as Charles placed his other hand on Doran's other shoulder.

Doran tried to struggle, tried to zap himself out of Charles's hold, but couldn't move. Charles leaned into his ear and whispered low enough so that only he could hear. "Listen up, God of the Celtic times, you're going to park your ass right here as I highly doubt you will be able to break my hold. I'm sure you've already tried to zap away and failed. I am far older than you can imagine and a hell of a lot stronger. Don't make me make you look like a pussy in front of Jensen or your girl. Yeah?"

He stilled completely and turned an interesting shade of pale. Nodding to Charles he turned his attention back to Kedah, who was pretty much reaching out for death's hand at this point. Whatever Charles was, he was most definitely older and a shit ton stronger, and he knew better than to fuck with that which he wasn't familiar with. "What's going on?" He asked, desperate for an answer. "Please. I'm begging for an answer."

"Jensen is about to save her life but to do so, he must take it first." Charles gave a squeeze on Doran's shoulders and continued. "Be still Celtic God, things are about to go to hell but I promise, she's strong enough to make it back." He tightened his hold on Doran as they sat in silence and watched the next actions unfold. Jensen struck out with a knife, slicing a thin line across both of Kedah's carotid arteries. She gasped, shuddered, and began to bleed out. Quickly.

Everyone watched in horror as Jensen held Kedah's head in his hand, keeping her upright as she continued to bleed. Her color drained to pale and they watched as her life began to slip away. Her breathing began to become labored and as she took her final breaths, everyone remained quiet, not knowing what to expect.

Doran's body collapsed onto the ground as he felt his soulmate's life force weaken and fade. Everything in him demanded that he run to her, to try and save her life, but he was forced to resist the call. He trusted that whatever was going on, it was the right thing to do. He had to trust Charles, if only because he'd never met anyone older than he.

Kedah's eyes flashed open in a panic as she searched to find his, locking gazes with him. He watched as a single tear formed and dropped down her cheek, right before she took a huge gulp of air and her last breath shuddered away.

"Now." Charles said calmly.

Kedah's eyes closed as her body went completely limp in Jensen's grasp.

Quickly, and with precise movements, Jensen ripped open his wrist with his fangs and shoved his blood into Kedah's mouth. Nothing happened. He rolled her to her back, keeping her head upright, but tilted and kept his arm at her lips, letting his blood fill her mouth, praying it would trickle down her throat.

Everyone in the room stopped breathing when nothing happened. Doran's eyes were panicked as he desperately searched her body for signs of life. Jensen ripped open his wrist again to allow more blood to flow down her throat.

No one moved.

No one breathed.

She remained stock still and pale.

Nothing was happening.

After what seemed like days, but was possibly just seconds, Charles looked over at Kedah with a crooked smile. "There she is." He muttered right before she gasped, grabbed onto Jensen's arm, and held it forcefully to her mouth, taking long hard pulls from his vein.

Doran actually felt tears well up in his eyes as he watched her body do what needed to be done. Though her eyes never opened, her body acted on vampire instinct, taking all it needed to survive.

Doran watched silently as she fed for a full minute. Once Jensen released her from his arm, he nodded to Doran, who shot off like a rocket, gathering her in his arms and cradling her like a newborn. He backed himself against a wall, holding her close, blankly staring off into the distance.

"What the hell did I just witness?" He asked.

Jensen knelt down, a little unsteadily, and placed a hand on Kedah's cheek. "I have made her my child. Free from Max. If she survives." He looked into Doran's eyes and after a moment of the two of them simply staring at one another, nodded.

Charles came into his line of sight next and knelt down. "Tell her. Tell her what she means to you. Your soul will heal hers."

"How do you know?" He asked quietly, a tear rolling down his cheek.

"Because I do." Charles stood and helped Jensen to his feet, leading him to the other side of the room where a vein was waiting for him.

He looked down at the fragile little body he was holding and cried anew. He didn't even care if the people there saw him crying at this point. Fuck it. She came so close to dying, several times, and if she had she'd never have known how he felt. Even now there seemed to be no guarantee that she'd survive. How could he have ever let this happen?

Her body was pale and limp. Her breathing was uneven and slow. Her wounds from the silver were still open and bleeding. And yet, she was the most beautiful creature he'd ever laid eyes on and he loved her.

Loved that she drove him crazy with worry. Loved that she was clumsy and could trip over air if she wasn't careful. Loved that hidden underneath all her clumsiness and doubt was a warrior of old, desperate to be let loose.

He loved the way her hair fell to her shoulders and was a tangled mess in the mornings when she first woke up. The way her eyes sparkled with life whenever anything new or interesting crossed her path. The way it made him look at things in a new light. He loved her soft curves and determined heart. She loved a good pizza over a salad, didn't mind cheerios and adored ice cream.

Yet, he never said any of these things to her. He loved her with his entire being and she had no idea.

"Kedah. I don't really know how to say what I need to, or even if you can hear me. I'm such a shit with words and you'd think that after thousands of years being alive I'd be better. Truthfully, I never had a reason to be better. But now, now I do. Now I have a reason to be better at everything. You're my reason and I'm really going to need you to stay with me."

"You asked me once what I was waiting for. What I was longing for. It was you. It's always been you and will continue to always be you. My people, the Celts, yearn to find their Anam Cara, or soul friend. The

277

one person we can truly commit to on the deepest of levels within our very souls."

"That's you, Kedah. You are my Anam Cara and I want to spend eternity showing you how much you mean to me. I've been waiting and longing for over 2000 years for you to appear, and suddenly you were there. Hair a wild mess, clumsy to a fault, adorable and genuine. What you bring to the world, what you bring to me, is a spark of wonderment. You look at everything with eyes that can see the greatest achievement in the smallest of deeds."

"Donnea leave me alone, lass. My heart. My soul. The world. My world. We canna bear it if you left. Please, Kitten, donnea leave me now. Not when I just found you."

Doran looked down at her lifeless body, a body that was still breathing with difficulty and injured, and loved her even more. If she could just make it through this, he knew she'd be fine. Shit may happen again, and trouble will find her, but she'd be able to take care of herself and he'd be able to help. Because he knew that she'd never tolerate him doing all the fighting and protecting. It wasn't in her nature to sit back and leave the control to someone else.

"I love you, Kitten." Leaning down, he placed the briefest of kisses on her lips, being as gentle as he could be. "Come back to me."

A few moments passed and nothing happened. "I don't know what else to do." He muttered, seemingly talking to no one but himself.

Charles strode over and placed a hand on Doran's shoulder, giving him a reassuring squeeze. "Take her to bed. Tuck her in. Force down bags of blood every few hours and let her sort through it on her own. She's basically turning again, so her body will need time to heal and process. You, we, have done everything that can be done at this point."

"Thank you." He said. "Thank you to the both of you." Jensen nodded to him, still a little drained from his side of things and Charles just smiled.

"I'ma head back to work. That place really goes to hell if I'm gone too long." He laughed as he zapped himself from the room.

"We going to talk about exactly who that is at some point?" Doran asked.

Jensen just shook his head. "I'm not."

"Alrighty. I'm taking Kedah home. I'll call you when she wakes up."

"Scotland?"

"Yeah." He gathered her up and zapped them to his room, laying her on his bed while he grabbed some supplies. He could always come back if needed, but preferred to stay with her until she was awake and talking.

Grabbing a pack from his closet, he zapped over to Kedah's room, grabbed some clothes from her closet and dresser, got back to his room, grabbed some of his stuff and shoved it all in the bag. Next up he found a cooler, a picnic sized one, and went to the kitchen and got enough blood to fill it, hoping it would stay good in the Scotland winter that was going on.

There was nothing else he needed, so he scooped her up and went home. It wasn't exactly the homecoming he expected to have when he brought his Anam Cara there, but it would do. At least she was here with him and hopefully didn't go into a panic when she woke up.

If she woke up.

No, he thought. She'd wake. He would just have to wait.

Tucking her into his bed, he piled blankets and pillows around her, dragged up a chair and made himself comfortable. He waited a few thousand years for her, what was a few more days. Right?

CHAPTER
thirty-one

Several days had passed since the night with Kedah and the raid and Jensen still had no idea if she had lived or not. Assuming the change in Sire worked, she would now be his child and ideally he should be aware if she survived. However, with her being across the world, he just couldn't be sure. Since Doran hadn't shown up in a ball of rage, he would just continue to believe she was still recovering. Maybe later he'd call and check to give him some peace of mind.

The raid on one of Max's facilities led to some interesting discoveries, though not Max himself. Nor his second in command, James. They recovered more than a fair number of prisoners that were used as test subjects, too many dead bodies, and a handful of documents about exploring cross breeding for a new species of warrior.

Of course, Max wouldn't keep all the pieces of his puzzle in the same location, but at least this was more to go on than what they previously had. They also, temporarily, had more residents within the Estate than before the raid. So many of the living were in such bad shape that they had to convert one of the basement floors to a medical/detention ward.

Most were in no shape to escape or run, but just in case loyalties were still leaning towards Max, guards were posted by the only exit.

They were stretched thin for guards and security as it was, and this stretched them further. Max hadn't been active since the raid, but it was only a matter of time before he kicked things up again.

Sitting behind his desk with his computer open, a stack of printed emails piled high, and the answering machine blinking, Jensen really felt drained and had no desire to do anything. He needed to take a few days off, clear his head, and regain some amount of control and composure. Surely he could sneak away for a day or two, go to his cabin in the mountains and just sleep. Maybe read a book. Certainly not open a computer or take a call. The invention of both those things caused more hell in the world than it actually helped.

You know what, he muttered to himself, that's what I'll do. Others in the Estate could hold down the fort for a few days. Since Doran wasn't here, Aiden was next in line to be trusted to watch the place and make sure no one burned it down.

As he rose and pushed the stack of papers aside, Aiden walked in carrying a small pet carrier, smiling. "Hey boss, I brought you a present."

"Not your boss and I don't need a present." He commented lightly, eyeing the carrier with concern.

"Well, you kinda are the head boss around here, so boss just seems to fit." Aiden laughed while setting the carrier on the desk.

"You are a pack master in your own right, Aiden. I am not your boss." He was not interested in this debate nor was he interested in what was in the carrier. He just wanted to leave.

"Fine. You're older then. Anyways, I brought you a present. Enjoy." Aiden laughed.

"I don't want it Aiden, whatever it is." He muttered, trying to inch his way from behind the desk so he could escape.

"Just take a look before you say no." Aiden had a smile about him that was all trouble. Whatever this was, he was sure it was more complicated than he wanted it to be. Taking a step around his desk, he peered into the carrier and cringed. His knee jerk reaction was to get the animal inside out as quickly as possible, but he stopped himself. The person who used to be allergic to such animals had long since gone but the mark of protection he felt never left. It never would. "Why did you bring me a cat?"

"I thought vampires and cats got along? Don't you want it?" Aiden said.

"No, I really don't." He answered. "Aiden. Please, I am very busy. Why did you bring this to me?" His patience was wearing thin. Very, very thin.

"Look closer." Aiden insisted.

Sighing, loudly, he knelt and looked closer. The cat within, was a beautiful long haired cat with fur that seemed to shift from white to brown to gray every time it moved. It was pacing inside the carrier, clearly as irritated as he was. Looking closer he saw its eyes, a wondrously rare combination of one blue and one green. It stopped pacing long enough to really look back at him, and that's when its magic filled the air. Jensen paused, looking down at the cat, his curiosity now piqued.

"Alright, I'll bite. Why do you have a werecat trapped in a carrier?" He asked, standing and looking back at Aiden.

"I found her wandering the streets, causing a little bit of hell. She can't shift back to her human form." Aiden explained. The cat, clearly sensing the conversation, hissed and started scratching at the carrier, desperate for an escape.

"What do you mean she can't shift back to her human form?" He asked, now invested into the situation.

"Exactly that. She's a were and as such should be able to go from cat to human, without any problems. She can't. As a pack master, I possess the ability to force that shift if needed and I can't get past her mental shield to do it. I've never encountered this, personally, but have known of it happening." Aiden explained.

"And you brought her here because?" He inquired of Aiden. What Jensen could do about it he hadn't a clue. Vampires didn't normally mingle with weres much, so he had very little experience in this department.

"We have a werecat on the grounds, don't we?" Aiden asked, taking a seat on the couch, stretching out his long legs on the coffee table. Jensen walked casually over to Aiden and slapped his legs off his table, because he was that irritated and Aiden just happened to be the one here to take the brunt of it. Aiden gave him a look and rolled his eyes.

"We do." Jensen answered. They had one in residence but he kept very much to himself and occupied a cottage in the very back part of the property. True to the nature of a cat, he liked to be secluded and alone, only coming to the main house when he needed something specific or to work his rotation.

"Better call him. He may have more luck than I, or you, would."

"Why can't you call him? I really am busy." Jensen demanded. He knew the answer, but was getting frustrated and just wanted to leave.

"You know the answer to that." Aiden quipped.

"Fine." He walked back to his desk and picked up his phone, calling their local cat. He answered, he always did and promised to be there shortly. Lev was a good man, but not anywhere near what you'd expect from a cat. "On his way."

"Great. I'll just leave her with you then," Aiden started but Jensen held up a hand and stopped him.

"You are not going anywhere. You brought this mess to me, you're helping to rid me of it. Her." He muttered. Another headache was brewing. Stepping over to his cooler, he grabbed a bag of blood, tossed it into the microwave and looked around for his favorite glass that was suddenly missing. "God damn it, George. Stop messing with my stuff." He grunted into the air while opening a cabinet to find another glass.

Aiden snorted and looked around. "George causing trouble again?"

"Who knows? He's about due for a reappearance as I've not seen or heard from him in a while." George was the resident ghost, well poltergeist per se. He loved to hide things and rearrange furniture when he was feeling particularly feisty. Looks like he was on the hunt tonight, starting in Jensen's office.

283

Finding a mug that would do for now, he poured out the blood and sipped it while he sat back in his office chair, closing his eyes. Just one day. That's all he wanted. One day to be away from responsibilities. Hell, at this point he'd take just an hour of nothing.

He'd never get it here, which was why he wanted to go to his cabin. No one knew about it, no one could bother him, not a soul could reach him unless he wished it. Except Doran and he was otherwise occupied. "While we wait, I need you to do me a favor."

"Sure." Aiden said, his voice a hint of concern. Rightfully so too, he could ask anything of him.

"Can you look after the Estate for me for a night or two?" He asked, eyes still closed. "I need to go out."

"Out as in fighting bad guys out? Or out as in need to get laid out?" Aiden questioned with a smirk.

"Out as in I need to go out and it's really none of your damn business." He shot back at him, trying to keep frustrations to a minimum.

"Boss you sound stressed. You need to get laid." Aiden muttered happily.

Without skipping a beat, he answered, utterly serious. "Or I need to kill something. Are you volunteering?"

"Nope." Aiden shot out.

"Just make sure no one burns down the property." He asked. "Please."

"Speaking of burning the place down and people who would probably do it on accident, how's Kedah?" Aiden asked.

"No idea. Haven't heard from Doran yet." Jensen answered.

"Ouch, bet he's a mess." Aiden muttered sympathetically.

Jensen didn't answer and kept his eyes shut while waiting. Minutes passed as they sat in silence, listening to a very angry feline hiss and scratch at the cage she was trapped in. He felt bad for her, being trapped as she was, but if she was stuck in her cat form, it could only be because of neglect or torture. Neither were great options to be dealing with.

Lev walked into the office, completely unannounced, and without prompting went straight for the cage. Jensen popped his eyes open and watched as Lev knelt down and peered in, looking at their new feline friend. She stopped hissing and moved to the front of the cage, eyeing Lev warily. The two of them looked at each other for a long moment before she hissed and stuck a paw through the crate and swatted at Lev, who moved back before getting scratched.

"What the hell was that about?" Aiden asked, having had, at some point, moved himself a little further away from the two cats. Some things almost never changed and the instinctive reaction that wolves, or dogs, had to cats, and vice versa, was almost comical at times. Like two positives of a magnet, instantly repelling each other.

Lev stood and faced Aiden, instantly filling the room. For a cat, he was a big guy. Standing at about six foot five, he had the build of a solid athlete and the personality that didn't match. Quiet and soft spoken, Lev was damn handy to have on the security teams but almost not even worth trying to have a conversation with. He'd not say but a few words.

"She's spooked." Lev spoke quietly.

"Obviously." Aiden muttered shaking his head. "Can you get a read on her?"

"Yes." Lev responded.

"Care to share with the class?" Aiden inquired, looking a little irritated. He didn't have much interaction with Lev, not like Jensen did, so this was bound to drive him nuts. And quickly.

"No." Lev muttered and turned his attention back to the cat. He then looked up at Jensen. "I'll see what I can do."

"That's appreciated, thank you." He replied. At least then he wouldn't have to worry about her.

"One small problem, though." Lev muttered.

Of course there was. There was always a problem to be had. "And that would be?"

"Whoever has kept her in her cat form, for however long that has been, will be looking for her." Lev remarked casually.

He had thought of that already but hadn't said anything just yet. Looks like everyone was on the same page.

Aiden spoke before Jensen could. "Thought of that, so I made sure I wasn't followed by magic or otherwise. However, whoever lost her, will probably start poking around. I'll make sure my boys are aware when they go out. If someone seems to be missing a cat, they aren't to be trusted and to be brought in."

At least someone seemed to be on top of things, Jensen thought. Good. "I'll let people on my end know as well. Do we think she's a product of Max?"

"I'd say that's a pretty good bet." Aiden commented. "You guys got this? I need to leave; the cat stench is just too much." He said with a sly smile.

"Just as well, you smell like a wet dog who played in the swamp." Lev commented, still looking at the other cat and not turning his attention elsewhere.

Jensen couldn't help but laugh. He tried to keep it in, but couldn't help it. Laughing he shook his head and smiled as Aiden left, wide eyed and amused. No one had ever really heard Lev speak more than a few words, so this new development was going to be the talk of the pack for a long time. He'd put money on them trying to poke Lev until he spoke again. He'd feel bad if he didn't know that Lev could absolutely take out half the pack, single handedly.

"I can take her back to my place and see what I can do." Lev said, rising and turning to face him.

"Thank you. Do you need anything from me?" He asked.

"No. I'll keep you posted." Lev took the cage, and a very pissed off inhabitant of the cage, and walked out of the room, saying nothing more.

Well, at least that problem seemed to have solved itself. Now was his chance to get away, if it was meant to be. Only one thing he wanted to do before taking a car and making himself invisible for the night. Grabbing his phone off of the desk, he dialed Doran's number, praying he didn't wake the man or interrupt anything.

"What?" a muffled quiet voice demanded from the other line.

"I was just calling to check on Kedah. How is she?" He asked.

"Still asleep." Doran answered.

It had been three days since they had left and she was still out. That probably wasn't a good sign. "Everything seem okay?" He gently asked.

"Fine. She just won't wake." Doran grumbled.

"I'm sure she's fine, Doran. Just give it some more time." He said, trying to console the man. He was probably beside himself with worry and more than likely hadn't slept a bit since returning home. "If you could, let me know when she awakes. Okay?"

"Sure." Doran said and hung up. It was an odd day indeed that he got more words out of the cat than he did Doran. Sighing, he pocketed his phone and left the office, heading to the garage.

Just one day, that's all he needed. One day to collect himself and he'd be back, diving head first into the mess that Max was creating and whatever other hell decided to break loose. Not even one day, he just needed one night. To whatever gods were listening, just one night of nothing was all he was asking for.

Epilogue

Kedah lay out on a beach, the sun warming her skin while water lapped at her toes. She was at peace. She was content. The sun caressed her face and she sighed happily, knowing that its golden rays could never harm her. She was already dead, after all.

She paused. She was dead?

Wait, what? Her mind repeated those words over and over, trying to comprehend them. The sun dropped out of the sky and a blood moon rose, turning everything scarlet and shadowed. It should have been mildly terrifying and yet she felt nothing but comfort.

This darkness was her home while the light was a danger.

Then, a little voice in the back of her head reminded her that she was a vampire and needed to start acting like it. Whatever this little slice of heaven was, she didn't belong and she needed to go back to where she did.

She had been resting in this world of sun and sand, water and peacefulness for days, letting her body feel the warmth and renewal it offered. That was okay for those days, but now she needed to wake up.

She needed to go home. She knew that. Accepted it. But, she'd miss the sun. It was her only regret. The sea she could feel again, but not the sun. Smiling at her surroundings, she waved a goodbye and willed herself to open her eyes.

The warmth she felt when she came back into her body seemed to be a combination of two things, and neither was the sun that she had in her dream, but felt pretty close to it. One was the incredible amount of blankets and comforters that covered her body. The second was the massive body of a male that she was snuggled up against. Snuggled may not have been the right word, more like held against. It was as if he was guarding her, protecting her from some unseen force while she slept.

It felt wonderful. She felt wonderful. Healed. Relaxed. Different.

Opening her eyes wider she peeked out from under the covers enough to realize she had absolutely no idea where she was. Not a single thing that she saw was familiar. As far as she could tell, everything was made of wood and stone and she could see no hint of anything remotely modern. As if the past week hadn't been weird enough, did she fall back in time too?

Wouldn't that just suck on a whole new level.

Leaving that random thought aside, she began stretching out her legs, straightening her body, and moaned as her muscles tensed in protest. It felt like she hadn't moved in days or maybe even weeks. But, that couldn't be right, right? Arching her back, she groaned while her spine adjusted and cracked back into place.

A strong hand came down onto her stomach, holding her still in mid movement of adjusting her back. "Lass," Doran said in a sleepy voice, thick with his native accent. "Donna move like that against me again or I'll not be held responsible for my actions."

She blushed and carefully lowered herself back onto the bed, understanding his meaning and not regretting it one bit. Plus, that accent of his that slipped out every once in a while was just sexy and added to the moment. "Sorry."

"Donna be. I don't mind. No man in their right mind would if they were waking to the stretching and yawning of a beautiful woman in their bed." He grinned down at her, the sleep slowly fading from his eyes. "How are you feeling? Not going to lie here, Kitten, you scared the hell outta me and a few others."

"I feel, fine, actually." She said while yawning again. "Wait, why do I feel fine? Shouldn't I feel like hell?" Nothing hurt, her stomach wasn't empty, she wasn't hungry, for blood or food, and she felt rested.

"You've been asleep and/or in a coma for nearly four days." He muttered, frowning slightly.

"Four days? Seriously?" She exclaimed.

"Do you remember what happened?" He asked, his voice a little more cautious than normal.

She thought back, trying to remember exactly what her last memory was. Everything was spotty and nothing formed a coherent thought. "No, not really. I remember you coming to get me. I remember the silver. Pain." She closed her eyes as a wave of emotion washed over her. "I remember those that died. Then, nothing." She looked further into her mind and a few more images popped up. "I took Jensen's vein. Lots of pain."

He smiled lazily at her. "The cliff notes are as follows. I came and rescued you. You were in pretty bad shape, but despite that you managed to throw knives at, and impressively nail, James in both eyes. I'd assume he survived, though I am sure he wishes he may not have. I'm not too sure eyes grow back. Then we got back to the Estate and Charles was there."

"Charles?" She interrupted.

"You know him as Cook." He answered.

"Oh, I thought I remembered him there. Why was he there?" She questioned.

"Charles is much older than I am and a hell of a lot more mysterious. He knew he needed to be there, so he was. It's a little more complicated than that, so I'll explain it better another time, or you can always try and ask him." He smiled and rested his hand on her cheek, which was something the two of them tended to do in tender moments. She closed her eyes briefly and savored the warmth and love that he was showing, something she knew was absolutely genuine, but didn't know why she knew that. "So, anyway, and I guess you knew about this because I sure as hell didn't, your Sire has changed."

"It worked?" She said, snapping her eyes open, shocked.

"Dunno how, but I'd say aye, it worked. We won't know until we go back home and Jensen has a look at you, but, again, I'm going with yes. Why didn't you tell me you knew about that?" He questioned gently.

"Truthfully? Because it seemed like such a long shot." She muttered honestly. She couldn't believe that her luck may finally be on the up and that she was out from Max's control. He'd be raging pissed, and they'd all have to deal with that, but at least he couldn't make her do things or say things against her will anymore.

"Well, you may be one of the only ones on record to survive it. And that's it. I brought you here to recover." He brushed some stray hair from her face, his fingers lingering on her skin.

Everything he said rang true, because somehow she could hear the truth in his words, and yet she felt like he was leaving something major out. Something personal. She wanted to pry, but if it had been four days of her sleeping it off then she really needed a toothbrush and a shower. And maybe to know where she was, exactly. A toilet would also be helpful. "So, where are we?"

"Scotland. My home. My real home." He said with a lazy smile. He looked so much more comfortable here, like he could finally be himself. It was comforting to finally see a true smile from him.

"Scotland? How did we get here?" She squealed in surprise. "I don't have a passport!"

"Lass, traveling with me you don't really need one. We get to skip the customs lines and baggage claim takes less than two seconds." He laughed, and the sound was like magic to her ears.

"Oh. Is that why your accent is so thick? Because you're home?" She questioned, not that she really minded the accent. No one in their right mind would.

He laughed and shook his head. "Nah. Comes on when I'm just waking up, really comfortable with someone or just stressed."

"Right. Okay, well, I could use a shower, and a toothbrush. Oh and why am I not hungry, for blood?" For a moment she blissfully thought maybe she wasn't a vampire anymore, but the thought faded as her fangs gave her a subtle reminder by poking into her bottom lip.

Doran nodded to her arm where she saw an IV port had been put into place. No bag was hooked up at the moment, but a few dead bags laid across the floor. "You thrash in your sleep, so I had to put a port in so that when you were calm I could get blood into your system. I tried to force it down your throat, but you kept spitting it out. Made quit the mess."

"Shit, I'm sorry." She muttered as she sat up and put her legs over the side of the bed, debating on whether or not she'd actually be able to stand. Gingerly, she put her feet down and took a few steps, pleased to see them in working order.

"Better spitting it out than to go after my vein." He muttered as he rose from the bed as well.

It was toasty warm in the room, thanks to a roaring fire in a hearth that was larger than her. She'd never seen anything like it outside history books. "Is this a castle?"

"Aye, but just a small one. Called a manor." He said as he led her to the bathroom, opening the door for her. "Shower's in here, take your time. Sorry it's a bit of a mess, I didn't have indoor plumbing until about a day or so ago. Girly stuff is in there and your toothbrush and stuff is by the sink."

"You brought all this stuff for me? Why not just take me home?" She asked, though to be truthful this felt like home. He felt like home. Something had changed between them. Something good, though she wasn't sure what.

"I did and we'll talk after. I'll go get some food." He gave her a wink and closed the door.

The first thing she did, right after turning the water on was to go pee. Damn those meds for silver poisoning and how they make you want to pee for a year. If she'd been asleep for four days, she really didn't want to think of what her body did to eject the silver, but it was what it was. Doran didn't look put out by her or grossed out, so whatever happened during those days must not have been terrifying.

Once relieved of about six gallons of water, she stripped down and climbed into the steady stream of heat, sighing contently as the spray caressed her skin. It was the best shower she had ever taken. Seriously. The best. Despite the mess, which honestly wasn't bad for a one day project, it was marvelous.

She washed her body of four days' worth of funk and yuck, plus whatever still lingered from the aftermath of the incident at the Estate and the dried blood from the IV port she still had nestled into her arm. That was going to come out as soon as Doran was back and could yank it out. She'd do it, but no. Needle in the arm wasn't on her list of things she felt confident about, despite the brief amount of medical training she had. She was happy to note that her skin seemed to be intact, as the last memory she had she vaguely thought chunks came off with the silver chains that were wrapped around her.

Shutting off the water, she stepped out and wrapped a towel snuggly around her body. Glancing at the sink, she spied her toothbrush and gave her mouth a good cleaning, several times. Once that was done and she felt about as clean as she could be, she found Doran's robe hanging on the wall and switched from the towel to it. It was super soft and smelled like him, which was a win in her book.

Stepping back out into the room, she smiled at Doran who had set up a blanket by the hearth and set food out for them. He sat by the fire, staring off into the distance until he caught her movements and looked over at her.

He took her breath away. The love and devotion in his face conveyed more than words ever could. She wasn't sure why he cared so much, or why he was doing everything that seemed so not Doran, but at this very moment, she'd take it.

Smiling, she took his outstretched hand and sat down beside him, gathering her legs under her so that she wouldn't flash him, only now remembering she was wearing only the robe and a smile. "This looks great. Thank you."

"I wasn't sure exactly what you like because I think the only meal we have ever had together was pizza and cheerios." He said, amused.

"I'm not too picky." She said truthfully. She looked up at his face, as he looked down at her, and for the first time she noticed that his eye color matched hers. It looked like a swirl of the two colors. Then she remembered Sadie bringing up that her eyes had changed. "Side note. Why do our eyes match now?"

"Um, it's a little complicated. You don't remember anything I said to you, after we got back to the Estate?" He asked, changing the subject.

"No. Images and feelings, but not words." Something passed on his face, some emotion that she couldn't place. It was gone before she could think further on it. "What am I not remembering, Doran? What are you still not telling me?"

His heart sunk to his stomach and stayed there like a ton of bricks at the bottom of the ocean. By her facial expression, and sheer curiosity, she really couldn't remember anything he had said to her. She remembered emotions, which was okay, but the words were lost.

A part of him was extremely hurt by this knowledge, but another part was grateful. He didn't want to be outright rejected. Who would? However, it was time she at least knew some of what was going on. Enough for her to take some sort of action for herself, or at least to make decisions for herself. Soulmates could be tricky and not everyone that had a soulmate had a happily ever after.

He assumed they would, but, maybe not. She was still so young, so new at being a vampire, and even newer at trying to figure out who and what she was going to be someday. If he didn't tread lightly, he would lose her out of a sheer panic. "Why don't I start by answering at least one question that I know has to be bugging you? One question that not a single other person living on solid ground knows."

She sat up a little straighter while picking up some fruit and eating it quietly. "Alright."

"I am a God. Celtic, to be a little more specific. Well, former Celtic god, but that's where things get complicated." He said, his nerves on edge. It was true, not a single other person, aside from those still residing in the heavens, knew exactly who he was, and he meant to keep it that way. It could be dangerous, if not deadly, for people to know.

"A god?" She said blankly. "Like a god god? Not sure I expected that. At. All." Setting the fruit she had in her hand back down, she shifted her body until she was completely facing him, her wet hair framing out her beautifully soft face. "Really? A God?"

"Really, a God. More former God than current God, but basically still one. I retained almost all my, talents, when I fell." The knot in his stomach was starting to slowly unwind when he realized she wasn't going to run screaming from the room or lock herself in the bathroom.

"So you are, well were, a Celtic God." She said slowly. "Which one?"

"Ah Kitten. There is a lot of power in knowing the true name of someone, even more so with a God." He said with a thoughtful sigh. And that was damn truth. If she knew, she had the power to absolutely destroy him and would also carry a target that shone just as brightly as the one he carried everywhere he went.

"Good power or bad power?" She curiously asked.

"Depends on the person, Kitten. Depends on where their loyalties lie." He said truthfully.

"Alright. I'll settle for just a Celtic God, for now. I don't need that kind of power over you. Maybe not ever. That's terrifying if we're being honest." She said.

"Aye, it's more terrifying than you can realize, but maybe one day you will know. After all, you are my soulmate. You have the power to keep me secret or expose me for what I was and am." There, he said it. His heart was going to hammer out of his chest, but he said it. "And that answers the eyes questions. Soulmates eye color sometimes merges, like ours did."

She stilled, but didn't move away from him. She didn't even take a breath. This was bad. Maybe he shouldn't have said anything. Maybe he needed to keep talking. Explain a bit more. He watched the rise and fall of her chest and watched carefully for any signs of rejection or disapproval. He never wanted someone to talk as much as he wanted her to say something, even just one word, right now.

He watched as she bit at her bottom lip, something she did when she was in deep concentration, and probably wasn't as aware of it as he was, and held his breath.

Fuck, maybe he made a mistake. An epic one, but, what was said was said and there was nothing he could do about it now. And as if things couldn't get just a little tenser, his phone rang. Cursing, he took it out, saw the caller ID and put it back in his pocket. They could all fucking wait ten minutes until he and Kedah could work some things out.

He watched as a million different emotions crossed her face before she settled down with just a smile. She showed no fear, no reservation, and no concerns. Smiling, she reached out and laid a palm on his cheek, like she did back in her room, those few nights ago. Like he had just done to her when she awoke. "Soulmates, huh? That's what all of this was about?

"That's what, what?" He stammered, tripping over his own words. "Kitten I donna think you understand the gravity of what I just said or why I have been so reserved. I've been on Earth for over 2000 years and never thought I'd find you. Then I did and you hit me like a Mack truck to a dandelion." His voice came out as a little breathless and his thoughts were spinning out of control.

"What I meant was, why didn't you just say something right off the bat? Why didn't you at least say you liked me, even just a little?" She said calmly while scooting closer to him.

"Why?" He stuttered out before shutting his mouth. He hadn't a damn clue as to why he didn't say anything. "I don't know."

"Doran, I am not going to deny I feel an attraction to you. It's like there's a tether tied between us and I can always feel you near, drawing you back to me. I want to be around you, stubborn and all." She commented, her words steady and clear.

"But. . ." It was in her voice, the 'but' that he knew was coming.

"But I'm not sure how committed I can be to a full blown relationship." She took a deep breath and smiled wider. "But, I will try my very best. You just have to understand that I have no idea who or what I want to be and what I want to do with my life. I'm still young, and by vampire and god standards, I'd imagine I'm still a baby. I need to discover who I'm meant to be. Which means you're going to have to let me fall. You're going to have to let me make mistakes and learn. Try new things. Now, this isn't saying that at the end of the night I want to be anywhere other than your bed, because let's face it, I'm not an idiot. But you're going to have to give me some time. Can you do that?"

All the breaths he'd been holding in since the day he met her escaped in a quiet whoosh. He felt relieved. Renewed. Revived. "Yes, I can try, but you're going to have to work with me too. I'm going to be an asshole and I'm going to make bad choices. Because, Kitten, I'll want to catch you when you fall and protect you when you tell me not to. Lass, I've waited a long time for you and I'm willing to wait awhile more if that's what you need from me." He laid his hand on hers and closed his eyes.

"Well then, Celtic God, why don't you come and kiss me and we'll make this official?" She said and before the last thought came out, his mouth covered hers.

She was everything amazing that the world had to offer. No doubt she was going to be stubborn, hard to handle, a challenge, and clumsy beyond belief. But, she would be all those things wrapped in love, compassion, empathy, curiosity and a will to truly live all that life was going to offer her.

He couldn't wait.

74158936R00179

Made in the USA
Columbia, SC
29 July 2017